THE WORKS OF
ROBERT LOUIS STEVENSON
VAILIMA EDITION
VOLUME XI

AMS PRESS

NEW YORK

FLEEMING JENKIN

THE MERRY MEN AND OTHER TALES
MEMOIR OF FLEEMING JENKIN

BY
ROBERT LOUIS STEVENSON

NEW YORK
CHARLES SCRIBNER'S SONS
LONDON : WILLIAM HEINEMANN:
IN ASSOCIATION WITH CHATTO AND WINDUS:
CASSELL AND COMPANY LIMITED: AND
LONGMANS, GREEN AND COMPANY.
MCMXXII

HOUSTON PUBLIC LIBRARY

Library of Congress Cataloging in Publication Data

Stevenson, Robert Louis, 1850-1894.
    The works of Robert Louis Stevenson.

    Reprint of the 1921-23 ed. published by Scribner,
New York.
    Vol. 26 includes index.
    CONTENTS: v. 1. An inland voyage. Travels with a
donkey. Edinburgh, picturesque notes.—v. 2. Virginibus
puerisque. The amateur emigrant. The Pacific capitals.
Silverado squatters.—v. 3. New Arabian nights. The
pavilion on the links, and other tales. [etc.]
PR5480.F74   828'.8'09   70-143897
ISBN 0-404-08750-7

Reprinted by special arrangement with Charles Scribner's Sons

Reprinted from the edition of 1922, New York
First AMS edition published, 1974
Manufactured in the United States of America

International Standard Book Number:
Complete Set: 0-404-08750-7
Volume 11: 0-404-08761-2

AMS PRESS, INC.
NEW YORK, N.Y. 10003

CONTENTS

VOLUME XI

THE MERRY MEN

AND OTHER TALES

The Merry Men and Other Tales appeared first in a collected edition in 1887.
The tales had been originally printed as
follows:

PREFATORY NOTE

IN a vague quest for "a house . . . a burn within reach; heather and a fir or two," we came upon "Kinnaird Cottage," near Pitlochry, where Professor Blackie, a picturesque and well-known figure in Scotland, had been in the habit of spending his vacations. For some reason the cottage was vacant during the summer of 1881; we were very glad indeed, to engage it, though our landlady and her daughter, who were to attend to our domestic affairs, made it plain to us that we were not to be considered in the same breath with the eccentric professor. Kinnaird Cottage possessed more advantages than my husband had demanded when he agreed to go to the Highlands with his people, for the house stood a few yards from "a little green glen with a burn,—a wonderful burn, gold and green and snow white, singing loud and low in different steps of its career, now pouring over miniature crags, now fretting itself to death in a maze of rocky stairs and pots; never was so sweet a little river. Behind, great purple moorlands reaching to Ben Vrackie."

PREFATORY NOTE

Although it was the seventh of June when we moved into the cottage, as yet we had had nothing but cold rains and penetrating winds; and in all innocence (this being my first season in this beautiful and inclement region) I asked when the spring would begin. "The spring!" said my mother-in-law; "why, *this* is the spring." "And the summer," I inquired anxiously,—"when will the summer be here?" "Well," returned my mother-in-law doubtfully, "we must wait for St. Swithin's day; it all depends on what kind of weather we have then." St. Swithin's day came and went in a storm of wind and rain. "I am afraid," confessed my mother-in-law, "that the summer is past, and we shall have no more good weather." And so it turned out. Between showers she and I wandered over the moor and along the banks of the burn, but always with umbrellas in our hands, and generally returning drenched.

My husband, who had come to the Highlands solely for the sunshine and bracing air, was condemned to spend the most of his time in our small, stuffy sitting-room, with no amusement or occupation other than that afforded by his writing materials. The only books we had with us were two large volumes of the life of Voltaire, which did not tend to raise our already depressed spirits. Even these, removed from us by my husband's parents one dreary Sunday as not being proper "Sabba'-day reading," were annexed by the elder couple, each taking a volume. Thrown entirely on our own resources for amusement, we decided to write stories and read them to each other; naturally, these tales, coloured by our surroundings, were of a sombre cast.

As my husband was then writing only for our mutual entertainment, without thought of publication, he put his first tale, *Thrawn Janet*, in the vernacular of the country. "I doubt if this is good enough for my father to hear," he said, as he began reading it to me. But he took heart as he went on. That evening is as clear in my memory as though it were yesterday,—the dim light of our one candle, with the acrid smell of the wick we forgot to snuff, the shadows in the corners of the "lang, laigh, mirk chalmer, perishing cauld," the driving rain on the roof close above our heads, and the gusts of wind that shook our windows. The very sound of the names—Murdock Soulis, The Hangin' Shaw in the beild of the Black Hill, Balweary in the vale of Dule—sent a "cauld grue" along my bones. By the time the tale was finished my husband had fairly frightened himself, and we crept down the stairs clinging hand in hand like two scared children. My father-in-law's unexpected praise of *Thrawn Janet* caused my husband to regard it with more favour; and after a few corrections he began to feel that he had really, as he said, "pulled it off."

For some time he had had it in his mind to weave a thread of a story round The Merry Men of Aros

PREFATORY NOTE

Roost. The summer having apparently slipped past us without stopping, and the rain hardly ceasing after St. Swithin's day (in my mother-in-law's diary I find recorded "weather wet," almost immediately after "have had bad weather," "still wet," "afraid to venture out," "pouring rain," and so on, almost without variation) my husband had nothing to distract his attention from the work in hand, and *The Merry Men* was soon under way. The story itself, overshadowed by its surroundings, did not come so easily as *Thrawn Janet*, and never quite satisfied its author, who believed that he had succeeded in giving the terror of the sea, but had failed to get a real grip on his story.

The continual cold rains having seriously affected my husband's health, we finally left Kinnaird Cottage, and by the doctor's orders settled for a time in Braemar. The two stories were sent to the *Cornhill Magazine*, where *Thrawn Janet* was published in October, 1881, *The Merry Men* appearing serially from June, 1882.

F. V. DE G. S.

CONTENTS

CONTENTS

THE TREASURE OF FRANCHARD

My dear Lady Taylor:

To your name, if I wrote on brass, I could add nothing; it has been already written higher than I could dream to reach, by a strong and a dear hand; and if I now dedicate to you these tales, it is not as the writer who brings you his work, but as the friend who would remind you of his affection.

Robert Louis Stevenson.

Skerryvore,
   Bournemouth.

Facsimile of first page of
Markheim

Markheim

"Yes," said the dealer, "our windfalls are of various kinds. Some customers are ignorant, and then I touch a dividend on my superior knowledge. Some are dishonest," and here he held up the candle, so that the light fell strongly on his visitor, "and in that case," he continued, "I profit by my virtue."

Markheim had but just entered from the daylight streets, and his eyes had not yet grown familiar with the mingled shine and darkness in the shop. At these pointed words, and before the near presence of the flame, he blinked painfully and looked aside.

The dealer chuckled. "You come to me on Christmas Day," he resumed, "when you know that I am alone in my house, put up my shutters, and make a point of refusing business. Well, you will have to pay for that; you will have to pay for my derangement, when I should be balancing my books; you will have to pay, besides, for a kind of manner that I remark in you today very strongly. I am the essence of discretion, and ask no awkward questions; but when a customer cannot look me in the eye, he has to pay for it." The dealer once more

Facsimile of first page of
Markheim

THE MERRY MEN

CHAPTER I

EILEAN AROS

T was a beautiful morning in the late July when I set forth on foot for the last time for Aros. A boat had put me ashore the night before at Grisapol; I had such breakfast as the little inn afforded, and, leaving all my baggage till I had an occasion to come round for it by sea, struck right across the promontory with a cheerful heart.

I was far from being a native of these parts, springing, as I did, from an unmixed Lowland stock. But an uncle of mine, Gordon Darnaway, after a poor, rough youth, and some years at sea, had married a young wife in the islands; Mary Maclean she was called, the last of her family; and when she died in giving birth to a daughter, Aros, the sea-girt farm, had remained in his possession. It brought him in nothing but the means of life, as I was well aware; but he was a man

11

whom ill-fortune had pursued; he feared, cumbered as he was with the young child, to make a fresh adventure upon life; and remained in Aros, biting his nails at destiny. Years passed over his head in that isolation, and brought neither help nor contentment. Meantime our family was dying out in the Lowlands; there is little luck for any of that race; and perhaps my father was the luckiest of all, for not only was he one of the last to die, but he left a son to his name and a little money to support it. I was a student of Edinburgh University, living well enough at my own charges, but without kith or kin; when some news of me found its way to Uncle Gordon on the Ross of Grisapol; and he, as he was a man who held blood thicker than water, wrote to me the day he heard of my existence, and taught me to count Aros as my home. Thus it was that I came to spend my vacations in that part of the country, so far from all society and comfort, between the codfish and the moorcocks; and thus it was that now, when I had done with my classes, I was returning thither with so light a heart that July day.

The Ross, as we call it, is a promontory neither wide nor high, but as rough as God made it to this day; the deep sea on either hand of it, full of rugged isles and reefs most perilous to seamen —all overlooked from the eastward by some very high cliffs and the great peak of Ben Kyaw. *The Mountain of the Mist*, they say the words signify

in the Gaelic tongue; and it is well named. For
that hill-top, which is more than three thousand
feet in height, catches all the clouds that come
blowing from the seaward; and, indeed, I used
often to think that it must make them for itself;
since when all heaven was clear to the sea-level,
there would ever be a streamer on Ben Kyaw.
It brought water, too, and was mossy[1] to the top
in consequence. I have seen us sitting in broad
sunshine on the Ross, and the rain falling black
like crape upon the mountain. But the wetness
of it made it often appear more beautiful to my
eyes; for when the sun struck upon the hillsides,
there were many wet rocks and watercourses that
shone like jewels even as far as Aros, fifteen miles
away.

The road that I followed was a cattle-track.
It twisted so as nearly to double the length of
my journey; it went over rough boulders so that
a man had to leap from one to another, and
through soft bottoms where the moss came nearly
to the knee. There was no cultivation anywhere
and not one house in the ten miles from Grisapol
to Aros. Houses of course there were—three at
least; but they lay so far on the one side or the
other that no stranger could have found them
from the track. A large part of the Ross is
covered with big granite rocks, some of them
larger than a two-roomed house, one beside another, with fern and deep heather in between

[1]Boggy.

13

them where the vipers breed. Any way the wind was, it was always sea-air, as salt as on a ship; the gulls were as free as moorfowl over all the Ross; and whenever the way rose a little, your eye would kindle with the brightness of the sea. From the very midst of the land, on a day of wind and a high spring, I have heard the Roost roaring like a battle where it runs by Aros, and the great and fearful voices of the breakers that we call the Merry Men.

Aros itself—Aros Jay, I have heard the natives call it, and they say it means *the House of God*—Aros itself was not properly a piece of the Ross, nor was it quite an islet. It formed the south-west corner of the land, fitted close to it, and was in one place only separated from the coast by a little gut of the sea, not forty feet across the narrowest. When the tide was full, this was clear and still, like a pool on a land river; only there was a difference in the weeds and fishes and the water itself was green instead of brown; but when the tide went out, in the bottom of the ebb, there was a day or two in every month when you could pass dryshod from Aros to the mainland. There was some good pasture, where my uncle fed the sheep he lived on; perhaps the feed was better because the ground rose higher on the islet than the main level of the Ross, but this I am not skilled enough to settle. The house was a good one for that country, two stories high. It looked westward over a bay, with a pier hard

14

by for a boat, and from the door you could watch
the vapours blowing on Ben Kyaw.

On all this part of the coast, and especially
near Aros, these great granite rocks that I have
spoken of go down together in troops into the sea,
like cattle on a summer's day. There they stand,
for all the world like their neighbours ashore;
only the salt water sobbing between them instead
of the quiet earth, and clots of sea-pink blooming
on their sides instead of heather; and the great
sea-conger to wreathe about the base of them instead of the poisonous viper of the land. On calm
days you can go wandering between them in a
boat for hours, echoes following you about the
labyrinth; but when the sea is up, Heaven help
the man that hears that caldron boiling.

Off the south-west end of Aros these blocks are
very many, and much greater in size. Indeed,
they must grow monstrously bigger out to sea,
for there must be ten sea-miles of open water
sown with them as thick as a country place with
houses, some standing thirty feet above the tides,
some covered, but all perilous to ships; so that
on a clear, westerly blowing day, I have counted,
from the top of Aros, the great rollers breaking
white and heavy over as many as six-and-forty
buried reefs. But it is nearer in shore that the
danger is worst; for the tide, here running like
a mill-race, makes a long belt of broken water
—a *Roost* we call it—at the tail of the land. I
have often been out there in a dead calm at the

slack of the tide; and a strange place it is, with the sea swirling and combing up and boiling like the caldrons of a linn, and now and again a little dancing mutter of sound as though the *Roost* were talking to itself. But when the tide begins to run again, and above all in heavy weather, there is no man could take a boat within half a mile of it, nor a ship afloat that could either steer or live in such a place. You can hear the roaring of it six miles away. At the seaward end there comes the strongest of the bubble; and it's here that these big breakers dance together—the dance of death, it may be called—that have got the name, in these parts, of the Merry Men. I have heard it said that they run fifty feet high; but that must be the green water only, for the spray runs twice as high as that. Whether they got the name from their movements, which are swift and antic, or from the shouting they make about the turn of the tide, so that all Aros shakes with it, is more than I can tell.

The truth is, that in a south-westerly wind, that part of our archipelago is no better than a trap. If a ship got through the reefs, and weathered the Merry Men, it would be to come ashore on the south coast of Aros, in Sandag Bay, where so many dismal things befell our family, as I propose to tell. The thought of all these dangers, in the place I knew so long, makes me particularly welcome the works now going forward to set lights upon the headlands and buoys along

16

the channels of our iron-bound, inhospitable islands.

The country people had many a story about Aros, as I used to hear from my uncle's man, Rorie, an old servant of the Macleans, who had transferred his services without afterthought on the occasion of the marriage. There was some tale of an unlucky creature, a sea-kelpie, that dwelt and did business in some fearful manner of his own among the boiling breakers of the Roost. A mermaid had once met a piper on Sandag beach, and there sang to him a long, bright midsummer's night, so that in the morning he was found stricken crazy, and from thenceforward, till the day he died, said only one form of words; what they were in the original Gaelic I cannot tell, but they were thus translated: "Ah, the sweet singing out of the sea." Seals that haunted on that coast have been known to speak to man in his own tongue, presaging great disasters. It was here that a certain saint first landed on his voyage out of Ireland to convert the Hebrideans. And, indeed, I think he had some claim to be called saint; for, with the boats of that past age, to make so rough a passage, and land on such a ticklish coast, was surely not far short of the miraculous. It was to him, or to some of his monkish underlings who had a cell there, that the islet owes its holy and beautiful name, the House of God.

Among these old wives' stories there was one

which I was inclined to hear with more credulity. As I was told, in that tempest which scattered the ships of the Invincible Armada over all the north and west of Scotland, one great vessel came ashore on Aros, and before the eyes of some solitary people on a hill-top, went down in a moment with all hands, her colours flying even as she sank. There was some likelihood in this tale; for another of that fleet lay sunk on the north side, twenty miles from Grisapol. It was told, I thought, with more detail and gravity than its companion stories, and there was one particularity which went far to convince me of its truth: the name, that is, of the ship was still remembered, and sounded, in my ears, Spanishly. The *Espirito Santo* they called it, a great ship of many decks of guns, laden with treasure and grandees of Spain, and fierce soldadoes, that now lay fathom deep to all eternity, done with her wars and voyages, in Sandag Bay, upon the west of Aros. No more salvos of ordnance for that tall ship, the "Holy Spirit," no more fair winds or happy ventures; only to rot there deep in the sea-tangle and hear the shoutings of the Merry Men as the tide ran high about the island. It was a strange thought to me first and last, and only grew stranger as I learned the more of the way in which she had set sail with so proud a company, and King Philip, the wealthy king, that sent her on that voyage.

And now I must tell you, as I walked from

Grisapol that day, the *Espirito Santo* was very much in my reflections. I had been favourably remarked by our then Principal in Edinburgh College, the famous writer, Dr. Robertson, and by him had been set to work on some papers of an ancient date to rearrange and sift of what was worthless; and in one of these, to my great wonder, I found a note of this very ship, the *Espirito Santo*, with her captain's name, and how she carried a great part of the Spaniard's treasure, and had been lost upon the Ross of Grisapol; but in what particular spot, the wild tribes of that place and period would give no information to the King's inquiries. Putting one thing with another, and taking our island tradition together with this note of old King Jamie's perquisitions after wealth, it had come strongly on my mind that the spot for which he sought in vain could be no other than the small bay of Sandag on my uncle's land; and being a fellow of a mechanical turn, I had ever since been plotting how to weigh that good ship up again with all her ingots, ounces, and doubloons, and bring back our house of Darnaway to its long-forgotten dignity and wealth.

This was a design of which I soon had reason to repent. My mind was sharply turned on different reflections; and since I became the witness of a strange judgment of God's the thought of dead men's treasures has been intolerable to my conscience. But even at that time I must acquit myself of sordid greed; for if I desired riches, it was not for their own sake, but for the sake of a person who was dear to my heart—my uncle's daughter, Mary Ellen. She had been educated well, and had been a time to school upon the mainland; which, poor girl, she would have been happier without. For Aros was no place for her with old Rorie the servant, and her father, who was one of the unhappiest men in Scotland, plainly bred up in a country place among Cameronians, long a skipper sailing out of the Clyde about the islands, and now, with infinite discontent, managing his sheep and a little 'long-shore fishing for the necessary bread. If it was sometimes weariful to me, who was there but a month or two, you may fancy what it was to her who dwelt in that same desert all the year round, with the sheep and flying seagulls, and the Merry Men singing and dancing in the Roost!

CHAPTER II

IT was half-flood when I got the length of Aros;
and there was nothing for it but to stand on
the far shore and whistle for Rorie with the boat.
I had no need to repeat the signal. At the first
sound, Mary was at the door flying a handker-
chief by way of answer, and the old long-legged
serving-man was shambling down the gravel to
the pier. For all his hurry, it took him a long
while to pull across the bay; and I observed him
several times to pause, go into the stern, and
look over curiously into the wake. As he came
nearer, he seemed to me aged and haggard, and
I thought he avoided my eye. The coble had
been repaired, with two new thwarts and several
patches of some rare and beautiful foreign wood,
the name of it unknown to me.

"Why, Rorie," said I, as we began the return
voyage, "this is fine wood. How came you by
that?"

"It will be hard to cheesel," Rorie opined re-
luctantly; and just then, dropping the oars, he

21

made another of those dives into the stern which I had remarked as he came across to fetch me, and, leaning his hand on my shoulder, stared with an awful look into the waters of the bay.

"What is wrong?" I asked, a good deal startled.

"It will be a great feesh," said the old man, returning to his oars; and nothing more could I get out of him, but strange glances and an ominous nodding of the head. In spite of myself, I was infected with a measure of uneasiness; I turned also, and studied the wake. The water was still and transparent, but, out here in the middle of the bay, exceeding deep. For some time I could see naught; but at last it did seem to me as if something dark—a great fish, or perhaps only a shadow—followed studiously in the track of the moving coble. And then I remembered one of Rorie's superstitions: how in a ferry in Morven, in some great, exterminating feud among the clans, a fish, the like of it unknown in all our waters, followed for some years the passage of the ferry-boat, until no man dared to make the crossing.

"He will be waiting for the right man," said Rorie.

Mary met me on the beach, and led me up the brae and into the house of Aros. Outside and inside there were many changes. The garden was fenced with the same wood that I had noted in the boat; there were chairs in the kitchen

covered with strange brocade; curtains of brocade hung from the window; a clock stood silent
on the dresser; a lamp of brass was swinging
from the roof; the table was set for dinner with
the finest of linen and silver; and all these new
riches were displayed in the plain old kitchen
that I knew so well, with the high-backed settle,
and the stools, and the closet-bed for Rorie; with
the wide chimney the sun shone into, and the
clear-smouldering peats; with the pipes on the
mantelshelf and the three-cornered spittoons,
filled with sea-shells instead of sand, on the floor;
with the bare stone walls and the bare wooden
floor, and the three patchwork rugs that were
of yore its sole adornment—poor man's patchwork, the like of it unknown in cities, woven
with homespun, and Sunday black, and sea-
cloth polished on the bench of rowing. The
room, like the house, had been a sort of wonder
in that country-side, it was so neat and habit-
able; and to see it now, shamed by these incongruous additions, filled me with indignation and
a kind of anger. In view of the errand I had
come upon to Aros, the feeling was baseless and
unjust; but it burned high, at the first moment,
in my heart.

"Mary, girl," said I, "this is the place I
had learned to call my home, and I do not
know it."

"It is my home by nature, not by the learning," she replied; "the place I was born and the

place I'm like to die in; and I neither like these changes, nor the way they came, nor that which came with them. I would have liked better, under God's pleasure, they had gone down into the sea, and the Merry Men were dancing on them now."

Mary was always serious; it was perhaps the only trait that she shared with her father; but the tone with which she uttered these words was even graver than of custom.

"Ay," said I, "I feared it came by wreck, and that's by death; yet when my father died, I took his goods without remorse."

"Your father died a clean-strae death, as the folk say," said Mary.

"True," I returned; "and a wreck is like a judgment. What was she called?"

"They ca'd her the *Christ-Anna*," said a voice behind me; and, turning round, I saw my uncle standing in the doorway.

He was a sour, small, bilious man, with a long face and very dark eyes; fifty-six years old, sound and active in body, and with an air somewhat between that of a shepherd and that of a man following the sea. He never laughed, that I heard; read long at the Bible; prayed much, like the Cameronians he had been brought up among; and indeed, in many ways, used to remind me of one of the hill-preachers in the killing times before the Revolution. But he never got much comfort, nor even, as I used to think, much

24

guidance, by his piety. He had his black fits when he was afraid of hell; but he had led a rough life, to which he would look back with envy, and was still a rough, cold, gloomy man.

As he came in at the door out of the sunlight, with his bonnet on his head and a pipe hanging in his button-hole, he seemed, like Rorie, to have grown older and paler, the lines were deeplier ploughed upon his face, and the whites of his eyes were yellow, like old stained ivory, or the bones of the dead.

"Ay," he repeated, dwelling upon the first part of the word, "the *Christ-Anna*. It's an awfu' name."

I made him my salutations, and complimented him upon his look of health; for I feared he had perhaps been ill.

"I'm in the body," he replied, ungraciously enough; "aye in the body and the sins of the body, like yoursel'. Denner," he said abruptly to Mary, and then ran on to me: "They're grand braws, thir that we hae gotten, are they no'? Yon's a bonny knock,[1] but it'll no gang; and the napery's by ordnar. Bonny, bairnly braws; it's for the like o' them folk sells the peace of God that passeth understanding; it's for the like o' them, an' maybe no' even sae muckle worth, folk daunton God to His face and burn in muckle hell; and it's for that reason the Scripture ca's them, as I read the passage, the accursed thing.

[1] Clock.

25

Mary, ye girzie," he interrupted himself to cry with some asperity, "what for hae ye no' put out the twa candlesticks?"

"Why should we need them at high noon?" she asked.

But my uncle was not to be turned from his idea. "We'll bruik[1] them while we may," he said; and so two massive candlesticks of wrought silver were added to the table equipage, already so unsuited to that rough sea-side farm.

"She cam' ashore Februar' 10, about ten at nicht," he went on to me. "There was nae wind, and a sair run o' sea; and she was in the sook o' the Roost, as I jaloose. We had seen her a' day, Rorie and me, beating to the wind. She wasna a handy craft, I 'm thinking, that *Christ-Anna;* for she would neither steer nor stey wi' them. A sair day they had of it; their hands was never aff the sheets, and it perishin' cauld—ower cauld to snaw; and aye they would get a bit nip o' wind, and awa' again, to pit the emp'y hope into them. Eh, man! but they had a sair day for the last o't! He would have had a prood, prood heart that won ashore upon the back o' that."

"And were all lost?" I cried. "God help them!"

"Wheesht!" he said sternly. "Nane shall pray for the deid on my hearth-stane."

I disclaimed a Popish sense for my ejaculation; and he seemed to accept my disclaimer with un-

[1]Enjoy.

26

usual facility, and ran on once more upon what had evidently become a favourite subject.

"We fand her in Sandag Bay, Rorie an' me, and a' thae braws in the inside of her. There's a kittle bit, ye see, about Sandag; whiles the sook rins strong for the Merry Men; an' whiles again, when the tide's makin' hard an' ye can hear the Roost blawin' at the far-end of Aros, there comes a back-spang of current straucht into Sandag Bay. Weel, there's the thing that got the grip on the *Christ-Anna*. She but to have come in ram-stam an' stern forrit; for the bows of her are aften under, and the back-side of her is clear at hie-water o' neaps. But, man! the dunt that she cam doon wi' when she struck! Lord save us a'! but it's an unco life to be a sailor—a cauld, wan-chancy life. Mony's the gliff I got mysel' in the great deep; and why the Lord should hae made yon unco water is mair than ever I could win to understand. He made the vales and the pastures, the bonny green yaird, the halesome, canty land—

> "And now they shout and sing to Thee,
> For Thou hast made them glad,"

as the Psalms say in the metrical version. No' that I would preen my faith to that clink neither; but it's bonny, and easier to mind. 'Who go to sea in ships,' they hae 't again—

> "and in
> Great waters trading be,
> Within the deep these men God's works
> And His great wonders see."

Weel, it's easy sayin' sae. Maybe Dauvit wasna very weel acquaint wi' the sea. But troth,
if it wasna prentit in the Bible, I wad whiles be
temp'it to think it wasna the Lord, but the
muckle, black deil that made the sea. There's
naething good comes oot o't but the fish; an' the
spentacle o' God riding on the tempest, to be
shüre, whilk would be what Dauvit was likely
ettling at. But, man, they were sair wonders
that God showed to the *Christ-Anna*—wonders,
do I ca' them? Judgments, rather: judgments in
the mirk nicht among the draygons o' the deep.
And their souls—to think o' that—their souls,
man, maybe no prepared! The sea—a muckle
yett to hell!"

I observed, as my uncle spoke, that his voice
was unnaturally moved and his manner unwont-
edly demonstrative. He leaned forward at these
last words, for example, and touched me on the
knee with his spread fingers, looking up into my
face with a certain pallor, and I could see that
his eyes shone with a deep-seated fire, and that
the lines about his mouth were drawn and
tremulous.

Even the entrance of Rorie, and the beginning
of our meal, did not detach him from his train
of thought beyond a moment. He conde-
scended, indeed, to ask me some questions as to
my success at college, but I thought it was with
half his mind; and even in his extempore grace,
which was, as usual, long and wandering, I could

find the trace of his preoccupation, praying, as he did, that God would "remember in mercy fower puir, feckless, fiddling, sinful creatures here by their lee-lane beside the great and dowie waters."

Soon there came an interchange of speeches between him and Rorie.

"Was it there?" asked my uncle.

"Ou, ay!" said Rorie.

I observed that they both spoke in a manner of aside, and with some show of embarrassment, and that Mary herself appeared to colour, and looked down on her plate. Partly to show my knowledge, and so relieve the party from an awkward strain, partly because I was curious, I pursued the subject.

"You mean the fish?" I asked.

"Whatten fish?" cried my uncle. "Fish, quo' he! Fish! Your een are fu' o' fatness, man; your heid dozened wi' carnal leir. Fish! it's a bogle!"

He spoke with great vehemence, as though angry; and perhaps I was not very willing to be put down so shortly, for young men are disputatious. At least I remember I retorted hotly, crying out upon childish superstitions.

"And ye come frae the College!" sneered Uncle Gordon. "Gude kens what they learn folk there; it's no muckle service onyway. Do ye think, man, that there's naething in a' yon saut wilderness o' a world oot wast there, wi' the

29

sea-grasses growin', an' the sea-beasts fechtin', an' the sun glintin' down into it, day by day? Na; the sea's like the land, but fearsomer. If there's folk ashore, there's folk in the sea—deid they may be, but they're folk whatever; and as for deils, there's nane that's like the sea-deils. There's no sae muckle harm in the land-deils, when a's said and done. Lang syne, when I was a callant in the south country, I mind there was an auld, bald bogle in the Peewie Moss. I got a glisk o' him mysel', sittin' on his hunkers in a hag, as grey's a tombstane. An', troth, he was a fearsome-like taed. But he steered naebody. Nae doobt, if ane that was a reprobate, ane the Lord hated, had gane by there wi' his sin still upon his stamach, nae doobt the creature would hae lowped upo' the likes o' him. But there's deils in the deep sea would yoke on a communicant! Eh, sirs, if ye had gane doon wi' the puir lads in the *Christ-Anna*, ye would ken by now the mercy o' the seas. If ye had sailed it for as lang as me, ye would hate the thocht of it as I do. If ye had but used the een God gave ye, ye would hae learned the wickedness o' that fause, saut, cauld, bullering creature, and of a' that's in it by the Lord's permission: labsters an' partans, an' sic like, howking in the deid; muckle, gutsy, blawing whales; an' fish—the hale clan o' them —cauld-wamed, blind-eed uncanny ferlies. O sirs," he cried, "the horror—the horror o' the sea!"

We were all somewhat staggered by this outburst; and the speaker himself, after that last
hoarse apostrophe, appeared to sink gloomily
into his own thoughts. But Rorie, who was
greedy of superstitious lore, recalled him to the
subject by a question.

"You will not ever have seen a teevil of the
sea?" he asked.

"No clearly," replied the other, "I misdoobt
if a mere man could see ane clearly and conteenue
in the body. I hae sailed wi' a lad—they ca'd him
Sandy Gabart; he saw ane, shüre eneuch, an'
shüre eneuch it was the end of him. We were
seeven days oot frae the Clyde—a sair wark we
had had—gaun north wi' seeds an' braws an'
things for the Macleod. We had got in ower
near under the Cutchull'ns, an' had just gane
about by Soa, an' were off on a lang tack, we
thocht would maybe hauld as far's Copnahow.
I mind the nicht weel; a mune smoored wi' mist;
a fine gaun breeze upon the water, but no steedy;
an'—what nane o' us likit to hear—anither wund
gurlin' owerheid, amang thae fearsome, auld
stane craigs o' the Cutchull'ns. Weel, Sandy
was forrit wi' the jib sheet; we couldna see him
for the mains'l, that had just begude to draw,
when a' at ance he gied a skirl. I luffed for my
life, for I thocht we were ower near Soa; but na,
it wasna that, it was puir Sandy Gabart's deid
skreigh, or near-hand, for he was deid in half an
hour. A't he could tell was that a sea-deil, or

sea-bogle, or sea-spenster, or sic-like, had clum up by the bowsprit, an' gi'en him ae cauld, uncanny look. An', or the life was oot o' Sandy's body, we kent weel what the thing betokened, and why the wund gurled in the taps o' the Cutchull'ns; for doon it cam'—a wund do I ca' it! it was the wund o' the Lord's anger—an' a' that nicht we foucht like men dementit, and the niest that we kenned we were ashore in Loch Uskevagh, an' the cocks were crawing in Benbecula."

"It will have been a merman," Rorie said.

"A merman!" screamed my uncle, with immeasurable scorn. "Auld wives' clavers! There's nae sic things as mermen."

"But what was the creature like?" I asked.

"What like was it? Gude forbid that we suld ken what like it was! It had a kind of a heid upon it—man could say nae mair."

Then Rorie, smarting under the affront, told several tales of mermen, mermaids, and seahorses that had come ashore upon the islands and attacked the crews of boats upon the sea; and my uncle, in spite of his incredulity, listened with uneasy interest.

"Aweel, aweel," he said, "it may be sae; I may be wrang; but I find nae word o' mermen in the Scriptures."

"And you will find nae word of Aros Roost, maybe," objected Rorie, and his argument appeared to carry weight.

WHAT THE WRECK BROUGHT

When dinner was over, my uncle carried me forth with him to a bank behind the house. It was a very hot and quiet afternoon; scarce a ripple anywhere upon the sea, nor any voice but the familiar voice of sheep and gulls; and perhaps in consequence of this repose in nature, my kinsman showed himself more rational and tranquil than before. He spoke evenly and almost cheerfully of my career, with every now and then a reference to the lost ship or the treasures it had brought to Aros. For my part, I listened to him in a sort of trance, gazing with all my heart on that remembered scene, and drinking gladly the sea-air and the smoke of peats that had been lit by Mary.

Perhaps an hour had passed when my uncle, who had all the while been covertly gazing on the surface of the little bay, rose to his feet and bade me follow his example. Now I should say that the great run of tide at the south-west end of Aros exercises a perturbing influence round all the coast. In Sandag Bay, to the south, a strong current runs at certain periods of the flood and ebb respectively; but in this northern bay—Aros Bay, as it is called—where the house stands and on which my uncle was now gazing, the only sign of disturbance is towards the end of the ebb, and even then it is too slight to be remarkable. When there is any swell, nothing can be seen at all; but when it is calm, as it often is, there appear certain strange, undecipherable marks—sea-runes, as we may name them—on the glassy surface of the bay. The like is common in a thousand places on the coast; and many a boy must have amused himself as I did, seeking to read in them some reference to himself or those he loved. It was to these marks that my uncle now directed my attention, struggling as he did so, with an evident reluctance.

"Do ye see yon scart upo' the water?" he inquired; "yon ane wast the grey stane? Ay? Weel, it 'll no' be like a letter, wull it?"

"Certainly it is," I replied. "I have often remarked it. It is like a C."

He heaved a sigh as if heavily disappointed with my answer, and then added below his breath: "Ay, for the *Christ-Anna*."

"I used to suppose, sir, it was for myself," said I; "for my name is Charles."

"And so ye saw 't afore?" he ran on, not heeding my remark. "Weel, weel, but that's unco strange. Maybe, it's been there waitin', as a man wad say, through a' the weary ages. Man, but that's awfu'." And then, breaking off: "Ye 'll no' see anither, will ye?" he asked.

"Yes," said I. "I see another very plainly, near the Ross side, where the road comes down— an M."

"An M," he repeated very low; and then, again after another pause: "An' what wad ye make o' that?" he inquired.

"I had always thought it to mean Mary, sir,"

I answered, growing somewhat red, convinced as I was in my own mind that I was on the threshold of a decisive explanation.

But we were each following his own train of thought to the exclusion of the other's. My uncle once more paid no attention to my words: only hung his head and held his peace; and I might have been led to fancy that he had not heard me, if his next speech had not contained a kind of echo from my own.

"I would say naething o' thae clavers to Mary," he observed, and began to walk forward.

There is a belt of turf along the side of Aros Bay where walking is easy; and it was along this that I silently followed my silent kinsman. I was perhaps a little disappointed at having lost so good an opportunity to declare my love; but I was at the same time far more deeply exercised at the change that had befallen my uncle. He was never an ordinary, never, in the strict sense, an amiable, man; but there was nothing in even the worst that I had known of him before, to prepare me for so strange a transformation. It was impossible to close the eyes against one fact; that he had, as the saying goes, something on his mind; and as I mentally ran over the different words which might be represented by the letter M—misery, mercy, marriage, money, and the like—I was arrested with a sort of start by the word murder. I was still considering the ugly sound and fatal meaning of the word, when the direction of our walk brought us to a point from which a view was to be had to either side, back towards Aros Bay and homestead, and forward on the ocean, dotted to the north with isles, and lying to the southward blue and open to the sky. There my guide came to a halt, and stood staring for a while on that expanse. Then he turned to me and laid a hand on my arm.

"Ye think there's naething there?" he said, pointing with his pipe; and then cried out aloud, with a kind of exultation: "I'll tell ye, man! The deid are down there—thick like rattons!"

He turned at once, and, without another word, we retraced our steps to the house of Aros.

I was eager to be alone with Mary; yet it was not till after supper, and then but for a short while, that I could have a word with her. I lost no time beating about the bush, but spoke out plainly what was on my mind.

"Mary," I said, "I have not come to Aros without a hope. If that should prove well founded, we may all leave and go somewhere else, secure of daily bread and comfort; secure, perhaps, of something far beyond that, which it would seem extravagant in me to promise. But there's a hope that lies nearer to my heart than money." And at that I paused. "You can guess fine what that is, Mary," I said. She looked away from me in silence, and that was small encouragement, but I was not to be put off. "All my days I have thought the world of you," I continued; "the time goes on and I think always the more of you; I could not think to be happy or hearty in my life without you: you are the apple of my eye." Still she looked away, and said never a word; but I thought I saw that her hands shook. "Mary," I cried in fear, "do ye no' like me?"

"Oh, Charlie man," she said, "is this a time to speak of it? Let me be a while; let me be the way I am; it'll not be you that loses by the waiting!"

I made out by her voice that she was nearly weeping, and this put me out of any thought but to compose her. "Mary Ellen," I said, "say no more; I did not come to trouble you: your way shall be mine, and your time too; and you have told me all I wanted. Only just this one thing more: what ails you?"

She owned it was her father, but would enter into no particulars, only shook her head, and said he was not well and not like himself, and it was a great pity. She knew nothing of the wreck. "I havena been near it," said she. "What for would I go near it, Charlie lad? The poor souls are gone to their account long syne; and I would just have wished they had ta'en their gear with them—poor souls!"

This was scarcely any great encouragement for me to tell her of the *Espirito Santo;* yet I did so, and at the very first word she cried out in surprise. "There was a man at Grisapol," she said, "in the month of May—a little, yellow, black-avised body, they tell me, with gold rings upon his fingers, and a beard; and he was speiring high and low for that same ship."

It was towards the end of April that I had been given these papers to sort out by Dr. Robertson: and it came suddenly back upon my mind that they were thus prepared for a Spanish historian, or a man calling himself such, who had come with high recommendations to the Principal, on a mission of inquiry as to the dispersion of the great Armada. Putting one thing with another, I fancied that the visitor "with the gold rings upon his fingers" might be the same with Dr. Robertson's historian from Madrid. If that were so, he would be more likely after treasure for himself than information for a learned society. I made up my mind, I should lose no time over my undertaking; and if the ship lay sunk in Sandag Bay, as perhaps both he and I supposed, it should not be for the advantage of this ringed adventurer, but for Mary and myself, and for the good, old, honest, kindly family of the Darnaways.

CHAPTER III

LAND AND SEA IN SANDAG BAY

I WAS early afoot next morning; and as soon as I had a bite to eat, set forth upon a tour of exploration. Something in my heart distinctly told me that I should find the ship of the Armada; and although I did not give way entirely to such hopeful thoughts, I was still very light in spirits and walked upon air. Aros is a very rough islet, its surface strewn with great rocks and shaggy with fern and heather; and my way lay almost north and south across the highest knoll; and though the whole distance was inside of two miles, it took more time and exertion than four upon a level road. Upon the summit, I paused. Although not very high—not three hundred feet, as I think—it yet out-tops all the neighbouring lowlands of the Ross, and commands a great view of sea and islands. The sun, which had been up some time, was already hot upon my neck; the air was listless and thundery, although purely clear; away over the north-west, where the isles lie thickliest congregated, some half-a-dozen small and ragged clouds hung together in a covey; and the head of Ben Kyaw wore, not merely a few streamers, but a solid hood of vapour. There was a threat in the weather. The sea, it is true, was smooth like glass: even the Roost was but a seam on that wide mirror, and the Merry Men no more than caps of foam; but to my eye and ear, so long familiar with these places, the sea also seemed to lie uneasily; a sound of it, like a long sigh, mounted to me where I stood; and, quiet as it was, the Roost itself appeared to be revolving mischief. For I ought to say that all we dwellers in these parts attributed, if not prescience, at least a quality of warning, to that strange and dangerous creature of the tides.

I hurried on, then, with the greater speed, and had soon descended the slope of Aros to the part that we call Sandag Bay. It is a pretty large piece of water compared with the size of the isle; well sheltered from all but the prevailing wind; sandy and shoal and bounded by low sand-hills to the west, but to the eastward lying several fathoms deep along a ledge of rocks. It is upon that side that, at a certain time each flood, the current mentioned by my uncle sets so strong into the bay; a little later, when the Roost begins to work higher, an undertow runs still more strongly in the reverse direction; and it is the action of this last, as I suppose, that has scoured that part so deep. Nothing is to be seen out of Sandag Bay but one small segment of the horizon and, in heavy weather, the breakers flying high over a deep sea-reef.

From half-way down the hill, I had perceived the wreck of February last, a brig of considerable tonnage, lying, with her back broken, high and dry on the east corner of the sands; and I was making directly towards it, and already almost on the margin of the turf, when my eyes were suddenly arrested by a spot, cleared of fern and heather, and marked by one of those long, low, and almost human-looking mounds that we see so commonly in graveyards. I stopped like a man shot. Nothing had been said to me of any dead man or interment on the island; Rorie, Mary, and my uncle had all equally held their peace; of her at least, I was certain that she must be ignorant; and yet here, before my eyes, was proof indubitable of the fact. Here was a grave; and I had to ask myself, with a chill, what manner of man lay there in his last sleep, awaiting the signal of the Lord in that solitary, sea-beat resting-place? My mind supplied no answer but what I feared to entertain. Shipwrecked, at least, he must have been; perhaps, like the old Armada mariners, from some far and rich land over-sea; or perhaps one of my own race, perishing within eyesight of the smoke of home. I stood a while uncovered by his side, and I could have desired that it had lain in our religion to put up some prayer for that unhappy stranger, or, in the old classic way, outwardly to honour his misfortune.

41

I knew, although his bones lay there, a part of
Aros, till the trumpet sounded, his imperishable
soul was forth and far away, among the raptures
of the everlasting Sabbath or the pangs of hell;
and yet my mind misgave me even with a fear,
that perhaps he was near me where I stood,
guarding his sepulchre and lingering on the scene
of his unhappy fate.

Certainly it was with a spirit somewhat overshadowed that I turned away from the grave to
the hardly less melancholy spectacle of the wreck.
Her stem was above the first arc of the flood; she
was broken in two a little abaft the foremast—
though indeed she had none, both masts having
broken short in her disaster; and as the pitch of
the beach was very sharp and sudden, and the
bows lay many feet below the stern, the fracture
gaped widely open, and you could see right
through her poor hull upon the farther side. Her
name was much defaced, and I could not make
out clearly whether she was called *Christiania*,
after the Norwegian city, or *Christiana*, after the
good woman, Christian's wife, in that old book
the *Pilgrim's Progress*. By her build she was
a foreign ship, but I was not certain of her nation-
ality. She had been painted green, but the colour was faded and weathered, and the paint peel-
ing off in strips. The wreck of the mainmast lay
alongside, half-buried in sand. She was a forlorn sight, indeed, and I could not look without
emotion at the bits of rope that still hung about

her, so often handled of yore by shouting seamen; or the little scuttle where they had passed
up and down to their affairs; or that poor nose-
less angel of a figure-head that had dipped into
so many running billows.

I do not know whether it came most from the
ship or from the grave, but I fell into some melancholy scruples, as I stood there, leaning with
one hand against the battered timbers. The
homelessness of men, and even of inanimate
vessels, cast away upon strange shores, came
strongly in upon my mind. To make a profit of
such pitiful misadventures seemed an unmanly
and a sordid act; and I began to think of my then
quest as of something sacrilegious in its nature.
But when I remembered Mary, I took heart
again. My uncle would never consent to an
imprudent marriage, nor would she, as I was
persuaded, wed without his full approval. It behoved me, then, to be up and doing for my wife;
and I thought with a laugh how long it was since
that great sea-castle, the *Espirito Santo*, had left
her bones in Sandag Bay, and how weak it would
be to consider rights so long extinguished and
misfortunes so long forgotten in the process of
time.

I had my theory of where to seek for her remains. The set of the current and the soundings
both pointed to the east side of the bay under the
ledge of rocks. If she had been lost in Sandag
Bay, and if, after these centuries, any portion of

her held together, it was there that I should find
it. The water deepens, as I have said, with
great rapidity, and even close alongside the rocks
several fathoms may be found. As I walked
upon the edge I could see far and wide over the
sandy bottom of the bay; the sun shone clear and
green and steady in the deeps; the bay seemed
rather like a great transparent crystal, as one
sees them in a lapidary's shop; there was naught
to show that it was water but an internal trembling, a hovering within of sun-glints and netted
shadows, and now and then a faint lap and a
dying bubble round the edge. The shadows of
the rocks lay out for some distance at their feet,
so that my own shadow, moving, pausing, and
stooping on the top of that, reached sometimes
half across the bay. It was above all in this
belt of shadows that I hunted for the *Espirito
Santo;* since it was there the undertow ran
strongest, whether in or out. Cool as the whole
water seemed this broiling day, it looked, in that
part, yet cooler, and had a mysterious invitation
for the eyes. Peer as I pleased, however, I
could see nothing but a few fishes or a bush of
sea-tangle, and here and there a lump of rock
that had fallen from above and now lay separate
on the sandy floor. Twice did I pass from one
end to the other of the rocks, and in the whole
distance I could see nothing of the wreck, nor
any place but one where it was possible for it to
be. This was a large terrace in five fathoms of

water, raised off the surface of the sand to a considerable height, and looking from above like a mere outgrowth of the rocks on which I walked. It was one mass of great sea-tangles like a grove, which prevented me judging of its nature, but in shape and size it bore some likeness to a vessel's hull. At least it was my best chance. If the *Espirito Santo* lay not there under the tangles, it lay nowhere at all in Sandag Bay; and I prepared to put the question to the proof, once and for all, and either go back to Aros a rich man or cured for ever of my dreams of wealth.

I stripped to the skin, and stood on the extreme margin with my hands clasped, irresolute. The bay at that time was utterly quiet; there was no sound but from a school of porpoises somewhere out of sight behind the point; yet a certain fear withheld me on the threshold of my venture. Sad sea-feelings, scraps of my uncle's superstitions, thoughts of the dead, of the grave, of the old broken ships, drifted through my mind, But the strong sun upon my shoulders warmed me to the heart, and I stooped forward and plunged into the sea.

It was all that I could do to catch a trail of the sea-tangle that grew so thickly on the terrace; but once so far anchored I secured myself by grasping a whole armful of these thick and slimy stalks, and, planting my feet against the edge, I looked around me. On all sides the clear sand stretched forth unbroken; it came to the foot of

the rocks, scoured into the likeness of an alley in
a garden by the action of the tides; and before
me, for as far as I could see, nothing was visible
but the same many-folded sand upon the sun-
bright bottom of the bay. Yet the terrace to
which I was then holding was as thick with
strong sea-growths as a tuft of heather, and the
cliff from which it bulged hung draped below the
water-line with brown lianas. In this complex-
ity of forms, all swaying together in the current,
things were hard to be distinguished; and I was
still uncertain whether my feet were pressed upon
the natural rock or upon the timbers of the Armada treasure-ship, when the whole tuft of tangle came away in my hand, and in an instant I
was on the surface, and the shores of the bay and
the bright water swam before my eyes in a glory
of crimson.

I clambered back upon the rocks, and threw
the plant of tangle at my feet. Something at the
same moment rang sharply, like a falling coin. I
stooped, and there, sure enough, crusted with the
red rust, there lay an iron shoe-buckle. The
sight of this poor human relic thrilled me to the
heart, but not with hope nor fear, only with a
desolate melancholy. I held it in my hand, and
the thought of its owner appeared before me like
the presence of an actual man. His weather-
beaten face, his sailor's hands, his sea-voice
hoarse with singing at the capstan, the very foot
that had once worn that buckle and trod so much

along the swerving decks—the whole human fact
of him, as a creature like myself, with hair and
blood and seeing eyes, haunted me in that sunny,
solitary place, not like a spectre, but like some
friend whom I had basely injured. Was the
great treasure-ship indeed below there, with her
guns and chain and treasure, as she had sailed
from Spain; her decks a garden for the sea-weed,
her cabin a breeding-place for fish, soundless but
for the dredging water, motionless but for the
waving of the tangle upon her battlements—that
old, populous, sea-riding castle, now a reef in
Sandag Bay? Or, as I thought it likelier, was
this a waif from the disaster of the foreign brig—
was this shoe-buckle bought but the other day
and worn by a man of my own period in the
world's history, hearing the same news from day
to day, thinking the same thoughts, praying,
perhaps, in the same temple with myself?   However it was, I was assailed with dreary thoughts;
my uncle's words, "the dead are down there,"
echoed in my ears; and though I determined
to dive once more, it was with a strong repugnance that I stepped forward to the margin of
the rocks.

A great change passed at that moment over
the appearance of the bay.   It was no more that
clear, visible interior, like a house roofed with
glass, where the green, submarine sunshine slept
so stilly. A breeze, I suppose, had flawed the
surface, and a sort of trouble and blackness filled

its bosom, where flashes of light and clouds of shadow tossed confusedly together. Even the terrace below obscurely rocked and quivered. It seemed a graver thing to venture on this place of ambushes; and when I leaped into the sea the second time it was with a quaking in my soul.

I secured myself as at first, and groped among the waving tangle. All that met my touch was cold and soft and gluey. The thicket was alive with crabs and lobsters, trundling to and fro lop-sidedly, and I had to harden my heart against the horror of their carrion neighbourhood. On all sides I could feel the grain and the clefts of hard, living stone; no planks, no iron, not a sign of any wreck; the *Espirito Santo* was not there. I remember I had almost a sense of relief in my disappointment, and I was about ready to leave go, when something happened that sent me to the surface with my heart in my mouth. I had already stayed somewhat late over my explorations; the current was freshening with the change of the tide, and Sandag Bay was no longer a safe place for a single swimmer. Well, just at the last moment there came a sudden flush of current, dredging through the tangles like a wave. I lost one hold, was flung sprawling on my side, and, instinctively grasping for a fresh support, my fingers closed on something hard and cold. I think I knew at that moment what it was. At least I instantly left hold of the tangle, leaped for the surface, and clambered out next moment on the friendly rocks with the bone of a man's leg in my grasp.

Mankind is a material creature, slow to think and dull to perceive connections. The grave, the wreck of the brig, and the rusty shoe-buckle were surely plain advertisements. A child might have read their dismal story, and yet it was not until I touched that actual piece of mankind that the full horror of the charnel ocean burst upon my spirit. I laid the bone beside the buckle, picked up my clothes, and ran as I was along the rocks towards the human shore. I could not be far enough from the spot; no fortune was vast enough to tempt me back again. The bones of the drowned dead should henceforth roll undisturbed by me, whether on tangle or minted gold. But as soon as I trod the good earth again and had covered my nakedness against the sun, I knelt down over against the ruins of the brig, and out of the fulness of my heart prayed long and passionately for all poor souls upon the sea. A generous prayer is never presented in vain; the petition may be refused, but the petitioner is always, I believe, rewarded by some gracious visitation. The horror, at least, was lifted from my mind; I could look with calm of spirit on that great bright creature, God's ocean; and as I set off homeward up the rough sides of Aros, nothing remained of any concern beyond a deep determination to meddle no more with the spoils of wrecked vessels or the treasures of the dead.

I was already some way up the hill before I paused to breathe and look behind me. The sight that met my eyes was doubly strange.

For, first, the storm that I had foreseen was now advancing with almost tropical rapidity. The whole surface of the sea had been dulled from its conspicuous brightness to an ugly hue of corrugated lead; already in the distance the white waves, the "skipper's daughters," had begun to flee before a breeze that was still insensible on Aros; and already along the curve of Sandag Bay there was a splashing run of sea that I could hear from where I stood. The change upon the sky was even more remarkable. There had begun to arise out of the south-west a huge and solid continent of scowling cloud; here and there, through rents in its contexture, the sun still poured a sheaf of spreading rays; and here and there, from all its edges, vast inky streamers lay forth along the yet unclouded sky. The menace was express and imminent. Even as I gazed, the sun was blotted out. At any moment the tempest might fall upon Aros in its might.

The suddenness of this change of weather so fixed my eyes on heaven that it was some seconds before they alighted on the bay, mapped out below my feet, and robbed a moment later of the sun. The knoll which I had just surmounted overflanked a little amphitheatre of lower hillocks sloping towards the sea, and beyond that the yellow arc of beach and the whole extent of

Sandag Bay. It was a scene on which I had
often looked down, but where I had never before beheld a human figure. I had but just
turned my back upon it and left it empty, and
my wonder may be fancied when I saw a boat
and several men in that deserted spot. The
boat was lying by the rocks. A pair of fellows,
bareheaded, with their sleeves rolled up, and
one with a boat-hook, kept her with difficulty to
her moorings, for the current was growing brisker
every moment. A little way off upon the ledge
two men in black clothes, whom I judged to be
superior in rank, laid their heads together over
some task which at first I did not understand, but
a second after I had made it out—they were taking bearings with the compass; and just then I
saw one of them unroll a sheet of paper and lay
his finger down, as though identifying features in
a map. Meanwhile a third was walking to and
fro, poking among the rocks and peering over the
edge into the water. While I was still watching
them with the stupefaction of surprise, my mind
hardly yet able to work on what my eyes reported, this third person suddenly stooped and
summoned his companions with a cry so loud
that it reached my ears upon the hill. The
others ran to him, even dropping the compass
in their hurry, and I could see the bone and the
shoe-buckle going from hand to hand, causing
the most unusual gesticulations of surprise and
interest. Just then I could hear the seamen

crying from the boat, and saw them point westward to that cloud continent which was ever the
more rapidly unfurling its blackness over heaven.
The others seemed to consult; but the danger
was too pressing to be braved, and they bundled
into the boat carrying my relics with them, and
set forth out of the bay with all speed of oars.

I made no more ado about the matter, but
turned and ran for the house. Whoever these
men were, it was fit my uncle should be instantly
informed. It was not then altogether too late
in the day for a descent of the Jacobites; and
maybe Prince Charlie, whom I knew my uncle to
detest, was one of the three superiors whom I
had seen upon the rock. Yet as I ran, leaping
from rock to rock, and turned the matter loosely
in my mind, this theory grew ever the longer the
less welcome to my reason. The compass, the
map, the interest awakened by the buckle, and
the conduct of that one among the strangers who
had looked so often below him in the water, all
seemed to point to a different explanation of
their presence on that outlying, obscure islet of
the western sea. The Madrid historian, the
search instituted by Dr. Robertson, the bearded
stranger with the rings, my own fruitless search
that very morning in the deep water of Sandag
Bay, ran together, piece by piece, in my memory,
and I made sure that these strangers must be
Spaniards in quest of ancient treasure and the
lost ship of the Armada. But the people living

in outlying islands, such as Aros, are answerable
for their own security; there is none near by to
protect or even to help them; and the presence
in such a spot of a crew of foreign adventurers—
poor, greedy, and most likely lawless—filled
me with apprehensions for my uncle's money,
and even for the safety of his daughter.   I was
still wondering how we were to get rid of them
when I came, all breathless, to the top of Aros.
The whole world was shadowed over; only in
the extreme east, on a hill of the mainland, one
last gleam of sunshine lingered like a jewel; rain
had begun to fall, not heavily, but in great drops;
the sea was rising with each moment, and already
a band of white encircled Aros and the nearer
coasts of Grisapol.   The boat was still pulling
seaward, but I now became aware of what had
been hidden from me lower down—a large,
heavily sparred, handsome schooner, lying to at
the south end of Aros.   Since I had not seen her
in the morning when I had looked around so
closely at the signs of the weather, and upon
these lone waters where a sail was rarely visible,
it was clear she must have lain last night behind
the uninhabited Eilean Gour, and this proved
conclusively that she was manned by strangers
to our coast, for that anchorage, though good
enough to look at, is little better than a trap for
ships.   With such ignorant sailors upon so wild
a coast, the coming gale was not unlikely to
bring death upon its wings.

CHAPTER IV

THE GALE

I FOUND my uncle at the gable-end, watching the signs of the weather, with a pipe in his fingers.

"Uncle," said I, "there were men ashore at Sandag Bay——"

I had no time to go further; indeed, I not only forgot my words, but even my weariness, so strange was the effect on Uncle Gordon. He dropped his pipe and fell back against the end of the house with his jaw fallen, his eyes staring, and his long face as white as paper. We must have looked at one another silently for a quarter of a minute, before he made answer in this extraordinary fashion: "Had he a hair kep on?"

I knew as well as if I had been there that the man who now lay buried at Sandag had worn a hairy cap, and that he had come ashore alive. For the first and only time I lost toleration for the man who was my benefactor and the father of the woman I hoped to call my wife.

"These were living men," said I, "perhaps Jacobites, perhaps the French, perhaps pirates,

54

perhaps adventurers come here to seek the Spanish treasure-ship; but, whatever they may be, dangerous at least to your daughter and my cousin. As for your own guilty terrors, man, the dead sleeps well where you have laid him. I stood this morning by his grave; he will not wake before the trump of doom."

My kinsman looked upon me, blinking, while I spoke; then he fixed his eyes for a little on the ground, and pulled his fingers foolishly; but it was plain that he was past the power of speech.

"Come," said I. "You must think for others. You must come up the hill with me, and see this ship."

He obeyed without a word or a look, following slowly after my impatient strides. The spring seemed to have gone out of his body, and he scrambled heavily up and down the rocks, instead of leaping, as he was wont, from one to another. Nor could I, for all my cries, induce him to make better haste. Only once he replied to me complainingly, and like one in bodily pain: "Ay, ay, man, I'm coming." Long before we had reached the top, I had no other thought for him but pity. If the crime had been monstrous, the punishment was in proportion.

At last we emerged above the sky-line of the hill, and could see around us. All was black and stormy to the eye; the last gleam of sun had vanished; a wind had sprung up, not yet high, but gusty and unsteady to the point; the rain, on the other hand, had ceased. Short as was the interval, the sea already ran vastly higher than when I had stood there last; already it had begun to break over some of the outward reefs, and already it moaned aloud in the sea-caves of Aros. I looked, at first in vain, for the schooner.

"There she is," I said at last. But her new position, and the course she was now lying, puzzled me. "They cannot mean to beat to sea," I cried.

"That's what they mean," said my uncle, with something like joy; and just then the schooner went about and stood upon another tack, which put the question beyond the reach of doubt. These strangers, seeing a gale on hand, had thought first of sea-room. With the wind that threatened, in these reef-sown waters and contending against so violent a stream of tide, their course was certain death.

"Good God!" said I, "they are all lost."

"Ay," returned my uncle, "a'—a' lost. They hadna a chance but to rin for Kyle Dona. The gate they're gaun the noo, they couldna win through an the muckle deil were there to pilot them. Eh, man," he continued, touching me on the sleeve, "it's a braw nicht for a shipwreck! Twa in ae twalmonth! Eh, but the Merry Men'll dance bonny!"

I looked at him, and it was then that I began to fancy him no longer in his right mind. He was peering up to me, as if for sympathy, a timid joy in his eyes. All that had passed between us was already forgotten in the prospect of this fresh disaster.

"If it were not too late," I cried with indignation, "I would take the coble and go out to warn them."

"Na, na," he protested, "ye maunna interfere; ye maunna meddle wi' the like o' that. It's His"—doffing his bonnet—"His wull. And, eh, man! but it's a braw nicht for 't!"

Something like fear began to creep into my soul; and, reminding him that I had not yet dined, I proposed we should return to the house. But no; nothing would tear him from his place of outlook.

"I maun see the hail thing, man, Cherlie," he explained; and then as the schooner went about a second time, "Eh, but they han'le her bonny!" he cried. "The *Christ-Anna* was naething to this."

Already the men on board the schooner must have begun to realise some part, but not yet the twentieth, of the dangers that environed their doomed ship. At every lull of the capricious wind they must have seen how fast the current swept them back. Each tack was made shorter, as they saw how little it prevailed. Every moment the rising swell began to boom and foam upon another sunken reef; and ever and again a breaker would fall in sounding ruin under the very bows of her, and the brown reef and stream-

ing tangle appear in the hollow of the wave. I
tell you, they had to stand to their tackle; there
was no idle man aboard that ship, God knows.
It was upon the progress of a scene so horrible
to any human-hearted man that my misguided
uncle now pored and gloated like a connoisseur.
As I turned to go down the hill, he was lying
on his belly on the summit, with his hands
stretched forth and clutching in the heather.
He seemed rejuvenated, mind and body.

When I got back to the house already dismally
affected, I was still more sadly downcast at the
sight of Mary. She had her sleeves rolled up
over her strong arms, and was quietly making
bread. I got a bannock from the dresser and
sat down to eat it in silence.

"Are ye wearied, lad?" she asked after a while.

"I am not so much wearied, Mary," I replied,
getting on my feet, "as I am weary of delay, and
perhaps of Aros too. You know me well enough
to judge me fairly, say what I like. Well, Mary,
you may be sure of this: you had better be anywhere but here."

"I'll be sure of one thing," she returned: "I'll
be where my duty is."

"You forget, you have a duty to yourself," I
said.

"Ay, man?" she replied, pounding at the
dough; "will you have found that in the Bible,
now?"

"Mary," I said solemnly, "you must not laugh

at me just now. God knows I am in no heart for laughing. If we could get your father with us, it would be best; but with him or without him, I want you far away from here, my girl; for your own sake, and for mine, ay, and for your father's too, I want you far—far away from here. I came with other thoughts; I came here as a man comes home; now it is all changed, and I have no desire nor hope but to flee—for that's the word —flee, like a bird out of the fowler's snare, from this accursed island."

She had stopped her work by this time.

"And do you think, now," said she, "do ye think, now, I have neither eyes nor ears? Do ye think I havena broken my heart to have these braws (as he calls them, God forgive him!) thrown into the sea? Do ye think I have lived with him, day in, day out, and not seen what you saw in an hour or two? No," she said, "I know there's wrong in it; what wrong, I neither know nor want to know. There was never an ill thing made better by meddling, that I could hear of. But, my lad, you must never ask me to leave my father. While the breath is in his body, I'll be with him. And he's not long for here, either: that I can tell you, Charlie—he's not long for here. The mark is on his brow; and better so— maybe better so."

I was a while silent, not knowing what to say; and when I roused my head at last to speak, she got before me.

"Charlie," she said, "what's right for me, needna be right for you. There's sin upon this house and trouble; you are a stranger; take your things upon your back and go your ways to better places and to better folk, and if you were ever minded to come back, though it were twenty years syne, you would find me aye waiting."

"Mary Ellen," I said, "I asked you to be my wife, and you said as good as yes. That's done for good. Wherever you are, I am; as I shall answer to my God."

As I said the words, the winds suddenly burst out raving, and then seemed to stand still and shudder round the house of Aros. It was the first squall, or prologue, of the coming tempest, and as we started and looked about us, we found that a gloom, like the approach of evening, had settled round the house.

"God pity all poor folks at sea!" she said. "We'll see no more of my father till the morrow's morning."

And then she told me, as we sat by the fire and hearkened to the rising gusts, of how this change had fallen upon my uncle. All last winter he had been dark and fitful in his mind. Whenever the Roost ran high, or, as Mary said, whenever the Merry Men were dancing, he would lie out for hours together on the Head, if it were at night, or on the top of Aros by day, watching the tumult of the sea, and sweeping the horizon for a sail. After February the tenth, when the

wealth-bringing wreck was cast ashore at Sandag, he had been at first unnaturally gay, and
his excitement had never fallen in degree, but
only changed in kind from dark to darker. He
neglected his work, and kept Rorie idle. They
two would speak together by the hour at the
gable-end, in guarded tones and with an air of
secrecy and almost of guilt; and if she questioned
either, as at first she sometimes did, her inquiries
were put aside with confusion. Since Rorie had
first remarked the fish that hung about the ferry,
his master had never set foot but once upon the
mainland of the Ross. That once—it was in
the height of the springs—he had passed dryshod while the tide was out; but, having lingered
over-long on the far side, found himself cut off
from Aros by the returning waters. It was with
a shriek of agony that he had leaped across the
gut, and he had reached home thereafter in a
fever-fit of fear. A fear of the sea, a constant
haunting thought of the sea, appeared in his talk
and devotions, and even in his looks when he
was silent.

Rorie alone came in to supper; but a little later
my uncle appeared, took a bottle under his arm,
put some bread in his pocket, and set forth again
to his outlook, followed this time by Rorie. I
heard that the schooner was losing ground, but
the crew were still fighting every inch with hopeless ingenuity and courage; and the news filled
my mind with blackness.

A little after sundown the full fury of the gale broke forth, such a gale as I have never seen in summer, nor, seeing how swiftly it had come, even in winter. Mary and I sat in silence, the house quaking overhead, the tempest howling without, the fire between us sputtering with raindrops. Our thoughts were far away with the poor fellows on the schooner, or my not less unhappy uncle, houseless on the promontory; and yet ever and again we were startled back to ourselves, when the wind would rise and strike the gable like a solid body, or suddenly fall and draw away, so that the fire leaped into flame and our hearts bounded in our sides. Now the storm in its might would seize and shake the four corners of the roof, roaring like Leviathan in anger. Anon, in a lull, cold eddies of tempest moved shudderingly in the room, lifting the hair upon our heads and passing between us as we sat. And again the wind would break forth in a chorus of melancholy sounds, hooting low in the chimney, wailing with flutelike softness round the house.

It was perhaps eight o'clock when Rorie came in and pulled me mysteriously to the door. My uncle, it appeared, had frightened even his constant comrade; and Rorie, uneasy at his extravagance, prayed me to come out and share the watch. I hastened to do as I was asked; the more readily as, what with fear and horror, and the electrical tension of the night, I was myself restless and disposed for action. I told Mary to be under no alarm, for I should be a safeguard on her father; and wrapping myself warmly in a plaid, I followed Rorie into the open air.

The night, though we were so little past midsummer, was as dark as January. Intervals of a groping twilight alternated with spells of utter blackness; and it was impossible to trace the reason of these changes in the flying horror of the sky. The wind blew the breath out of a man's nostrils; all heaven seemed to thunder overhead like one huge sail; and when there fell a momentary lull on Aros, we could hear the gusts dismally sweeping in the distance. Over all the lowlands of the Ross, the wind must have blown as fierce as on the open sea; and God only knows the uproar that was raging around the head of Ben Kyaw. Sheets of mingled spray and rain were driven in our faces. All round the isle of Aros the surf, with an incessant, hammering thunder, beat upon the reefs and beaches. Now louder in one place, now lower in another, like the combinations of orchestral music, the constant mass of sound was hardly varied for a moment. And loud above all this hurly-burly I could hear the changeful voices of the Roost and the intermittent roaring of the Merry Men. At that hour, there flashed into my mind the reason of the name that they were called. For the noise of them seemed almost mirthful, as it outtopped the other noises of the night; or if not

mirthful, yet instinct with a portentous joviality.
Nay, and it seemed even human. As when savage men have drunk away their reason, and, discarding speech, bawl together in their madness by the hour; so, to my ears, these deadly breakers shouted by Aros in the night.

Arm in arm, and staggering against the wind, Rorie and I won every yard of ground with conscious effort. We slipped on the wet sod, we fell together sprawling on the rocks. Bruised, drenched, beaten, and breathless, it must have taken us near half an hour to get from the house down to the Head that overlooks the Roost. There, it seemed, was my uncle's favourite observatory. Right in the face of it, where the cliff is highest and most sheer, a hump of earth, like a parapet, makes a place of shelter from the common winds, where a man may sit in quiet and see the tide and the mad billows contending at his feet. As he might look down from the window of a house upon some street disturbance, so, from this post, he looks down upon the tumbling of the Merry Men. On such a night, of course, he peers upon a world of blackness, where the waters wheel and boil, where the waves joust together with the noise of an explosion and the foam towers and vanishes in the twinkling of an eye. Never before had I seen the Merry Men thus violent. The fury, height, and transiency of their spoutings was a thing to be seen and not recounted. High over our heads on the cliff

rose their white columns in the darkness; and the
same instant, like phantoms, they were gone.
Sometimes three at a time would thus aspire
and vanish; sometimes a gust took them, and the
spray would fall about us, heavy as a wave.
And yet the spectacle was rather maddening in
its levity than impressive by its force.   Thought
was beaten down by the confounding uproar; a
gleeful vacancy possessed the brains of men, a
state akin to madness; and I found myself at
times following the dance of the Merry Men as
it were a tune upon a jigging instrument.

I first caught sight of my uncle when we were
still some yards away in one of the flying glimpses
of twilight that chequered the pitch darkness of
the night.   He was standing up behind the parapet, his head thrown back and the bottle to his
mouth.   As he put it down, he saw and recognised us with a toss of one hand fleeringly above
his head.

"Has he been drinking?" shouted I to Rorie.

"He will aye be drunk when the wind blaws,"
returned Rorie in the same high key, and it was
all that I could do to hear him.

"Then—was he so—in February?" I inquired.

Rorie's "Ay" was a cause of joy to me.   The
murder, then, had not sprung in cold blood from
calculation; it was an act of madness no more to
be condemned than to be pardoned.   My uncle
was a dangerous madman, if you will, but he was
not cruel and base as I had feared.   Yet what a

scene for a carouse, what an incredible vice was
this that the poor man had chosen! I have
always thought drunkenness a wild and almost
fearful pleasure, rather demoniacal than human;
but drunkenness, out here in the roaring blackness, on the edge of a cliff above that hell of waters, the man's head spinning like the Roost, his
foot tottering on the edge of death, his ear watching for the signs of shipwreck, surely that, if it
were credible in any one, was morally impossible
in a man like my uncle, whose mind was set upon
a damnatory creed and haunted by the darkest
superstitions. Yet so it was; and, as we reached
the bight of shelter and could breathe again, I
saw the man's eye shining in the night with an
unholy glimmer.

"Eh, Charlie man, it's grand!" he cried.
"See to them!" he continued, dragging me to
the edge of the abyss from whence arose that
deafening clamour and those clouds of spray;
"see to them dancin', man! Is that no' wicked?"

He pronounced the word with gusto, and I
thought it suited with the scene.

"They're yowlin' for thon schooner," he went
on, his thin, insane voice clearly audible in the
shelter of the bank, "an' she's comin' aye nearer,
aye nearer, aye nearer an' nearer an' nearer; an'
they ken't, the folk kens it, they ken weel it's
by wi' them. Charlie, lad, they're a' drunk in
yon schooner, a' dozened wi' drink. They were
a' drunk in the *Christ-Anna*, at the hinder end.

There's nane could droon at sea wantin' the brandy. Hoot awa, what do you ken?" with a sudden blast of anger. "I tell ye, it canna be; they daurna droon withoot it. Ha'e," holding out the bottle, "tak' a sowp."

I was about to refuse, but Rorie touched me as if in warning; and indeed I had already thought better of the movement. I took the bottle, therefore, and not only drank freely myself, but contrived to spill even more as I was doing so. It was pure spirit, and almost strangled me to swallow. My kinsman did not observe the loss, but, once more throwing back his head, drained the remainder to the dregs. Then, with a loud laugh, he cast the bottle forth among the Merry Men, who seemed to leap up, shouting, to receive it.

"Ha'e, bairns!" he cried, "there's your han'sel. Ye'll get bonnier nor that, or morning."

Suddenly, out in the black night before us, and not two hundred yards away, we heard, at a moment when the wind was silent, the clear note of a human voice. Instantly the wind swept howling down upon the Head, and the Roost bellowed, and churned, and danced with a new fury. But we had heard the sound, and we knew, with agony, that this was the doomed ship now close on ruin, and that what we had heard was the voice of her master issuing his last command. Crouching together on the edge, we waited, straining every sense, for the inevitable end. It was long, however, and to us it seemed like ages, ere the schooner suddenly appeared for one brief instant, relieved against a tower of glimmering foam. I still see her reefed mainsail flapping loose, as the boom fell heavily across the deck; I still see the black outline of the hull, and still think I can distinguish the figure of a man stretched upon the tiller. Yet the whole sight we had of her passed swifter than lightning; the very wave that disclosed her fell burying her for ever; the mingled cry of many voices at the point of death rose and was quenched in the roaring of the Merry Men. And with that the tragedy was at an end. The strong ship, with all her gear, and the lamp perhaps still burning in the cabin, the lives of so many men, precious surely to others, dear, at least, as heaven to themselves, had all, in that one moment, gone down into the surging waters. They were gone like a dream. And the wind still ran and shouted, and the senseless waters in the Roost still leaped and tumbled as before.

How long we lay there together, we three, speechless and motionless, is more than I can tell, but it must have been for long. At length, one by one, and almost mechanically, we crawled back into the shelter of the bank. As I lay against the parapet, wholly wretched and not entirely master of my mind, I could hear my kinsman maundering to himself in an altered and melancholy mood. Now he would repeat to himself with maudlin iteration, "Sic a fecht as they had—sic a sair fecht as they had, puir lads, puir lads!" and anon he would bewail that "a' the gear was as gude's tint," because the ship had gone down among the Merry Men instead of stranding on the shore; and throughout, the name—the *Christ-Anna*—would come and go in his divagations, pronounced with shuddering awe. The storm all this time was rapidly abating. In half an hour the wind had fallen to a breeze, and the change was accompanied or caused by a heavy, cold, and plumping rain. I must then have fallen asleep, and when I came to myself, drenched, stiff, and unrefreshed, day had already broken, grey, wet, discomfortable day; the wind blew in faint and shifting capfuls, the tide was out, the Roost was at its lowest, and only the strong beating surf round all the coasts of Aros remained to witness of the furies of the night.

CHAPTER V

A MAN OUT OF THE SEA

RORIE set out for the house in search of warmth and breakfast; but my uncle was bent upon examining the shores of Aros, and I felt it a part of duty to accompany him throughout. He was now docile and quiet, but tremulous and weak in mind and body; and it was with the eagerness of a child that he pursued his exploration. He climbed far down upon the rocks; on the beaches, he pursued the retreating breakers. The merest broken plank or rag of cordage was a treasure in his eyes to be secured at the peril of his life. To see him, with weak and stumbling footsteps, expose himself to the pursuit of the surf, or the snares and pitfalls of the weedy rock, kept me in a perpetual terror. My arm was ready to support him, my hand clutched him by the skirt, I helped him to draw his pitiful discoveries beyond the reach of the returning wave; a nurse accompanying a child of seven would have had no different experience.

Yet, weakened as he was by the reaction from

70

his madness of the night before, the passions that smouldered in his nature were those of a strong man. His terror of the sea, although conquered for the moment, was still undiminished; had the sea been a lake of living flames, he could not have shrunk more panically from its touch; and once, when his foot slipped and he plunged to the mid-leg into a pool of water, the shriek that came up out of his soul was like the cry of death. He sat still for a while, panting like a dog, after that; but his desire for the spoils of shipwreck triumphed once more over his fears; once more he tottered among the curded foam; once more he crawled upon the rocks among the bursting bubbles; once more his whole heart seemed to be set on drift-wood, fit, if it was fit for anything, to throw upon the fire. Pleased as he was with what he found, he still incessantly grumbled at his ill-fortune.

"Aros," he said, "is no' a place for wrecks ava' —no' ava'. A' the years I 've dwalt here, this ane maks the second; and the best o' the gear clean tint!"

"Uncle," said I, for we were now on a stretch of open sand, where there was nothing to divert his mind, "I saw you last night as I never thought to see you—you were drunk."

"Na, na," he said, "no' as bad as that. I had been drinking, though. And to tell ye the God's truth, it 's a thing I canna mend. There 's nae soberer man than me in my ordnar; but when

I hear the wind blaw in my lug, it's my belief that I gang gyte."

"You are a religious man," I replied, "and this is sin."

"Ou," he returned, "if it wasna sin, I dinna ken that I would care for 't. Ye see, man, it's defiance. There's a sair spang o' the auld sin o' the warld in yon sea; it's an unchristian business at the best o't; an' whiles when it gets up, an' the wind skreighs—the wind an' her are a kind of sib, I'm thinkin'—an' thae Merry Men, the daft callants, blawin' and lauchin', and puir souls in the deid thraws warstlin' the leelang nicht wi' their bit ships—weel, it comes ower me like a glamour. I'm a deil, I ken't. But I think naething o' the puir sailor lads; I'm wi' the sea, I'm just like ane o' her ain Merry Men."

I thought I should touch him in a joint of his harness. I turned me towards the sea; the surf was running gaily, wave after wave, with their manes blowing behind them, riding one after another up the beach, towering, curving, falling one upon another on the trampled sand. Without, the salt air, the scared gulls, the widespread army of the sea-chargers, neighing to each other, as they gathered together to the assault of Aros; and close before us, that line on the flat sands that, with all their number and their fury, they might never pass.

"Thus far shalt thou go," said I, "and no farther." And then I quoted as solemnly as I

72

was able a verse that I had often before fitted to
the chorus of the breakers:

> "But yet the Lord that is on high,
>   Is more of might by far,
> Than noise of many waters is,
>   Or great sea-billows are."

"Ay," said my kinsman, "at the hinder end,
the Lord will triumph; I dinna misdoobt that.
But here on earth, even silly men-folk daur Him
to His face. It is no' wise; I am no' sayin' that
it's wise; but it's the pride of the eye, and it's
the lust o' life, an' it's the wale o' pleesures."

I said no more, for we had now begun to cross
a neck of land that lay between us and Sandag;
and I withheld my last appeal to the man's better
reason till we should stand upon the spot associated with his crime. Nor did he pursue the
subject; but he walked beside me with a firmer
step. The call that I had made upon his mind
acted like a stimulant, and I could see that he had
forgotten his search for worthless jetsam, in a profound, gloomy, and yet stirring train of thought.
In three or four minutes we had topped the
brae and begun to go down upon Sandag. The
wreck had been roughly handled by the sea;
the stem had been spun round and dragged a
little lower down; and perhaps the stern had been
forced a little higher, for the two parts now lay
entirely separate on the beach. When we came
to the grave I stopped, uncovered my head in

the thick rain, and, looking my kinsman in the face, addressed him.

"A man," said I, "was in God's providence suffered to escape from mortal dangers; he was poor, he was naked, he was wet, he was weary, he was a stranger; he had every claim upon the bowels of your compassion; it may be that he was the salt of the earth, holy, helpful, and kind; it may be he was a man laden with iniquities to whom death was the beginning of torment. I ask you in the sight of Heaven: Gordon Darnaway, where is the man for whom Christ died?"

He started visibly at the last words; but there came no answer, and his face expressed no feeling but a vague alarm.

"You were my father's brother," I continued: "you have taught me to count your house as if it were my father's house; and we are both sinful men walking before the Lord among the sins and dangers of this life. It is by our evil that God leads us into good; we sin, I dare not say by His temptation, but I must say with His consent; and to any but the brutish man his sins are the beginning of wisdom. God has warned you by this crime; He warns you still by the bloody grave between our feet; and if there shall follow no repentance, no improvement, no return to Him, what can we look for but the following of some memorable judgment?"

Even as I spoke the words, the eyes of my uncle wandered from my face. A change fell upon his looks that cannot be described; his features seemed to dwindle in size, the colour faded from his cheeks, one hand rose waveringly and pointed over my shoulder into the distance, and the oft-repeated name fell once more from his lips: "The *Christ-Anna!*"

I turned; and if I was not appalled to the same degree, as I return thanks to Heaven that I had not the cause, I was still startled by the sight that met my eyes. The form of a man stood upright on the cabin-hutch of the wrecked ship; his back was towards us; he appeared to be scanning the offing with shaded eyes, and his figure was relieved to its full height, which was plainly very great, against the sea and sky. I have said a thousand times that I am not superstitious; but at that moment, with my mind running upon death and sin, the unexplained appearance of a stranger on that sea-girt, solitary island filled me with a surprise that bordered close on terror. It seemed scarce possible that any human soul should have come ashore alive in such a sea as had raged last night along the coasts of Aros; and the only vessel within miles had gone down before our eyes among the Merry Men. I was assailed with doubts that made suspense unbearable, and, to put the matter to the touch at once, stepped forward and hailed the figure like a ship.

He turned about, and I thought he started to behold us. At this my courage instantly revived and I called and signed to him to draw near, and

he, on his part, dropped immediately to the sands
and began slowly to approach, with many stops
and hesitations. At each repeated mark of the
man's uneasiness I grew the more confident myself; and I advanced another step, encouraging
him as I did so with my head and hand. It was
plain the castaway had heard indifferent ac-
counts of our island hospitality; and indeed,
about this time, the people farther north had a
sorry reputation.

"Why," I said, "the man is black!"

And just at that moment, in a voice that I
could scarce have recognised, my kinsman began
swearing and praying in a mingled stream. I
looked at him; he had fallen on his knees, his
face was agonised; at each step of the castaway's
the pitch of his voice rose, the volubility of his
utterance and the fervour of his language redoubled. I call it prayer, for it was addressed
to God; but surely no such ranting incongruities
were ever before addressed to the Creator by a
creature: surely if prayer can be a sin, this mad
harangue was sinful. I ran to my kinsman, I
seized him by the shoulders, I dragged him to
his feet.

"Silence, man," said I, "respect your God in
words, if not in action. Here, on the very scene
of your transgressions, He sends you an occasion
of atonement. Forward and embrace it; welcome like a father yon creature who comes trembling to your mercy."

A MAN OUT OF THE SEA

With that, I tried to force him towards the
black; but he felled me to the ground, burst from
my grasp, leaving the shoulder of his jacket, and
fled up the hillside towards the top of Aros like
a deer. I staggered to my feet again, bruised
and somewhat stunned; the negro had paused in
surprise, perhaps in terror, some half-way between me and the wreck; my uncle was already
far away, bounding from rock to rock; and I thus
found myself torn for a time between two duties.
But I judged, and I pray Heaven that I judged
rightly, in favour of the poor wretch upon the
sands; his misfortune was at least not plainly of
his own creation; it was one, besides, that I could
certainly relieve; and I had begun by that time to
regard my uncle as an incurable and dismal lunatic. I advanced accordingly towards the black,
who now awaited my approach with folded arms,
like one prepared for either destiny. As I came
nearer, he reached forth his hand with a great
gesture, such as I had seen from the pulpit, and
spoke to me in something of a pulpit voice, but
not a word was comprehensible. I tried him
first in English, then in Gaelic, both in vain; so
that it was clear we must rely upon the tongue
of looks and gestures. Thereupon I signed to
him to follow me, which he did readily and with
a grave obeisance like a fallen king; all the while
there had come no shade of alteration in his face,
neither of anxiety while he was still waiting, nor
of relief now that he was reassured; if he were a

slave, as I supposed, I could not but judge he must have fallen from some high place in his own country, and fallen as he was, I could not but admire his bearing. As we passed the grave, I paused and raised my hands and eyes to heaven in token of respect and sorrow for the dead; and he, as if in answer, bowed low and spread his hands abroad; it was a strange motion, but done like a thing of common custom; and I supposed it was ceremonial in the land from which he came. At the same time he pointed to my uncle, whom he could just see perched upon a knoll, and touched his head to indicate that he was mad.

We took the long way round the shore, for I feared to excite my uncle if we struck across the island; and as we walked, I had time enough to mature the little dramatic exhibition by which I hoped to satisfy my doubts. Accordingly, pausing on a rock, I proceeded to imitate before the negro the action of the man whom I had seen the day before taking bearings with the compass at Sandag. He understood me at once, and, taking the imitation out of my hands, showed me where the boat was, pointed out seaward as if to indicate the position of the schooner, and then down along the edge of the rock with the words, "Espirito Santo," strangely pronounced, but clear enough for recognition. I had thus been right in my conjecture; the pretended historical inquiry had been but a cloak for treasure-hunting; the man who had played Dr. Robertson was the same as the foreigner who visited Grisapol in spring, and now, with many others, lay dead under the Roost of Aros: there had their greed brought them, there should their bones be tossed for ever-more. In the meantime the black continued his imitation of the scene, now looking up skyward as though watching the approach of the storm; now, in the character of a seaman, waving the rest to come aboard; now as an officer, running along the rock and entering the boat; and anon bending over imaginary oars with the air of a hurried boatman; but all with the same solemnity of manner, so that I was never even moved to smile. Lastly, he indicated to me, by a panto-mime not to be described in words, how he himself had gone up to examine the stranded wreck, and, to his grief and indignation, had been deserted by his comrades; and thereupon folded his arms once more, and stooped his head, like one accepting fate.

The mystery of his presence being thus solved for me, I explained to him by means of a sketch the fate of the vessel and of all aboard her. He showed no surprise nor sorrow, and, with a sudden lifting of his open hand, seemed to dismiss his former friends or masters (whichever they had been) into God's pleasure. Respect came upon me and grew stronger, the more I observed him; I saw he had a powerful mind and a sober and severe character, such as I loved to commune with; and before we reached the house of Aros

I had almost forgotten, and wholly forgiven him, his uncanny colour.

To Mary I told all that had passed without suppression, though I own my heart failed me; but I did wrong to doubt her sense of justice. "You did the right," she said. "God's will be done." And she set out meat for us at once.

As soon as I was satisfied, I bade Rorie keep an eye upon the castaway, who was still eating, and set forth again myself to find my uncle. I had not gone far before I saw him sitting in the same place, upon the very topmost knoll, and seemingly in the same attitude as when I had last observed him. From that point, as I have said, the most of Aros and the neighbouring Ross would be spread below him like a map; and it was plain that he kept a bright look-out in all directions, for my head had scarcely risen above the summit of the first ascent before he had leaped to his feet and turned as if to face me. I hailed him at once, as well as I was able, in the same tones and words as I had often used before, when I had come to summon him to dinner. He made not so much as a movement in reply. I passed on a little farther, and again tried parley, with the same result. But when I began a second time to advance, his insane fears blazed up again, and still in dead silence, but with incredible speed, he began to flee from before me along the rocky summit of the hill. An hour before, he had been dead weary, and I had been compara-

tively active. But now his strength was re-
cruited by the fervour of insanity, and it would
have been vain for me to dream of pursuit. Nay,
the very attempt, I thought, might have inflamed his terrors, and thus increased the miseries of our position. And I had nothing left but
to turn homeward and make my sad report to
Mary.

She heard it, as she had heard the first, with a
concerned composure, and, bidding me lie down
and take that rest of which I stood so much in
need, set forth herself in quest of her misguided
father. At that age it would have been a strange
thing that put me from either meat or sleep; I
slept long and deep; and it was already long past
noon before I awoke and came down-stairs into
the kitchen. Mary, Rorie, and the black castaway were seated about the fire in silence; and I
could see that Mary had been weeping. There
was cause enough, as I soon learned, for tears.
First she, and then Rorie, had been forth to seek
my uncle; each in turn had found him perched
upon the hill-top, and from each in turn he had
silently and swiftly fled. Rorie had tried to
chase him, but in vain; madness lent a new vigour
to his bounds; he sprang from rock to rock
over the widest gullies; he scoured like the wind
along the hill-tops; he doubled and twisted like a
hare before the dogs; and Rorie at length gave
in; and the last that he saw, my uncle was seated
as before upon the crest of Aros. Even during

the hottest excitement of the chase, even when
the fleet-footed servant had come, for a moment,
very near to capture him, the poor lunatic had
uttered not a sound. He fled, and he was silent,
like a beast; and this silence had terrified his
pursuer.

There was something heart-breaking in the situation. How to capture the madman, how to
feed him in the meanwhile, and what to do with
him when he was captured, were the three difficulties that we had to solve.

"The black," said I, "is the cause of this attack. It may even be his presence in the house
that keeps my uncle on the hill. We have done
the fair thing; he has been fed and warmed under
this roof; now I propose that Rorie put him
across the bay in the coble, and take him through
the Ross as far as Grisapol."

In this proposal Mary heartily concurred; and
bidding the black follow us, we all three descended to the pier. Certainly, Heaven's will
was declared against Gordon Darnaway; a thing
had happened, never paralleled before in Aros;
during the storm, the coble had broken loose, and
striking on the rough splinters of the pier, now
lay in four feet of water with one side stove in.
Three days of work at least would be required
to make her float. But I was not to be beaten.
I led the whole party round to where the gut was
narrowest, swam to the other side, and called
to the black to follow me. He signed, with the

same clearness and quiet as before, that he knew
not the art; and there was truth apparent in his
signals, it would have occurred to none of us
to doubt his truth; and that hope being over, we
must all go back even as we came to the house
of Aros, the negro walking in our midst without
embarrassment.

All we could do that day was to make one more
attempt to communicate with the unhappy madman. Again he was visible on his perch; again
he fled in silence. But food and a great cloak
were at least left for his comfort; the rain, besides, had cleared away, and the night promised
to be even warm. We might compose ourselves,
we thought, until the morrow; rest was the chief
requisite, that we might be strengthened for
unusual exertions; and as none cared to talk, we
separated at an early hour.

I lay long awake, planning a campaign for the
morrow. I was to place the black on the side of
Sandag, whence he should head my uncle towards
the house; Rorie in the west, I on the east, were
to complete the cordon, as best we might. It
seemed to me, the more I recalled the configura-
tion of the island, that it should be possible,
though hard, to force him down upon the low
ground along Aros Bay; and once there, even
with the strength of his madness, ultimate escape
was hardly to be feared. It was on his terror of
the black that I relied; for I made sure, however
he might run, it would not be in the direction of

the man whom he supposed to have returned
from the dead, and thus one point of the compass
at least would be secure.

When at length I fell asleep, it was to be awakened shortly after by a dream of wrecks, black
men, and submarine adventure; and I found myself so shaken and fevered that I arose, descended
the stair, and stepped out before the house.
Within, Rorie and the black were asleep together
in the kitchen; outside was a wonderful clear
night of stars, with here and there a cloud still
hanging, last stragglers of the tempest. It was
near the top of the flood, and the Merry Men
were roaring in the windless quiet of the night.
Never, not even in the height of the tempest, had
I heard their song with greater awe. Now,
when the winds were gathered home, when the
deep was dandling itself back into its summer
slumber, and when the stars rained their gentle
light over land and sea, the voice of these tide-
breakers was still raised for havoc. They
seemed, indeed, to be a part of the world's evil
and the tragic side of life. Nor were their meaningless vociferations the only sounds that broke
the silence of the night. For I could hear, now
shrill and thrilling and now almost drowned, the
note of a human voice that accompanied the
uproar of the Roost. I knew it for my kinsman's; and a great fear fell upon me of God's
judgments, and the evil in the world. I went
back again into the darkness of the house as into

a place of shelter, and lay long upon my bed, pondering these mysteries.

It was late when I again woke, and I leaped into my clothes and hurried to the kitchen. No one was there; Rorie and the black had both stealthily departed long before; and my heart stood still at the discovery. I could rely on Rorie's heart, but I placed no trust in his discretion. If he had thus set out without a word, he was plainly bent upon some service to my uncle. But what service could he hope to render even alone, far less in the company of the man in whom my uncle found his fears incarnated? Even if I were not already too late to prevent some deadly mischief, it was plain I must delay no longer. With the thought I was out of the house; and often as I have run on the rough sides of Aros, I never ran as I did that fatal morning. I do not believe I put twelve minutes to the whole ascent.

My uncle was gone from his perch. The basket had indeed been torn open and the meat scattered on the turf; but, as we found afterwards, no mouthful had been tasted; and there was not another trace of human existence in that wide field of view. Day had already filled the clear heavens; the sun already lighted in a rosy bloom upon the crest of Ben Kyaw; but all below me the rude knolls of Aros and the shield of the sea lay steeped in the clear darkling twilight of the dawn.

"Rorie!" I cried; and again "Rorie!" My voice died in the silence, but there came no answer back. If there were indeed an enterprise afoot to catch my uncle, it was plainly not in fleetness of foot, but in dexterity of stalking, that the hunters placed their trust. I ran on farther, keeping the higher spurs, and looking right and left, nor did I pause again till I was on the mount above Sandag. I could see the wreck, the uncovered belt of sand, the waves idly beating the long ledge of rocks, and on either hand the tumbled knolls, boulders, and gullies of the island. But still no human thing.

At a stride the sunshine fell on Aros, and the shadows and colours leaped into being. Not half a moment later, below me to the west, sheep began to scatter as in a panic. There came a cry. I saw my uncle running. I saw the black jump up in hot pursuit; and before I had time to understand, Rorie also had appeared, calling directions in Gaelic as to a dog herding sheep.

I took to my heels to interfere, and perhaps I had done better to have waited where I was, for I was the means of cutting off the madman's last escape. There was nothing before him from that moment but the grave, the wreck, and the sea in Sandag Bay. And yet Heaven knows that what I did was for the best.

My uncle Gordon saw in what direction, horrible to him, the chase was driving him. He doubled, darting to the right and left; but high as

the fever ran in his veins, the black was still the
swifter.   Turn where he would, he was still fore-
stalled, still driven toward the scene of his crime.
Suddenly he began to shriek aloud, so that the
coast re-echoed; and now both I and Rorie were
calling on the black to stop.   But all was vain,
for it was written otherwise.   The pursuer still
ran, the chase still sped before him screaming;
they avoided the grave, and skimmed close past
the timbers of the wreck; in a breath they had
cleared the sand; and still my kinsman did not
pause, but dashed straight into the surf; and the
black, now almost within reach, still followed
swiftly behind him.   Rorie and I both stopped,
for the thing was now beyond the hands of men,
and these were the decrees of God that came to
pass before our eyes.   There was never a sharper
ending.   On that steep beach they were beyond
their depth at a bound; neither could swim; the
black rose once for a moment with a throttling
cry; but the current had them, racing seaward;
and if ever they came up again, which God alone
can tell, it would be ten minutes after, at the
far end of Aros Roost, where the sea-birds hover
fishing.

WILL O' THE MILL

THE PLAIN AND THE STARS

THE Mill where Will lived with his adopted parents stood in a falling valley between pine-woods and great mountains. Above, hill after hill soared upwards until they soared out of the depth of the hardiest timber, and stood naked against the sky. Some way up, a long grey village lay like a seam or a rag of vapour on a wooded hillside; and when the wind was favourable, the sound of the church bells would drop down, thin and silvery, to Will. Below, the valley grew ever steeper and steeper, and at the same time widened out on either hand; and from an eminence beside the mill it was possible to see its whole length and away beyond it over a wide plain, where the river turned and shone, and moved on from city to city on its voyage towards the sea. It chanced that over this valley there lay a pass into a neighbouring kingdom, so that, quiet and rural as it was, the road that ran along beside the river was a high thoroughfare between two splendid and powerful societies. All through the summer, travelling-carriages came crawling

up, or went plunging briskly downwards past the
mill; and as it happened that the other side was
very much easier of ascent, the path was not
much frequented, except by people going in one
direction; and of all the carriages that Will saw
go by, five-sixths were plunging briskly downwards and only one-sixth crawling up. Much
more was this the case with foot-passengers. All
the light-footed tourists, all the pedlars laden
with strange wares, were tending downward like
the river that accompanied their path. Nor
was this all; for when Will was yet a child a disastrous war arose over a great part of the world.
The newspapers were full of defeats and victories,
the earth rang with cavalry hoofs, and often for
days together and for miles around the coil of
battle terrified good people from their labours in
the field. Of all this, nothing was heard for a
long time in the valley; but at last one of the
commanders pushed an army over the pass by
forced marches, and for three days horse and
foot, cannon and tumbril, drum and standard,
kept pouring downward past the mill. All day
the child stood and watched them on their passage—the rhythmical stride, the pale, unshaven
faces tanned about the eyes, the discoloured
regimentals and the tattered flags, filled him with
a sense of weariness, pity, and wonder; and all
night long, after he was in bed, he could hear the
cannon pounding and the feet trampling, and
the great armament sweeping onward and down-

ward past the mill. No one in the valley ever heard the fate of the expedition, for they lay out of the way of gossip in those troublous times; but Will saw one thing plainly, that not a man returned. Whither had they all gone? Whither went all the tourists and pedlars with strange wares? whither all the brisk barouches with servants in the dicky? whither the water of the stream, ever coursing downward and ever renewed from above? Even the wind blew oftener down the valley, and carried the dead leaves along with it in the fall. It seemed like a great conspiracy of things animate and inanimate; they all went downward, fleetly and gaily downward, and only he, it seemed, remained behind, like a stock upon the wayside. It sometimes made him glad when he noticed how the fishes kept their heads up stream. They, at least, stood faithfully by him, while all else were posting downward to the unknown world.

One evening he asked the miller where the river went.

"It goes down the valley," answered he, "and turns a power of mills—six-score mills, they say, from here to Unterdeck—and it none the wearier after all. And then it goes out into the lowlands, and waters the great corn country, and runs through a sight of fine cities (so they say) where kings live all alone in great palaces, with a sentry walking up and down before the door. And it goes under bridges with stone men upon them, looking down and smiling so curious at the water, and living folks leaning their elbows on the wall and looking over too. And then it goes on and on, and down through marshes and sands, until at last it falls into the sea, where the ships are that bring parrots and tobacco from the Indies. Ay, it has a long trot before it as it goes singing over our weir, bless its heart!"

"And what is the sea?" asked Will.

"The sea!" cried the miller. "Lord help us all, it is the greatest thing God made! That is where all the water in the world runs down into a great salt lake. There it lies, as flat as my hand and as innocent-like as a child; but they do say when the wind blows it gets up into water-mountains bigger than any of ours, and swallows down great ships bigger than our mill, and makes such a roaring that you can hear it miles away upon the land. There are great fish in it five times bigger than a bull, and one old serpent as long as our river and as old as all the world, with whiskers like a man, and a crown of silver on her head."

Will thought he had never heard anything like this, and he kept on asking question after question about the world that lay away down the river, with all its perils and marvels, until the old miller became quite interested himself, and at last took him by the hand and led him to the hill-top that overlooks the valley and the plain. The sun was near setting, and hung low down in a cloudless sky. Everything was defined and glorified in golden light. Will had never seen so great an expanse of country in his life; he stood and gazed with all his eyes. He could see the cities, and the woods and fields, and the bright curves of the river, and far away to where the rim of the plain trenched along the shining heavens. An overmastering emotion seized upon the boy, soul and body; his heart beat so thickly that he could not breathe; the scene swam before his eyes; the sun seemed to wheel round and round, and throw off, as it turned, strange shapes which disappeared with the rapidity of thought, and were succeeded by others. Will covered his face with his hands, and burst into a violent fit of tears; and the poor miller, sadly disappointed and perplexed, saw nothing better for it than to take him up in his arms and carry him home in silence.

From that day forward Will was full of new hopes and longings. Something kept tugging at his heartstrings; the running water carried his desires along with it as he dreamed over its fleeting surface; the wind, as it ran over innumerable tree-tops, hailed him with encouraging words; branches beckoned downward; the open road, as it shouldered round the angles and went turning and vanishing faster and faster down the valley, tortured him with its solicitations. He spent long whiles on the eminence, looking down the river shed and abroad on the flat lowlands, and watched the clouds that travelled forth upon the sluggish wind and trailed their purple shadows on the plain; or he would linger by the wayside, and follow the carriages with his eyes as they rattled downward by the river. It did not matter what it was; everything that went that way, were it cloud or carriage, bird or brown water in the stream, he felt his heart flow out after it in an ecstasy of longing.

We are told by men of science that all the ventures of mariners on the sea, all that countermarching of tribes and races that confounds old history with its dust and rumour, sprang from nothing more abstruse than the laws of supply and demand, and a certain natural instinct for cheap rations. To any one thinking deeply, this will seem a dull and pitiful explanation. The tribes that came swarming out of the North and East, if they were indeed pressed onward from behind by others, were drawn at the same time by the magnetic influence of the South and West. The fame of other lands had reached them; the name of the eternal city rang in their ears; they were not colonists, but pilgrims; they travelled towards wine and gold and sunshine, but their hearts were set on something higher. That divine unrest, that old stinging trouble of humanity that makes all high achievements and all miserable failure, the same that spread wings with Icarus, the same that sent Columbus into the desolate Atlantic, inspired and supported

these barbarians on their perilous march. There
is one legend which profoundly represents their
spirit, of how a flying party of these wanderers
encountered a very old man shod with iron. The
old man asked them whither they were going;
and they answered with one voice: "To the
Eternal City!" He looked upon them gravely.
"I have sought it," he said, "over the most part
of the world. Three such pairs as I now carry
on my feet have I worn out upon this pilgrimage,
and now the fourth is growing slender underneath my steps. And all this while I have not
found the city." And he turned and went his
own way alone, leaving them astonished.

And yet this would scarcely parallel the intensity of Will's feeling for the plain. If he could
only go far enough out there, he felt as if his eyesight would be purged and clarified, as if his hearing would grow more delicate, and his very
breath would come and go with luxury. He was
transplanted and withering where he was; he lay
in a strange country and was sick for home. Bit
by bit, he pieced together broken notions of the
world below; of the river, ever moving and growing until it sailed forth into the majestic ocean;
of the cities, full of brisk and beautiful people,
playing fountains, bands of music and marble
palaces, and lighted up at night from end to end
with artificial stars of gold; of the great churches,
wise universities, brave armies, and untold
money lying stored in vaults; of the high-flying

vice that moved in the sunshine, and the stealth and swiftness of midnight murder. I have said he was sick as if for home: the figure halts. He was like some one lying in twilit, formless pre-existence, and stretching out his hands lovingly towards many-coloured, many-sounding life. It was no wonder he was unhappy, he would go and tell the fish; they were made for their life, wished for no more than worms and running water, and a hole below a falling bank; but he was differently designed, full of desires and aspirations, itching at the fingers, lusting with the eyes, whom the whole variegated world could not satisfy with aspects. The true life, the true bright sunshine, lay far out upon the plain. And O! to see this sunlight once before he died! to move with a jocund spirit in a golden land! to hear the trained singers and sweet church bells, and see the holiday gardens! "And O fish!" he would cry, "if you would only turn your noses down stream, you could swim so easily into the fabled waters and see the vast ships passing over your head like clouds, and hear the great water-hills making music over you all day long!" But the fish kept looking patiently in their own direction, until Will hardly knew whether to laugh or cry.

Hitherto the traffic on the road had passed by Will, like something seen in a picture: he had perhaps exchanged salutations with a tourist, or caught sight of an old gentleman in a travelling-cap at a carriage window; but for the most part it had been a mere symbol, which he contemplated from apart and with something of a superstitious feeling. A time came at last when this was to be changed. The miller, who was a greedy man in his way, and never forewent an opportunity of honest profit, turned the mill-house into a little wayside inn, and, several pieces of good fortune falling in opportunely, built stables and got the position of post master on the road. It now became Will's duty to wait upon people, as they sat to break their fasts in the little arbour at the top of the mill garden; and you may be sure that he kept his ears open, and learned many new things about the outside world as he brought the omelette or the wine. Nay, he would often get into conversation with single guests, and by adroit questions and polite attention, not only gratify his own curiosity, but win the goodwill of the travellers. Many complimented the old couple on their serving-boy; and a professor was eager to take him away with him, and have him properly educated in the plain. The miller and his wife were mightily astonished and even more pleased. They thought it a very good thing that they should have opened their inn. "You see," the old man would remark, "he has a kind of talent for a publican; he never would have made anything else!" And so life wagged on in the valley, with high satisfaction to all concerned but Will.

Every carriage that left the inn-door seemed to take a part of him away with it; and when people jestingly offered him a lift, he could with difficulty command his emotion. Night after night he would dream that he was awakened by flustered servants, and that a splendid equipage waited at the door to carry him down into the plain; night after night; until the dream, which had seemed all jollity to him at first, began to take on a colour of gravity, and the nocturnal summons and waiting equipage occupied a place in his mind as something to be both feared and hoped for.

One day, when Will was about sixteen, a fat young man arrived at sunset to pass the night. He was a contented-looking fellow, with a jolly eye, and carried a knapsack. While dinner was preparing, he sat in the arbour to read a book; but as soon as he had begun to observe Will, the book was laid aside; he was plainly one of those who prefer living people to people made of ink and paper. Will, on his part, although he had not been much interested in the stranger at first sight, soon began to take a great deal of pleasure in his talk, which was full of good-nature and good-sense, and at last conceived a great respect for his character and wisdom. They sat far into the night; and about two in the morning Will opened his heart to the young man, and told him how he longed to leave the valley and what bright hopes he had connected with the cities of the plain. The young man whistled, and then broke into a smile.

"My young friend," he remarked, "you are a very curious little fellow, to be sure, and wish a great many things which you will never get. Why, you would feel quite ashamed if you knew how the little fellows in these fairy cities of yours are all after the same sort of nonsense, and keep breaking their hearts to get up into the mountains. And let me tell you, those who go down into the plains are a very short while there before they wish themselves heartily back again. The air is not so light nor so pure; nor is the sun any brighter. As for the beautiful men and women, you would see many of them in rags and many of them deformed with horrible disorders; and a city is so hard a place for people who are poor and sensitive that many choose to die by their own hand."

"You must think me very simple," answered Will. "Although I have never been out of this valley, believe me, I have used my eyes. I know how one thing lives on another; for instance, how the fish hangs in the eddy to catch his fellows; and the shepherd, who makes so pretty a picture carrying home the lamb, is only carrying it home for dinner. I do not expect to find all things right in your cities. That is not what troubles me; it might have been that once upon a time; but although I live here always, I have asked many questions and learned a great deal in these last years, and certainly enough to cure me of my old fancies. But you would not have me die like a dog and not see all that is to be seen, and do all that a man can do, let it be good or evil? you would not have me spend all my days between this road here and the river, and not so much as make a motion to be up and live my life?—I would rather die out of hand," he cried, "than linger on as I am doing."

"Thousands of people," said the young man, "live and die like you, and are none the less happy."

"Ah!" said Will, "if there are thousands who would like, why should not one of them have my place?"

It was quite dark; there was a hanging lamp in the arbour which lit up the table and the faces of the speakers; and along the arch, the leaves upon the trellis stood out illuminated against the night sky, a pattern of transparent green upon a dusky purple. The fat young man rose, and, taking Will by the arm, led him out under the open heavens.

"Did you ever look at the stars?" he asked, pointing upwards.

"Often and often," answered Will.

"And do you know what they are?"

"I have fancied many things."

"They are worlds like ours," said the young man. "Some of them less; many of them a million times greater; and some of the least sparkles that you see are not only worlds, but whole clusters of worlds turning about each other in the midst of space. We do not know what there may be in any of them; perhaps the answer to all our difficulties or the cure of all our sufferings: and yet we can never reach them; not all the skill of the craftiest of men can fit out a ship for the nearest of these our neighbours, nor would the life of the most aged suffice for such a journey. When a great battle has been lost or a dear friend is dead, when we are hipped or in high spirits, there they are unweariedly shining overhead. We may stand down here, a whole army of us together, and shout until we break our hearts, and not a whisper reaches them. We may climb the highest mountain, and we are no nearer them. All we can do is to stand down here in the garden and take off our hats; the starshine lights upon our heads, and where mine is a little bald, I dare say you can see it glisten in the darkness. The mountain and the mouse. That is like to be all we shall ever have to do with Arcturus or Aldebaran. Can you apply a parable?" he added, laying his hand upon Will's shoulder. "It is not the same thing as a reason, but usually vastly more convincing."

Will hung his head a little, and then raised it once more to heaven. The stars seemed to expand and emit a sharper brilliancy; and as he kept turning his eyes higher and higher, they seemed to increase in multitude under his gaze.

"I see," he said, turning to the young man. "We are in a rat-trap."

"Something of that size. Did you ever see a squirrel turning in a cage? and another squirrel sitting philosophically over his nuts? I needn't ask you which of them looked more of a fool."

THE PARSON'S MARJORY

After some years the old people died, both in one winter, very carefully tended by their adopted son, and very quietly mourned when they were gone. People who had heard of his roving fancies supposed he would hasten to sell the property, and go down the river to push his fortunes. But there was never any sign of such an intention on the part of Will. On the contrary, he had the inn set on a better footing, and hired a couple of servants to assist him in carrying it on; and there he settled down, a kind, talkative, inscrutable young man, six feet three in his stockings, with an iron constitution and a friendly voice. He soon began to take rank in the district as a bit of an oddity: it was not much to be wondered at from the first, for he was always full of notions, and kept calling the plainest common sense in question; but what most raised the report upon him was the odd circumstance of his courtship with the parson's Marjory.

The parson's Marjory was a lass about nineteen, when Will would be about thirty; well enough looking, and much better educated than any other girl in that part of the country, as became her parentage. She held her head very high, and had already refused several offers of marriage with a grand air, which had got her hard names among the neighbours. For all that she was a good girl, and one that would have made any man well contented.

Will had never seen much of her; for although the church and parsonage were only two miles from his own door, he was never known to go there but on Sundays. It chanced, however, that the parsonage fell into disrepair, and had to be dismantled; and the parson and his daughter took lodgings for a month or so, on very much reduced terms, at Will's inn. Now, what with the inn, and the mill, and the old miller's savings, our friend was a man of substance; and besides that, he had a name for good temper and shrewdness which make a capital portion in marriage; and so it was currently gossiped, among their ill-wishers, that the parson and his daughter had not chosen their temporary lodging with their eyes shut. Will was about the last man in the world to be cajoled or frightened into marriage. You had only to look into his eyes, limpid and still like pools of water, and yet with a sort of clear light that seemed to come from within, and you would understand at once that here was one who knew his own mind, and would stand to it immovably. Marjory herself was no weakling by her looks, with strong, steady eyes and a resolute and quiet bearing. It might be a question whether she was not Will's match in steadfastness, after all, or which of them would rule the roast in marriage. But Marjory had never given it a thought, and accompanied her father with the most unshaken innocence and unconcern.

The season was still so early that Will's customers were few and far between; but the lilacs were already flowering, and the weather was so mild that the party took dinner under the trellis, with the noise of the river in their ears and the woods ringing about them with the songs of birds. Will soon began to take a particular pleasure in these dinners. The parson was rather a dull companion, with a habit of dozing at table; but nothing rude or cruel ever fell from his lips. And as for the parson's daughter, she suited her surroundings with the best grace imaginable; and whatever she said seemed so pat and pretty that Will conceived a great idea of her talents. He could see her face, as she leaned forward, against a background of rising pinewoods; her eyes shone peaceably; the light lay around her hair like a kerchief; something that was hardly a smile rippled her pale cheeks, and Will could not contain himself from gazing on her in an agreeable dismay. She looked, even in her quietest moments, so complete in herself, and so quick with life down to her finger-tips and the very skirts of her dress, that the remainder of

created things became no more than a blot by
comparison; and if Will glanced away from her
to her surroundings, the trees looked inanimate
and senseless, the clouds hung in heaven like
dead things, and even the mountain-tops were
disenchanted. The whole valley could not compare in looks with this one girl.

Will was always observant in the society of his
fellow-creatures; but his observation became almost painfully eager in the case of Marjory. He
listened to all she uttered, and read her eyes, at
the same time, for the unspoken commentary.
Many kind, simple, and sincere speeches found
an echo in his heart. He became conscious of a
soul beautifully poised upon itself, nothing doubt-
ing, nothing desiring, clothed in peace. It was
not possible to separate her thoughts from her
appearance. The turn of her wrist, the still
sound of her voice, the light in her eyes, the lines
of her body, fell in tune with her grave and gentle
words, like the accompaniment that sustains
and harmonises the voice of the singer. Her
influence was one thing, not to be divided or
discussed, only to be felt with gratitude and joy.
To Will, her presence recalled something of his
childhood, and the thought of her took its place
in his mind beside that of dawn, of running
water, and of the earliest violets and lilacs. It
is the property of things seen for the first time,
or for the first time after long, like the flowers in
spring, to reawaken in us the sharp edge of sense

and that impression of mystic strangeness which otherwise passes out of life with the coming of years; but the sight of a loved face is what renews a man's character from the fountain upwards.

One day after dinner Will took a stroll among the firs; a grave beatitude possessed him from top to toe, and he kept smiling to himself and the landscape as he went. The river ran between the stepping-stones with a pretty wimple; a bird sang loudly in the wood; the hill-tops looked immeasurably high, and as he glanced at them from time to time seemed to contemplate his movements with a beneficent but awful curiosity. His way took him to the eminence which overlooked the plain; and there he sat down upon a stone, and fell into deep and pleasant thought. The plain lay abroad with its cities and silver river; everything was asleep, except a great eddy of birds which kept rising and falling and going round and round in the blue air. He repeated Marjory's name aloud, and the sound of it gratified his ear. He shut his eyes, and her image sprang up before him, quietly luminous and attended with good thoughts. The river might run for ever; the birds fly higher and higher till they touched the stars. He saw it was empty bustle after all; for here, without stirring a foot, waiting patiently in his own narrow valley, he also had attained the better sunlight.

The next day Will made a sort of declaration

across the dinner-table, while the parson was filling his pipe.

"Miss Marjory," he said, "I never knew any
one I liked so well as you. I am mostly a cold,
unkindly sort of man; not from want of heart,
but out of strangeness in my way of thinking;
and people seem far away from me. 'Tis as if
there were a circle round me, which kept every
one out but you; I can hear the others talking
and laughing; but you come quite close. — Maybe this is disagreeable to you?" he asked.

Marjory made no answer.

"Speak up, girl," said the parson.

"Nay, now," returned Will, "I wouldn't
press her, parson. I feel tongue-tied myself,
who am not used to it; and she's a woman, and
little more than a child, when all is said. But
for my part, as far as I can understand what
people mean by it, I fancy I must be what they
call in love. I do not wish to be held as com-
mitting myself; for I may be wrong; but that is
how I believe things are with me. And if Miss
Marjory should feel any otherwise on her part,
mayhap she would be so kind as shake her head."

Marjory was silent, and gave no sign that she
had heard.

"How is that, parson?" asked Will.

"The girl must speak," replied the parson, laying down his pipe. "Here's our neighbour who
says he loves you, Madge. Do you love him, ay
or no?"

"I think I do," said Marjory, faintly.

"Well then, that's all that could be wished!" cried Will, heartily. And he took her hand across the table, and held it a moment in both of his with great satisfaction.

"You must marry," observed the parson, replacing his pipe in his mouth.

"Is that the right thing to do, think you?" demanded Will.

"It is indispensable," said the parson.

"Very well," replied the wooer.

Two or three days passed away with great delight to Will, although a bystander might scarce have found it out. He continued to take his meals opposite Marjory, and to talk with her and gaze upon her in her father's presence; but he made no attempt to see her alone, nor in any other way changed his conduct towards her from what it had been since the beginning. Perhaps the girl was a little disappointed, and perhaps not unjustly; and yet if it had been enough to be always in the thoughts of another person, and so pervade and alter his whole life, she might have been thoroughly contented. For she was never out of Will's mind for an instant. He sat over the stream, and watched the dust of the eddy, and the poised fish, and straining weeds; he wandered out alone into the purple even, with all the blackbirds piping round him in the wood; he rose early in the morning; and saw the sky turn from grey to gold, and the light

leap upon the hill-tops; and all the while he kept
wondering if he had never seen such things before, or how it was that they should look so different now. The sound of his own mill-wheel,
or of the wind among the trees, confounded
and charmed his heart. The most enchanting
thoughts presented themselves unbidden in his
mind. He was so happy that he could not sleep
at night, and so restless that he could hardly
sit still out of her company. And yet it seemed
as if he avoided her rather than sought her out.

One day, as he was coming home from a ramble, Will found Marjory in the garden picking
flowers, and as he came up with her, slackened
his pace and continued walking by her side.

"You like flowers?" he said.

"Indeed I love them dearly," she replied. "Do
you?"

"Why, no," said he, "not so much. They are
a very small affair, when all is done. I can fancy
people caring for them greatly, but not doing as
you are just now."

"How?" she asked, pausing and looking up at
him.

"Plucking them," said he. "They are a deal
better off where they are, and look a deal prettier,
if you go to that."

"I wish to have them for my own," she answered, "to carry them near my heart, and keep
them in my room. They tempt me when they
grow here; they seem to say, 'Come and do some-

thing with us'; but once I have cut them and put them by, the charm is laid, and I can look at them with quite an easy heart."

"You wish to possess them," replied Will, "in order to think no more about them. It's a bit like killing the goose with the golden eggs. It's a bit like what I wished to do when I was a boy. Because I had a fancy for looking out over the plain, I wished to go down there—where I couldn't look out over it any longer. Was not that fine reasoning? Dear, dear, if they only thought of it, all the world would do like me; and you would let your flowers alone, just as I stay up here in the mountains." Suddenly he broke off sharp. "By the Lord!" he cried. And when she asked him what was wrong, he turned the question off, and walked away into the house with rather a humorous expression of face.

He was silent at table; and after the night had fallen and the stars had come out overhead, he walked up and down for hours in the courtyard and garden with an uneven pace. There was still a light in the window of Marjory's room: one little oblong patch of orange in a world of dark blue hills and silver starlight. Will's mind ran a great deal on the window; but his thoughts were not very lover-like. "There she is in her room," he thought, "and there are the stars overhead:—a blessing upon both!" Both were good influences in his life; both soothed and braced him in his profound contentment with the world.

And what more should he desire with either?
The fat young man and his councils were so present to his mind, that he threw back his head,
and, putting his hands before his mouth, shouted
aloud to the populous heavens. Whether from
the position of his head or the sudden strain of
the exertion, he seemed to see a momentary
shock among the stars, and a diffusion of frosty
light pass from one to another along the sky. At
the same instant, a corner of the blind was lifted
up and lowered again at once. He laughed a
loud ho-ho! "One and another!" thought Will.
"The stars tremble, and the blind goes up. Why,
before Heaven, what a great magician I must be!
Now if I were only a fool, should not I be in a
pretty way?" And he went off to bed, chuckling
to himself: "If I were only a fool!"

The next morning, pretty early, he saw her
once more in the garden, and sought her out.

"I have been thinking about getting married,"
he began abruptly; "and after having turned it
all over, I have made up my mind it's not worth
while."

She turned upon him for a single moment; but
his radiant, kindly appearance would, under the
circumstances, have disconcerted an angel, and
she looked down again upon the ground in silence. He could see her tremble.

"I hope you don't mind," he went on, a little
taken aback. "You ought not. I have turned
it all over, and upon my soul there's nothing in it.

We should never be one whit nearer than we are just now, and, if I am a wise man, nothing like so happy."

"It is unnecessary to go round about with me," she said. "I very well remember that you refused to commit yourself; and now that I see you were mistaken, and in reality have never cared for me, I can only feel sad that I have been so far misled."

"I ask your pardon," said Will stoutly; "you do not understand my meaning. As to whether I have ever loved you or not, I must leave that to others. But for one thing, my feeling is not changed; and for another, you may make it your boast that you have made my whole life and character something different from what they were. I mean what I say; no less. I do not think getting married is worth while. I would rather you went on living with your father, so that I could walk over and see you once, or maybe twice a week, as people go to church, and then we should both be all the happier between whiles. That 's my notion. But I 'll marry you if you will," he added.

"Do you know that you are insulting me?" she broke out.

"Not I, Marjory," said he; "if there is anything in a clear conscience, not I. I offer all my heart's best affections; you can take it or want it, though I suspect it 's beyond either your power or mine to change what has once been done, and set me fancy-free. I'll marry you, if you like; but I tell you again and again, it's not worth while, and we had best stay friends. Though I am a quiet man I have noticed a heap of things in my life. Trust in me, and take things as I propose; or, if you don't like that, say the word, and I'll marry you out of hand."

There was a considerable pause, and Will, who began to feel uneasy, began to grow angry in consequence.

"It seems you are too proud to say your mind," he said. "Believe me that's a pity. A clean shrift makes simple living. Can a man be more downright or honourable to a woman than I have been? I have said my say, and given you your choice. Do you want me to marry you? or will you take my friendship, as I think best? or have you had enough of me for good? Speak out for the dear God's sake! You know your father told you a girl should speak her mind in these affairs."

She seemed to recover herself at that, turned without a word, walked rapidly through the garden, and disappeared into the house, leaving Will in some confusion as to the result. He walked up and down the garden, whistling softly to himself. Sometimes he stopped and contemplated the sky and hill-tops; sometimes he went down to the tail of the weir and sat there, looking foolishly in the water. All this dubiety and perturbation was so foreign to his nature and the life

which he had resolutely chosen for himself, that
he began to regret Marjory's arrival. "After
all," he thought, "I was as happy as a man need
be. I could come down here and watch my fishes
all day long if I wanted: I was as settled and contented as my old mill."

Marjory came down to dinner, looking very
trim and quiet; and no sooner were all three at
table than she made her father a speech, with her
eyes fixed upon her plate, but showing no other
sign of embarrassment or distress.

"Father," she began, "Mr. Will and I have
been talking things over. We see that we have
each made a mistake about our feelings, and he
has agreed, at my request, to give up all idea of
marriage, and be no more than my very good
friend, as in the past. You see, there is no
shadow of a quarrel, and indeed I hope we shall
see a great deal of him in the future, for his visits
will always be welcome in our house. Of course,
father, you will know best, but perhaps we should
do better to leave Mr. Will's house for the present. I believe, after what has passed, we should
hardly be agreeable inmates for some days."

Will, who had commanded himself with difficulty from the first, broke out upon this into an
inarticulate noise, and raised one hand with an
appearance of real dismay, as if he were about
to interfere and contradict. But she checked
him at once, looking up at him with a swift
glance and an angry flush upon her cheek.

"You will perhaps have the good grace," she said, "to let me explain these matters for myself."

Will was put entirely out of countenance by her expression and the ring of her voice. He held his peace, concluding that there were some things about this girl beyond his comprehension—in which he was exactly right.

The poor parson was quite crestfallen. He tried to prove that this was no more than a true lovers' tiff, which would pass off before night; and when he was dislodged from that position, he went on to argue that where there was no quarrel there could be no call for a separation; for the good man liked both his entertainment and his host. It was curious to see how the girl managed them, saying little all the time, and that very quietly, and yet twisting them round her finger and insensibly leading them wherever she would by feminine tact and generalship. It scarcely seemed to have been her doing—it seemed as if things had merely so fallen out— that she and her father took their departure that same afternoon in a farm-cart, and went farther down the valley, to wait, until their own house was ready for them, in another hamlet. But Will had been observing closely, and was well aware of her dexterity and resolution. When he found himself alone he had a great many curious matters to turn over in his mind. He was very sad and solitary, to begin with. All the interest

had gone out of his life, and he might look up at
the stars as long as he pleased, he somehow failed
to find support or consolation. And then he
was in such a turmoil of spirit about Marjory.
He had been puzzled and irritated at her behaviour, and yet he could not keep himself from
admiring it. He thought he recognised a fine,
perverse angel in that still soul which he had
never hitherto suspected; and though he saw it
was an influence that would fit but ill with his
own life of artificial calm, he could not keep himself from ardently desiring to possess it. Like a
man who has lived among shadows and now
meets the sun, he was both pained and delighted.

As the days went forward he passed from one
extreme to another; now pluming himself on the
strength of his determination, now despising his
timid and silly caution. The former was, perhaps, the true thought of his heart, and represented the regular tenor of the man's reflections;
but the latter burst forth from time to time with
an unruly violence, and then he would forget
all consideration, and go up and down his house
and garden or walk among the fir-woods like one
who is beside himself with remorse. To equable,
steady-minded Will this state of matters was
intolerable; and he determined, at whatever cost,
to bring it to an end. So, one warm summer
afternoon he put on his best clothes, took a thorn
switch in his hand, and set out down the valley
by the river. As soon as he had taken his deter-

mination, he had regained at a bound his customary peace of heart, and he enjoyed the bright weather and the variety of the scene without any admixture of alarm or unpleasant eagerness. It was nearly the same to him how the matter turned out. If she accepted him he would have to marry her this time, which perhaps was all for the best. If she refused him, he would have done his utmost, and might follow his own way in the future with an untroubled conscience. He hoped, on the whole, she would refuse him; and then, again, as he saw the brown roof which sheltered her, peeping through some willows at an angle of the stream, he was half inclined to reverse the wish, and more than half ashamed of himself for this infirmity of purpose.

Marjory seemed glad to see him, and gave him her hand without affectation or delay.

"I have been thinking about this marriage," he began.

"So have I," she answered. "And I respect you more and more for a very wise man. You understood me better than I understood myself; and I am now quite certain that things are all for the best as they are."

"At the same time——" ventured Will.

"You must be tired," she interrupted. "Take a seat and let me fetch you a glass of wine. The afternoon is so warm; and I wish you not to be displeased with your visit. You must come quite often; once a week, if you can spare the time; I am always so glad to see my friends."

"Oh, very well," thought Will to himself. "It appears I was right after all." And he paid a very agreeable visit, walked home again in capital spirits, and gave himself no further concern about the matter.

For nearly three years Will and Marjory continued on these terms, seeing each other once or twice a week without any word of love between them; and for all that time I believe Will was nearly as happy as a man can be. He rather stinted himself the pleasure of seeing her; and he would often walk half-way over to the parsonage, and then back again, as if to whet his appetite. Indeed, there was one corner of the road, whence he could see the church-spire wedged into a crevice of the valley between sloping fir-woods, with a triangular snatch of plain by way of background, which he greatly affected as a place to sit and moralise in before returning homewards; and the peasants got so much into the habit of finding him there in the twilight that they gave it the name of "Will o' the Mill's Corner."

At the end of the three years Marjory played him a sad trick by suddenly marrying somebody else. Will kept his countenance bravely, and merely remarked that, for as little as he knew of women, he had acted very prudently in not marrying her himself three years before. She plainly knew very little of her own mind, and, in spite of a deceptive manner, was as fickle and flighty as the rest of them. He had to congratulate himself on an escape, he said, and would take a higher opinion of his own wisdom in consequence. But at heart, he was reasonably displeased, moped a good deal for a month or two, and fell away in flesh, to the astonishment of his serving-lads.

It was perhaps a year after this marriage that Will was awakened late one night by the sound of a horse galloping on the road, followed by precipitate knocking at the inn-door. He opened his window and saw a farm servant, mounted and holding a led horse by the bridle, who told him to make what haste he could and go along with him; for Marjory was dying, and had sent urgently to fetch him to her bedside. Will was no horseman, and made so little speed upon the way that the poor young wife was very near her end before he arrived. But they had some minutes' talk in private, and he was present and wept very bitterly while she breathed her last.

DEATH

Year after year went away into nothing, with great explosions and outcries in the cities on the plain: red revolt springing up and being suppressed in blood, battle swaying hither and thither, patient astronomers in observatory towers picking out and christening new stars, plays being performed in lighted theatres, people

being carried into hospitals on stretchers, and
all the usual turmoil and agitation of men's lives
in crowded centres. Up in Will's valley only
the winds and seasons made an epoch; the fish
hung in the swift stream, the birds circled overhead, the pine-tops rustled underneath the stars,
the tall hills stood over all; and Will went to and
fro, minding his wayside inn, until the snow
began to thicken on his head. His heart was
young and vigorous; and if his pulses kept a
sober time, they still beat strong and steady in
his wrists. He carried a ruddy stain on either
cheek, like a ripe apple; he stooped a little, but
his step was still firm; and his sinewy hands were
reached out to all men with a friendly pressure.
His face was covered with those wrinkles which
are got in open air, and which, rightly looked at,
are no more than a sort of permanent sunburn-
ing; such wrinkles heighten the stupidity of stupid faces; but to a person like Will, with his clear
eyes and smiling mouth, only give another charm
by testifying to a simple and easy life. His talk
was full of wise sayings. He had a taste for
other people; and other people had a taste for
him. When the valley was full of tourists in the
season, there were merry nights in Will's arbour;
and his views, which seemed whimsical to his
neighbours, were often enough admired by
learned people out of towns and colleges. Indeed,
he had a very noble old age, and grew daily better
known; so that his fame was heard of in the cities

of the plain; and young men who had been summer travellers spoke together in *cafés* of Will o'
the Mill and his rough philosophy. Many and
many an invitation, you may be sure, he had;
but nothing could tempt him from his upland
valley. He would shake his head and smile over
his tobacco-pipe with a deal of meaning. "You
come too late," he would answer. "I am a dead
man now: I have lived and died already. Fifty
years ago you would have brought my heart into
my mouth; and now you do not even tempt me.
But that is the object of long living, that man
should cease to care about life." And again:
"There is only one difference between a long life
and a good dinner: that, in the dinner, the sweets
come last." Or once more: "When I was a boy,
I was a bit puzzled, and hardly knew whether
it was myself or the world that was curious and
worth looking into. Now, I know it is myself,
and stick to that."

He never showed any symptom of frailty, but
kept stalwart and firm to the last; but they say
he grew less talkative towards the end, and would
listen to other people by the hour in an amused
and sympathetic silence. Only, when he did
speak, it was more to the point and more charged
with old experience. He drank a bottle of wine
gladly; above all, at sunset on the hill-top or
quite late at night under the stars in the arbour.
The sight of something attractive and unattain-
able seasoned his enjoyment, he would say; and

he professed he had lived long enough to admire a candle all the more when he could compare it with a planet.

One night, in his seventy-second year, he awoke in bed, in such uneasiness of body and mind that he arose and dressed himself and went out to meditate in the arbour. It was pitch dark, without a star; the river was swollen, and the wet woods and meadows loaded the air with perfume. It had thundered during the day, and it promised more thunder for the morrow. A murky, stifling night for a man of seventy-two! Whether it was the weather or the wakefulness, or some little touch of fever in his old limbs, Will's mind was besieged by tumultuous and crying memories. His boyhood, the night with the fat young man, the death of his adopted parents, the summer days with Marjory, and many of those small circumstances, which seem nothing to another, and are yet the very gist of a man's own life to himself—things seen, words heard, books misconstrued—arose from their forgotten corners and usurped his attention. The dead themselves were with him, not merely taking part in this thin show of memory that defiled before his brain, but revisiting his bodily senses as they do in profound and vivid dreams. The fat young man leaned his elbows on the table opposite; Marjory came and went with an apronful of flowers between the garden and the arbour; he could hear the old parson knocking

out his pipe or blowing his resonant nose. The
tide of his consciousness ebbed and flowed; he
was sometimes half asleep and drowned in his
recollections of the past; and sometimes he was
broad awake, wondering at himself. But about
the middle of the night he was startled by the
voice of the dead miller calling to him out of the
house as he used to do on the arrival of custom.
The hallucination was so perfect that Will sprang
from his seat and stood listening for the summons
to be repeated; and as he listened he became conscious of another noise besides the brawling of
the river and the ringing in his feverish ears.
It was like the stir of the horses and the creaking
of harness, as though a carriage with an impatient team had been brought up upon the road
before the courtyard gate. At such an hour,
upon this rough and dangerous pass, the suppo-
sition was no better than absurd; and Will dismissed it from his mind, and resumed his seat
upon the arbour chair; and sleep closed over him
again like running water. He was once again
awakened by the dead miller's call, thinner and
more spectral than before; and once again he
heard the noise of an equipage upon the road.
And so thrice and four times, the same dream,
or the same fancy, presented itself to his senses:
until at length, smiling to himself as when one
humours a nervous child, he proceeded towards
the gate to set his uncertainty at rest.

From the arbour to the gate was no great dis-

tance, and yet it took Will some time; it seemed
as if the dead thickened around him in the court,
and crossed his path at every step. For, first, he
was suddenly surprised by an overpowering
sweetness of heliotropes; it was as if his garden
had been planted with this flower from end to
end, and the hot, damp night had drawn forth
all their perfumes in a breath. Now the helio-
trope had been Marjory's favourite flower, and
since her death not one of them had ever been
planted in Will's ground.

"I must be going crazy," he thought. "Poor
Marjory and her heliotropes!"

And with that he raised his eyes towards the
window that had once been hers. If he had been
bewildered before, he was now almost terrified;
for there was a light in the room; the window
was an orange oblong as of yore; and the corner
of the blind was lifted and let fall as on the night
when he stood and shouted to the stars in his
perplexity. The illusion only endured an instant; but it left him somewhat unmanned, rub-
bing his eyes and staring at the outline of the
house and the black night behind it. While he
thus stood, and it seemed as if he must have
stood there quite a long time, there came a re-
newal of the noises on the road: and he turned in
time to meet a stranger, who was advancing to
meet him across the court. There was something like the outline of a great carriage dis-
cernible on the road behind the stranger, and,

above that, a few black pine-tops, like so many plumes.

"Master Will?" asked the new-comer, in brief military fashion.

"That same, sir," answered Will. "Can I do anything to serve you?"

"I have heard you much spoken of, Master Will," returned the other; "much spoken of, and well. And though I have both hands full of business, I wish to drink a bottle of wine with you in your arbour. Before I go, I shall introduce myself."

Will led the way to the trellis, and got a lamp lighted and a bottle uncorked. He was not altogether unused to such complimentary interviews, and hoped little enough for this one, being schooled by many disappointments. A sort of cloud had settled on his wits and prevented him from remembering the strangeness of the hour. He moved like a person in his sleep; and it seemed as if the lamp caught fire and the bottle came uncorked with the facility of thought. Still, he had some curiosity about the appearance of his visitor, and tried in vain to turn the light into his face; either he handled the lamp clumsily, or there was a dimness over his eyes; but he could make out little more than a shadow at table with him. He stared and stared at this shadow, as he wiped out the glasses, and began to feel cold and strange about the heart. The silence weighed upon him, for he could hear nothing now, not even the river, but the drumming of his own arteries in his ears.

"Here's to you," said the stranger, roughly.

"Here is my service, sir," replied Will, sipping his wine, which somehow tasted oddly.

"I understand you are a very positive fellow," pursued the stranger.

Will made answer with a smile of some satisfaction and a little nod.

"So am I," continued the other; "and it is the delight of my heart to tramp on people's corns. I will have nobody positive but myself; not one. I have crossed the whims, in my time, of kings and generals and great artists. And what would you say," he went on, "if I had come up here on purpose to cross yours?"

Will had it on his tongue to make a sharp rejoinder; but the politeness of an old innkeeper prevailed; and he held his peace and made answer with a civil gesture of the hand.

"I have," said the stranger. "And if I did not hold you in a particular esteem, I should make no words about the matter. It appears you pride yourself on staying where you are. You mean to stick by your inn. Now I mean you shall come for a turn with me in my barouche; and before this bottle's empty, so you shall."

"That would be an odd thing, to be sure," replied Will, with a chuckle. "Why, sir, I have grown here like an old oaktree; the devil himself could hardly root me up: and for all I perceive you are a very entertaining old gentleman, I would wager you another bottle you lose your pains with me."

The dimness of Will's eyesight had been increasing all this while; but he was somehow conscious of a sharp and chilling scrutiny which irritated and yet overmastered him.

"You need not think," he broke out suddenly, in an explosive, febrile manner that startled and alarmed himself, "that I am a stay-at-home, because I fear anything under God. God knows I am tired enough of it all; and when the time comes for a longer journey than ever you dream of, I reckon I shall find myself prepared."

The stranger emptied his glass and pushed it away from him. He looked down for a little, and then, leaning over the table, tapped Will three times upon the forearm with a single finger. "The time has come!" he said solemnly.

An ugly thrill spread from the spot he touched. The tones of his voice were dull and startling, and echoed strangely in Will's heart.

"I beg your pardon," he said, with some discomposure. "What do you mean?"

"Look at me, and you will find your eyesight swim. Raise your hand; it is dead-heavy. This is your last bottle of wine, Master Will, and your last night upon the earth."

"You are a doctor?" quavered Will.

"The best that ever was," replied the other;

"for I cure both mind and body with the same prescription. I take away all pain and I forgive all sins; and where my patients have gone wrong in life, I smooth out all complications and set them free again upon their feet."

"I have no need of you," said Will.

"A time comes for all men, Master Will," replied the doctor, "when the helm is taken out of their hands. For you, because you were prudent and quiet, it has been long of coming, and you have had long to discipline yourself for its reception. You have seen what is to be seen about your mill; you have sat close all your days like a hare in its form; but now that is at an end; and," added the doctor, getting on his feet, "you must arise and come with me."

"You are a strange physician," said Will, looking steadfastly upon his guest.

"I am a natural law," he replied, "and people call me Death."

"Why did you not tell me so at first?" cried Will. "I have been waiting for you these many years. Give me your hand, and welcome."

"Lean upon my arm," said the stranger, "for already your strength abates. Lean on me heavily as you need; for though I am old, I am very strong. It is but three steps to my carriage, and there all your trouble ends. Why, Will," he added, "I have been yearning for you as if you were my own son; and of all the men that ever I came for in my long days, I have come for you

127

most gladly. I am caustic, and sometimes offend people at first sight; but I am a good friend at heart to such as you."

"Since Marjory was taken," returned Will, "I declare before God you were the only friend I had to look for."

So the pair went arm-in-arm across the courtyard.

One of the servants awoke about this time and heard the noise of horses pawing before he dropped asleep again; all down the valley that night there was a rushing as of a smooth and steady wind descending towards the plain; and when the world rose next morning, sure enough Will o' the Mill had gone at last upon his travels.

MARKHEIM

"YES," said the dealer, "our windfalls are of various kinds. Some customers are ignorant, and then I touch a dividend of my superior knowledge. Some are dishonest," and here he held up the candle, so that the light fell strongly on his visitor, "and in that case," he continued, "I profit by my virtue."

Markheim had but just entered from the daylight streets, and his eyes had not yet grown familiar with the mingled shine and darkness in the shop. At these pointed words, and before the near presence of the flame, he blinked painfully and looked aside.

The dealer chuckled. "You come to me on Christmas Day," he resumed, "when you know that I am alone in my house, put up my shutters, and make a point of refusing business. Well, you will have to pay for that; you will have to pay for my loss of time, when I should be balancing my books; you will have to pay, besides, for a kind of manner that I remark in you to-day very strongly. I am the essence of discretion, and ask

MARKHEIM

no awkward questions; but when a customer cannot look me in the eye, he has to pay for it." The dealer once more chuckled; and then, changing to his usual business voice, though still with a note of irony, "You can give, as usual, a clear account of how you came into the possession of the object?" he continued. "Still your uncle's cabinet? A remarkable collector, sir!"

And the little pale, round-shouldered dealer stood almost on tiptoe, looking over the top of his gold spectacles, and nodding his head with every mark of disbelief. Markheim returned his gaze with one of infinite pity, and a touch of horror.

"This time," said he, "you are in error. I have not come to sell, but to buy. I have no curios to dispose of; my uncle's cabinet is bare to the wainscot; even were it still intact, I have done well on the Stock Exchange, and should more likely add to it than otherwise, and my errand to-day is simplicity itself. I seek a Christmas present for a lady," he continued, waxing more fluent as he struck into the speech he had prepared; "and certainly I owe you every excuse for thus disturbing you upon so small a matter. But the thing was neglected yesterday; I must produce my little compliment at dinner; and, as you very well know, a rich marriage is not a thing to be neglected."

There followed a pause, during which the dealer seemed to weigh this statement incredulously. The ticking of many clocks among the

curious lumber of the shop, and the faint rushing
of the cabs in a near thoroughfare, filled up the
interval of silence.

"Well, sir," said the dealer, "be it so. You
are an old customer after all; and if, as you say,
you have the chance of a good marriage, far be
it from me to be an obstacle.—Here is a nice
thing for a lady now," he went on, "this hand
glass—fifteenth century, warranted; comes from
a good collection, too; but I reserve the name, in
the interests of my customer, who was just like
yourself, my dear sir, the nephew and sole heir
of a remarkable collector."

The dealer, while he thus ran on in his dry and
biting voice, had stooped to take the object from
its place; and, as he had done so, a shock had
passed through Markheim, a start both of hand
and foot, a sudden leap of many tumultuous passions to the face. It passed as swiftly as it came,
and left no trace beyond a certain trembling of
the hand that now received the glass.

"A glass," he said hoarsely, and then paused,
and repeated it more clearly. "A glass? For
Christmas? Surely not?"

"And why not?" cried the dealer. "Why not
a glass?"

Markheim was looking upon him with an indefinable expression. "You ask me why not?"
he said. "Why, look here—look in it—look at
yourself! Do you like to see it? No! nor I—
nor any man."

The little man had jumped back when Markheim had so suddenly confronted him with the mirror; but now, perceiving there was nothing worse on hand, he chuckled. "Your future lady, sir, must be pretty hard-favoured," said he.

"I ask you," said Markheim, "for a Christmas present, and you give me this—this damned reminder of years, and sins and follies—this hand-conscience! Did you mean it? Had you a thought in your mind? Tell me. It will be better for you if you do. Come, tell me about yourself. I hazard a guess now, that you are in secret a very charitable man?"

The dealer looked closely at his companion. It was very odd, Markheim did not appear to be laughing; there was something in his face like an eager sparkle of hope, but nothing of mirth.

"What are you driving at?" the dealer asked.

"Not charitable?" returned the other, gloomily. "Not charitable; not pious; not scrupulous; unloving, unbeloved; a hand to get money, a safe to keep it. Is that all? Dear God, man, is that all?"

"I will tell you what it is," began the dealer, with some sharpness, and then broke off again into a chuckle. "But I see this is a love-match of yours, and you have been drinking the lady's health."

"Ah!" cried Markheim, with a strange curiosity. "Ah, have you been in love? Tell me about that."

"I," cried the dealer. "I in love! I never had the time, nor have I the time to-day for all this nonsense. Will you take the glass?"

"Where is the hurry?" returned Markheim. "It is very pleasant to stand here talking; and life is so short and insecure that I would not hurry away from any pleasure—no, not even from so mild a one as this. We should rather cling, cling to what little we can get, like a man at a cliff's edge. Every second is a cliff, if you think upon it—a cliff a mile high—high enough, if we fall, to dash us out of every feature of humanity. Hence it is best to talk pleasantly. Let us talk of each other; why should we wear this mask? Let us be confidential. Who knows we might become friends?"

"I have just one word to say to you," said the dealer. "Either make your purchase, or walk out of my shop."

"True, true," said Markheim. "Enough fooling. To business. Show me something else."

The dealer stooped once more, this time to replace the glass upon the shelf, his thin blond hair falling over his eyes as he did so. Markheim moved a little nearer, with one hand in the pocket of his great-coat; he drew himself up and filled his lungs; at the same time many different emotions were depicted together on his face— terror, horror, and resolve, fascination and a physical repulsion; and through a haggard lift of his upper lip, his teeth looked out.

"This, perhaps, may suit," observed the dealer; and then, as he began to re-arise, Markheim bounded from behind upon his victim. The long, skewer-like dagger flashed and fell. The dealer struggled like a hen, striking his temple on the shelf, and then tumbled on the floor in a heap.

Time had some score of small voices in that shop, some stately and slow as was becoming to their great age; others garrulous and hurried. All these told out the seconds in an intricate chorus of tickings. Then the passage of a lad's feet, heavily running on the pavement, broke in upon these smaller voices and startled Markheim into the consciousness of his surroundings. He looked about him awfully. The candle stood on the counter, its flame solemnly wagging in a draught; and by that inconsiderable movement, the whole room was filled with noiseless bustle and kept heaving like a sea: the tall shadows nodding, the gross blots of darkness swelling and dwindling as with respiration, the faces of the portraits and the china gods changing and wavering like images in water. The inner door stood ajar, and peered into that leaguer of shadows with a long slit of daylight like a pointing finger.

From these fear-stricken rovings, Markheim's eyes returned to the body of his victim, where it lay both humped and sprawling, incredibly small and strangely meaner than in life. In these poor, miserly clothes, in that ungainly attitude, the dealer lay like so much sawdust. Markheim had

feared to see it, and, lo! it was nothing. And
yet, as he gazed, this bundle of old clothes and
pool of blood began to find eloquent voices.
There it must lie; there was none to work the
cunning hinges or direct the miracle of locomo-
tion—there it must lie till it was found. Found!
ay, and then? Then would this dead flesh lift
up a cry that would ring over England, and fill
the world with the echoes of pursuit. Ay, dead
or not, this was still the enemy. "Time was that
when the brains were out," he thought; and the
first word struck into his mind. Time, now that
the deed was accomplished—time, which had
closed for the victim, had become instant and
momentous for the slayer.

The thought was yet in his mind, when, first
one and then another, with every variety of pace
and voice—one deep as the bell from a cathedral
turret, another ringing on its treble notes the pre-
lude of a waltz—the clocks began to strike the
hour of three in the afternoon.

The sudden outbreak of so many tongues in
that dumb chamber staggered him. He began
to bestir himself, going to and fro with the candle,
beleaguered by moving shadows, and startled to
the soul by chance reflections. In many rich
mirrors, some of home designs, some from Venice
or Amsterdam, he saw his face repeated and repeated, as it were an army of spies; his own eyes
met and detected him; and the sound of his own
steps, lightly as they fell, vexed the surrounding

quiet. And still as he continued to fill his pockets, his mind accused him, with a sickening iteration, of the thousand faults of his design. He should have chosen a more quiet hour; he should have prepared an alibi; he should not have used a knife; he should have been more cautious, and only bound and gagged the dealer, and not killed him; he should have been more bold, and killed the servant also; he should have done all things otherwise; poignant regrets, weary, incessant toiling of the mind to change what was unchangeable, to plan what was now useless, to be the architect of the irrevocable past. Meanwhile, and behind all this activity, brute terrors, like the scurrying of rats in a deserted attic, filled the more remote chambers of his brain with riot; the hand of the constable would fall heavy on his shoulder, and his nerves would jerk like a hooked fish; or he beheld, in galloping defile, the dock, the prison, the gallows, and the black coffin.

Terror of the people in the street sat down before his mind like a besieging army. It was impossible, he thought, but that some rumour of the struggle must have reached their ears and set on edge their curiosity; and now, in all the neighbouring houses, he divined them sitting motionless and with uplifted ear—solitary people, condemned to spend Christmas dwelling alone on memories of the past, and now startlingly recalled from that tender exercise; happy family parties, struck into silence round the table, the mother still with raised finger: every degree and age and humour, but all, by their own hearts, prying and hearkening and weaving the rope that was to hang him. Sometimes it seemed to him he could not move too softly; the clink of the tall Bohemian goblets rang out loudly like a bell; and alarmed by the bigness of the ticking, he was tempted to stop the clocks. And then, again, with a swift transition of his terrors, the very silence of the place appeared a source of peril, and a thing to strike and freeze the passer-by; and he would step more boldly, and bustle aloud among the contents of the shop, and imitate, elaborate bravado, the movements of a busy man at ease in his own house.

But he was now so pulled about by different alarms that, while one portion of his mind was still alert and cunning, another trembled on the brink of lunacy. One hallucination in particular took a strong hold on his credulity. The neighbour hearkening with white face beside his window, the passer-by arrested by a horrible surmise on the pavement—these could at worst suspect, they could not know; through the brick walls and shuttered windows only sounds could penetrate. But here, within the house, was he alone? He knew he was; he had watched the servant set forth sweethearting, in her poor best, "out for the day" written in every ribbon and smile. Yes, he was alone, of course; and yet, in the bulk of empty house above him, he could surely hear a stir of delicate footing—he was surely conscious, inexplicably conscious of some presence. Ay, surely; to every room and corner of the house his imagination followed it; and now it was a faceless thing, and yet had eyes to see with; and again it was a shadow of himself; and yet again behold the image of the dead dealer, reinspired with cunning and hatred.

At times, with a strong effort, he would glance at the open door which still seemed to repel his eyes. The house was tall, the skylight small and dirty, the day blind with fog; and the light that filtered down to the ground story was exceedingly faint, and showed dimly on the threshold of the shop. And yet, in that strip of doubtful brightness, did there not hang wavering a shadow?

Suddenly, from the street outside, a very jovial gentleman began to beat with a staff on the shop-door, accompanying his blows with shouts and railleries in which the dealer was continually called upon by name. Markheim, smitten into ice, glanced at the dead man. But no! he lay quite still; he was fled away far beyond ear-shot of these blows and shoutings; he was sunk beneath seas of silence; and his name, which would once have caught his notice above the howling of a storm, had become an empty sound. And presently the jovial gentleman desisted from his knocking and departed.

Here was a broad hint to hurry what remained

to be done, to get forth from this accusing neighbourhood, to plunge into a bath of London multitudes, and to reach, on the other side of day,
that haven of safety and apparent innocence—
his bed. One visitor had come: at any moment
another might follow and be more obstinate. To
have done the deed, and yet not to reap the profit
would be too abhorrent a failure. The money,
that was now Markheim's concern; and as a
means to that, the keys.

He glanced over his shoulder at the open door,
where the shadow was still lingering and shivering; and with no conscious repugnance of the
mind, yet with a tremor of the belly, he drew
near the body of his victim. The human character had quite departed. Like a suit half
stuffed with bran, the limbs lay scattered, the
trunk doubled, on the floor; and yet the thing re-
pelled him. Although so dingy and inconsiderable to the eye, he feared it might have more
significance to the touch. He took the body by
the shoulders, and turned it on its back. It
was strangely light and supple, and the limbs,
as if they had been broken, fell into the oddest
postures. The face was robbed of all expression;
but it was as pale as wax, and shockingly smeared
with blood about one temple. That was, for
Markheim, the one displeasing circumstance.
It carried him back, upon the instant, to a certain fair day in a fishers' village: a grey day, a
piping wind, a crowd upon the street, the blare

of brasses, the booming of drums, the nasal voice
of a ballad-singer; and a boy going to and fro,
buried over head in the crowd and divided between interest and fear, until, coming out upon
the chief place of concourse, he beheld a booth
and a great screen with pictures, dismally designed, garishly coloured: Brownrigg with her
apprentice; the Mannings with their murdered
guest; Weare in the death-grip of Thurtell; and
a score besides of famous crimes. The thing
was as clear as an illusion; he was once again
that little boy; he was looking once again, and
with the same sense of physical revolt, at these
vile pictures; he was still stunned by the thump-
ing of the drums. A bar of that day's music returned upon his memory; and at that, for the
first time, a qualm came over him, a breath of
nausea, a sudden weakness of the joints, which
he must instantly resist and conquer.

He judged it more prudent to confront than to
flee from these considerations; looking the more
hardily in the dead face, bending his mind to
realise the nature and greatness of his crime. So
little a while ago that face had moved with every
change of sentiment, that pale mouth had spoken,
that body had been all on fire with governable
energies; and now, and by his act, that piece of
life had been arrested, as the horologist, with in-
terjected finger, arrests the beating of the clock.
So he reasoned in vain; he could rise to no more
remorseful consciousness; the same heart which

had shuddered before the painted effigies of crime
looked on its reality unmoved.   At best, he felt
a gleam of pity for one who had been endowed in
vain with all those faculties that can make the
world a garden of enchantment, one who had
never lived and who was now dead.   But of
penitence, no, not a tremor.

With that, shaking himself clear of these considerations, he found the keys and advanced towards the open door of the shop.   Outside, it had
begun to rain smartly; and the sound of the
shower upon the roof had banished silence.   Like
some dripping cavern, the chambers of the house
were haunted by an incessant echoing, which
filled the ear and mingled with the ticking of
the clocks.   And, as Markheim approached the
door, he seemed to hear, in answer to his own
cautious tread, the steps of another foot with-
drawing up the stair.   The shadow still palpi-
tated loosely on the threshold.   He threw a ton's
weight of resolve upon his muscles, and drew
back the door.

The faint, foggy daylight glimmered dimly on
the bare floor and stairs; on the bright suit of
armour posted, halbert in hand, upon the landing; and on the dark wood-carvings and framed
pictures that hung against the yellow panels of
the wainscot.   So loud was the beating of the
rain through all the house that, in Markheim's
ears, it began to be distinguished into many different sounds.   Footsteps and sighs, the tread

of regiments marching in the distance, the chink of money in the counting, and the creaking of doors held stealthily ajar, appeared to mingle with the patter of the drops upon the cupola and the gushing of the water in the pipes. The sense that he was not alone grew upon him to the verge of madness. On every side he was haunted and begirt by presences. He heard them moving in the upper chambers; from the shop, he heard the dead man getting to his legs; and as he began with a great effort to mount the stairs, feet fled quietly before him and followed stealthily behind. If he were but deaf, he thought, how tranquilly he would possess his soul! And then again, and hearkening with ever fresh attention, he blessed himself for that unresting sense which held the outposts and stood a trusty sentinel upon his life. His head turned continually on his neck; his eyes, which seemed starting from their orbits, scouted on every side, and on every side were half rewarded as with the tail of something nameless vanishing. The four-and-twenty steps to the first floor were four-and-twenty agonies.

On that first story, the doors stood ajar, three of them like three ambushes, shaking his nerves like the throats of cannon. He could never again, he felt, be sufficiently immured and fortified from men's observing eyes; he longed to be home, girt in by walls, buried among bedclothes, and invisible to all but God. And at that thought he wondered a little, recollecting tales of other murderers and the fear they were said to entertain of heavenly avengers. It was not so, at least, with him. He feared the laws of nature, lest, in their callous and immutable procedure, they should preserve some damning evidence of his crime. He feared tenfold more, with a slavish, superstitious terror, some scission in the continuity of man's experience, some wilful illegality of nature. He played a game of skill, depending on the rules, calculating consequence from cause; and what if nature, as the defeated tyrant overthrew the chess-board, should break the mould of their succession? The like had befallen Napoleon (so writers said) when the winter changed the time of its appearance. The like might befall Markheim: the solid walls might become transparent and reveal his doings like those of bees in a glass hive; the stout planks might yield under his foot like quicksands and detain him in their clutch; ay, and there were soberer accidents that might destroy him: if, for instance, the house should fall and imprison him beside the body of his victim; or the house next door should fly on fire, and the firemen invade him from all sides. These things he feared; and, in a sense, these things might be called the hands of God reached forth against sin. But about God himself he was at ease; his act was doubtless exceptional, but so were his excuses, which God knew; it was there, and not among men, that he felt sure of justice.

When he had got safe into the drawing-room, and shut the door behind him, he was aware of a respite from alarms. The room was quite dismantled, uncarpeted besides, and strewn with packing-cases and incongruous furniture; several great pier-glasses, in which he beheld himself at various angles, like an actor on a stage; many pictures, framed and unframed, standing, with their faces to the wall; a fine Sheraton sideboard, a cabinet of marquetry, and a great old bed, with tapestry hangings. The windows opened to the floor; but by great good-fortune the lower part of the shutters had been closed, and this concealed him from the neighbours. Here, then, Markheim drew in a packing-case before the cabinet, and began to search among the keys. It was a long business, for there were many; and it was irksome, besides; for, after all, there might be nothing in the cabinet, and time was on the wing. But the closeness of the occupation sobered him. With the tail of his eye he saw the door—even glanced at it from time to time directly, like a besieged commander pleased to verify the good estate of his defences. But in truth he was at peace. The rain falling in the street sounded natural and pleasant. Presently, on the other side, the notes of a piano were wakened to the music of a hymn, and the voices of many children took up the air and words. How stately, how comfortable was the melody! How fresh the youthful voices! Markheim

gave ear to it smilingly, as he sorted out the keys;
and his mind was thronged with answerable
ideas and images; church-going children and
the pealing of the high organ; children afield,
bathers by the brookside, ramblers on the bram-
bly common, kite-fliers in the windy and cloud-
navigated sky; and then, at another cadence of the
hymn, back again to church, and the somnolence
of summer Sundays, and the high genteel voice of
the parson (which he smiled a little to recall) and
the painted Jacobean tombs, and the dim letter-
ing of the Ten Commandments in the chancel.

And as he sat thus, at once busy and absent, he
was startled to his feet. A flash of ice, a flash of
fire, a bursting gush of blood, went over him, and
then he stood transfixed and thrilling. A step
mounted the stair slowly and steadily, and presently a hand was laid upon the knob, and the
lock clicked, and the door opened.

Fear held Markheim in a vice. What to expect he knew not, whether the dead man walking,
or the official ministers of human justice, or some
chance witness blindly stumbling in to consign
him to the gallows. But when a face was thrust
into the aperture, glanced round the room,
looked at him, nodded and smiled as if in friendly
recognition, and then withdrew again, and the
door closed behind it, his fear broke loose from
his control in a hoarse cry. At the sound of this
the visitant returned.

"Did you call me?" he asked, pleasantly, and

with that he entered the room and closed the door behind him.

Markheim stood and gazed at him with all his eyes. Perhaps there was a film upon his sight, but the outlines of the new-comer seemed to change and waver like those of the idols in the wavering candle-light of the shop; and at times he thought he knew him; and at times he thought he bore a likeness to himself; and always, like a lump of living terror, there lay in his bosom the conviction that this thing was not of the earth and not of God.

And yet the creature had a strange air of the commonplace, as he stood looking on Markheim with a smile; and when he added: "You are looking for the money, I believe?" it was in the tones of every-day politeness.

Markheim made no answer.

"I should warn you," resumed the other, "that the maid has left her sweetheart earlier than usual and will soon be here. If Mr. Markheim be found in this house, I need not describe to him the consequences."

"You know me?" cried the murderer.

The visitor smiled. "You have long been a favourite of mine," he said; "and I have long observed and often sought to help you."

"What are you?" cried Markheim: "the devil?"

"What I may be," returned the other, "cannot affect the service I propose to render you."

"It can," cried Markheim; "it does! Be helped by you? No, never; not by you! You do not know me yet; thank God, you do not know me!"

"I know you," replied the visitant, with a sort of kind severity or rather firmness. "I know you to the soul."

"Know me!" cried Markheim. "Who can do so? My life is but a travesty and slander on myself. I have lived to belie my nature. All men do; all men are better than this disguise that grows about and stifles them. You see each dragged away by life, like one whom bravos have seized and muffled in a cloak. If they had their own control—if you could see their faces, they would be altogether different, they would shine out for heroes and saints! I am worse than most; my self is more overlaid; my excuse is known to me and God. But, had I the time, I could disclose myself."

"To me?" inquired the visitant.

"To you before all," returned the murderer. "I supposed you were intelligent. I thought—since you exist—you would prove a reader of the heart. And yet you would propose to judge me by my acts! Think of it; my acts! I was born and I have lived in a land of giants; giants have dragged me by the wrists since I was born out of my mother—the giants of circumstance. And you would judge me by my acts! But can you not look within? Can you not understand that

evil is hateful to me? Can you not see within
me the clear writing of conscience, never blurred
by any wilful sophistry, although too often dis-
regarded? Can you not read me for a thing that
surely must be common as humanity—the unwilling sinner?"

"All this is very feelingly expressed," was the
reply, "but it regards me not. These points of
consistency are beyond my province, and I care
not in the least by what compulsion you may
have been dragged away, so as you are but carried in the right direction. But time flies; the
servant delays, looking in the faces of the crowd
and at the pictures on the hoardings, but still she
keeps moving nearer; and remember, it is as if
the gallows itself was striding towards you
through the Christmas streets! Shall I help
you; I, who know all? Shall I tell you where to
find the money?"

"For what price?" asked Markheim.

"I offer you the service for a Christmas gift,"
returned the other.

Markheim could not refrain from smiling with
a kind of bitter triumph. "No," said he, "I will
take nothing at your hands; if I were dying of
thirst, and it was your hand that put the pitcher
to my lips, I should find the courage to refuse. It
may be credulous, but I will do nothing to commit myself to evil."

"I have no objection to a death-bed repentance," observed the visitant.

"Because you disbelieve their efficacy!" Markheim cried.

"I do not say so," returned the other; "but I look on these things from a different side, and when the life is done my interest falls. The man has lived to serve me, to spread black looks under colour of religion, or to sow tares in the wheatfield, as you do, in a course of weak compliance with desire. Now that he draws so near to his deliverance, he can add but one act of service— to repent, to die smiling, and thus to build up in confidence and hope the more timorous of my surviving followers. I am not so hard a master. Try me. Accept my help. Please yourself in life as you have done hitherto; please yourself more amply, spread your elbows at the board; and when the night begins to fall and the curtains to be drawn, I tell you, for your greater comfort, that you will find it even easy to compound your quarrel with your conscience, and to make a truckling peace with God. I came but now from such a death-bed, and the room was full of sincere mourners, listening to the man's last words: and when I looked into that face, which had been set as a flint against mercy, I found it smiling with hope."

"And do you, then, suppose me such a creature?" asked Markheim. "Do you think I have no more generous aspirations than to sin, and sin, and sin, and, at last, sneak into heaven? My heart rises at the thought. Is this, then, your experience of mankind? or is it because you find me with red hands that you presume such baseness? and is this crime of murder indeed so impious as to dry up the very springs of good?"

"Murder is to me no special category," replied the other. "All sins are murder, even as all life is war. I behold your race, like starving mariners on a raft, plucking crusts out of the hands of famine and feeding on each other's lives. I follow sins beyond the moment of their acting; I find in all that the last consequence is death; and to my eyes, the pretty maid who thwarts her mother with such taking graces on a question of a ball, drips no less visibly with human gore than such a murderer as yourself. Do I say that I follow sins? I follow virtues also; they differ not by the thickness of a nail, they are both scythes for the reaping angel of Death. Evil, for which I live, consists not in action but in character. The bad man is dear to me; not the bad act, whose fruits, if we could follow them far enough down the hurtling cataract of the ages, might yet be found more blessed than those of the rarest virtues. And it is not because you have killed a dealer, but because you are Markheim, that I offered to forward your escape."

"I will lay my heart open to you," answered Markheim. "This crime on which you find me is my last. On my way to it I have learned many lessons; itself is a lesson, a momentous lesson. Hitherto I have been driven with revolt to what I would not; I was a bond-slave to poverty, driven and scourged. There are robust virtues that can stand in these temptations; mine was not so: I had a thirst of pleasure. But to-day, and out of this deed, I pluck both warning and riches—both the power and a fresh resolve to be myself. I become in all things a free actor in the world; I begin to see myself all changed, these hands the agents of good, this heart at peace. Something comes over me out of the past; something of what I have dreamed on Sabbath evenings to the sound of the church organ, of what I forecast when I shed tears over noble books, or talked, an innocent child, with my mother. There lies my life; I have wandered a few years, but now I see once more my city of destination."

"You are to use this money on the Stock Exchange, I think?" remarked the visitor; "and there, if I mistake not, you have already lost some thousands?"

"Ah," said Markheim, "but this time I have a sure thing."

"This time, again, you will lose," replied the visitor quietly.

"Ah, but I keep back the half!" cried Markheim.

"That also you will lose," said the other.

The sweat started upon Markheim's brow.

"Well, then, what matter?" he exclaimed. "Say it be lost, say I am plunged again in poverty, shall one part of me, and that the worst, continue until the end to over-ride the better? Evil and good run strong in me, haling me both ways. I do not love the one thing, I love all. I can conceive great deeds, renunciations, martyrdoms; and though I be fallen to such a crime as murder, pity is no stranger to my thoughts. I pity the poor; who knows their trials better than myself? I pity and help them; I prize love, I love honest laughter; there is no good thing nor true thing on earth but I love it from my heart. And are my vices only to direct my life, and my virtues to lie without effect, like some passive lumber of the mind? Not so; good, also, is a spring of acts."

But the visitant raised his finger. "For six-and-thirty years that you have been in this world," said he, "through many changes of fortune and varieties of humour, I have watched you steadily fall. Fifteen years ago you would have started at a theft. Three years back you would have blenched at the name of murder. Is there any crime, is there any cruelty or meanness, from which you still recoil?—five years from now I shall detect you in the fact! Downward, downward, lies your way; nor can anything but death avail to stop you."

"It is true," Markheim said huskily, "I have in some degree complied with evil. But it is so with all: the very saints, in the mere exercise of living, grow less dainty and take on the tone of their surroundings."

"I will propound to you one simple question," said the other; "and as you answer, I shall read to you your moral horoscope. You have grown in many things more lax; possibly you do right to be so; and at any account, it is the same with all men. But granting that, are you in any one particular, however trifling, more difficult to please with your own conduct, or do you go in all things with a looser rein?"

"In any one?" repeated Markheim, with an anguish of consideration. "No," he added, with despair, "in none! I have gone down in all."

"Then," said the visitor, "content yourself with what you are, for you will never change; and the words of your part on this stage are irrevocably written down."

Markheim stood for a long while silent, and indeed it was the visitor who first broke the silence. "That being so," he said, "shall I show you the money?"

"And grace?" cried Markheim.

"Have you not tried it?" returned the other. "Two or three years ago, did I not see you on the platform of revival meetings, and was not your voice the loudest in the hymn?"

"It is true," said Markheim; "and I see clearly what remains for me by way of duty. I thank you for these lessons from my soul; my eyes are

153

opened, and I behold myself at last for what I am."

At this moment, the sharp note of the door-bell rang through the house; and the visitant, as though this were some concerted signal for which he had been waiting, changed at once in his de-meanour. "The maid!" he cried. "She has returned, as I forewarned you, and there is now before you one more difficult passage. Her master, you must say, is ill; you must let her in, with an assured but rather serious countenance—no smiles, no over-acting, and I promise you suc-cess! Once the girl within, and the door closed, the same dexterity that has already rid you of the dealer will relieve you of this last danger in your path. Thenceforward you have the whole evening—the whole night, if needful—to ransack the treasures of the house and to make good your safety. This is help that comes to you with the mask of danger. Up!" he cried: "up, friend; your life hangs trembling in the scales: up, and act!"

Markheim steadily regarded his counsellor. "If I be condemned to evil acts," he said, "there is still one door of freedom open—I can cease from action. If my life be an ill thing, I can lay it down. Though I be, as you say truly, at the beck of every small temptation, I can yet, by one decisive gesture, place myself beyond the reach of all. My love of good is damned to barrenness; it may, and let it be! But I have still my hatred of evil; and from that, to your galling disappointment, you shall see that I can draw both energy and courage."

The features of the visitor began to undergo a wonderful and lovely change: they brightened and softened with a tender triumph; and, even as they brightened, faded and dislimned. But Markheim did not pause to watch or understand the transformation. He opened the door and went down-stairs very slowly, thinking to himself. His past went soberly before him; he beheld it as it was, ugly and strenuous like a dream, random as chance-medley—a scene of defeat. Life, as he thus reviewed it, tempted him no longer; but on the further side he perceived a quiet haven for his bark. He paused in the passage, and looked into the shop, where the candle still burned by the dead body. It was strangely silent. Thoughts of the dealer swarmed into his mind, as he stood gazing. And then the bell once more broke out into impatient clamour.

He confronted the maid upon the threshold with something like a smile.

"You had better go for the police," said he: "I have killed your master."

THRAWN JANET

THE Reverend Murdoch Soulis was long minister of the moorland parish of Balweary, in the vale of Dule. A severe, bleak-faced old man, dreadful to his hearers, he dwelt in the last years of his life, without relative or servant or any human company, in the small and lonely manse under the Hanging Shaw. In spite of the iron composure of his features, his eye was wild, scared, and uncertain; and when he dwelt, in private admonition, on the future of the impenitent, it seemed as if his eye pierced through the storms of time to the terrors of eternity. Many young persons, coming to prepare themselves against the season of the Holy Communion, were dreadfully affected by his talk. He had a sermon on 1st Peter, v. and 8th, "The devil as a roaring lion," on the Sunday after every seventeenth of August, and he was accustomed to surpass himself upon that text both by the appalling nature of the matter and the terror of his bearing in the pulpit. The children were frightened into fits, and the old looked more than usually oracular, and were, all that day, full of those hints that Hamlet deprecated. The manse itself, where it stood by the water of Dule among some thick trees, with the Shaw overhanging it on the one side, and on the other many cold, moorish hill-tops rising toward the sky, had begun, at a very early period of Mr. Soulis's ministry, to be avoided in the dusk hours by all who valued themselves upon their prudence; and guidmen sitting at the clachan alehouse shook their heads together at the thought of passing late by that uncanny neighbourhood. There was one spot, to be more particular, which was regarded with especial awe. The manse stood between the highroad and the water of Dule, with a gable to each; its back was towards the kirktown of Balweary, nearly half a mile away; in front of it, a bare garden, hedged with thorn, occupied the land between the river and the road. The house was two stories high, with two large rooms on each. It opened not directly on the garden, but on a causewayed path, or passage, giving on the road on the one hand, and closed on the other by the tall willows and elders that bordered on the stream. And it was this strip of causeway that enjoyed among the young parishioners of Balweary so infamous a reputation. The minister walked there often after dark, sometimes groaning aloud in the instancy of his unspoken prayers; and when he was from home, and the manse door was locked, the more daring schoolboys ventured, with beating hearts, to "follow my leader" across that legendary spot.

This atmosphere of terror, surrounding, as it did, a man of God of spotless character and orthodoxy, was a common cause of wonder and subject of inquiry among the few strangers who were led by chance or business into that unknown, outlying country. But many even of the people of the parish were ignorant of the strange events which had marked the first year of Mr. Soulis's ministrations; and among those who were better informed, some were naturally reticent, and others shy of that particular topic. Now and again, only, one of the older folk would warm into courage over his third tumbler, and recount the cause of the minister's strange looks and solitary life.

Fifty years syne, when Mr. Soulis cam' first into Ba'weary, he was still a young man—a callant, the folk said—fu' o' book-learnin' an' grand at the exposition, but, as was natural in sae young a man, wi' nae leevin' experience in religion. The younger sort were greatly taken wi' his gifts and his gab; but auld, concerned, serious men and women were moved even to prayer for the young man, whom they took to be a self-deceiver, and the parish that was like to be sae ill-supplied. It was before the days o' the moderates—weary fa' them; but ill things are like guid—they baith come bit by bit, a pickle at a

158

time; and there were folk even then that said
the Lord had left the college professors to their
ain devices, an' the lads that went to study wi'
them wad hae done mair an' better sittin' in a
peat-bog, like their forbears of the persecution,
wi' a Bible under their oxter an' a speerit o'
prayer in their heart. There was nae doubt
onyway, but that Mr. Soulis had been ower lang
at the college. He was careful and troubled for
mony things besides the ae thing needful. He
had a feck o' books wi' him—mair than had ever
been seen before in a' that presbytery; and a sair
wark the carrier had wi' them, for they were a'
like to have smoored in the De'il's Hag between
this and Kilmackerlie. They were books o'
divinity, to be sure, or so they ca'd them; but
the serious were o' opinion there was little service for sae mony, when the hail o' God's Word
would gang in the neuk o' a plaid. Then he wad
sit half the day and half the nicht forbye, which
was scant decent—writin', nae less; an' first
they were feared he wad read his sermons; an'
syne it proved he was writin' a book himsel',
which was surely no' fittin' for ane o' his years
an' sma' experience.

Onyway it behoved him to get an auld, decent
wife to keep the manse for him an' see to his bit
deeners; an' he was recommended to an auld
limmer—Janet M'Clour, they ca'd her—an' sae
far left to himsel' as to be ower persuaded.
There was mony advised him to the contrar, for

THRAWN JANET

Janet was mair than suspeckit by the best folk in
Ba'weary. Lang or that, she had had a wean to
a dragoon; she hadna come forrit[1] for maybe
thretty year; and bairns had seen her mumblin'
to hersel' up on Key's Loan in the gloamin',
whilk was an unco time an' place for a God-
fearin' woman. Howsoever, it was the laird
himsel' that had first tauld the minister o' Janet;
an' in thae days he wad hae gane a far gate to
pleesure the laird. When folk tauld him that
Janet was sib to the de'il, it was a' superstition
by his way o' it; an' when they cast up the Bible
to him an' the witch of Endor, he wad threep it
doun their thrapples that thir days were a' gane
by, an' the de'il was mercifully restrained.

Weel, when it got about the clachan that Janet
M'Clour was to be servant at the manse, the folk
were fair mad wi' her an' him thegither; an'
some o' the guidwives had nae better to dae than
get round her door-cheeks and chairge her wi' a'
that was ken't again' her, frae the sodger's bairn
to John Tamson's twa kye. She was nae great
speaker; folk usually let her gang her ain gate,
an' she let them gang theirs, wi' neither Fair-
guid-een nor Fair-guid-day; but when she buckled
to, she had a tongue to deave the miller. Up she
got, an' there wasna an auld story in Ba'weary
but she gart somebody lowp for it that day; they
couldna say ae thing but she could say twa to it;
till, at the hinder end, the guidwives up an'

[1] "To come forrit"—to offer oneself as a communicant.

160

claught haud of her, an' clawed the coats aff her back, and pu'd her doun the clachan to the water o' Dule, to see if she were a witch or no, soom or droun. The carline skirled till ye could hear her at the Hangin' Shaw, an' she focht like ten; there was mony a guidwife bure the mark o' her neist day an' mony a lang day after; an' just in the hettest o' the collieshangie, wha suld come up (for his sins) but the new minister!

"Women," said he (an' he had a grand voice), "I charge you in the Lord's name to let her go."

Janet ran to him—she was fair wud wi' terror —an' clang to him, an' prayed him, for Christ's sake, save her frae the cummers; an' they, for their pairt, tauld him a' that was ken't, an' maybe mair.

"Woman," says he to Janet, "is this true?"

"As the Lord sees me," says she, "as the Lord made me, no' a word o't. Forbye the bairn," says she, "I 've been a decent woman a' my days."

"Will you," says Mr. Soulis, "in the name of God, and before me, His unworthy minister, renounce the devil and his works?"

Weel, it wad appear that when he askit that, she gave a girn that fairly frichtit them that saw her, an' they could hear her teeth play dirl the-gither in her chafts; but there was naething for it but the ae way or the ither; an' Janet lifted up her hand an' renounced the de'il before them a'.

"And now," says Mr. Soulis to the guidwives, "home with ye, one and all, and pray to God for His forgiveness."

An' he gied Janet his arm, though she had little on her but a sark, and took her up the clachan to her ain door like a leddy o' the land; an' her screighin' an' laughin' as was a scandal to be heard.

There were mony grave folk lang ower their prayers that nicht; but when the morn cam' there was sic a fear fell upon a' Ba'weary that the bairns hid theirsels, an' even the men-folk stood an' keekit frae their doors. For there was Janet comin' doun the clachan—her or her likeness, nane could tell—wi' her neck thrawn, an' her heid on ae side, like a body that has been hangit, an' a girn on her face like an unstreakit corp. By an' by they got used wi' it, an' even speered at her to ken what was wrang; but frae that day forth she couldna speak like a Christian woman, but slavered an' played click wi' her teeth like a pair o' shears; an' frae that day forth the name o' God cam' never on her lips. Whiles she wad try to say it, but it michtna be. Them that kenned best said least; but they never gied that Thing the name o' Janet M'Clour; for the auld Janet, by their way o't, was in muckle hell that day. But the minister was neither to haud nor to bind; he preached about naething but the folk's cruelty that had gi'en her a stroke of the palsy; he skelpit the bairns that meddled

her; an' he had her up to the manse that same
nicht, an' dwalled there a' his lane wi' her under
the Hangin' Shaw.

Weel, time gaed by: and the idler sort commenced to think mair lichtly o' that black business. The minister was weel thocht o'; he was
aye late at the writing, folk wad see his can'le
doon by the Dule water after twal' at e'en; and
he seemed pleased wi' himsel' an' upsitten as at
first, though a' body could see that he was dwin-
ing. As for Janet she cam' an' she gaed; if she
didna speak muckle afore, it was reason she
should speak less then; she meddled naebody;
but she was an eldritch thing to see, an' nane
wad hae mistrysted wi' her for Ba'weary glebe.

About the end o' July there cam' a spell o'
weather, the like o't never was in that country-
side; it was lown an' het an' heartless; the herds
couldna win up the Black Hill, the bairns were
ower weariet to play; an' yet it was gousty too,
wi' claps o' het wund that rumm'led in the glens,
and bits o' shouers that slockened naething. We
aye thocht it bût to thun'er on the morn; but the
morn cam', an' the morn's morning, an' it was
aye the same uncanny weather, sair on folks and
bestial. O' a' that were the waur, nane suffered
like Mr. Soulis; he could neither sleep nor eat,
hé tauld his elders; an' when he wasna writin'
at his weary book, he wad be stravaguin' ower a'
the country-side like a man possessed, when a'
body else was blithe to keep caller ben the house.

THRAWN JANET

Abune Hangin' Shaw, in the bield o' the Black
Hill, there 's a bit enclosed grund wi' an iron yett;
an' it seems, in the auld days, that was the kirkyaird o' Ba'weary, an' consecrated by the
Papists before the blessed licht shone upon the
kingdom. It was a great howff, o' Mr. Soulis's
onyway; there he wad sit an' consider his sermons; an' indeed it's a bieldy bit. Weel, as he
cam' ower the wast end o' the Black Hill, ae day,
he saw first twa, an' syne fower, an' syne seeven
corbie craws fleein' round an' round abune the
auld kirkyaird. They flew laigh an' heavy, an'
squawked to ither as they gaed; an' it was clear
to Mr. Soulis that something had put them frae
their ordinar. He wasna easy fleyed, an' gaed
straucht up to the wa's; an' what suld he find
there but a man, or the appearance o' a man,
sittin' in the inside upon a grave. He was of a
great stature, an' black as hell, and his e'en were
singular to see.[1] Mr. Soulis had heard tell o'
black men, mony's the time; but there was something unco about this black man that daunted
him. Het as he was, he took a kind o' cauld
grue in the marrow o' his banes; but up he spak
for a' that; an' says he: "My friend, are you a
stranger in this place?" The black man answered never a word; he got upon his feet, an'
begoud on to hirsle to the wa' on the far side; but

[1] It was a common belief in Scotland that the devil appeared
as a black man. This appears in several witch trials and I think
in Law's *Memorials*, that delightful storehouse of the quaint and
grisly.

he aye lookit at the minister; an' the minister
stood an' lookit back; till a' in a meenit the
black man was ower the wa' an' rinnin' for the
bield o' the trees. Mr. Soulis, he hardly kenned
why, ran after him; but he was fair forjeskit wi'
his walk an' the het, unhalesome weather; an'
rin as he likit, he got nae mair than a glisk o' the
black man amang the birks, till he won doun to
the foot o' the hillside, an' there he saw him ance
mair, gaun, hap-step-an'-lawp, ower Dule water
to the manse.

Mr. Soulis wasna weel pleased that this fearsome gangrel suld mak' sae free wi' Ba'weary
manse; an' he ran the harder, an', wet shoon,
ower the burn, an' up the walk; but the de'il a
black man was there to see. He stepped out
upon the road, but there was naebody there; he
gaed a' ower the gairden, but na, nae black man.
At the hinder end, an' a bit feared as was but
natural, he lifted the hasp an' into the manse;
and there was Janet M'Clour before his e'en, wi'
her thrawn craig, an' nane sae pleased to see
him. An' he aye minded sinsyne, when first he
set his e'en upon her, he had the same cauld and
deidly grue.

"Janet," says he, "have you seen a black
man?"

"A black man!" quo' she. "Save us a'!
Ye're no wise, minister. There's nae black man
in a' Ba'weary."

But she didna speak plain, ye maun understand; but yam-yammered, like a powney wi' the bit in its moo.

"Weel," says he, "Janet, if there was nae black man, I have spoken with the Accuser of the Brethren."

An' he sat doun like ane wi' a fever, an' his teeth chittered in his heid.

"Hoots," says she, "think shame to yoursel', minister"; an' gied him a drap brandy that she keepit aye by her.

Syne Mr. Soulis gaed into his study amang a' his books. It 's a lang, laigh, mirk chalmer, perishin' cauld in winter, an' no' very dry even in the top o' the simmer, for the manse stands near the burn. Sae doun he sat, and thocht of a' that had come an' gane since he was in Ba'weary, an' his hame, an' the days when he was a bairn an' ran daffin' on the braes; an' that black man aye ran in his heid like the owercome of a sang. Aye the mair he thocht, the mair he thocht o' the black man. He tried the prayer, an' the words wouldna come to him; an' he tried, they say, to write at his book, but he couldna mak' nae mair o' that. There was whiles he thocht the black man was at his oxter, an' the swat stood upon him cauld as well-water; and there was ither whiles, when he cam' to himsel' like a christened bairn an' minded naething.

The upshot was that he gaed to the window an' stood glowrin' at Dule water. The trees are unco thick, an' the water lies deep an' black under the manse; an' there was Janet washin' the cla'es wi' her coats kilted. She had her back to the minister, an' he, for his pairt, hardly kenned what he was lookin' at. Syne she turned round, an' shawed her face; Mr. Soulis had the same cauld grue as twice that day afore, an' it was borne in upon him what folk said, that Janet was deid lang syne, an' this was a bogle in her clay-cauld flesh. He drew back a pickle and he scanned her narrowly. She was tramp-trampin' in the cla'es croonin' to hersel'; and eh! Gude guide us, but it was a fearsome face. Whiles she sang louder, but there was nae man born o' woman that could tell the words o' her sang; an' whiles she lookit side-lang doun, but there was naething there for her to look at. There gaed a scunner through the flesh upon his banes; an' that was Heeven's advertisement. But Mr. Soulis just blamed himsel', he said, to think sae ill o' a puir, auld afflicted wife that hadna a freend forbye himsel'; an' he put up a bit prayer for him an' her, an' drank a little caller water—for his heart rose again' the meat—an' gaed up to his naked bed in the gloamin'.

That was a nicht that has never been forgotten in Ba'weary, the nicht o' the seeventeenth o' August, seeventeen hun'er' an' twal'. It had been het afore, as I hae said, but that nicht it was hetter than ever. The sun gaed doun amang unco-lookin' clouds; it fell as mirk as the pit; no' a star, no' a breath o' wund; ye couldna see your han' afore your face, an' even the auld folk cuist the covers frae their beds an' lay pechin' for their breath. Wi' a' that he had upon his mind, it was gey an' unlikely Mr. Soulis wad get muckle sleep. He lay an' he tummled; the gude, caller bed that he got into brunt his very banes; whiles he slept, an' whiles he waukened; whiles he heard the time o' nicht, an' whiles a tyke yowlin' up the muir, as if somebody was deid; whiles he thocht he heard bogles claverin' in his lug, an' whiles he saw spunkies in the room. He behoved, he judged, to be sick; an' sick he was—little he jaloosed the sickness.

At the hinder end, he got a clearness in his mind, sat up in his sark on the bed-side, an' fell thinkin' ance mair o' the black man an' Janet. He couldna weel tell how—maybe it was the cauld to his feet—but it cam' in upon him wi' a spate that there was some connection between thir twa, an' that either or baith o' them were bogles. An' just at that moment, in Janet's room, which was neist to his, there cam' a stramp o' feet as if men were wars'lin', an' then a loud bang; an' then a wund gaed reishling round the fower quarters o' the house; an' then a' was ance mair as seelent as the grave.

Mr. Soulis was feared for neither man nor de'il. He got his tinder-box, an' lit a can'le, an' made three steps o't ower to Janet's door. It was on the hasp, an' he pushed it open, an' keeked bauldly in. It was a big room, as big as

the minister's ain, an' plenished wi' grand, auld
solid gear, for he had naething else.   There was a
fower-posted bed wi' auld tapestry; an' a braw
cabinet o' aik, that was fu' o' the minister's divinity books, an' put there to be out o' the gate;
an' a wheen duds o' Janet's lying here an' there
about the floor.   But nae Janet could Mr. Soulis
see; nor ony sign o' a contention.   In he gaed
(an' there's few that wad hae followed him) an'
lookit a' round, an' listened.   But there was naething to be heard, neither inside the manse nor
in a' Ba'weary parish, an' naething to be seen but
the muckle shadows turnin' round the can'le.
An' then, a' at aince, the minister's heart played
dunt an' stood stock-still; an' a cauld wund blew
amang the hairs o' his heid.   Whaten a weary
sicht was that for the puir man's e'en!   For there
was Janet hangin' frae a nail beside the auld aik
cabinet: her heid aye lay on her shouther, her
e'en were steekit, the tongue projected frae her
mouth, an' her heels were twa feet clear abune
the floor.

"God forgive us all!" thocht Mr. Soulis, "poor
Janet's dead."

He cam' a step nearer to the corp; an' then his
heart fair whammled in his inside.   For by what
cantrip it wad ill beseem a man to judge, she
was hangin' frae a single nail an' by a single
wursted thread for darnin' hose.

It's a awfu' thing to be your lane at nicht wi'
siccan prodigies o' darkness; but Mr. Soulis was

strong in the Lord. He turned an' gaed his ways
oot o' that room, an' lockit the door ahint him;
an' step by step, doun the stairs, as heavy as
leed; and set doun the can'le on the table at the
stairfoot. He couldna pray, he couldna think,
he was dreepin' wi' caul' swat, an' naething could
he hear but the dunt-dunt-duntin' o'' his ain
heart. He micht maybe hae stood there an hour,
or maybe twa, he minded sae little; when a' o' a
sudden, he heard a laigh, uncanny steer up-stairs;
a foot gaed to an' fro in the chalmer whaur
the corp was hangin'; syne the door was opened,
though he minded weel that he had lockit it; an'
syne there was a step upon the landin', an' it
seemed to him as if the corp was lookin' ower
the rail and doun upon him whaur he stood.

He took up the can'le again (for he couldna
want the licht), an' as saftly as ever he could,
gaed straucht out o' the manse an' to the far end
o' the causeway. It was aye pit-mirk; the flame
o' the can'le, when he set it on the grund, brunt
steedy and clear as in a room; naething moved,
but the Dule water seepin' and sabbin' doun the
glen, an' yon unhaly footstep that cam' ploddin'
doun the stairs inside the manse. He kenned the
foot ower weel, for it was Janet's; an' at ilka
step that cam' a wee thing nearer, the cauld got
deeper in his vitals. He commended his soul to
Him that made an' keepit him; "and, O Lord,"
said he, "give me strength this night to war
against the powers of evil."

By this time the foot was comin' through the passage for the door; he could hear a hand skirt alang the wa', as if the fearsome thing was feelin' for its way. The saughs tossed an' maned thegither, a long sigh cam' ower the hills, the flame o' the can'le was blawn aboot; an' there stood the corp of Thrawn Janet, wi' her grogram goun an' her black mutch, wi' the heid aye upon the shouther, an' the girn still upon the face o't—leevin', ye wad hae said—deid, as Mr. Soulis weel kenned—upon the threshold o' the manse.

It's a strange thing that the soul of man should be that thirled into his perishable body; but the minister saw that, an' his heart didna break.

She didna stand there lang; she began to move again an' cam' slowly towards Mr. Soulis whaur he stood under the saughs. A' the life o' his body, a' the strength o' his speerit, were glowerin' frae his e'en. It seemed she was gaun to speak, but wanted words, an' made a sign wi' the left hand. There cam' a clap o' wund, like a cat's fuff; oot gaed the can'le, the saughs skreighed like folk; an' Mr. Soulis kenned that, live or die, this was the end o't.

"Witch, beldame, devil!" he cried, "I charge you, by the power of God, begone—if you be dead, to the grave—if you be damned, to hell."

An' at that moment the Lord's ain hand out o' the Heevens struck the Horror whaur it stood; the auld, deid, desecrated corp o' the witch-wife, sae lang keepit frae the grave and hirsled round by de'ils, lowed up like a brunstane spunk an' fell in ashes to the grund; the thunder followed, peal on dirling peal, the rairin' rain upon the back o' that; and Mr. Soulis lowped through the garden hedge, an' ran, wi' skelloch upon skelloch, for the clachan.

That same mornin', John Christie saw the Black Man pass the Muckle Cairn as it was chappin' six; before eicht, he gaed by the change-house at Knockdow; an' no' lang after, Sandy M'Lellan saw him gaun linkin' doun the braes frae Kilmackerlie. There's little doubt but it was him that dwalled sae lang in Janet's body; but he was awa' at last; an' sinsyne the de'il has never fashed us in Ba'weary.

But it was a sair dispensation for the minister; lang, lang he lay ravin' in his bed; an' frae that hour to this, he was the man ye ken the day.

OLALLA

"NOW," said the doctor, "my part is done, and, I may say, with some vanity, well done. It remains only to get you out of this cold and poisonous city, and to give you two months of a pure air and an easy conscience. The last is your affair. To the first I think I can help you. It falls indeed rather oddly; it was but the other day the Padre came in from the country; and as he and I are old friends, although of contrary professions, he applied to me in a matter of distress among some of his parishioners. This was a family—but you are ignorant of Spain, and even the names of our grandees are hardly known to you; suffice it, then, that they were once great people, and are now fallen to the brink of destitution. Nothing now belongs to them but the residencia, and certain leagues of desert mountain, in the greater part of which not even a goat could support life. But the house is a fine old place, and stands at a great height among the hills, and most salubriously; and I had no sooner heard my friend's tale than I remembered you.

I told him I had a wounded officer, wounded in the good cause, who was now able to make a change; and I proposed that his friends should take you for a lodger. Instantly the Padre's face grew dark, as I had maliciously foreseen it would. It was out of the question, he said. Then let them starve, said I, for I have no sympathy with tatterdemalion pride. Thereupon we separated, not very content with one another; but yesterday, to my wonder, the Padre returned and made a submission: the difficulty, he said, he had found upon inquiry to be less than he had feared; or, in other words, these proud people had put their pride in their pocket. I closed with the offer; and, subject to your approval, I have taken rooms for you in the residencia. The air of these mountains will renew your blood; and the quiet in which you will there live is worth all the medicines in the world."

"Doctor," said I, "you have been throughout my good angel, and your advice is a command. But tell me, if you please, something of the family with which I am to reside."

"I am coming to that," replied my friend; "and, indeed, there is a difficulty in the way. These beggars are, as I have said, of very high descent and swollen with the most baseless vanity; they have lived for some generations in a growing isolation, drawing away, on either hand, from the rich who had now become too high for them, and from the poor, whom they still regarded as too low; and even to-day, when poverty forces them to unfasten their door to a guest, they cannot do so without a most ungracious stipulation. You are to remain, they say, a stranger; they will give you attendance, but they refuse from the first the idea of the smallest intimacy."

I will not deny that I was piqued, and perhaps the feeling strengthened my desire to go, for I was confident that I could break down that barrier if I desired. "There is nothing offensive in such a stipulation," said I; "and I even sympathise with the feeling that inspired it."

"It is true, they have never seen you," returned the doctor politely; "and if they knew you were the handsomest and the most pleasant man that ever came from England (where I am told that handsome men are common, but pleasant ones not so much so), they would doubtless make you welcome with a better grace. But since you take the thing so well, it matters not. To me, indeed, it seems discourteous. But you will find yourself the gainer. The family will not much tempt you. A mother, a son, and a daughter; an old woman said to be half-witted, a country lout, and a country girl, who stands very high with her confessor, and is, therefore," chuckled the physician, "most likely plain; there is not much in that to attract the fancy of a dashing officer."

"And yet you say they are high-born," I objected.

"Well, as to that, I should distinguish," returned the doctor. "The mother is; not so the children. The mother was the last representative of a princely stock, degenerate both in parts and fortune. Her father was not only poor, he was mad: and the girl ran wild about the residencia till his death. Then, much of the fortune having died with him, and the family being quite extinct, the girl ran wilder than ever, until at last she married, Heaven knows whom, a muleteer some say, others a smuggler; while there are some who uphold there was no marriage at all, and that Felipe and Olalla are bastards. The union, such as it was, was tragically dissolved some years ago; but they live in such seclusion, and the country at that time was in so much disorder, that the precise manner of the man's end is known only to the priest—if even to him."

"I begin to think I shall have strange experiences," said I.

"I would not romance, if I were you," replied the doctor; "you will find, I fear, a very grovelling and commonplace reality. Felipe, for instance, I have seen. And what am I to say? He is very rustic, very cunning, very loutish, and, I should say, an innocent; the others are probably to match. No, no, señor commandante, you must seek congenial society among the great sights of our mountains; and in these at least, if you are at all a lover of the works of nature, I promise you will not be disappointed."

OLALLA

The next day Felipe came for me in a rough country cart, drawn by a mule; and a little before the stroke of noon, after I had said farewell to the doctor, the innkeeper, and different good souls who had befriended me during my sickness, we set forth out of the city by the eastern gate, and began to ascend into the Sierra. I had been so long a prisoner, since I was left behind for dying after the loss of the convoy, that the mere smell of the earth set me smiling. The country through which we went was wild and rocky, partially covered with rough woods, now of the cork-tree, and now of the great Spanish chestnut, and frequently intersected by the beds of mountain torrents. The sun shone, the wind rustled joyously; and we had advanced some miles, and the city had already shrunk into an inconsiderable knoll upon the plain behind us, before my attention began to be diverted to the companion of my drive. To the eye, he seemed but a diminutive, loutish, well-made country lad, such as the doctor had described, mighty quick and active, but devoid of any culture; and this first impression was with most observers final. What began to strike me was his familiar, chattering talk; so strangely inconsistent with the terms on which I was to be received; and partly from his imperfect enunciation, partly from the sprightly incoherence of the matter, so very difficult to follow clearly without an effort of the mind. It is true I had before talked with persons of a similar mental constitution; persons who seemed to live (as he did) by the senses, taken and possessed by the visual object of the moment and unable to discharge their minds of that impression. His seemed to me (as I sat, distantly giving ear) a kind of conversation proper to drivers, who pass much of their time in a great vacancy of the intellect and threading the sights of a familiar country. But this was not the case of Felipe; by his own account he was a homekeeper. "I wish I was there now," he said; and then spying a tree by the wayside, he broke off to tell me that he had once seen a crow among its branches.

"A crow?" I repeated, struck by the ineptitude of the remark, and thinking I had heard imperfectly.

But by this time he was already filled with a new idea; hearkening with a rapt intentness, his head on one side, his face puckered; and he struck me rudely, to make me hold my peace. Then he smiled and shook his head.

"What did you hear?" I asked.

"Oh, it is all right," he said; and began encouraging his mule with cries that echoed unhumanly up the mountain walls.

I looked at him more closely. He was superlatively well-built, light, and lithe and strong; he was well-featured; his yellow eyes were very large, though, perhaps, not very expressive; take him altogether, he was a pleasant-looking lad, and I had no fault to find with him, beyond that

he was of a dusky hue, and inclined to hairiness;
two characteristics that I disliked. It was his
mind that puzzled, and yet attracted me. The
doctor's phrase—an innocent—came back to me;
and I was wondering if that were, after all, the
true description, when the road began to go
down into the narrow and naked chasm of a tor-
rent. The waters thundered tumultuously in
the bottom; and the ravine was filled full of the
sound, the thin spray, and the claps of wind,
that accompanied their descent. The scene
was certainly impressive; but the road was in
that part very securely walled in; the mule went
steadily forward; and I was astonished to perceive the paleness of terror in the face of my
companion. The voice of that wild river was
inconstant, now sinking lower as if in weariness,
now doubling its hoarse tones; momentary fresh-
ets seemed to swell its volume, sweeping down
the gorge, raving and booming against the barrier walls; and I observed it was at each of
these accessions to the clamour, that my driver
more particularly winced and blanched. Some
thoughts of Scottish superstition and the river-
kelpie passed across my mind; I wondered if
perchance the like were prevalent in that part
of Spain; and turning to Felipe, sought to draw
him out.

"What is the matter?" I asked.

"Oh, I am afraid," he replied.

"Of what are you afraid?" I returned. "This

seems one of the safest places on this very dangerous road."

"It makes a noise," he said, with a simplicity of awe that set my doubts at rest.

The lad was but a child in intellect; his mind was like his body, active and swift, but stunted in development; and I began from that time forth to regard him with a measure of pity, and to listen, at first with indulgence, and at last even with pleasure, to his disjointed babble.

By about four in the afternoon we had crossed the summit of the mountain line, said farewell to the western sunshine, and began to go down upon the other side, skirting the edge of many ravines and moving through the shadow of dusky woods. There rose upon all sides the voice of falling water, not condensed and formidable as in the gorge of the river, but scattered and sounding gaily and musically from glen to glen. Here, too, the spirits of my driver mended, and he began to sing aloud in a falsetto voice, and with a singular bluntness of musical perception, never true either to melody or key, but wandering at will, and yet somehow with an effect that was natural and pleasing, like that of the song of birds. As the dusk increased, I fell more and more under the spell of this artless warbling, listening and waiting for some articulate air, and still disappointed; and when at last I asked him what it was he sang—"Oh," cried he, "I am just singing!" Above all, I was taken with a trick he had of unweariedly repeating the same note at little intervals; it was not so monotonous as you would think, or, at least, not disagreeable; and it seemed to breathe a wonderful contentment with what is, such as we love to fancy in the attitude of trees or the quiescence of a pool.

Night had fallen dark before we came out upon a plateau, and drew up, a little after, before a certain lump of superior blackness which I could only conjecture to be the residencia. Here my guide, getting down from the cart, hooted and whistled for a long time in vain; until at last an old peasant man came towards us from somewhere in the surrounding dark, carrying a candle in his hand. By the light of this I was able to perceive a great arched doorway of a Moorish character: it was closed by iron-studded gates, in one of the leaves of which Felipe opened a wicket. The peasant carried off the cart to some out-building; but my guide and I passed through the wicket which was closed again behind us; and by the glimmer of the candle, passed through a court, up a stone stair, along a section of an open gallery, and up more stairs again, until we came at last to the door of a great and somewhat bare apartment. This room, which I understood was to be mine, was pierced by three windows, lined with some lustrous wood disposed in panels, and carpeted with the skins of many savage animals. A bright fire burned in the chimney, and shed abroad a changeable flicker; close up to the blaze there was drawn a table, laid for supper; and in the far end a bed stood ready. I was pleased by these preparations, and said so to Felipe; and he, with the same simplicity of disposition that I had already remarked in him, warmly re-echoed my praises. "A fine room," he said; "a very fine room. And fire, too; fire is good; it melts out the pleasure in your bones. And the bed," he continued, carrying over the candle in that direction—"see what fine sheets—how soft, how smooth, smooth"; and he passed his hand again and again over their texture, and then laid down his head and rubbed his cheeks among them with a grossness of content that somehow offended me. I took the candle from his hand (for I feared he would set the bed on fire) and walked back to the supper table, where, perceiving a measure of wine, I poured out a cup and called to him to come and drink of it. He started to his feet at once and ran to me with a strong expression of hope; but when he saw the wine, he visibly shuddered.

"Oh no," he said, "not that; that is for you. I hate it."

"Very well, Señor," said I; "then I will drink to your good health, and to the prosperity of your house and family. Speaking of which," I added, after I had drunk, "shall I not have the pleasure of laying my salutations in person at the feet of the Señora, your mother?"

But at these words all the childishness passed

out of his face, and was succeeded by a look of indescribable cunning and secrecy. He backed away from me at the same time, as though I were an animal about to leap or some dangerous fellow with a weapon, and when he had got near the door, glowered at me sullenly with contracted pupils. "No," he said at last, and the next moment was gone noiselessly out of the room; and I heard his footing die away down-stairs as light as rainfall, and silence closed over the house.

After I had supped I drew up the table nearer to the bed and began to prepare for rest; but in the new position of the light, I was struck by a picture on the wall. It represented a woman, still young. To judge by her costume and the mellow unity which reigned over the canvas, she had long been dead; to judge by the vivacity of the attitude, the eyes and the features, I might have been beholding in a mirror the image of life. Her figure was very slim and strong, and of a just proportion; red tresses lay like a crown over her brow; her eyes, of a very golden brown, held mine with a look; and her face, which was perfectly shaped, was yet marred by a cruel, sullen, and sensual expression. Something in both face and figure, something exquisitely intangible, like the echo of an echo, suggested the features and bearing of my guide; and I stood a while, unpleasantly attracted and wondering at the oddity of the resemblance. The common, carnal stock of that race, which had been originally designed for such high dames as the one now looking on me from the canvas, had fallen to baser uses, wearing country clothes, sitting on the shaft and holding the reins of a mule cart, to bring home a lodger. Perhaps an actual link subsisted; perhaps some scruple of the delicate flesh that was once clothed upon with the satin and brocade of the dead lady, now winced at the rude contact of Felipe's frieze.

The first light of the morning shone full upon the portrait, and, as I lay awake, my eyes continued to dwell upon it with growing complacency; its beauty crept about my heart insidiously, silencing my scruples one after another; and while I knew that to love such a woman were to sign and seal one's own sentence of degeneration, I still knew that, if she were alive, I should love her. Day after day the double knowledge of her wickedness and of my weakness grew clearer. She came to be the heroine of many day-dreams, in which her eyes led on to, and sufficiently rewarded, crimes. She cast a dark shadow on my fancy; and when I was out in the free air of heaven, taking vigorous exercise and healthily renewing the current of my blood, it was often a glad thought to me that my enchantress was safe in the grave, her wand of beauty broken, her lips closed in silence, her philtre spilt. And yet I had a half-lingering terror that she might not be dead after all, but re-arisen in the body of some descendant.

Felipe served my meals in my own apartment; and his resemblance to the portrait haunted me. At times it was not; at times, upon some change of attitude or flash of expression, it would leap out upon me like a ghost. It was above all in his ill tempers that the likeness triumphed. He certainly liked me; he was proud of my notice, which he sought to engage by many simple and childlike devices; he loved to sit close before my fire, talking his broken talk or singing his odd, endless, wordless songs, and sometimes drawing his hand over my clothes with an affectionate manner of caressing that never failed to cause in me an embarrassment of which I was ashamed. But for all that, he was capable of flashes of causeless anger and fits of sturdy sullenness. At a word of reproof, I have seen him upset the dish of which I was about to eat, and this not surreptitiously, but with defiance; and similarly at a hint of inquisition. I was not unnaturally curious, being in a strange place and surrounded by strange people, but at the shadow of a question, he shrank back, lowering and dangerous. Then it was that, for a fraction of a second, this rough lad might have been the brother of the lady in the frame. But these humours were swift to pass; and the resemblance died along with them.

In these first days I saw nothing of any one but Felipe, unless the portrait is to be counted; and since the lad was plainly of weak mind, and had moments of passion, it may be wondered

that I bore his dangerous neighbourhood with
equanimity. As a matter of fact, it was for
some time irksome; but it happened before long
that I obtained over him so complete a mastery
as set my disquietude at rest.

It fell in this way. He was by nature sloth-
ful and much of a vagabond, and yet he kept by
the house, and not only waited upon my wants,
but laboured every day in the garden or small
farm to the south of the residencia. Here he
would be joined by the peasant whom I had seen
on the night of my arrival, and who dwelt at the
far end of the enclosure, about half a mile away,
in a rude out-house; but it was plain to me that,
of these two, it was Felipe who did most; and
though I would sometimes see him throw down
his spade and go to sleep among the very plants
he had been digging, his constancy and energy
were admirable in themselves, and still more so
since I was well assured they were foreign to his
disposition and the fruit of an ungrateful effort.
But while I admired, I wondered what had called
forth in a lad so shuttle-witted this enduring
sense of duty. How was it sustained? I asked
myself, and to what length did it prevail over
his instincts? The priest was possibly his in-
spirer; but the priest came one day to the residencia. I saw him both come and go after an
interval of close upon an hour, from a knoll
where I was sketching, and all that time Felipe
continued to labour undisturbed in the garden.

OLALLA

At last, in a very unworthy spirit, I determined to debauch the lad from his good resolutions, and, waylaying him at the gate, easily persuaded him to join me in a ramble. It was a fine day, and the woods to which I led him were green and pleasant and sweet-smelling and alive with the hum of insects. Here he discovered himself in a fresh character, mounting up to heights of gaiety that abashed me, and displaying an energy and grace of movement that delighted the eye. He leaped, he ran round me in mere glee; he would stop, and look and listen, and seemed to drink in the world like a cordial; and then he would suddenly spring into a tree with one bound, and hang and gambol there like one at home. Little as he said to me, and that of not much import, I have rarely enjoyed more stirring company; the sight of his delight was a continual feast; the speed and accuracy of his movements pleased me to the heart; and I might have been so thoughtlessly unkind as to make a habit of these walks, had not chance prepared a very rude conclusion to my pleasure. By some swiftness or dexterity the lad captured a squirrel in a tree-top. He was then some way ahead of me, but I saw him drop to the ground and crouch there, crying aloud for pleasure like a child. The sound stirred my sympathies, it was so fresh and innocent; but as I bettered my pace to draw near, the cry of the squirrel knocked upon my heart. I have heard and seen much

187

of the cruelty of lads, and above all of peasants;
but what I now beheld struck me into a passion
of anger. I thrust the fellow aside, plucked the
poor brute out of his hands, and with swift
mercy killed it. Then I turned upon the tor-
turer, spoke to him long out of the heat of my
indignation, calling him names at which he
seemed to wither; and at length, pointing toward the residencia, bade him begone and leave
me, for I chose to walk with men, not with ver-
min. He fell upon his knees, and, the words
coming to him with more clearness than usual,
poured out a stream of the most touching sup-
plications, begging me in mercy to forgive him,
to forget what he had done, to look to the future. "Oh, I try so hard," he said. "Oh, commandante, bear with Felipe this once; he will
never be a brute again!" Thereupon, much
more affected than I cared to show, I suffered
myself to be persuaded, and at last shook hands
with him and made it up. But the squirrel,
by way of penance, I made him bury; speaking
of the poor thing's beauty, telling him what pains
it had suffered, and how base a thing was the
abuse of strength. "See, Felipe," said I, "you
are strong indeed; but in my hands you are as
helpless as that poor thing of the trees. Give
me your hand in mine. You cannot remove it.
Now suppose that I were cruel like you, and
took a pleasure in pain. I only tighten my hold,
and see how you suffer." He screamed aloud,

his face stricken ashy and dotted with needle points of sweat; and when I set him free, he fell to the earth and nursed his hand and moaned over it like a baby. But he took the lesson in good part; and whether from that, or from what I had said to him, or the higher notion he now had of my bodily strength, his original affection was changed into a dog-like, adoring fidelity.

Meanwhile I gained rapidly in health. The residencia stood on the crown of a stony plateau; on every side the mountains hemmed it about; only from the roof, where was a bartizan, there might be seen between two peaks, a small segment of plain blue, with extreme distance. The air in these altitudes moved freely and largely; great clouds congregated there, and were broken up by the wind and left in tatters on the hill-tops; a hoarse and yet faint rumbling of torrents rose from all round; and one could there study all the ruder and more ancient characters of nature in something of their pristine force. I delighted from the first in the vigorous scenery and changeful weather; nor less in the antique and dilapidated mansion where I dwelt. This was a large oblong, flanked at two opposite corners by bastion-like projections, one of which commanded the door, while both were loopholed for musketry. The lower story was, besides, naked of windows, so that the building, if garrisoned, could not be carried without artillery.

It enclosed an open court planted with pomegranate trees. From this a broad flight of marble stairs ascended to an open gallery, running all round and resting, towards the court, on slender pillars. Thence again, several enclosed stairs led to the upper stories of the house, which were thus broken up into distinct divisions. The windows, both within and without, were closely shuttered; some of the stonework in the upper parts had fallen; the roof, in one place, had been wrecked in one of the flurries of wind which were common in these mountains; and the whole house, in the strong, beating sunlight, and standing out above a grove of stunted cork-trees, thickly laden and discoloured with dust, looked like the sleeping palace of the legend. The court, in particular, seemed the very home of slumber. A hoarse cooing of doves haunted about the eaves; the winds were excluded, but when they blew outside, the mountain dust fell here as thick as rain, and veiled the red bloom of the pomegranates; shuttered windows and the closed doors of numerous cellars, and the vacant arches of the gallery, enclosed it; and all day long the sun made broken profiles on the four sides, and paraded the shadow of the pillars on the gallery floor. At the ground level there was, however, a certain pillared recess, which bore the marks of human habitation. Though it was open in front upon the court, it was yet provided with a chimney, where a wood fire

would be always prettily blazing; and the tile
floor was littered with the skins of animals.

It was in this place that I first saw my hostess.
She had drawn one of the skins forward and sat
in the sun, leaning against a pillar. It was her
dress that struck me first of all, for it was rich
and brightly coloured, and shone out in that
dusty courtyard with something of the same relief as the flowers of the pomegranates. At a
second look it was her beauty of person that
took hold of me. As she sat back—watching me,
I thought, though with invisible eyes—and
wearing at the same time an expression of almost imbecile good-humour and contentment,
she showed a perfectness of feature and a quiet
nobility of attitude that were beyond a statue's.
I took off my hat to her in passing, and her face
puckered with suspicion as swiftly and lightly as
a pool ruffles in the breeze; but she paid no heed
to my courtesy. I went forth on my customary walk a trifle daunted, her idol-like impassiv-
ity haunting me; and when I returned, although
she was still in much the same posture, I was
half surprised to see that she had moved as far
as the next pillar, following the sunshine. This
time, however, she addressed me with some tri-
vial salutation, civilly enough conceived, and
uttered in the same deep-chested, and yet indis-
tinct and lisping tones, that had already baffled
the utmost niceness of my hearing from her son.
I answered rather at a venture; for not only did

I fail to take her meaning with precision, but the sudden disclosure of her eyes disturbed me. They were unusually large, the iris golden like Felipe's, but the pupil at that moment so distended that they seemed almost black; and what affected me was not so much their size as (what was perhaps its consequence) the singular insignificance of their regard. A look more blankly stupid I have never met. My eyes dropped before it even as I spoke, and I went on my way up-stairs to my own room, at once baffled and embarrassed. Yet, when I came there and saw the face of the portrait, I was again reminded of the miracle of family descent. My hostess was, indeed, both older and fuller in person; her eyes were of a different colour; her face, besides, was not only free from the ill-significance that offended and attracted me in the painting; it was devoid of either good or bad—a moral blank expressing literally naught. And yet there was a likeness, not so much speaking as immanent, not so much in any particular feature as upon the whole. It should seem, I thought, as if when the master set his signature to that grave canvas, he had not only caught the image of one smiling and false-eyed woman, but stamped the essential quality of a race.

From that day forth, whether I came or went, I was sure to find the Señora seated in the sun against a pillar, or stretched on a rug before the fire; only at times she would shift her station to

the top round of the stone staircase, where she
lay with the same nonchalance right across my
path. In all these days, I never knew her to
display the least spark of energy beyond what
she expended in brushing and re-brushing her
copious copper-coloured hair, or in lisping out,
in the rich and broken hoarseness of her voice,
her customary idle salutations to myself. These,
I think, were her two chief pleasures, beyond
that of mere quiescence. She seemed always
proud of her remarks, as though they had been
witticisms: and, indeed, though they were empty
enough, like the conversation of many respectable persons, and turned on a very narrow range
of subjects, they were never meaningless or in-
coherent; nay, they had a certain beauty of
their own, breathing as they did, of her entire
contentment. Now she would speak of the
warmth in which (like her son) she greatly delighted; now of the flowers of the pomegranate
trees, and now of the white doves and long-
winged swallows that fanned the air of the court.
The birds excited her. As they raked the eaves
in their swift flight or skimmed sidelong past
her with a rush of wind, she would sometimes
stir, and sit a little up, and seem to awaken from
her doze of satisfaction. But for the rest of her
days she lay luxuriously folded on herself and
sunk in sloth and pleasure. Her invincible content at first annoyed me, but I came gradually
to find repose in the spectacle, until at last it

grew to be my habit to sit down beside her four times in the day, both coming and going, and to talk with her sleepily, I scarce knew of what. I had come to like her dull, almost animal neighbourhood; her beauty and her stupidity soothed and amused me. I began to find a kind of transcendental good-sense in her remarks, and her unfathomable good-nature moved me to admiration and envy. The liking was returned; she enjoyed my presence half unconsciously, as a man in deep meditation may enjoy the babbling of a brook. I can scarce say she brightened when I came, for satisfaction was written on her face eternally, as on some foolish statue's; but I was made conscious of her pleasure by some more intimate communication than the sight. And one day, as I sat within reach of her on the marble step, she suddenly shot forth one of her hands and patted mine. The thing was done, and she was back in her accustomed attitude, before my mind had received intelligence of the caress; and when I turned to look her in the face I could perceive no answerable sentiment. It was plain she attached no moment to the act, and I blamed myself for my own more uneasy consciousness.

The sight and (if I may so call it) the acquaintance of the mother confirmed the view I had already taken of the son. The family blood had been impoverished, perhaps by long in-breeding, which I knew to be a common error among the proud and the exclusive. No decline indeed, was to be traced in the body, which had been handed down unimpaired in shapeliness and strength; and the faces of to-day were struck as sharply from the mint as the face of two centuries ago that smiled upon me from the portrait. But the intelligence (that more precious heirloom) was degenerate; the treasure of ancestral memory ran low; and it had required the potent, plebeian crossing of a muleteer or mountain *contrabandista* to raise what approached hebetude in the mother into the active oddity of the son. Yet, of the two, it was the mother I preferred. Of Felipe, vengeful and placable, full of starts and shyings, inconstant as a hare, I could even conceive as a creature possibly noxious. Of the mother I had no thoughts but those of kindness. And indeed, as spectators are apt ignorantly to take sides, I grew something of a partisan in the enmity which I perceived to smoulder between them. True, it seemed mostly on the mother's part. She would sometimes draw in her breath as he came near, and the pupils of her vacant eyes would contract with horror or fear. Her emotions, such as they were, were much upon the surface and readily shared; and this latent repulsion occupied my mind, and kept me wondering on what grounds it rested, and whether the son was certainly in fault.

I had been about ten days in the residencia when there sprang up a high and harsh wind carrying clouds of dust. It came out of malarious lowlands, and over several snowy sierras. The nerves of those on whom it blew were strung and jangled; their eyes smarted with the dust; their legs ached under the burthen of their body and the touch of one hand upon another grew to be odious. The wind, besides, came down the gullies of the hills and stormed about the house with a great, hollow buzzing and whistling that was wearisome to the ear and dismally depressing to the mind. It did not so much blow in gusts as with the steady sweep of a waterfall, so that there was no remission of discomfort while it blew. But higher upon the mountain, it was probably of a more variable strength, with accesses of fury; for there came down at times a far-off wailing, infinitely grievous to hear; and at times, on one of the high shelves or terraces, there would start up, and then disperse, a tower of dust, like the smoke of an explosion.

I no sooner awoke in bed than I was conscious of the nervous tension and depression of the weather, and the effect grew stronger as the day proceeded. It was in vain that I resisted; in vain that I set forth upon my customary morning's walk; the irrational, unchanging fury of the storm had soon beat down my strength and wrecked my temper; and I returned to the residencia, glowing with dry heat, and foul and gritty with dust. The court had a forlorn appearance; now and then a glimmer of sun fled over it; now and then the wind swooped down upon the pomegranates, and scattered the blossoms, and set the window shutter clapping on the wall. In the recess the Señora was pacing to and fro with a flushed countenance and bright eyes; I thought, too, she was speaking to herself, like one in anger. But when I addressed her with my customary salutation, she only replied by a sharp gesture and continued her walk. The weather had distempered even this impassive creature; and as I went on up-stairs I was the less ashamed of my own discomposure.

All day the wind continued; and I sat in my room and made a feint of reading, or walked up and down, and listened to the riot overhead. Night fell, and I had not so much as a candle. I began to long for some society, and stole down to the court. It was now plunged in the blue of the first darkness; but the recess was redly lighted by the fire. The wood had been piled high, and was crowned by a shock of flames, which the draught of the chimney brandished to and fro. In this strong and shaken brightness the Señora continued pacing from wall to wall with disconnected gestures, clasping her hands, stretching forth her arms, throwing back her head as in appeal to heaven. In these disordered movements the beauty and grace of the woman showed more clearly; but there was a light in her eye that struck on me unpleasantly; and when I had looked on a while in silence, and seemingly unobserved, I turned tail as I had come, and groped my way back again to my own chamber.

By the time Felipe brought my supper and lights, my nerve was utterly gone; and, had the lad been such as I was used to seeing him, I should have kept him (even by force had that been necessary) to take off the edge from my distasteful solitude. But on Felipe, also, the wind had exercised its influence. He had been feverish all day; now that the night had come he was fallen into a low and tremulous humour that reacted on my own. The sight of his scared face, his starts and pallors and sudden hearkenings, unstrung me; and when he dropped and broke a dish, I fairly leaped out of my seat.

"I think we are all mad to-day," said I, affecting to laugh.

"It is the black wind," he replied dolefully. "You feel as if you must do something, and you don't know what it is."

I noted the aptness of the description; but, indeed, Felipe had sometimes a strange felicity in rendering into words the sensations of the body. "And your mother, too," said I; "she seems to feel this weather much. Do you not fear she may be unwell?"

He stared at me a little, and then said, "No," almost defiantly; and the next moment, carrying his hand to his brow, cried out lamentably on the wind and the noise that made his head go round like a mill-wheel. "Who can be well?" he cried; and, indeed, I could only echo his question, for I was disturbed enough myself.

I went to bed early, wearied with day-long restlessness: but the poisonous nature of the wind, and its ungodly and unintermittent uproar, would not suffer me to sleep. I lay there and tossed, my nerves and senses on the stretch. At times I would doze, dream horribly, and wake again; and these snatches of oblivion confused me as to time. But it must have been late on in the night, when I was suddenly startled by an outbreak of pitiable and hateful cries. I leaped from my bed, supposing I had dreamed; but the cries still continued to fill the house, cries of pain, I thought, but certainly of rage also, and so savage and discordant that they shocked the heart. It was no illusion; some living thing, some lunatic or some wild animal, was being foully tortured. The thought of Felipe and the squirrel flashed into my mind, and I ran to the door, but it had been locked from the outside; and I might shake it as I pleased, I was a fast prisoner. Still the cries continued. Now they would dwindle down into a moaning that seemed to be articulate, and at these times I made sure they must be human; and again they would break forth and fill the house with ravings worthy of hell. I stood at the door and gave ear to them, till at last they died away. Long after that, I still lingered and still continued to hear them mingle in fancy with the storming of the wind; and when at last I crept to my bed, it was with a deadly sickness and a blackness of horror on my heart.

It was little wonder if I slept no more. Why had I been locked in? What had passed? Who was the author of these indescribable and shocking cries? A human being? It was inconceivable. A beast? The cries were scarce quite bestial; and what animal, short of a lion or a tiger, could thus shake the solid walls of the residencia? And while I was thus turning over the elements of the mystery, it came into my mind that I had not yet set eyes upon the daughter of the house. What was more probable than that the daughter of the Señora, and the sister of Felipe, should be herself insane? Or, what more likely than that these ignorant and half-witted people should seek to manage an afflicted kinswoman by violence? Here was a solution; and yet when I called to mind the cries (which I never did without a shuddering chill) it seemed altogether insufficient: not even cruelty could wring such cries from madness. But of one thing I was sure: I could not live in a house where such a thing was half conceivable and not probe the matter home and, if necessary, interfere.

The next day came, the wind had blown itself out, and there was nothing to remind me of the business of the night. Felipe came to my bed-

side with obvious cheerfulness; as I passed
through the court, the Señora was sunning herself with her accustomed immobility; and when
I issued from the gateway, I found the whole
face of nature austerely smiling, the heavens of
a cold blue, and sown with great cloud islands,
and the mountain-sides mapped forth into prov-
inces of light and shadow. A short walk restored
me to myself, and renewed within me the resolve
to plumb this mystery; and when, from the van-
tage of my knoll, I had seen Felipe pass forth
to his labours in the garden, I returned at once
to the residencia to put my design in practice.
The Señora appeared plunged in slumber; I stood
a while and marked her, but she did not stir;
even if my design were indiscreet I had little to
fear from such a guardian; and turning away, I
mounted to the gallery and began my exploration of the house.

All morning I went from one door to another,
and entered spacious and faded chambers, some
rudely shuttered, some receiving their full charge
of daylight, all empty and unhomely. It was a
rich house, on which Time had breathed his tar-
nish and dust had scattered disillusion. The
spider swung there; the bloated tarantula scam-
pered on the cornices; ants had their crowded
highways on the floor of halls of audience; the
big and foul fly, that lives on carrion and is often
the messenger of death, had set up his nest in
the rotten woodwork, and buzzed heavily about

the rooms. Here and there a stool or two, a couch, a bed, or a great carved chair remained behind, like islets on the bare floors, to testify of man's by-gone habitation; and everywhere the walls were set with the portraits of the dead. I could judge, by these decaying effigies, in the house of what a great and what a handsome race I was then wandering. Many of the men wore orders on their breasts, and had the port of noble officers; the women were all richly attired; the canvases most of them by famous hands. But it was not so much these evidences of greatness that took hold upon my mind, even contrasted, as they were, with the present depopulation and decay of the great house. It was rather the parable of family life that I read in this succession of fair faces and shapely bodies. Never before had I so realised the miracle of the continued race, the creation and re-creation, the weaving and changing and handing down of fleshly elements. That a child should be born of its mother, that it should grow and clothe itself (we know not how) with humanity, and put on inherited looks, and turn its head with the manner of one ascendant, and offer its hand with the gesture of another, are wonders dulled for us by repetition. But in the singular unity of look, in the common features and common bearing, of all these painted generations on the walls of the residencia, the miracle started out and looked me in the face. And an ancient mirror falling opportunely in my way, I stood and read my own features a long while, tracing out on either hand the filaments of descent and the bonds that knit me with my family.

At last, in the course of these investigations, I opened the door of a chamber that bore the marks of habitation. It was of large proportions and faced to the north, where the mountains were most wildly figured. The embers of a fire smouldered and smoked upon the hearth, to which a chair had been drawn close. And yet the aspect of the chamber was ascetic to the degree of sternness; the chair was uncushioned; the floor and walls were naked; and beyond the books which lay here and there in some confusion, there was no instrument of either work or pleasure. The sight of books in the house of such a family exceedingly amazed me; and I began with a great hurry and in momentary fear of interruption, to go from one to another and hastily inspect their character. They were of all sorts, devotional, historical, and scientific, but mostly of a great age and in the Latin tongue. Some I could see to bear the marks of constant study; others had been torn across and tossed aside as if in petulance or disapproval. Lastly, as I cruised about that empty chamber, I espied some papers written upon with pencil on a table near the window. An unthinking curiosity led me to take one up. It bore a copy of verses, very roughly metred in the original

Spanish, and which I may render somewhat
thus—

"Pleasure approached with pain and shame,
Grief with a wreath of lilies came.
Pleasure showed the lovely sun;
Jesu dear, how sweet it shone!
Grief with her worn hand pointed on,
Jesu dear, to thee!"

Shame and confusion at once fell on me; and
laying down the paper, I beat an immediate re-
treat from the apartment. Neither Felipe nor
his mother could have read the books nor written
these rough but feeling verses. It was plain I
had stumbled with sacrilegious feet into the
room of the daughter of the house. God knows,
my own heart most sharply punished me for my
indiscretion. The thought that I had thus se-
cretly pushed my way into the confidence of a
girl so strangely situated, and the fear that she
might somehow come to hear of it, oppressed
me like guilt. I blamed myself besides for my
suspicions of the night before; wondered that I
should ever have attributed those shocking cries
to one of whom I now conceived as of a saint,
spectral of mien, wasted with maceration, bound
up in the practices of a mechanical devotion, and
dwelling in a great isolation of soul with her incongruous relatives; and as I leaned on the bal-
ustrade of the gallery and looked down into the
bright close of pomegranates and at the gaily
dressed and somnolent woman, who just then
stretched herself and delicately licked her lips

as in the very sensuality of sloth, my mind swiftly compared the scene with the cold chamber looking northward on the mountains, where the daughter dwelt.

That same afternoon, as I sat upon my knoll, I saw the Padre enter the gate of the residencia. The revelation of the daughter's character had struck home to my fancy, and almost blotted out the horrors of the night before; but at sight of this worthy man the memory revived. I descended, then, from the knoll, and making a circuit among the woods, posted myself by the wayside to await his passage. As soon as he appeared I stepped forth and introduced myself as the lodger of the residencia. He had a very strong, honest countenance, on which it was easy to read the mingled emotions with which he regarded me, as a foreigner, a heretic, and yet one who had been wounded for the good cause. Of the family at the residencia he spoke with reserve, and yet with respect. I mentioned that I had not yet seen the daughter, whereupon he remarked that that was as it should be, and looked at me a little askance. Lastly, I plucked up courage to refer to the cries that had disturbed me in the night. He heard me out in silence, and then stopped and partly turned about, as though to mark beyond doubt that he was dismissing me.

"Do you take tobacco-powder?" said he, offering his snuff-box; and then, when I had refused, "I am an old man," he added, "and I may be allowed to remind you that you are a guest."

"I have, then, your authority," I returned, firmly enough, although I flushed at the implied reproof, "to let things take their course, and not to interfere?"

He said "Yes," and with a somewhat uneasy salute turned and left me where I was. But he had done two things: he had set my conscience at rest, and he had awakened my delicacy. I made a great effort, once more dismissed the recollections of the night, and fell once more to brooding on my saintly poetess. At the same time, I could not quite forget that I had been locked in, and that night when Felipe brought me my supper I attacked him warily on both points of interest.

"I never see your sister," said I casually.

"Oh, no," said he; "she is a good, good girl," and his mind instantly veered to something else.

"Your sister is pious, I suppose," I asked in the next pause.

"Oh," he cried, joining his hands with extreme fervour, "a saint; it is she that keeps me up."

"You are very fortunate," said I, "for the most of us, I am afraid, and myself among the number, are better at going down."

"Señor," said Felipe earnestly, "I would not say that. You should not tempt your angel. If one goes down, where is he to stop?"

"Why, Felipe," said I, "I had no guess you were a preacher, and I may say a good one; but I suppose that is your sister's doing?"

He nodded at me with round eyes.

"Well, then," I continued, "she has doubtless reproved you for your sin of cruelty?"

"Twelve times!" he cried; for this was the phrase by which the odd creature expressed the sense of frequency. "And I told her you had done so—I remembered that," he added proudly —"and she was pleased."

"Then, Felipe," said I, "what were those cries that I heard last night? for surely they were cries of some creature in suffering."

"The wind," returned Felipe, looking in the fire.

I took his hand in mine, at which, thinking it to be a caress, he smiled with a brightness of pleasure that came near disarming my resolve. But I trod the weakness down. "The wind," I repeated; "and yet I think it was this hand," holding it up, "that had first locked me in." The lad shook visibly, but answered never a word. "Well," said I, "I am a stranger and a guest. It is not my part either to meddle or to judge in your affairs; in these you shall take your sister's counsel, which I cannot doubt to be excellent. But in so far as concerns my own I will be no man's prisoner, and I demand that key." Half an hour later my door was suddenly thrown open, and the key tossed ringing on the floor.

OLALLA

A day or two after I came in from a walk a little before the point of noon. The Señora was lying lapped in slumber on the threshold of the recess; the pigeons dozed below the eaves like snowdrifts; the house was under a deep spell of noontide quiet; and only a wandering and gentle wind from the mountain stole round the galleries, rustled among the pomegranates, and pleasantly stirred the shadows. Something in the stillness moved me to imitation, and I went very lightly across the court and up the marble staircase. My foot was on the topmost round, when a door opened, and I found myself face to face with Olalla. Surprise transfixed me; her loveliness struck to my heart; she glowed in the deep shadow of the gallery, a gem of colour; her eyes took hold upon mine and clung there, and bound us together like the joining of hands; and the moments we thus stood face to face, drinking each other in, were sacramental and the wedding of souls. I know not how long it was before I awoke out of a deep trance, and, hastily bowing, passed on into the upper stair. She did not move, but followed me with her great, thirsting eyes; and as I passed out of sight it seemed to me as if she paled and faded.

In my own room, I opened the window and looked out, and could not think what change had come upon that austere field of mountains that it should thus sing and shine under the lofty heaven. I had seen her—Olalla! And the stone crags answered, Olalla! and the dumb, unfathomable azure answered, Olalla! The pale saint of my dreams had vanished for ever; and in her place I beheld this maiden on whom God had lavished the richest colours and the most exuberant energies of life, whom he had made active as a deer, slender as a reed, and in whose great eyes he had lighted the torches of the soul. The thrill of her young life, strung like a wild animal's, had entered into me; the force of soul that had looked out from her eyes and conquered mine, mantled about my heart and sprang to my lips in singing. She passed through my veins: she was one with me.

I will not say that this enthusiasm declined; rather my soul held out in its ecstasy as in a strong castle, and was there besieged by cold and sorrowful considerations. I could not doubt but that I loved her at first sight, and already with a quivering ardour that was strange to my experience. What then was to follow? She was the child of an afflicted house, the Señora's daughter, the sister of Felipe; she bore it even in her beauty. She had the lightness and swiftness of the one, swift as an arrow, light as dew; like the other, she shone on the pale background of the world with the brilliancy of flowers. I could not call by the name of brother that half-witted lad, nor by the name of mother that immovable and lovely thing of flesh, whose silly eyes and perpetual simper now recurred to my mind like something hateful. And if I could not marry, what then? She was helplessly unprotected; her eyes, in that single and long glance which had been all our intercourse, had confessed a weakness equal to my own; but in my heart I knew her for the student of the cold northern chamber, and the writer of the sorrowful lines; and this was a knowledge to disarm a brute. To flee was more than I could find courage for; but I registered a vow of unsleeping circumspection.

As I turned from the window, my eyes alighted on the portrait. It had fallen dead, like a candle after sunrise; it followed me with eyes of paint. I knew it to be like, and marvelled at the tenacity of type in that declining race; but the likeness was swallowed up in difference. I remembered how it had seemed to me a thing unapproachable in the life, a creature rather of the painter's craft than of the modesty of nature, and I marvelled at the thought, and exulted in the image of Olalla. Beauty I had seen before, and not been charmed, and I had been often drawn to women, who were not beautiful except to me; but in Olalla all that I desired and had not dared to imagine was united.

I did not see her the next day, and my heart ached and my eyes longed for her, as men long for morning. But the day after, when I returned, about my usual hour, she was once more on the gallery, and our looks once more met and embraced. I would have spoken, I would have drawn near to her; but strongly as she plucked at my heart, drawing me like a magnet, something yet more imperious withheld me; and I could only bow and pass by; and she, leaving my salutation unanswered, only followed me with her noble eyes.

I had now her image by rote, and as I conned the traits in memory it seemed as if I read her very heart. She was dressed with something of her mother's coquetry, and love of positive colour. Her robe, which I knew she must have made with her own hands, clung about her with a cunning grace. After the fashion of that country, besides, her bodice stood open in the middle, in a long slit, and here, in spite of the poverty of the house, a gold coin, hanging by a ribbon, lay on her brown bosom. These were proofs, had any been needed, of her inborn delight in life and her own loveliness. On the other hand, in her eyes, that hung upon mine, I could read depth beyond depth of passion and sadness, lights of poetry and hope, blacknesses of despair, and thoughts that were above the earth. It was a lovely body, but the inmate, the soul, was more than worthy of that lodging. Should I leave this incomparable flower to wither unseen on these rough mountains? Should I despise the great gift offered me in the eloquent silence of her eyes? Here was a soul immured; should I not burst its prison? All side considerations fell off from me; were she the child of Herod I swore

I should make her mine; and that very evening
I set myself, with a mingled sense of treachery
and disgrace, to captivate the brother. Perhaps
I read him with more favourable eyes, perhaps
the thought of his sister always summoned up
the better qualities of that imperfect soul; but
he had never seemed to me so amiable, and his
very likeness to Olalla, while it annoyed, yet
softened me.

A third day passed in vain—an empty desert
of hours. I would not lose a chance, and loitered
all afternoon in the court where (to give myself
a countenance) I spoke more than usual with the
Señora. God knows it was with a most tender
and sincere interest that I now studied her; and
even as for Felipe, so now for the mother, I was
conscious of a growing warmth of toleration.
And yet I wondered. Even while I spoke with
her, she would doze off into a little sleep, and presently awake again without embarrassment; and
this composure staggered me. And again, as I
marked her make infinitesimal changes in her
posture, savouring and lingering on the bodily
pleasure of the moment, I was driven to wonder
at this depth of passive sensuality. She lived
in her body; and her consciousness was all sunk
into and disseminated through her members,
where it luxuriously dwelt. Lastly, I could not
grow accustomed to her eyes. Each time she
turned on me these great, beautiful, and meaningless orbs, wide open to the day, but closed

against human inquiry—each time I had occasion to observe the lively changes of her pupils which expanded and contracted in a breath—I know not what it was came over me, I can find no name for the mingled feeling of disappointment, annoyance, and distaste that jarred along my nerves. I tried her on a variety of subjects, equally in vain; and at last led the talk to her daughter. But even there she proved indifferent; said she was pretty, which (as with children) was her highest word of commendation, but was plainly incapable of any higher thought; and when I remarked that Olalla seemed silent, merely yawned in my face and replied that speech was of no great use when you had nothing to say. "People speak much, very much," she added, looking at me with expanded pupils; and then again yawned, and again showed me a mouth that was as dainty as a toy. This time I took the hint, and, leaving her to her repose, went up into my own chamber to sit by the open window, looking on the hills and not beholding them, sunk in lustrous and deep dreams, and hearkening in fancy to the note of a voice that I had never heard.

I awoke on the fifth morning with a brightness of anticipation that seemed to challenge fate. I was sure of myself, light of heart and foot, and resolved to put my love incontinently to the touch of knowledge. It should lie no longer under the bonds of silence, a dumb thing, living by the eye only, like the love of beasts; but should now put on the spirit, and enter upon the joys of the complete human intimacy. I thought of it with wild hopes, like a voyager to El Dorado; into that unknown and lovely country of her soul, I no longer trembled to adventure. Yet when I did indeed encounter her, the same force of passion descended on me and at once submerged my mind; speech seemed to drop away from me like a childish habit; and I but drew near to her as the giddy man draws near to the margin of a gulf. She drew back from me a little as I came; but her eyes did not waver from mine, and these lured me forward. At last, when I was already within reach of her, I stopped. Words were denied me; if I advanced I could but clasp her to my heart in silence; and all that was sane in me, all that was still unconquered, revolted against the thought of such an accost. So we stood for a second, all our life in our eyes, exchanging salvos of attraction and yet each resisting; and then, with a great effort of the will, and conscious at the same time of a sudden bitterness of disappointment, I turned and went away in the same silence.

What power lay upon me that I could not speak? And she, why was she also silent? Why did she draw away before me dumbly, with fascinated eyes? Was this love? or was it a mere brute attraction, mindless and inevitable, like that of the magnet for the steel? We had never

spoken, we were wholly strangers; and yet an
influence, strong as the grasp of a giant, swept
us silently together. On my side, it filled me
with impatience; and yet I was sure that she was
worthy; I had seen her books, read her verses,
and thus, in a sense, divined the soul of my mistress. But on her side, it struck me almost cold.
Of me, she knew nothing but my bodily favour;
she was drawn to me as stones fall to earth; the
laws that rule the earth conducted her, uncon-
senting, to my arms; and I drew back at the
thought of such a bridal, and began to be jealous for myself. It was not thus that I desired
to be loved. And then I began to fall into a
great pity for the girl herself. I thought how
sharp must be her mortification, that she, the
student, the recluse, Felipe's saintly monitress,
should have thus confessed an overweening
weakness for a man with whom she had never
exchanged a word. And at the coming of pity,
all other thoughts were swallowed up; and I
longed only to find and console and reassure her;
to tell her how wholly her love was returned on
my side, and how her choice, even if blindly
made, was not unworthy.

The next day it was glorious weather; depth
upon depth of blue over-canopied the mountains; the sun shone wide; and the wind in the
trees and the many falling torrents in the mountains filled the air with delicate and haunting
music. Yet I was prostrated with sadness. My

heart wept for the sight of Olalla, as a child weeps for its mother. I sat down on a boulder on the verge of the low cliffs that bound the plateau to the north. Thence I looked down into the wooded valley of a stream, where no foot came. In the mood I was in, it was even touching to behold the place untenanted; it lacked Olalla; and I thought of the delight and glory of a life passed wholly with her in that strong air, and among these rugged and lovely surroundings, at first with a whimpering sentiment, and then again with such a fiery joy that I seemed to grow in strength and stature, like a Samson.

And then suddenly I was aware of Olalla drawing near. She appeared out of a grove of cork-trees, and came straight towards me; and I stood up and waited. She seemed in her walking a creature of such life and fire and lightness as amazed me; yet she came quietly and slowly. Her energy was in the slowness; but for inimitable strength, I felt she would have run, she would have flown to me. Still, as she approached, she kept her eyes lowered to the ground; and when she had drawn quite near, it was without one glance that she addressed me. At the first note of her voice I started. It was for this I had been waiting; this was the last test of my love. And lo, her enunciation was precise and clear, not lisping and incomplete like that of her family; and the voice, though deeper than usual with women, was still both youthful and womanly. She spoke in a rich chord; golden contralto strains mingled with hoarseness, as the red threads were mingled with the brown among her tresses. It was not only a voice that spoke to my heart directly; but it spoke to me of her. And yet her words immediately plunged me back upon despair.

"You will go away," she said, "to-day."

Her example broke the bonds of my speech; I felt as lightened of a weight, or as if a spell had been dissolved. I know not in what words I answered; but, standing before her on the cliffs, I poured out the whole ardour of my love, telling her that I lived upon the thought of her, slept only to dream of her loveliness, and would gladly forswear my country, my language, and my friends, to live for ever by her side. And then, strongly commanding myself, I changed the note; I reassured, I comforted her; I told her I had divined in her a pious and heroic spirit, with which I was worthy to sympathise, and which I longed to share and lighten. "Nature," I told her, "was the voice of God, which men disobey at peril; and if we were thus dumbly drawn together, ay, even as by a miracle of love, it must imply a divine fitness in our souls; we must be made," I said—"made for one another. We should be mad rebels," I cried out—"mad rebels against God, not to obey this instinct."

She shook her head. "You will go to-day,"

she repeated, and then with a gesture, and in a sudden, sharp note—"no, not to-day," she cried, "to-morrow."

But at this sign of relenting, power came in upon me in a tide. I stretched out my arms and called upon her name; and she leaped to me and clung to me. The hills rocked about us, the earth quailed; a shock as of a blow went through me and left me blind and dizzy. And the next moment, she had thrust me back, broken rudely from my arms, and fled with the speed of a deer among the cork-trees.

I stood and shouted to the mountains; I turned and went back towards the residencia, walking upon air. She sent me away, and yet I had but to call upon her name and she came to me. These were but the weaknesses of girls, from which even she, the strangest of her sex, was not exempted. Go? Not I, Olalla—O, not I, Olalla, my Olalla! A bird sang near by; and in that season, birds were rare. It bade me be of good cheer. And once more the whole countenance of nature, from the ponderous and stable mountains down to the lightest leaf and the smallest darting fly in the shadow of the groves, began to stir before me and to put on the lineaments of life and wear a face of awful joy. The sunshine struck upon the hills, strong as a hammer on the anvil, and the hills shook; the earth, under that vigorous insolation, yielded up heady scents; the woods smouldered in the blaze. I felt a thrill of travail and delight run through the earth. Something elemental, something rude, violent, and savage, in the love that sang in my heart, was like a key to nature's secrets; and the very stones that rattled under my feet appeared alive and friendly. Olalla! Her touch had quickened, and renewed, and strung me up to the old pitch of concert with the rugged earth, to a swelling of the soul that men learn to forget in their polite assemblies. Love burned in me like rage; tenderness waxed fierce; I hated, I adored, I pitied, I revered her with ecstasy. She seemed the link that bound me in with dead things on the one hand, and with our pure and pitying God upon the other; a thing brutal and divine, and akin at once to the innocence and to the unbridled forces of the earth.

My head thus reeling, I came into the court-yard of the residencia, and the sight of the mother struck me like a revelation. She sat there, all sloth and contentment, blinking under the strong sunshine, branded with a passive enjoyment, a creature set quite apart, before whom my ardour fell away like a thing ashamed. I stopped a moment, and, commanding such shaken tones as I was able, said a word or two. She looked at me with her unfathomable kindness; her voice in reply sounded vaguely out of the realm of peace in which she slumbered, and there fell on my mind, for the first time, a sense of respect for one so uniformly innocent and happy, and I passed on in a kind of wonder at myself, that I should be so much disquieted.

On my table there lay a piece of the same yellow paper I had seen in the north room; it was written on with pencil in the same hand, Olalla's hand, and I picked it up with a sudden sinking of alarm, and read, "If you have any kindness for Olalla, if you have any chivalry for a creature sorely wrought, go from here to-day; in pity, in honour, for the sake of Him who died, I supplicate that you shall go." I looked at this a while in mere stupidity, then I began to awaken to a weariness and horror of life; the sunshine darkened outside on the bare hills, and I began to shake like a man in terror. The vacancy thus suddenly opened in my life unmanned me like a physical void. It was not my heart, it was not my happiness, it was life itself that was involved. I could not lose her. I said so, and stood repeating it. And then, like one in a dream, I moved to the window, put forth my hand to open the casement, and thrust it through the pane. The blood spirted from my wrist; and with an instantaneous quietude and command of myself, I pressed my thumb on the little leaping fountain, and reflected what to do. In that empty room there was nothing to my purpose; I felt, besides, that I required assistance. There shot into my mind a hope that Olalla herself might be my helper, and I turned and went down-stairs, still keeping my thumb upon the wound.

OLALLA

There was no sign of either Olalla or Felipe, and I addressed myself to the recess, whither the Señora had now drawn quite back and sat dozing close before the fire, for no degree of heat appeared too much for her.

"Pardon me," said I, "if I disturb you, but I must apply to you for help."

She looked up sleepily and asked me what it was, and with the very words, I thought she drew in her breath with a widening of the nostrils and seemed to come suddenly and fully alive.

"I have cut myself," I said, "and rather badly. See!" And I held out my two hands from which the blood was oozing and dripping.

Her great eyes opened wide, the pupils shrank into points; a veil seemed to fall from her face, and leave it sharply expressive and yet inscrutable. And as I still stood, marvelling a little at her disturbance, she came swiftly up to me, and stooped and caught me by the hand; and the next moment my hand was at her mouth, and she had bitten me to the bone. The pang of the bite, the sudden spirting of blood, and the monstrous horror of the act, flashed through me all in one, and I beat her back; and she sprang at me again and again, with bestial cries, cries that I recognised, such cries as had awakened me on the night of the high wind. Her strength was like that of madness; mine was rapidly ebbing with the loss of blood; my mind besides was whirling with the abhorrent strangeness of the onslaught, and I was already forced against the wall, when Olalla ran betwixt us, and Felipe, following at a bound, pinned down his mother on the floor.

A trance-like weakness fell upon me; I saw, heard, and felt, but I was incapable of movement. I heard the struggle roll to and fro upon the floor, the yells of that catamount ringing up to Heaven as she strove to reach me. I felt Olalla clasp me in her arms, her hair falling on my face, and, with the strength of a man, raise and half drag, half carry me up-stairs into my own room, where she cast me down upon the bed. Then I saw her hasten to the door and lock it, and stand an instant listening to the savage cries that shook the residencia. And then, swift and light as a thought, she was again beside me, binding up my hand, laying it in her bosom, moaning and mourning over it with dove-like sounds. They were not words that came to her, they were sounds more beautiful than speech, infinitely touching, infinitely tender; and yet as I lay there, a thought stung to my heart, a thought wounded me like a sword, a thought, like a worm in a flower, profaned the holiness of my love. Yes, they were beautiful sounds, and they were inspired by human tenderness; but was their beauty human?

All day I lay there. For a long time the cries of that nameless female thing, as she struggled

with her half-witted whelp, resounded through
the house, and pierced me with despairing sorrow and disgust. They were the death-cry of
my love; my love was murdered; it was not only
dead, but an offence to me; and yet, think as I
pleased, feel as I must, it still swelled within
me like a storm of sweetness, and my heart
melted at her looks and touch. This horror
that had sprung out, this doubt upon Olalla,
this savage and bestial strain that ran not only
through the whole behaviour of her family, but
found a place in the very foundations and story
of our love—though it appalled, though it
shocked and sickened me, was yet not of power
to break the knot of my infatuation.

When the cries had ceased, there came the
scraping at the door, by which I knew Felipe
was without; and Olalla went and spoke to him
—I know not what. With that exception, she
stayed close beside me, now kneeling by my bed
and fervently praying, now sitting with her eyes
upon mine. So then, for these six hours I drank
in her beauty, and silently perused the story
in her face. I saw the golden coin hover on her
breaths; I saw her eyes darken and brighten,
and still speak no language but that of an unfathomable kindness; I saw the faultless face,
and, through the robe, the lines of the faultless
body. Night came at last, and in the growing
darkness of the chamber, the sight of her slowly
melted; but even then the touch of her smooth

hand lingered in mine and talked with me. To lie thus in deadly weakness and drink in the traits of the beloved, is to re-awake to love from whatever shock of disillusion. I reasoned with myself; and I shut my eyes on horrors, and again I was very bold to accept the worst. What mattered it, if that imperious sentiment survived; if her eyes still beckoned and attached me; if now, even as before, every fibre of my dull body yearned and turned to her? Late on in the night some strength revived in me, and I spoke.

"Olalla," I said, "nothing matters; I ask nothing; I am content; I love you."

She knelt down a while and prayed, and I devoutly respected her devotions. The moon had begun to shine in upon one side of each of the three windows, and make a misty clearness in the room, by which I saw her indistinctly. When she re-arose she made the sign of the cross.

"It is for me to speak," she said, "and for you to listen, I know; you can but guess. I prayed, how I prayed for you to leave this place. I begged it of you, and I know you would have granted me even this; or if not, oh let me think so!"

"I love you," I said.

"And yet you have lived in the world," she said, after a pause, "you are a man and wise; and I am but a child. Forgive me, if I seem to teach, who am as ignorant as the trees of the mountain; but those who learn much do but skim the face of knowledge; they seize the laws, they conceive the dignity of the design—the horror of the living fact fades from their memory. It is we who sit at home with evil who remember, I think, and are warned and pity. Go, rather, go now, and keep me in mind. So I shall have a life in the cherished places of your memory: a life as much my own, as that which I lead in this body."

"I love you," I said once more; and reaching out my weak hand, took hers, and carried it to my lips, and kissed it. Nor did she resist, but winced a little; and I could see her look upon me with a frown that was not unkindly, only sad and baffled. And then it seemed she made a call upon her resolution; plucked my hand towards her, herself at the same time leaning somewhat forward, and laid it on the beating of her heart. "There!" she cried, "you feel the very footfall of my life. It only moves for you; it is yours. But is it even mine? It is mine indeed to offer you, as I might take the coin from my neck, as I might break a live branch from a tree, and give it you. And yet not mine! I dwell, or I think I dwell (if I exist at all), somewhere apart, an impotent prisoner, and carried about and deafened by a mob that I disown. This capsule, such as throbs against the sides of animals, knows you at a touch for its master; ay, it loves you! But my soul, does my soul? I think not; I know not, fearing to ask. Yet when you spoke to me your words were of the soul; it is of the soul that you ask—it is only from the soul that you would take me."

"Olalla," I said, "the soul and the body are one, and mostly so in love. What the body chooses, the soul loves; where the body clings, the soul cleaves; body for body, soul to soul, they come together at God's signal; and the lower part (if we can call aught low) is only the footstool and foundation of the highest."

"Have you," she said, "seen the portraits in the house of my fathers? Have you looked at my mother or at Felipe? Have your eyes ever rested on that picture that hangs by your bed? She who sat for it died ages ago; and she did evil in her life. But look again: there is my hand to the least line, there are my eyes and my hair. What is mine, then, and what am I? If not a curve in this poor body of mine (which you love, and for the sake of which you dotingly dream that you love me), not a gesture that I can frame, not a tone of my voice, not any look from my eyes, no, not even now when I speak to him I love, but has belonged to others? Others, ages dead, have wooed other men with my eyes; other men have heard the pleading of the same voice that now sounds in your ears. The hands of the dead are in my bosom; they move me, they pluck me, they guide me; I am a puppet at their command; and I but re-inform features and attributes that have long been laid aside from evil in the quiet of the grave. Is it me you love, friend? or the race that made me? The girl who does not know and cannot answer for the least portion of herself? or the stream of which she is a transitory eddy, the tree of which she is the passing fruit? The race exists; it is old, it is ever young, it carries its eternal destiny in its bosom; upon it, like waves upon the sea, individual succeeds to individual, mocked with a semblance of self-control, but they are nothing. We speak of the soul, but the soul is in the race."

"You fret against the common law," I said. "You rebel against the voice of God, which he has made so winning to convince, so imperious to command. Hear it, and how it speaks between us! Your hand clings to mine, your heart leaps at my touch, the unknown elements of which we are compounded awake and run together at a look; the clay of the earth remembers its independent life and yearns to join us; we are drawn together as the stars are turned about in space, or as the tides ebb and flow, by things older and greater than we ourselves."

"Alas!" she said, "what can I say to you? My fathers, eight hundred years ago, ruled all this province: they were wise, great, cunning, and cruel; they were a picked race of the Spanish; their flags led in war; the king called them his cousin; the people, when the rope was slung for them or when they returned and found their hovels smoking, blasphemed their name. Presently a change began. Man has risen; if he has sprung from the brutes, he can descend again to the same level. The breath of weariness blew on their humanity and the cords relaxed; they began to go down; their minds fell on sleep, their passions awoke in gusts, heady and senseless like the wind in the gutters of the mountains; beauty was still handed down, but no longer the guiding wit nor the human heart; the seed passed on, it was wrapped in flesh, the flesh covered the bones, but they were the bones and the flesh of brutes, and their mind was as the mind of flies. I speak to you as I dare; but you have seen for yourself how the wheel has gone backward with my doomed race. I stand, as it were, upon a little rising ground in this desperate descent, and see both before and behind, both what we have lost and to what we are condemned to go farther downward. And shall I—I that dwell apart in the house of the dead, my body, loathing its ways—shall I repeat the spell? Shall I bind another spirit, reluctant as my own, into this bewitched and tempest-broken tenement that I now suffer in? Shall I hand down this cursed vessel of humanity, charge it with fresh life as with fresh poison, and dash it, like a fire, in the faces of posterity? But my vow has been given; the race shall cease from off the earth. At this hour my brother is making ready; his foot will soon be on the stair; and you will go with him and pass out of my sight for ever. Think of me sometimes as one to whom the lesson of life was very harshly told, but who heard it with courage; as one who loved you indeed, but who hated herself so deeply that her love was hateful to her; as one who sent you away and yet would have longed to keep you for ever; who had no dearer hope than to forget you, and no greater fear than to be forgotten."

She had drawn towards the door as she spoke, her rich voice sounding softer and farther away; and with the last word, she was gone, and I lay alone in the moonlit chamber. What I might have done had not I lain bound by my extreme weakness, I know not; but as it was there fell upon me a great and blank despair. It was not long before there shone in at the door the ruddy glimmer of a lantern, and Felipe coming, charged me without a word upon his shoulders, and carried me down to the great gate, where the cart was waiting. In the moonlight the hills stood out sharply, as if they were of cardboard; on the glimmering surface of the plateau, and from among the low trees which swung together and sparkled in the wind, the great black cube of the residencia stood out bulkily, its mass only broken by three dimly lighted windows in the northern front above the gate. They were Olalla's windows, and as the cart jolted onwards I kept my eyes fixed upon them till, where the road dipped into a valley, they were lost to my view for ever. Felipe walked in silence beside the shafts, but from time to time he would check the mule and seem to look back upon me; and at length drew quite near and laid his hand upon my head. There was such kindness in the touch, and such a simplicity, as of the brutes, that tears broke from me like the bursting of an artery.

"Felipe," I said, "take me where they will ask no questions."

He said never a word, but he turned his mule about, end for end, retraced some part of the way we had gone, and, striking into another path, led me to the mountain village, which was, as we say in Scotland, the kirk-town of that thinly peopled district. Some broken memories dwell in my mind of the day breaking over the plain, of the cart stopping, of arms that helped me down, of a bare room into which I was carried, and of a swoon that fell upon me like sleep.

The next day and the days following, the old priest was often at my side with his snuff-box and prayer-book, and after a while, when I began to pick up strength, he told me that I was now on a fair way to recovery, and must as soon as possible hurry my departure; whereupon, without naming any reason, he took snuff and looked at me sideways. I did not affect ignorance. I knew he must have seen Olalla. "Sir," said I, "you know that I do not ask in wantonness. What of that family?"

He said they were very unfortunate; that it

seemed a declining race, and that they were very poor and had been much neglected.

"But she has not," I said. "Thanks, doubtless, to yourself, she is instructed and wise beyond the use of women."

"Yes," he said, "the Señorita is well-informed. But the family has been neglected."

"The mother?" I queried.

"Yes, the mother too," said the Padre, taking snuff. "But Felipe is a well-intentioned lad."

"The mother is odd?" I asked.

"Very odd," replied the priest.

"I think, sir, we beat about the bush," said I. "You must know more of my affairs than you allow. You must know my curiosity to be justified on many grounds. Will you not be frank with me?"

"My son," said the old gentleman, "I will be very frank with you on matters within my competence; on those of which I know nothing it does not require much discretion to be silent. I will not fence with you, I take your meaning perfectly; and what can I say, but that we are all in God's hands, and that His ways are not as our ways? I have even advised with my superiors in the church, but they, too, were dumb. It is a great mystery."

"Is she mad?" I asked.

"I will answer you according to my belief. She is not," returned the Padre, "or she was not. When she was young—God help me, I fear I neglected that wild lamb—she was surely sane; and yet, although it did not run to such heights, the same strain was already notable; it had been so before her in her father, ay, and before him, and this inclined me, perhaps, to think too lightly of it. But these things go on growing, not only in the individual but in the race."

"When she was young," I began, and my voice failed me for a moment, and it was only with a great effort that I was able to add, "was she like Olalla?"

"Now God forbid!" exclaimed the Padre. "God forbid that any man should think so slightingly of my favourite penitent! No, no; the Señorita (but for her beauty, which I wish most honestly she had less of) has not a hair's resemblance to what her mother was at the same age. I could not bear to have you think so; though, Heaven knows, it were, perhaps, better that you should."

At this, I raised myself in bed, and opened my heart to the old man; telling him of our love and of her decision, owning my own horrors, my own passing fancies, but telling him that these were at an end; and with something more than a purely formal submission, appealing to his judgment.

He heard me very patiently and without surprise; and when I had done, he sat for some time silent. Then he began: "The Church," and instantly broke off again to apologise. "I had forgotten, my child, that you were not a Christian," said he. "And indeed, upon a point so highly unusual, even the Church can scarce be said to have decided. But would you have my opinion? The Señorita is, in a matter of this kind, the best judge; I would accept her judgment."

On the back of that he went away, nor was he thenceforward so assiduous in his visits; indeed, even when I began to get about again, he plainly feared and deprecated my society, not as in distaste but much as a man might be disposed to flee from the riddling sphinx. The villagers, too, avoided me; they were unwilling to be my guides upon the mountain. I thought they looked at me askance, and I made sure that the more superstitious crossed themselves on my approach. At first I set this down to my heretical opinions; but it began at length to dawn upon me that if I was thus redoubted it was because I had stayed at the residencia. All men despise the savage notions of such peasantry; and yet I was conscious of a chill shadow that seemed to fall and dwell upon my love. It did not conquer, but I may not deny that it restrained my ardour.

Some miles westward of the village there was a gap in the sierra, from which the eye plunged direct upon the residencia; and thither it became my daily habit to repair. A wood crowned the summit; and just where the pathway issued from its fringes, it was overhung by a considerable shelf of rock, and that, in its turn, was surmounted by a crucifix of the size of life and more than usually painful in design. This was my perch; thence, day after day, I looked down upon the plateau, and the great old house, and could see Felipe, no bigger than a fly, going to and fro about the garden. Sometimes mists would draw across the view, and be broken up again by mountain winds; sometimes the plain slumbered below me in unbroken sunshine; it would sometimes be all blotted out by rain. This distant post, these interrupted sights of the place where my life had been so strangely changed suited the indecision of my humour. I passed whole days there, debating with myself the various elements of our position; now leaning to the suggestions of love, now giving an ear to prudence, and in the end halting irresolute between the two.

One day, as I was sitting on my rock, there came by that way a somewhat gaunt peasant wrapped in a mantle. He was a stranger, and plainly did not know me even by repute; for, instead of keeping the other side, he drew near and sat down beside me, and we had soon fallen in talk. Among other things he told me he had been a muleteer, and in former years had much frequented these mountains; later on, he had followed the army with his mules, had realised a competence, and was now living retired with his family.

"Do you know that house?" I inquired, at last, pointing to the residencia, for I readily wearied of any talk that kept me from the thought of Olalla.

He looked at me darkly and crossed himself.

"Too well," he said, "it was there that one of my comrades sold himself to Satan; the Virgin shield us from temptations! He has paid the price; he is now burning in the reddest place in hell!"

A fear came upon me; I could answer nothing; and presently the man resumed, as if to himself. "Yes," he said, "O yes, I know it. I have passed its doors. There was snow upon the pass, the wind was driving it; sure enough there was death that night upon the mountains, but there was worse beside the hearth. I took him by the arm, Señor, and dragged him to the gate; I conjured him, by all he loved and respected, to go forth with me; I went on my knees before him in the snow; and I could see he was moved by my entreaty. And just then she came out on the gallery, and called him by his name; and he turned, and there was she standing with a lamp in her hand and smiling on him to come back. I cried out aloud to God, and threw my arms about him, but he put me by, and left me alone. He had made his choice; God help us. I would pray for him, but to what end? there are sins that not even the Pope can loose."

"And your friend," I asked, "what became of him?"

"Nay, God knows," said the muleteer. "If all be true that we hear, his end was like his sin, a thing to raise the hair."

"Do you mean that he was killed?" I asked.

"Sure enough, he was killed," returned the man. "But how? Ay, how? But these are things that it is sin to speak of."

"The people of that house . . ." I began.

But he interrupted me with a savage outburst. "The people?" he cried. "What people? There are neither men nor women in that house of Satan's! What? have you lived here so long, and never heard?" And here he put his mouth to my ear and whispered, as if even the fowls of the mountain might have overheard and been stricken with horror.

What he told me was not true, nor was it even original; being, indeed, but a new edition, vamped up again by village ignorance and superstition, of stories nearly as ancient as the race of man. It was rather the application that appalled me. In the old days, he said, the Church would have burned out that nest of basilisks; but the arm of the Church was now shortened; his friend Miguel had been unpunished by the hands of men, and left to the more awful judgment of an offended God. This was wrong; but it should be so no more. The Padre was sunk in age; he was even bewitched himself; but the eyes of his flock were now awake to their own danger; and some day—ay, and before long—the smoke of that house should go up to heaven.

He left me filled with horror and fear. Which way to turn I knew not; whether first to warn the Padre, or to carry my ill-news direct to the threatened inhabitants of the residencia. Fate was to decide for me; for, while I was still hesitating, I beheld the veiled figure of a woman drawing near to me up the pathway. No veil could deceive my penetration; by every line and every movement I recognised Olalla; and keeping hidden behind a corner of the rock, I suffered her to gain the summit. Then I came forward. She knew me and paused, but did not speak; I, too, remained silent; and we continued for some time to gaze upon each other with a passionate sadness.

"I thought you had gone," she said at length. "It is all that you can do for me—to go. It is all I ever asked of you. And you still stay. But do you know, that every day heaps up the peril of death, not only on your head, but on ours? A report has gone about the mountain; it is thought you love me, and the people will not suffer it."

I saw she was already informed of her danger, and I rejoiced at it. "Olalla," I said, "I am ready to go this day, this very hour, but not alone."

She stepped aside and knelt down before the

crucifix to pray, and I stood by and looked now at her and now at the object of her adoration, now at the living figure of the penitent, and now at the ghastly, daubed countenance, the painted wounds, and the projected ribs of the image. The silence was only broken by the wailing of some large birds that circled sidelong, as if in surprise or alarm, about the summit of the hills. Presently Olalla rose again, turned towards me, raised her veil, and, still leaning with one hand on the shaft of the crucifix, looked upon me with a pale and sorrowful countenance.

"I have laid my hand upon the cross," she said. "The Padre says you are no Christian; but look up for a moment with my eyes, and behold the face of the Man of Sorrows. We are all such as He was—the inheritors of sin; we must all bear and expiate a past which was not ours; there is in all of us—ay, even in me—a sparkle of the divine. Like Him, we must endure for a little while, until morning returns bringing peace. Suffer me to pass on upon my way alone; it is thus that I shall be least lonely, counting for my friend Him who is the friend of all the distressed; it is thus that I shall be the most happy, having taken my farewell of earthly happiness, and willingly accepted sorrow for my portion."

I looked at the face of the crucifix, and, though I was no friend to images, and despised that imitative and grimacing art of which it was a rude

238

example, some sense of what the thing implied was carried home to my intelligence. The face looked down upon me with a painful and deadly contraction; but the rays of a glory encircled it, and reminded me that the sacrifice was voluntary. It stood there, crowning the rock, as it still stands on so many highway-sides, vainly preaching to passers-by, an emblem of sad and noble truths; that pleasure is not an end, but an accident; that pain is the choice of the magnanimous; that it is best to suffer all things and do well. I turned and went down the mountain in silence; and when I looked back for the last time before the wood closed about my path, I saw Olalla still leaning on the crucifix.

THE TREASURE OF
FRANCHARD

THE TREASURE OF
FRANCHARD

CHAPTER I

BY THE DYING MOUNTEBANK

THEY had sent for the doctor from Bourron before six. About eight some villagers
came round for the performance, and were told
how matters stood. It seemed a liberty for a
mountebank to fall ill like real people, and they
made off again in dudgeon. By ten Madame
Tentaillon was gravely alarmed, and had sent
down the street for Doctor Desprez.

The Doctor was at work over his manuscripts
in one corner of the little dining-room, and his
wife was asleep over the fire in another, when the
messenger arrived.

"*Sapristi!*" said the Doctor, "you should have
sent for me before. It was a case for hurry."
And he followed the messenger as he was, in his
slippers and skull-cap.

The inn was not thirty yards away, but the
messenger did not stop there; he went in at one
door and out by another into the court, and then
led the way by a flight of steps beside the stable,

243

to the loft where the mountebank lay sick. If Doctor Desprez were to live a thousand years, he would never forget his arrival in that room; for not only was the scene picturesque, but the moment made a date in his existence. We reckon our lives, I hardly know why, from the date of our first sorry appearance in society, as if from a first humiliation; for no actor can come upon the stage with a worse grace. Not to go further back, which would be judged too curious, there are subsequently many moving and decisive accidents in the lives of all, which would make as logical a period as this of birth. And here, for instance, Doctor Desprez, a man past forty, who had made what is called a failure in life, and was moreover married, found himself at a new point of departure when he opened the door of the loft above Tentaillon's stable.

It was a large place, lighted only by a single candle set upon the floor. The mountebank lay on his back upon a pallet; a large man, with a Quixotic nose inflamed with drinking. Madame Tentaillon stooped over him, applying a hot-water and mustard embrocation to his feet; and on a chair close by sat a little fellow of eleven or twelve, with his feet dangling. These three were the only occupants, except the shadows. But the shadows were a company in themselves; the extent of the room exaggerated them to a gigantic size, and from the low position of the candle the light struck upwards and produced deformed foreshortenings. The mountebank's profile was enlarged upon the wall in caricature, and it was strange to see his nose shorten and lengthen as the flame was blown about by draughts. As for Madame Tentaillon, her shadow was no more than a gross hump of shoulders, with now and again a hemisphere of head. The chair legs were spindled out as long as stilts, and the boy sat perched atop of them, like a cloud, in the corner of the roof.

It was the boy who took the Doctor's fancy. He had a great arched skull, the forehead and the hands of a musician, and a pair of haunting eyes. It was not merely that these eyes were large, or steady, or the softest ruddy brown. There was a look in them, besides, which thrilled the Doctor, and made him half uneasy. He was sure he had seen such a look before, and yet he could not remember how or where. It was as if this boy, who was quite a stranger to him, had the eyes of an old friend or an old enemy. And the boy would give him no peace; he seemed profoundly indifferent to what was going on, or rather abstracted from it in a superior contemplation, beating gently with his feet against the bars of the chair, and holding his hands folded on his lap. But, for all that, his eyes kept following the Doctor about the room with a thoughtful fixity of gaze. Desprez could not tell whether he was fascinating the boy, or the boy was fascinating him. He busied himself over the sick man: he put questions, he felt the pulse, he jested, he grew a little hot and swore: and still, whenever he looked round, there were the brown eyes waiting for his with the same inquiring, melancholy gaze.

At last the Doctor hit on the solution at a leap. He remembered the look now. The little fellow, although he was as straight as a dart, had the eyes that go usually with a crooked back; he was not at all deformed, and yet a deformed person seemed to be looking at you from below his brows. The Doctor drew a long breath, he was so much relieved to find a theory (for he loved theories) and to explain away his interest.

For all that, he despatched the invalid with unusual haste, and, still kneeling with one knee on the floor, turned a little round and looked the boy over at his leisure. The boy was not in the least put out, but looked placidly back at the Doctor.

"Is this your father?" asked Desprez.

"Oh, no," returned the boy; "my master."

"Are you fond of him?" continued the Doctor.

"No, sir," said the boy.

Madame Tentaillon and Desprez exchanged expressive glances.

"That is bad, my man," resumed the latter, with a shade of sternness. "Every one should be fond of the dying, or conceal their sentiments; and your master here is dying. If I have watched a bird a little while stealing my cherries, I have a thought of disappointment when he flies away over my garden wall, and I see him steer for the forest and vanish. How much more a creature such as this, so strong, so astute, so richly endowed with faculties! When I think that, in a few hours the speech will be silenced, the breath extinct, and even the shadow vanished from the wall, I who never saw him, this lady who knew him only as a guest, are touched with some affection."

The boy was silent for a little, and appeared to be reflecting.

"You did not know him," he replied at last. "He was a bad man."

"He is a little pagan," said the landlady. "For that matter, they are all the same, these mountebanks, tumblers, artists, and what not. They have no interior."

But the doctor was still scrutinising the little pagan, his eyebrows knotted and uplifted.

"What is your name?" he asked.

"Jean-Marie," said the lad.

Desprez leaped upon him with one of his sudden flashes of excitement, and felt his head all over from an ethnological point of view.

"Celtic, Celtic!" he said.

"Celtic!" cried Madame Tentaillon, who had perhaps confounded the word with hydrocephalous. "Poor lad! is it dangerous?"

"That depends," returned the Doctor, grimly. And then once more addressing the boy: "And

what do you do for your living, Jean-Marie?"
he inquired.

"I tumble," was the answer.

"So! Tumble?" repeated Desprez. "Probably healthful. I hazard the guess, Madame Tentaillon, that tumbling is a healthful way of life. And have you never done anything else but tumble?"

"Before I learned that, I used to steal," answered Jean-Marie gravely.

"Upon my word!" cried the Doctor. "You are a nice little man for your age. Madame, when my *confrère* comes from Bourron, you will communicate my unfavourable opinion. I leave the case in his hands; but of course, on any alarming symptom, above all if there should be a sign of rally, do not hesitate to knock me up. I am a doctor no longer, I thank God; but I have been one. Good-night, madame.—Good sleep to you, Jean-Marie."

CHAPTER II

DOCTOR DESPREZ always rose early. Before the smoke arose, before the first cart rattled over the bridge to the day's labour in the fields, he was to be found wandering in his garden. Now he would pick a bunch of grapes; now he would eat a big pear under the trellis; now he would draw all sorts of fancies on the path with the end of his cane; now he would go down and watch the river running endlessly past the timber landing-place at which he moored his boat. There was no time, he used to say, for making theories like the early morning. "I rise earlier than any one else in the village," he once boasted. "It is a fair consequence that I know more and wish to do less with my knowledge."

The Doctor was a connoisseur of sunrises, and loved a good theatrical effect to usher in the day. He had a theory of dew, by which he could predict the weather. Indeed, most things served him to that end: the sound of the bells from all the neighbouring villages, the smell of the forest, the visits and the behaviour of both birds and fishes, the look of the plants in his garden, the disposition of cloud, the colour of the light, and last, although not least, the arsenal of meteorological intruments in a louvre-boarded hutch upon the lawn. Ever since he had settled at Gretz, he had been growing more and more into the local meteorologist, the unpaid champion of the local climate. He thought at first there was no place so healthful in the arrondissement. By the end of the second year, he protested there was none so wholesome in the whole department. And for some time before he met Jean-Marie, he had been prepared to challenge all France and the better part of Europe for a rival to his chosen spot.

"Doctor," he would say—"doctor is a foul word. It should not be used to ladies. It implies disease. I remark it, as a flaw in our civilisation, that we have not the proper horror of disease. Now I, for my part, have washed my hands of it; I have renounced my laureation; I am no doctor; I am only a worshipper of the true goddess Hygieia. Ah, believe me, it is she who has the cestus! And here, in this exiguous hamlet, has she placed her shrine: here she dwells and lavishes her gifts; here I walk with her in the early morning, and she shows me how strong she has made the peasants, how fruitful she has made the fields, how the trees grow up tall and comely under her eyes, and the fishes in the river become clean and agile at her presence.—Rheumatism!" he would cry, on some malapert interruption, "oh, yes, I believe we do have a little rheumatism. That could hardly be avoided, you know, on a river. And of course the place stands a little low; and the meadows are marshy, there's no doubt. But, my dear sir, look at Bourron! Bourron stands high. Bourron is close to the forest; plenty of ozone there, you would say. Well, compared with Gretz, Bourron is a perfect shambles."

The morning after he had been summoned to the dying mountebank, the Doctor visited the wharf at the tail of his garden, and had a long look at the running water. This he called prayer; but whether his adorations were addressed to the goddess Hygieia or some more orthodox deity, never plainly appeared. For he had uttered doubtful oracles, sometimes declaring that a river was the type of bodily health, sometimes extolling it as the great moral preacher, continually preaching peace, continuity, and diligence to man's tormented spirits. After he had watched a mile or so of the clear water running by before his eyes, seen a fish or two come to the surface with a gleam of silver, and sufficiently admired the long shadows of the trees falling half across the river from the opposite bank, with patches of moving sunlight in between, he strolled once more up the garden and through his house into the street, feeling cool and renovated.

The sound of his feet upon the causeway began the business of the day; for the village was still sound asleep. The church tower looked very airy in the sunlight; a few birds that turned about it, seemed to swim in an atmosphere of more than usual rarity; and the Doctor, walking in long transparent shadows, filled his lungs amply, and proclaimed himself well contented with the morning.

On one of the posts before Tentaillon's carriage entry he espied a little dark figure perched in a meditative attitude, and immediately recognised Jean-Marie.

"Aha!" he said, stopping before him humorously, with a hand on either knee. "So we rise early in the morning, do we? It appears to me that we have all the vices of a philosopher."

The boy got to his feet and made a grave salutation.

"And how is our patient?" asked Desprez.

It appeared the patient was about the same.

"And why do you rise early in the morning?" he pursued.

Jean-Marie, after a long silence, professed that he hardly knew.

"You hardly know?" repeated Desprez. "We hardly know anything, my man, until we try to learn. Interrogate your consciousness. Come, push me this inquiry home. Do you like it?"

"Yes," said the boy slowly; "yes, I like it."

"And why do you like it?" continued the

252

Doctor. "(We are now pursuing the Socratic method.) Why do you like it?"

"It is quiet," answered Jean-Marie; "and I have nothing to do; and then I feel as if I were good."

Doctor Desprez took a seat on the post at the opposite side. He was beginning to take an interest in the talk, for the boy plainly thought before he spoke, and tried to answer truly. "It appears you have a taste for feeling good," said the Doctor. "Now, there you puzzle me extremely; for I thought you said you were a thief; and the two are incompatible."

"Is it very bad to steal?" asked Jean-Marie.

"Such is the general opinion, little boy," replied the Doctor.

"No; but I mean as I stole," exclaimed the other. "For I had no choice. I think it is surely right to have bread; it must be right to have bread, there comes so plain a want of it. And then they beat me cruelly if I returned with nothing," he added. "I was not ignorant of right and wrong; for before that I had been well taught by a priest, who was very kind to me." (The Doctor made a horrible grimace at the word "priest.") "But it seemed to me, when one had nothing to eat and was beaten, it was a different affair. I would not have stolen for tartlets, I believe; but any one would steal for baker's bread."

"And so I suppose," said the Doctor, with a

rising sneer, "you prayed God to forgive you, and explained the case to Him at length."

"Why, sir?" asked Jean-Marie. "I do not see."

"Your priest would see, however," retorted Desprez.

"Would he?" asked the boy, troubled for the first time. "I should have thought God would have known."

"Eh?" snarled the Doctor.

"I should have thought God would have understood me," replied the other. "You do not, I see; but then it was God that made me think so, was it not?"

"Little boy, little boy," said Doctor Desprez, "I told you already you had the vices of philosophy; if you display the virtues also, I must go. I am a student of the blessed laws of health, an observer of plain and temperate nature in her common walks; and I cannot preserve my equanimity in presence of a monster. Do you understand?"

"No, sir," said the boy.

"I will make my meaning clear to you," replied the Doctor. "Look there at the sky—behind the belfry first, where it is so light, and then up and up, turning your chin back, right to the top of the dome, where it is already as blue as at noon. Is not that a beautiful colour? Does it not please the heart? We have seen it all our lives, until it has grown in with our familiar thoughts. Now," changing his tone, "suppose that sky to become suddenly of a live and fiery amber, like the colour of clear coals, and growing scarlet towards the top—I do not say it would be any the less beautiful; but would you like it as well?"

"I suppose not," answered Jean-Marie.

"Neither do I like you," returned the Doctor, roughly. "I hate all odd people, and you are the most curious little boy in all the world."

Jean-Marie seemed to ponder for a while, and then he raised his head again and looked over at the Doctor with an air of candid inquiry. "But are not you a very curious gentleman?" he asked.

The Doctor threw away his stick, bounded on the boy, clasped him to his bosom, and kissed him on both cheeks. "Admirable, admirable imp!" he cried. "What a morning, what an hour for a theorist of forty-two! No," he continued, apostrophising heaven, "I did not know that such boys existed; I was ignorant they made them so; I had doubted of my race; and now! It is like," he added, picking up his stick, "like a lovers' meeting. I have bruised my favourite staff in that moment of enthusiasm. The injury, however, is not grave." He caught the boy looking at him in obvious wonder, embarrassment, and alarm. "Hullo!" said he, "why do you look at me like that? Egad, I believe the boy despises me. Do you despise me, boy?"

"Oh no," replied Jean-Marie, seriously; "only I do not understand."

"You must excuse me, sir," returned the Doctor, with gravity; "I am still so young. Oh, hang him!" he added to himself. And he took his seat again and observed the boy sardonically. "He has spoiled the quiet of my morning," thought he. "I shall be nervous all day, and have a febricule when I digest. Let me compose myself." And so he dismissed his preoccupations by an effort of the will which he had long practised, and let his soul roam abroad in the contemplation of the morning. He inhaled the air, tasting it critically as a connoisseur tastes a vintage, and prolonging the expiration with hygienic gusto. He counted the little flecks of cloud along the sky. He followed the movements of the birds round the church tower—making long sweeps, hanging poised, or turning airy somersaults in fancy, and beating the wind with imaginary pinions. And in this way he regained peace of mind and animal composure, conscious of his limbs, conscious of the sight of his eyes, conscious that the air had a cool taste, like a fruit, at the top of his throat; and at last, in complete abstraction, he began to sing. The Doctor had but one air—"Malbrouck s'en va-t-en guerre"; even with that he was on terms of mere politeness; and his musical exploits were always reserved for moments when he was alone and entirely happy.

He was recalled to earth rudely by a pained expression on the boy's face. "What do you think of my singing?" he inquired, stopping in the middle of a note; and then, after he had waited some little while and received no answer, "What do you think of my singing?" he repeated, imperiously.

"I do not like it," faltered Jean-Marie.

"Oh, come!" cried the Doctor. "Possibly you are a performer yourself?"

"I sing better than that," replied the boy.

The Doctor eyed him for some seconds in stupefaction. He was aware that he was angry, and blushed for himself in consequence, which made him angrier. "If this is how you address your master!" he said at last, with a shrug and a flourish of his arms.

"I do not speak to him at all," returned the boy. "I do not like him."

"Then you like me?" snapped Doctor Desprez, with unusual eagerness.

"I do not know," answered Jean-Marie.

The Doctor rose. "I shall wish you a good-morning," he said. "You are too much for me. Perhaps you have blood in your veins, perhaps celestial ichor, or perhaps you circulate nothing more gross than respirable air; but of one thing I am inexpugnably assured:—that you are no human being. No, boy"—shaking his stick at him—"you are not a human being. Write, write it in your memory—'I am not a human being—I have no pretension to be a human be-ing—I am a dive, a dream, an angel, an acrostic, an illusion—what you please, but not a human being.' And so accept my humble salutations and farewell!"

And with that the Doctor made off along the street in some emotion, and the boy stood, men-tally gaping, where he left him.

CHAPTER III

THE ADOPTION

MADAME DESPREZ, who answered to the Christian name of Anastasie, presented an agreeable type of her sex; exceedingly wholesome to look upon, a stout *brune*, with cool smooth cheeks, steady, dark eyes, and hands that neither art nor nature could improve. She was the sort of person over whom adversity passes like a summer cloud; she might, in the worst of conjunctions, knit her brows into one vertical furrow for a moment, but the next it would be gone. She had much of the placidity of a contented nun; with little of her piety, however; for Anastasie was of a very mundane nature, fond of oysters and old wine, and somewhat bold pleasantries, and devoted to her husband for her own sake rather than for his. She was imperturbably good-natured, but had no idea of self-sacrifice. To live in that pleasant old house, with a green garden behind and bright flowers about the window, to eat and drink of the best, to gossip with a neighbour for a quarter of an hour, never to wear stays or a dress except when she went to Fontainebleau shopping, to be kept in a continual supply of racy novels, and to be married to Doctor Desprez and have no ground of jealousy, filled the cup of her nature to the brim. Those who had known the Doctor in bachelor days, when he had aired quite as many theories, but of a different order, attributed his present philosophy to the study of Anastasie. It was her brute enjoyment that he rationalised and perhaps vainly imitated.

Madame Desprez was an artist in the kitchen, and made coffee to a nicety. She had a knack of tidiness, with which she had infected the Doctor; everything was in its place; everything capable of polish shone gloriously; and dust was a thing banished from her empire. Aline, their single servant, had no other business in the world but to scour and burnish. So Doctor Desprez lived in his house like a fatted calf, warmed and cosseted to his heart's content.

The midday meal was excellent. There was a ripe melon, a fish from the river in a memorable Béarnaise sauce, a fat fowl in a fricassee, and a dish of asparagus, followed by some fruit. The Doctor drank half a bottle *plus* one glass, the wife half a bottle *minus* the same quantity, which was a marital privilege, of an excellent Côte-Rôtie, seven years old. Then the coffee was brought, and a flask of Chartreuse for madame, for the Doctor despised and distrusted such de-

coctions; and then Aline left the wedded pair
to the pleasures of memory and digestion.

"It is a very fortunate circumstance, my
cherished one," observed the Doctor—"this coffee is adorable—a very fortunate circumstance
upon the whole—Anastasie, I beseech you, go
without that poison for to-day; only one day,
and you will feel the benefit, I pledge my reputation."

"What is this fortunate circumstance, my
friend?" inquired Anastasie, not heeding his protest, which was of daily recurrence.

"That we have no children, my beautiful," replied the Doctor. "I think of it more and more
as the years go on, and with more and more
gratitude towards the Power that dispenses such
afflictions. Your health, my darling, my studious quiet, our little kitchen delicacies, how they
would all have suffered, how they would all have
been sacrificed! And for what? Children are
the last word of human imperfection. Health
flees before their face. They cry, my dear; they
put vexatious questions; they demand to be fed,
to be washed, to be educated, to have their noses
blown; and then, when the time comes, they
break our hearts, as I break this piece of sugar.
A pair of professed egoists, like you and me,
should avoid offspring, like an infidelity."

"Indeed!" said she; and she laughed. "Now,
that is like you—to take credit for the thing you
could not help."

"My dear," returned the Doctor, solemnly, "we might have adopted."

"Never!" cried madame. "Never, Doctor, with my consent. If the child were my own flesh and blood, I would not say no. But to take another person's indiscretion on my shoulders, my dear friend, I have too much sense."

"Precisely," replied the Doctor. "We both had. And I am all the better pleased with our wisdom, because—because——" He looked at her sharply.

"Because what?" she asked, with a faint premonition of danger.

"Because I have found the right person," said the Doctor firmly, "and shall adopt him this afternoon."

Anastasie looked at him out of a mist. "You have lost your reason," she said; and there was a clang in her voice that seemed to threaten trouble.

"Not so, my dear," he replied; "I retain its complete exercise. To the proof: instead of attempting to cloak my inconsistency, I have, by way of preparing you, thrown it into strong relief. You will there, I think, recognise the philosopher who has the ecstasy to call you wife. The fact is, I have been reckoning all this while without an accident. I never thought to find a son of my own. Now, last night I found one. Do not unnecessarily alarm yourself, my dear; he is not a drop of blood to me that I know. It is his mind, darling, his mind that calls me father."

"His mind!" she repeated with a titter between scorn and hysterics. "His mind, indeed! Henri, is this an idiotic pleasantry, or are you mad? His mind! And what of my mind?"

"Truly," replied the Doctor with a shrug, "you have your finger on the hitch. He will be strikingly antipathetic to my beautiful Anastasie. She will never understand him; he will never understand her. You married the animal side of my nature, dear; and it is on the spiritual side that I find my affinity for Jean-Marie. So much so, that, to be perfectly frank, I stand in some awe of him myself. You will easily perceive that I am announcing a calamity for you. Do not," he broke out in tones of real solicitude —"do not give way to tears after a meal, Anastasie. You will certainly give yourself a false digestion."

Anastasie controlled herself. "You know how willing I am to humour you," she said, "in all reasonable matters. But on this point——"

"My dear love," interrupted the Doctor, eager to prevent a refusal, "who wished to leave Paris? Who made me give up cards, and the opera, and the boulevard, and my social relations, and all that was my life before I knew you? Have I been faithful? Have I been obedient? Have I not borne my doom with cheerfulness? In all honesty, Anastasie, have I not a right to a stip-

263

ulation on my side? I have, and you know it. I stipulate my son."

Anastasie was aware of defeat; she struck her colours instantly. "You will break my heart," she sighed.

"Not in the least," said he. "You will feel a trifling inconvenience for a month, just as I did when I was first brought to this vile hamlet; then your admirable sense and temper will prevail, and I see you already as content as ever, and making your husband the happiest of men."

"You know I can refuse you nothing," she said, with a last flicker of resistance; "nothing that will make you truly happier. But will this? Are you sure, my husband? Last night, you say, you found him! He may be the worst of humbugs."

"I think not," replied the Doctor. "But do not suppose me so unwary as to adopt him out of hand. I am, I flatter myself, a finished man of the world; I have had all possibilities in view; my plan is contrived to meet them all. I take the lad as stable-boy. If he pilfer, if he grumble, if he desire to change, I shall see I was mistaken; I shall recognise him for no son of mine, and send him tramping."

"You will never do so when the time comes," said his wife; "I know your good heart."

She reached out her hand to him, with a sigh; the Doctor smiled as he took it and carried it to his lips; he had gained his point with greater ease than he had dared to hope; for perhaps the twentieth time he had proved the efficacy of his trusty argument, his Excalibur, the hint of a return to Paris. Six months in the capital, for a man of the Doctor's antecedents and relations, implied no less a calamity than total ruin. Anastasie had saved the remainder of his fortune by keeping him strictly in the country. The very name of Paris put her in a blue fear; and she would have allowed her husband to keep a menagerie in the back-garden, let alone adopting a stable-boy, rather than permit the question of return to be discussed.

About four of the afternoon, the mountebank rendered up his ghost; he had never been conscious since his seizure. Doctor Desprez was present at his last passage, and declared the farce over. Then he took Jean-Marie by the shoulder and led him out into the inn garden where there was a convenient bench beside the river. Here he sat him down and made the boy place himself on his left.

"Jean-Marie," he said very gravely, "this world is exceedingly vast; and even France, which is only a small corner of it, is a great place for a little lad like you. Unfortunately it is full of eager, shouldering people moving on; and there are very few bakers' shops for so many eaters. Your master is dead; you are not fit to gain a living by yourself; you do not wish to steal? No. Your situation then is undesirable;

it is, for the moment, critical. On the other hand, you behold in me a man not old, though elderly, still enjoying the youth of the heart and the intelligence; a man of instruction; easily situated in this world's affairs; keeping a good table:—a man, neither as friend nor host, to be despised. I offer you your food and clothes, and to teach you lessons in the evening, which will be infinitely more to the purpose for a lad of your stamp than those of all the priests in Europe. I propose no wages, but if ever you take a thought to leave me, the door shall be open, and I will give you a hundred francs to start the world upon. In return, I have an old horse and chaise, which you would very speedily learn to clean and keep in order. Do not hurry yourself to answer, and take it or leave it as you judge aright. Only remember this, that I am no sentimentalist or charitable person, but a man who lives rigorously to himself; and that if I make the proposal, it is for my own ends—it is because I perceive clearly an advantage to myself. And now, reflect."

"I shall be very glad. I do not see what else I can do. I thank you, sir, most kindly, and I will try to be useful," said the boy.

"Thank you," said the Doctor warmly, rising at the same time and wiping his brow, for he had suffered agonies while the thing hung in the wind. A refusal, after the scene at noon, would have placed him in a ridiculous light before Anastasie. "How hot and heavy is the evening, to be sure! I have always had a fancy to be a fish in summer, Jean-Marie, here in the Loing beside Gretz. I should lie under a water-lily and listen to the bells, which must sound most delicately down below. That would be a life—do you not think so too?"

"Yes," said Jean-Marie.

"Thank God you have imagination!" cried the Doctor, embracing the boy with his usual effusive warmth, though it was a proceeding that seemed to disconcert the sufferer almost as much as if he had been an English schoolboy of the same age. "And now," he added, "I will take you to my wife."

Madame Desprez sat in the dining-room in a cool wrapper. All the blinds were down, and the tile floor had been recently sprinkled with water; her eyes were half shut, but she affected to be reading a novel as they entered. Though she was a bustling woman, she enjoyed repose between whiles and had a remarkable appetite for sleep.

The Doctor went through a solemn form of introduction, adding, for the benefit of both parties, "You must try to like each other for my sake."

"He is very pretty," said Anastasie.—"Will you kiss me, my pretty little fellow?"

The Doctor was furious, and dragged her into the passage. "Are you a fool, Anastasie?" he said. "What is all this I hear about the tact of women? Heaven knows, I have not met with it in my experience. You address my little philosopher as if he were an infant. He must be spoken to with more respect, I tell you; he must not be kissed and Georgy-porgy'd like an ordinary child."

"I only did it to please you, I am sure," replied Anastasie; "but I will try to do better."

The Doctor apologised for his warmth. "But I do wish him," he continued, "to feel at home among us. And really your conduct was so idiotic, my cherished one, and so utterly and distantly out of place, that a saint might have been pardoned a little vehemence in disapproval. Do, do try—if it is possible for a woman to understand young people—but of course it is not, and I waste my breath. Hold your tongue as much as possible at least, and observe my conduct narrowly; it will serve you for a model."

Anastasie did as she was bidden, and considered the Doctor's behaviour. She observed that he embraced the boy three times in the course of the evening, and managed generally to confound and abash the little fellow out of speech and appetite. But she had the true womanly heroism in little affairs. Not only did she refrain from the cheap revenge of exposing the Doctor's errors to himself, but she did her best to remove their ill-effect on Jean-Marie. When Desprez went out for his last breath of air before retiring for the night, she came over to the boy's side and took his hand.

"You must not be surprised nor frightened by my husband's manners," she said. "He is the kindest of men, but so clever that he is sometimes difficult to understand. You will soon grow used to him, and then you will love him, for that nobody can help. As for me, you may be sure, I shall try to make you happy, and will not bother you at all. I think we should be excellent friends, you and I. I am not clever, but I am very good-natured. Will you give me a kiss?"

He held up his face, and she took him in her arms and then began to cry. The woman had spoken in complaisance; but she had warmed to her own words, and tenderness followed. The Doctor, entering, found them enlaced: he concluded that his wife was in fault; and he was just beginning, in an awful voice, "Anastasie——," when she looked up at him, smiling, with an upraised finger; and he held his peace, wondering, while she led the boy to his attic.

CHAPTER IV

THE EDUCATION OF A PHILOSOPHER

THE installation of the adopted stable-boy was thus happily effected, and the wheels of life continued to run smoothly in the Doctor's house. Jean-Marie did his horse and carriage duty in the morning; sometimes helped in the housework; sometimes walked abroad with the Doctor, to drink wisdom from the fountain-head; and was introduced at night to the sciences and the dead tongues. He retained his singular placidity of mind and manner; he was rarely in fault; but he made only a very partial progress in his studies, and remained much of a stranger in the family.

The Doctor was a pattern of regularity. All forenoon he worked on his great book, the *Comparative Pharmacopœia, or Historical Dictionary of all Medicines*, which as yet consisted principally of slips of paper and pins. When finished, it was to fill many personable volumes and to combine antiquarian interest with professional utility. But the Doctor was studious of literary graces and the picturesque; an anecdote,

a touch of manners, a moral qualification, or a
sounding epithet was sure to be preferred before
a piece of science; a little more, and he would
have written the *Comparative Pharmacopœia* in
verse! The article "Mummia," for instance,
was already complete, though the remainder of
the work had not progressed beyond the letter
A. It was exceedingly copious and entertaining, written with quaintness and colour, exact,
erudite, a literary article; but it would hardly
have afforded guidance to a practising physician
of to-day. The feminine good-sense of his wife
had led her to point this out with uncompromis-
ing sincerity; for the Dictionary was duly read
aloud to her, betwixt sleep and waking, as it
proceeded towards an infinitely distant comple-
tion; and the doctor was a little sore on the subject of mummies, and sometimes resented an al-
lusion with asperity.

After the midday meal and a proper period of
digestion, he walked, sometimes alone, sometimes accompanied by Jean-Marie; for madame
would have preferred any hardship rather than
walk.

She was, as I have said, a very busy person,
continually occupied about material comforts,
and ready to drop asleep over a novel the instant
she was disengaged. This was the less objec-
tionable, as she never snored or grew distempered in complexion when she slept. On the
contrary, she looked the very picture of luxu-

rious and appetising ease, and woke without a
start to the perfect possession of her faculties.
I am afraid she was greatly an animal, but she
was a very nice animal to have about. In this
way, she had little to do with Jean-Marie; but
the sympathy which had been established between them on the first night remained unbroken; they held occasional conversations,
mostly on household matters; to the extreme
disappointment of the Doctor, they occasionally
sallied off together to that temple of debasing
superstition, the village church; madame and he,
both in their Sunday's best, drove twice a month
to Fontainebleau and returned laden with pur-
chases; and in short, although the Doctor still
continued to regard them as irreconcilably antipathetic, their relation was as intimate, friendly,
and confidential as their natures suffered.

I fear, however, that in her heart of hearts,
madame kindly despised and pitied the boy.
She had no admiration for his class of virtues;
she liked a smart, polite, forward, roguish sort
of boy, cap in hand, light of foot, meeting the
eye; she liked volubility, charm, a little vice—
the promise of a second Doctor Desprez. And it
was her indefeasible belief that Jean-Marie was
dull. "Poor dear boy," she had said once, "how
sad it is that he should be so stupid!" She had
never repeated that remark, for the Doctor had
raged like a wild bull, denouncing the brutal
bluntness of her mind, bemoaning his own fate

to be so unequally mated with an ass, and, what touched Anastasie more nearly, menacing the table china by the fury of his gesticulations. But she adhered silently to her opinion; and when Jean-Marie was sitting, stolid, blank, but not unhappy, over his unfinished tasks, she would snatch her opportunity in the Doctor's absence, go over to him, put her arms about his neck, lay her cheek to his, and communicate her sympathy with his distress. "Do not mind," she would say; "I, too, am not at all clever, and I can assure you that it makes no difference in life."

The Doctor's view was naturally different. That gentleman never wearied of the sound of his own voice, which was, to say the truth, agreeable enough to hear. He now had a listener, who was not so cynically indifferent as Anastasie, and who sometimes put him on his mettle by the most relevant objections. Besides, was he not educating the boy? And education, philosophers are agreed, is the most philosophical of duties. What can be more heavenly to poor mankind than to have one's hobby grow into a duty to the State? Then, indeed, do the ways of life become ways of pleasantness. Never had the Doctor seen reason to be more content with his endowments. Philosophy flowed smoothly from his lips. He was so agile a dialectician that he could trace his nonsense, when challenged, back to some root in sense, and prove it to be a sort of flower upon his system. He slipped out of antinomies like a fish, and left his disciple marvelling at the rabbi's depth.

Moreover, deep down in his heart the Doctor was disappointed with the ill-success of his more formal education. A boy, chosen by so acute an observer for his aptitude, and guided along the path of learning by so philosophic an instructor, was bound, by the nature of the universe, to make a more obvious and lasting advance. Now Jean-Marie was slow in all things, impenetrable in others; and his power of forgetting was fully on a level with his power to learn. Therefore the Doctor cherished his peripatetic lectures, to which the boy attended, which he generally appeared to enjoy, and by which he often profited.

Many and many were the talks they had together; and health and moderation proved the subject of the Doctor's divagations. To these he lovingly returned.

"I lead you," he would say, "by the green pastures. My system, my beliefs, my medicines, are resumed in one phrase—to avoid excess. Blessed nature, healthy, temperate nature, abhors and exterminates excess. Human law, in this matter, imitates at a great distance her provisions; and we must strive to supplement the efforts of the law. Yes, boy, we must be a law to ourselves and for our neighbours—*lex armata* —armed, emphatic, tyrannous law. If you see a crapulous human ruin snuffing, dash him from his box! The judge, though in a way an admission of disease, is less offensive to me than either the doctor or the priest. Above all the doctor —the doctor and the purulent trash and garbage of his pharmacopœia! Pure air—from the neighbourhood of a pinetum for the sake of the turpentine—unadulterated wine, and the reflections of an unsophisticated spirit in the presence of the works of nature—these, my boy, are the best medical appliances and the best religious comforts. Devote yourself to these. Hark! there are the bells of Bourron (the wind is in the north, it will be fair). How clear and airy is the sound! The nerves are harmonised and quieted; the mind attuned to silence; and observe how easily and regularly beats the heart! Your unenlightened doctor would see nothing in these sensations; and yet you yourself perceive they are a part of health.—Did you remember your cinchona this morning? Good. Cinchona also is a work of nature: it is, after all, only the bark of a tree which we might gather for ourselves if we lived in the locality.—What a world is this! Though a professed atheist, I delight to bear my testimony to the world. Look at the gratuitous remedies and pleasures that surround our path! The river runs by the garden end, our bath, our fish-pond, our natural system of drainage. There is a well in the court which sends up sparkling water from the earth's very heart, clean, cool, and, with a little wine, most wholesome. The district is notorious for its salubrity; rheumatism is the only prevalent complaint, and I myself, have never had a touch of it. I tell you—and my opinion is based upon the coldest, clearest processes of reason—if I, if you, desired to leave this home of pleasures, it would be the duty, it would be the privilege, of our best friend to prevent us with a pistol bullet."

One beautiful June day they sat upon the hill outside the village. The river, as blue as heaven, shone here and there among the foliage. The indefatigable birds turned and flickered about Gretz church-tower. A healthy wind blew from over the forest, and the sound of innumerable thousands of tree-tops and innumerable millions on millions of green leaves was abroad in the air, and filled the ear with something between whispered speech and singing. It seemed as if every blade of grass must hide a cigale; and the fields rang merrily with their music, jingling far and near as with the sleigh-bells of the fairy queen. From their station on the slope the eye embraced a large space of poplar'd plain upon the one hand, the waving hill-tops of the forest on the other, and Gretz itself in the middle, a handful of roofs. Under the bestriding arch of the blue heavens, the place seemed dwindled to a toy. It seemed incredible that people dwelt, and could find room to turn or air to breathe, in such a corner of the world. The thought came home to the boy, perhaps for the first time, and he gave it words.

"How small it looks!" he sighed.

"Ay," replied the Doctor, "small enough now. Yet it was once a walled city; thriving, full of furred burgesses and men in armour, humming with affairs;—with tall spires, for aught that I know, and portly towers along the battlements. A thousand chimneys ceased smoking at the curfew bell. There were gibbets at the gate as thick as scarecrows. In time of war, the assault swarmed against it with ladders, the arrows fell like leaves, the defenders sallied hotly over the drawbridge, each side uttered its cry as they plied their weapons. Do you know that the walls extended as far as the Commanderie? Tradition so reports. Alas, what a long way off is all this confusion—nothing left of it but my quiet words spoken in your ear—and the town itself shrunk to the hamlet underneath us! By and by came the English wars—you shall hear more of the English, a stupid people, who sometimes blundered into good—and Gretz was taken, sacked, and burned. It is the history of many towns; but Gretz never rose again; it was never rebuilt; its ruins were a quarry to serve the growth of rivals; and the stones of Gretz are now erect along the streets of Nemours. It gratifies me that our old house was the first to rise after the calamity; when the town had come to an end, it inaugurated the hamlet."

"I, too, am glad of that," said Jean-Marie.

"It should be the temple of the humbler vir-

tues," responded the Doctor with a savoury gusto. "Perhaps one of the reasons why I love my little hamlet as I do, is that we have a similar history, she and I. Have I told you that I was once rich?"

"I do not think so," answered Jean-Marie. "I do not think I should have forgotten. I am sorry you should have lost your fortune."

"Sorry?" cried the Doctor. "Why, I find I have scarce begun your education after all. Listen to me! Would you rather live in the old Gretz or in the new, free from the alarms of war, with the green country at the door, without noise, passports, the exactions of the soldiery, or the jangle of the curfew bell to send us off to bed by sundown?"

"I suppose I should prefer the new," replied the boy.

"Precisely," returned the Doctor; "so do I. And, in the same way, I prefer my present moderate fortune to my former wealth. Golden mediocrity! cried the adorable ancients; and I subscribe to their enthusiasm. Have I not good wine, good food, good air, the fields and the forest for my walk, a house, an admirable wife, a boy whom I protest I cherish like a son? Now, if I were still rich, I should indubitably make my residence in Paris—you know Paris—Paris and Paradise are not convertible terms. This pleasant noise of the wind streaming among leaves changed into the grinding Babel of the street, the stupid glare of plaster substituted for this quiet pattern of greens and greys, the nerves shattered, the digestion falsified—picture the fall! Already you perceive the consequences; the mind is stimulated, the heart steps to a different measure, and the man is himself no longer. I have passionately studied myself—the true business of philosophy. I know my character as the musician knows the ventages of his flute. Should I return to Paris, I should ruin myself gambling; nay, I go further—I should break the heart of my Anastasie with infidelities."

This was too much for Jean-Marie. That a place should so transform the most excellent of men transcended his belief. Paris, he protested, was even an agreeable place of residence. "Nor when I lived in that city did I feel much difference," he pleaded.

"What!" cried the Doctor: "Did you not steal when you were there?"

But the boy could never be brought to see that he had done anything wrong when he stole. Nor, indeed, did the Doctor think he had; but that gentleman was never very scrupulous when in want of a retort.

"And now," he concluded, "do you begin to understand? My only friends were those who ruined me. Gretz has been my academy, my sanatorium, my heaven of innocent pleasures. If millions are offered me, I wave them back: *Retro, Sathanas!*—evil one, begone! Fix your mind on my example; despise riches, avoid the debasing influence of cities. Hygiene—hygiene and mediocrity of fortune—these be your watchwords during life!"

The Doctor's system of hygiene strikingly coincided with his tastes; and his picture of the perfect life was a faithful description of the one he was leading at the time. But it is easy to convince a boy, whom you supply with all the facts for the discussion. And besides, there was one thing admirable in the philosophy, and that was the enthusiasm of the philosopher. There was never any one more vigorously determined to be pleased; and if he was not a great logician, and so had no right to convince the intellect, he was certainly something of a poet, and had a fascination to seduce the heart. What he could not achieve in his customary humour of a radiant admiration of himself and his circumstances, he sometimes effected in his fits of gloom.

"Boy," he would say, "avoid me to-day. If I were superstitious, I should even beg for an interest in your prayers. I am in the black fit; the evil spirit of King Saul, the hag of the merchant Abudah, the personal devil of the mediæval monk, is with me—is in me," tapping on his breast. "The vices of my nature are now uppermost; innocent pleasures woo me in vain; I long for Paris, for my wallowing in the mire. See," he would continue, producing a handful of silver, "I denude myself, I am not to be trusted with the price of a fare. Take it, keep it for me, squander it on deleterious candy, throw it in the deepest of the river—I will homologate your action. Save me from that part of myself which I disown. If you see me falter, do not hesitate; if necessary, wreck the train! I speak, of course, by a parable. Any extremity were better than for me to reach Paris alive."

Doubtless the Doctor enjoyed these little scenes, as a variation in his part; they represented the Byronic element in the somewhat artificial poetry of his existence; but to the boy, though he was dimly aware of their theatricality, they represented more. The Doctor made perhaps too little, the boy possibly too much, of the reality and gravity of these temptations.

One day a great light shone for Jean-Marie. "Could not riches be used well?" he asked.

"In theory, yes," replied the Doctor. "But it is found in experience that no one does so. All the world imagine they will be exceptional when they grow wealthy; but possession is debasing, new desires spring up; and the silly taste for ostentation eats out the heart of pleasure."

"Then you might be better if you had less," said the boy.

"Certainly not," replied the Doctor; but his voice quavered as he spoke.

"Why?" demanded pitiless innocence.

Doctor Desprez saw all the colours of the rainbow in a moment; the stable universe appeared to

be about capsizing with him. "Because," said he
—affecting deliberation after an obvious pause—
"because I have formed my life for my present
income. It is not good for men of my years to
be violently dissevered from their habits."

That was a sharp brush. The Doctor breathed
hard, and fell into taciturnity for the afternoon.
As for the boy, he was delighted with the resolution of his doubts; even wondered that he had
not foreseen the obvious and conclusive answer.
His faith in the Doctor was a stout piece of goods.
Desprez was inclined to be a sheet in the wind's
eye after dinner, especially after Rhone wine, his
favourite weakness. He would then remark on
the warmth of his feeling for Anastasie, and with
inflamed cheeks and a loose, flustered smile, de-
bate upon all sorts of topics, and be feebly and
indiscreetly witty. But the adopted stable-boy
would not permit himself to entertain a doubt
that savoured of ingratitude. It is quite true
that a man may be a second father to you, and
yet take too much to drink; but the best natures
are ever slow to accept such truths.

The Doctor thoroughly possessed his heart, but
perhaps he exaggerated his influence over his
mind. Certainly Jean-Marie adopted some of
his master's opinions, but I have yet to learn
that he ever surrendered one of his own. Con-
victions existed in him by divine right; they
were virgin, unwrought, the brute metal of decision. He could add others indeed, but he

could not put away; neither did he care if they were perfectly agreed among themselves; and his spiritual pleasures had nothing to do with turning them over or justifying them in words. Words were with him a mere accomplishment, like dancing. When he was by himself, his pleasures were almost vegetable. He would slip into the woods towards Achères, and sit in the mouth of a cave among grey birches. His soul stared straight out of his eyes; he did not move or think; sunlight, thin shadows moving in the wind, the edge of firs against the sky, occupied and bound his faculties. He was pure unity, a spirit wholly abstracted. A single mood filled him, to which all the objects of sense contributed, as the colours of the spectrum merge and disappear in white light.

So while the Doctor made himself drunk with words, the adopted stable-boy bemused himself with silence.

CHAPTER V

THE Doctor's carriage was a two-wheeled gig with a hood; a kind of vehicle in much favour among country doctors. On how many roads has one not seen it, a great way off between the poplars!—in how many village streets, tied to a gate-post! This sort of chariot is affected —particularly at the trot—by a kind of pitching movement to and fro across the axle, which well entitles it to the style of a noddy. The hood describes a considerable arc against the landscape, with a solemnly absurd effect on the contemplative pedestrian. To ride in such a carriage cannot be numbered among the things that appertain to glory; but I have no doubt it may be useful in liver complaint. Thence, perhaps, its wide popularity among physicians.

One morning early, Jean-Marie led forth the Doctor's noddy, opened the gate, and mounted to the driving-seat. The Doctor followed, arrayed from top to toe in spotless linen, armed with an immense flesh-coloured umbrella, and girt with a botanical case on a baldric; and the

equipage drove off smartly in a breeze of its own
provocation. They were bound for Franchard,
to collect plants, with an eye to the *Comparative
Pharmacopœia.*

A little rattling on the open roads, and they
came to the borders of the forest and struck into
an unfrequented track; the noddy yawed softly
over the sand, with an accompaniment of snapping twigs. There was a great, green, softly
murmuring cloud of congregated foliage overhead. In the arcades of the forest the air retained the freshness of the night. The athletic
bearing of the trees, each bearing its leafy mountain, pleased the mind like so many statues, and
the lines of the trunk led the eye admiringly up-
ward to where the extreme leaves sparkled in a
patch of azure. Squirrels leaped in mid-air. It
was a proper spot for a devotee of the goddess
Hygieia.

"Have you been to Franchard, Jean-Marie?"
inquired the Doctor. "I fancy not."

"Never," replied the boy.

"It is ruin in a gorge," continued Desprez,
adopting his expository voice; "the ruin of a
hermitage and chapel. History tells us much of
Franchard; how the recluse was often slain by
robbers; how he lived on a most insufficient diet;
how he was expected to pass his days in prayer.
A letter is preserved, addressed to one of these
solitaries by the superior of his order, full of admirable hygienic advice; bidding him go from

his book to praying, and so back again, for variety's sake, and when he was weary of both to stroll about his garden and observe the honey bees. It is to this day my own system. You must have often remarked me leaving the *Pharmacopœia*—often even in the middle of a phrase —to come forth into the sun and air. I admire the writer of that letter from my heart; he was a man of thought on the most important subjects. But, indeed, had I lived in the Middle Ages (I am heartily glad that I did not) I should have been an eremite myself—if I had not been a professed buffoon, that is. These were the only philosophical lives yet open: laughter or prayer; sneers, we might say, and tears. Until the sun of the Positive arose, the wise man had to make his choice between these two."

"I have been a buffoon, of course," observed Jean-Marie.

"I cannot imagine you to have excelled in your profession," said the Doctor, admiring the boy's gravity. "Do you ever laugh?"

"Oh, yes," replied the other. "I laugh often. I am very fond of jokes."

"Singular being!" said Desprez. "But I divagate (I perceive in a thousand ways that I grow old). Franchard was at length destroyed in the English wars, the same that levelled Gretz. But—here is the point—the hermits (for there were already more than one) had foreseen the danger and carefully concealed the sacrificial vessels. These vessels were of monstrous value, Jean-Marie — monstrous value — priceless, we may say; exquisitely worked, of exquisite material. And now, mark me, they have never been found. In the reign of Louis Quatorze some fellows were digging hard by the ruins. Suddenly—tock!—the spade hit upon an obstacle. Imagine the men looking one to another; imagine how their hearts bounded, how their colour came and went. It was a coffer, and in Franchard the place of buried treasure! They tore it open like famished beasts. Alas! it was not the treasure; only some priestly robes, which, at the touch of the eating air, fell upon themselves and instantly wasted into dust. The perspiration of these good fellows turned cold upon them, Jean-Marie. I will pledge my reputation, if there was anything like a cutting wind, one or other had a pneumonia for his trouble."

"I should like to have seen them turning into dust," said Jean-Marie. "Otherwise, I should not have cared so greatly."

"You have no imagination," cried the Doctor. "Picture to yourself the scene. Dwell on the idea—a great treasure lying in the earth for centuries: the material for a giddy, copious, opulent existence not employed; dresses and exquisite pictures unseen; the swiftest galloping horses not stirring a hoof, arrested by a spell; women with the beautiful faculty of smiles, not smiling; cards, dice, opera singing, orchestras, castles, beautiful parks and gardens, big ships with a tower of sailcloth, all lying unborn in a coffin—and the stupid trees growing overhead in the sunlight, year after year. The thought drives one frantic."

"It is only money," replied Jean-Marie. "It would do harm."

"Oh, come!" cried Desprez, "that is philosophy; it is all very fine, but not to the point just now. And besides, it is not 'only money,' as you call it; there are works of art in the question; the vessels were carved. You speak like a child. You weary me exceedingly, quoting my words out of all logical connection, like a parroquet."

"And at any rate, we have nothing to do with it," returned the boy submissively.

They struck the Route Ronde at that moment; and the sudden change to the rattling causeway combined, with the doctor's irritation, to keep him silent. The noddy jigged along; the trees went by, looking on silently, as if they had something on their minds. The Quadrilateral was passed; then came Franchard. They put up the horse at the little solitary inn, and went forth strolling; the gorge was dyed deeply with heather; the rocks and birches standing luminous in the sun. A great humming of bees about the flowers disposed Jean-Marie to sleep, and he sat down against a clump of heather, while the doctor went briskly to and fro, with quick turns, culling his simples.

The boy's head had fallen a little forward, his eyes were closed, his fingers had fallen lax about his knees, when a sudden cry called him to his feet. It was a strange sound, thin and brief; it fell dead, and silence returned as though it had never been interrupted. He had not recognised the Doctor's voice; but, as there was no one else in all the valley, it was plainly the Doctor who had given utterance to the sound. He looked right and left, and there was Desprez, standing in a niche between two boulders, and looking round on his adopted son with a countenance as white as paper.

"A viper!" cried Jean-Marie, running towards him. "A viper! You are bitten!"

The Doctor came down heavily out of the cleft, and advanced in silence to meet the boy, whom he took roughly by the shoulder.

"I have found it," he said, with a gasp.

"A plant?" asked Jean-Marie.

Desprez had a fit of unnatural gaiety, which the rocks took up and mimicked. "A plant!" he repeated scornfully. "Well—yes—a plant. And here," he added suddenly, showing his right hand, which he had hitherto concealed behind his back—"here is one of the bulbs."

Jean-Marie saw a dirty platter, coated with earth.

"That?" said he. "It is a plate!"

"It is a coach and horses," cried the Doctor. "Boy," he continued, growing warmer, "I pluck-

ed away a great pad of moss from between these
boulders, and disclosed a crevice; and when I
looked in, what do you suppose I saw? I saw a
house in Paris with a court and garden, I saw
my wife shining with diamonds, I saw myself a
deputy, I saw you—well, I—I saw your future,"
he concluded, rather feebly. "I have just discovered America," he added.

"But what is it?" asked the boy.

"The Treasure of Franchard," cried the Doctor; and, throwing his brown straw hat upon the
ground, he whooped like an Indian and sprang
upon Jean-Marie, whom he suffocated with em-
braces and bedewed with tears. Then he flung
himself down among the heather and once more
laughed until the valley rang.

But the boy had now an interest of his own, a
boy's interest. No sooner was he released from
the Doctor's accolade than he ran to the boulders,
sprang into the niche, and, thrusting his hand
into the crevice, drew forth one after another,
encrusted with the earth of ages, the flagons,
candlesticks and patens of the hermitage of
Franchard. A casket came last, tightly shut
and very heavy.

"Oh what fun, what fun!" he cried.

But when he looked back at the Doctor, who
had followed close behind and was silently observing, the words died from his lips. Desprez was
once more the colour of ashes; his lip worked and
trembled; a sort of bestial greed possessed him.

"This is childish," he said. "We lose precious time. Back to the inn, harness the trap, and bring it to yon bank. Run for your life, and remember—not one whisper. I stay here to watch."

Jean-Marie did as he was bid, though not without surprise. The noddy was brought round to the spot indicated; and the two gradually transported the treasure from its place of concealment to the boot below the driving-seat. Once it was all stored the Doctor recovered his gaiety.

"I pay my grateful duties to the genius of this dell," he said. "Oh, for a live coal, a heifer, and a jar of country wine! I am in the vein for sacrifice, for a superb libation. Well, and why not? We are at Franchard. English pale ale is to be had—not classical, indeed, but excellent. Boy, we shall drink ale."

"But I thought it was so unwholesome," said Jean-Marie, "and very dear besides."

"Fiddle-de-dee!" exclaimed the Doctor gaily. "To the inn!"

And he stepped into the noddy, tossing his head, with an elastic, youthful air. The horse was turned, and in a few seconds they drew up beside the palings of the inn garden.

"Here," said Desprez—"here, near the stable, so that we may keep an eye upon things."

They tied the horse, and entered the garden, the Doctor singing, now in fantastic high notes, now producing deep reverberations from his chest. He took a seat, rapped loudly on the table, assailed the waiter with witticisms; and when the bottle of Bass was at length produced, far more charged with gas than the most delirious champagne, he filled out a long glassful of froth and pushed it over to Jean-Marie. "Drink," he said; "drink deep."

"I would rather not," faltered the boy, true to his training.

"What?" thundered Desprez.

"I am afraid of it," said Jean-Marie; "my stomach——"

"Take it or leave it," interrupted Desprez fiercely; "but understand it once for all—there is nothing so contemptible as a precisian."

Here was a new lesson! The boy sat bemused, looking at the glass but not tasting it, while the Doctor emptied and refilled his own, at first with clouded brow, but gradually yielding to the sun, the heady, prickling beverage, and his own predisposition to be happy.

"Once in a way," he said at last, by way of a concession to the boy's more rigorous attitude, "once in a way, and at so critical a moment, this ale is a nectar for the gods. The habit, indeed, is debasing; wine, the juice of the grape, is the true drink of the Frenchman, as I have often had occasion to point out; and I do not know that I can blame you for refusing this outlandish stimulant. You can have some wine and cakes. Is

the bottle empty? Well, we will not be proud;
we will have pity on your glass."

The beer being done, the Doctor chafed bitterly
while Jean-Marie finished his cakes. "I burn to
be gone," he said, looking at his watch. "Good
God, how slow you eat!" And yet to eat slowly
was his own particular prescription, the main
secret of longevity!

His martyrdom, however, reached an end at
last; the pair resumed their places in the buggy,
and Desprez, leaning luxuriously back, announced his intention of proceeding to Fontainebleau.

"To Fontainebleau?" repeated Jean-Marie.

"My words are always measured," said the
Doctor. "On!"

The Doctor was driven through the glades of
paradise; the air, the light, the shining leaves,
the very movements of the vehicle, seemed to
fall in tune with his golden meditations; with his
head thrown back, he dreamed a series of sunny
visions, ale and pleasure dancing in his veins.
At last he spoke.

"I shall telegraph for Casimir," he said.
"Good Casimir! a fellow of the lower order of intelligence, Jean-Marie, distinctly not creative,
not poetic; and yet he will repay your study; his
fortune is vast, and is entirely due to his own
exertions. He is the very fellow to help us to
dispose of our trinkets, find us a suitable house
in Paris, and manage the details of our installa-

tion. Admirable Casimir, one of my oldest comrades! It was on his advice, I may add, that I invested my little fortune in Turkish bonds; when we have added these spoils of the mediæval church to our stake in the Mahometan empire, little boy, we shall positively roll among doubloons, positively roll! Beautiful forest," he cried, "farewell! Though called to other scenes, I will not forget thee. Thy name is graven in my heart. Under the influence of prosperity I become dithyrambic, Jean-Marie. Such is the impulse of the natural soul; such was the constitution of primæval man. And I— well, I will not refuse the credit—I have preserved my youth like a virginity; another, who should have led the same snoozing, countrified existence for these years, another had become rusted, become stereotyped; but I, I praise my happy constitution, retain the spring unbroken. Fresh opulence and a new sphere of duties find me unabated in ardour and only more mature by knowledge. For this prospective change, Jean-Marie—it may probably have shocked you. Tell me now, did it not strike you as an inconsistency? Confess—it is useless to dissemble —it pained you?"

"Yes," said the boy.

"You see," returned the Doctor, with sublime fatuity, "I read your thoughts! Nor am I surprised—your education is not yet complete; the higher duties of men have not been yet presented

to you fully. A hint—till we have leisure—
must suffice. Now that I am once more in possession of a modest competence; now that I have
so long prepared myself in silent meditation, it
becomes my superior duty to proceed to Paris.
My scientific training, my undoubted command
of language, mark me out for the service of my
country. Modesty in such a case would be a
snare. If sin were a philosophical expression, I
should call it sinful. A man must not deny his
manifest abilities, for that is to evade his obligations. I must be up and doing; I must be no
skulker in life's battle."

So he rattled on, copiously greasing the joint
of his inconsistency with words; while the boy
listened silently, his eyes fixed on the horse, his
mind seething. It was all lost eloquence; no
array of words could unsettle a belief of Jean-
Marie's; and he drove into Fontainebleau filled
with pity, horror, indignation, and despair.

In the town Jean-Marie was kept a fixture on
the driving-seat to guard the treasure; while the
Doctor, with a singular, slightly tipsy airiness of
manner, fluttered in and out of cafés, where he
shook hands with garrison officers, and mixed an
absinthe with the nicety of old experience; in and
out of shops, from which he returned laden with
costly fruits, real turtle, a magnificent piece of
silk for his wife, a preposterous cane for himself,
and a képi of the newest fashion for the boy; in
and out of the telegraph office, whence he des-

patched his telegram, and where three hours
later he received an answer promising a visit on
the morrow; and generally pervaded Fontainebleau with the first fine aroma of his divine good-
humour.

The sun was very low when they set forth
again; the shadows of the forest trees extended
across the broad white road that led them home;
the penetrating odour of the evening wood had
already arisen, like a cloud of incense, from that
broad field of tree-tops; and even in the streets
of the town, where the air had been baked all
day between white walls, it came in whiffs and
pulses, like a distant music. Half-way home,
the last gold flicker vanished from a great oak
upon the left; and when they came forth beyond
the borders of the wood, the plain was already
sunken in pearly greyness, and a great, pale
moon came swinging skyward through the filmy
poplars.

The Doctor sang, the Doctor whistled, the
Doctor talked. He spoke of the woods, and the
wars, and the deposition of dew; he brightened
and babbled of Paris; he soared into cloudy
bombast on the glories of the political arena.
All was to be changed; as the day departed, it
took with it the vestiges of an outworn existence,
and to-morrow's sun was to inaugurate the new.
"Enough," he cried, "of this life of maceration!"
His wife (still beautiful, or he was sadly partial)
was to be no longer buried; she should now shine

before society. Jean-Marie would find the world at his feet; the roads open to success, wealth, honour, and posthumous renown. "And oh, by the way," said he, "for God's sake keep your tongue quiet! You are, of course, a very silent fellow; it is a quality I gladly recognise in you—silence, golden silence! But this is a matter of gravity. No word must get abroad; none but the good Casimir is to be trusted; we shall probably dispose of the vessels in England."

"But are they not even ours?" the boy said, almost with a sob—it was the only time he had spoken.

"Ours in this sense, that they are nobody else's," replied the Doctor. "But the State would have some claim. If they were stolen, for instance, we should be unable to demand their restitution; we should have no title; we should be unable even to communicate with the police. Such is the monstrous condition of the law.[1] It is a mere instance of what remains to be done, of the injustices that may yet be righted by an ardent, active, and philosophical deputy."

Jean-Marie put his faith in Madame Desprez; and as they drove forward down the road from Bourron, between the rustling poplars, he prayed in his teeth, and whipped up the horse to an unusual speed. Surely, as soon as they arrived, madame would assert her character, and bring this waking nightmare to an end.

[1] Let it be so, for my tale!

Their entrance into Gretz was heralded and accompanied by a most furious barking; all the dogs in the village seemed to smell the treasure in the noddy. But there was no one in the street, save three lounging landscape-painters at Tentaillon's door. Jean-Marie opened the green gate and led in the horse and carriage; and almost at the same moment Madame Desprez came to the kitchen threshold with a lighted lantern; for the moon was not yet high enough to clear the garden walls.

"Close the gates, Jean-Marie!" cried the Doctor, somewhat unsteadily alighting.—"Anastasie, where is Aline?"

"She has gone to Montereau to see her parents," said madame.

"All is for the best!" exclaimed the Doctor fervently. "Here, quick, come near to me; I do not wish to speak too loud," he continued. "Darling, we are wealthy!"

"Wealthy!" repeated the wife.

"I have found the treasure of Franchard," replied her husband. "See, here are the first-fruits; a pineapple, a dress for my ever-beautiful —it will suit her—trust a husband's, trust a lover's, taste! Embrace me, darling! This grimy episode is over; the butterfly unfolds its painted wings. To-morrow Casimir will come; in a week we may be in Paris—happy at last! You shall have diamonds. Jean-Marie, take it out of the boot, with religious care, and bring

298

it piece by piece into the dining-room. We shall have plate at table! Darling, hasten and prepare this turtle; it will be a whet—it will be an addition to our meagre ordinary. I myself will proceed to the cellar. We shall have a bottle of that little Beaujolais you like, and finish with the Hermitage; there are still three bottles left. Worthy wine for a worthy occasion."

"But, my husband; you put me in a whirl," she cried. "I do not comprehend."

"The turtle, my adored, the turtle!" cried the Doctor; and he pushed her towards the kitchen, lantern and all.

Jean-Marie stood dumbfounded. He had pictured to himself a different scene—a more immediate protest, and his hope began to dwindle on the spot.

The Doctor was everywhere, a little doubtful on his legs, perhaps, and now and then taking the wall with his shoulder; for it was long since he had tasted absinthe, and he was even then reflecting that the absinthe had been a misconception. Not that he regretted excess on such a glorious day, but he made a mental memorandum to beware; he must not, a second time, become the victim of a deleterious habit. He had his wine out of the cellar in a twinkling; he arranged the sacrificial vessels, some on the white table-cloth, some on the sideboard, still crusted with historic earth. He was in and out of the kitchen, plying Anastasie with vermouth, heat-ing her with glimpses of the future, estimating their new wealth at ever larger figures; and before they sat down to supper, the lady's virtue had melted in the fire of his enthusiasm, her timidity had disappeared; she, too, had begun to speak disparagingly of the life at Gretz; and as she took her place and helped the soup, her eyes shone with the glitter of prospective diamonds.

All through the meal, she and the doctor made and unmade fairy plans. They bobbed and bowed and pledged each other. Their faces ran over with smiles; their eyes scattered sparkles, as they projected the doctor's political honours and the lady's drawing-room ovations.

"But you will not be a Red!" cried Anastasie.

"I am Left Centre to the core," replied the Doctor.

"Madame Gastein will present us—we shall find ourselves forgotten," said the lady.

"Never," protested the Doctor. "Beauty and talent leave a mark."

"I have positively forgotten how to dress," she sighed.

"Darling, you make me blush," cried he. "Yours has been a tragic marriage!"

"But your success—to see you appreciated, honoured, your name in all the papers, that will be more than pleasure—it will be heaven!" she cried.

"And once a week," said the Doctor, archly

scanning the syllables, "once a week—one good little game of baccarat?"

"Only once a week?" she questioned, threatening him with a finger.

"I swear it by my political honour," cried he.

"I spoil you," she said, and gave him her hand. He covered it with kisses.

Jean-Marie escaped into the night. The moon swung high over Gretz. He went down to the garden end and sat on the jetty. The river ran by with eddies of oily silver, and a low, monotonous song. Faint veils of mist moved among the poplars on the farther side. The reeds were quietly nodding. A hundred times already had the boy sat, on such a night, and watched the streaming river with untroubled fancy. And this perhaps was to be the last. He was to leave this familiar hamlet, this green, rustling country, this bright and quiet stream; he was to pass into the great city; his dear lady mistress was to move bedizened into saloons; his good, garrulous, kind-hearted master to become a brawling deputy; and both be lost for ever to Jean-Marie and their better selves. He knew his own defects; he knew he must sink into less and less consideration in the turmoil of a city life; sink more and more from the child into the servant. And he began dimly to believe the doctor's prophecies of evil. He could see a change in both. His generous incredulity failed him for this once; a child must have perceived that the Hermitage had completed what the absinthe had begun. If this were the first day, what would be the last? "If necessary, wreck the train," thought he, remembering the Doctor's parable. He looked round on the delightful scene; he drank deep of the charmed night air, laden with the scent of hay. "If necessary, wreck the train," he repeated. And he rose and returned to the house.

CHAPTER VI

A CRIMINAL INVESTIGATION
IN TWO PARTS

THE next morning there was a most unusual outcry in the Doctor's house. The last thing before going to bed, the Doctor had locked up some valuables in the dining-room cupboard; and behold, when he rose again, as he did about four o'clock, the cupboard had been broken open, and the valuables in question had disappeared. Madame and Jean-Marie were summoned from their rooms, and appeared in hasty toilettes; they found the Doctor raving, calling the heavens to witness and avenge his injury, pacing the room barefooted, with the tails of his night-shirt flirting as he turned.

"Gone!" he said: "the things are gone, the fortune gone! We are paupers once more. Boy! what do you know of this? Speak up, sir, speak up. Do you know of it? Where are they?" He had him by the arm, shaking him like a bag, and the boy's words, if he had any, were jolted forth in inarticulate murmurs. The Doctor, with a revulsion from his own violence,

303

set him down again. He observed Anastasie in tears. "Anastasie," he said, in quite an altered voice, "compose yourself, command your feelings. I would not have you give way to passion like the vulgar. This—this trifling accident must be lived down. Jean-Marie, bring me my smaller medicine chest. A gentle laxative is indicated."

And he dosed the family all round, leading the way himself with a double quantity. The wretched Anastasie, who had never been ill in the whole course of her existence, and whose soul recoiled from remedies, wept floods of tears as she sipped, and shuddered, and protested, and then was bullied and shouted at until she sipped again. As for Jean-Marie, he took his portion down with stoicism.

"I have given him a less amount," observed the Doctor, "his youth protecting him against emotion. And now that we have thus parried any morbid consequences, let us reason."

"I am so cold," wailed Anastasie.

"Cold!" cried the Doctor. "I give thanks to God that I am made of fierier material. Why, madame, a blow like this would set a frog into a transpiration. If you're cold, you can retire; and, by the way, you might throw me down my trousers. It is chilly for the legs."

"Oh, no!" protested Anastasie; "I will stay with you."

"Nay, madame, you shall not suffer for your devotion," said the Doctor. "I will myself fetch

you a shawl." And he went up-stairs and returned more fully clad and with an armful of
wraps for the shivering Anastasie. "And now,"
he resumed, "to investigate this crime. Let us
proceed by induction. Anastasie, do you know
anything that can help us?" Anastasie knew
nothing. "Or you, Jean-Marie?"

"Not I," replied the boy steadily.

"Good," returned the Doctor. "We shall now
turn our attention to the material evidences. (I
was born to be a detective; I have the eye and
the systematic spirit.) First, violence has been
employed. The door was broken open; and it
may be observed, in passing, that the lock was
dear indeed at what I paid for it: a crow to pluck
with Master Goguelat. Second, here is the
instrument employed, one of our own table-
knives, one of our best, my dear; which seems
to indicate no preparation on the part of the
gang—if gang it was. Thirdly, I observe that
nothing has been removed except the Franchard
dishes and the casket; our own silver has been
minutely respected. This is wily; it shows intelligence, a knowledge of the code, a desire to
avoid legal consequences. I argue from this
fact that the gang numbers persons of respectability—outward, of course, and merely outward,
as the robbery proves. But I argue, second,
that we must have been observed at Franchard
itself by some occult observer, and dogged
throughout the day with a skill and patience

that I venture to qualify as consummate. No ordinary man, no occasional criminal, would have shown himself capable of this combination. We have in our neighbourhood, it is far from improbable, a retired bandit of the highest order of intelligence."

"Good heaven!" cried the horrified Anastasie. "Henri, how can you!"

"My cherished one, this is a process of induction," said the Doctor. "If any of my steps are unsound, correct me. You are silent? Then do not, I beseech you, be so vulgarly illogical as to revolt from my conclusion. We have now arrived," he resumed, "at some idea of the composition of the gang—for I incline to the hypothesis of more than one—and we now leave this room, which can disclose no more, and turn our attention to the court and garden. (Jean-Marie, I trust you are observantly following my various steps; this is an excellent piece of education for you.) Come with me to the door. No steps on the court; it is unfortunate our court should be paved. On what small matters hangs the destiny of these delicate investigations! Hey! What have we here? I have led you to the very spot," he said, standing grandly backward and indicating the green gate. "An escalade, as you can now see for yourselves, has taken place."

Sure enough, the green paint was in several places scratched and broken; and one of the panels preserved the print of a nailed shoe. The foot had slipped, however, and it was difficult to estimate the size of the shoe, and impossible to distinguish the pattern of the nails.

"The whole robbery," concluded the Doctor, "step by step, has been reconstituted. Inductive science can no further go."

"It is wonderful," said his wife. "You should indeed have been a detective, Henri. I had no idea of your talents."

"My dear," replied Desprez, condescendingly, "a man of scientific imagination combines the lesser faculties; he is a detective just as he is a publicist or a general; these are but local applications of his special talent. But now," he continued, "would you have me go further? Would you have me lay my finger on the culprits—or rather, for I cannot promise quite so much, point out to you the very house where they consort? It may be a satisfaction, at least it is all we are likely to get, since we are denied the remedy of law. I reach the further stage in this way. In order to fill my outline of the robbery, I require a man of education, I require a man superior to considerations of morality. The three requisites all centre in Tentaillon's boarders. They are painters, therefore they are continually lounging in the forest. They are painters, therefore they are not unlikely to have some smattering of education. Lastly, because they are painters, they are probably immoral. And this

307

I prove in two ways. First, painting is an art which merely addresses the eye; it does not in any particular exercise the moral sense. And second, painting, in common with all the other arts, implies the dangerous quality of imagination. A man of imagination is never moral; he outsoars literal demarcations and reviews life under too many shifting lights to rest content with the invidious distinctions of the law!"

"But you always say—at least, so I understood you"—said madame, "that these lads display no imagination whatever."

"My dear, they displayed imagination, and of a very fantastic order, too," returned the Doctor, "when they embraced their beggarly profession. Besides—and this is an argument exactly suited to your intellectual level—many of them are English and American. Where else should we expect to find a thief?—And now you had better get your coffee. Because we have lost a treasure, there is no reason for starving. For my part, I shall break my fast with white wine. I feel unaccountably heated and thirsty to-day. I can only attribute it to the shock of the discovery. And yet, you will bear me out, I supported the emotion nobly."

The Doctor had now talked himself back into an admirable humour; and as he sat in the arbour and slowly imbibed a large allowance of white wine and picked a little bread and cheese with no very impetuous appetite, if a third of his meditations ran upon the missing treasure, the other two-thirds were more pleasingly busied in the retrospect of his detective skill.

About eleven Casimir arrived; he had caught an early train to Fontainebleau, and driven over to save time; and now his cab was stabled at Tentaillon's, and he remarked, studying his watch, that he could spare an hour and a half. He was much the man of business, decisively spoken, given to frowning in an intellectual manner. Anastasie's born brother, he did not waste much sentiment on the lady, gave her an English family kiss, and demanded a meal without delay.

"You can tell me your story while we eat," he observed. "Anything good to-day, Stasie?"

He was promised something good. The trio sat down to table in the arbour, Jean-Marie waiting as well as eating, and the Doctor recounted what had happened in his richest narrative manner. Casimir heard it with explosions of laughter.

"What a streak of luck for you, my good brother," he observed, when the tale was over. "If you had gone to Paris, you would have played dick-duck-drake with the whole consignment in three months. Your own would have followed; and you would have come to me in a procession like the last time. But I give you warning—Stasie may weep and Henri ratiocinate—it will not serve you twice. Your next collapse will be fatal. I thought I had told you so, Stasie? Hey? No sense?"

The Doctor winced and looked furtively at Jean-Marie; but the boy seemed apathetic.

"And then again," broke out Casimir, "what children you are—vicious children, my faith! How could you tell the value of this trash? It might have been worth nothing, or next door."

"Pardon me," said the Doctor. "You have your usual flow of spirits, I perceive, but even less than your usual deliberation. I am not entirely ignorant of these matters."

"Not entirely ignorant of anything ever I heard of," interrupted Casimir, bowing, and raising his glass with a sort of pert politeness.

"At least," resumed the Doctor, "I gave my mind to the subject—that you may be willing to believe—and I estimated that our capital would be doubled." And he described the nature of the find.

"My word of honour!" said Casimir, "I half believe you! But much would depend on the quality of the gold."

"The quality, my dear Casimir, was——" And the Doctor, in default of language, kissed his finger-tips.

"I would not take your word for it, my good friend," retorted the man of business. "You are a man of very rosy views. But this robbery," he continued—"this robbery is an odd thing. Of course I pass over your nonsense about gangs and landscape-painters. For me, that is a dream. Who was in the house last night?"

"None but ourselves," replied the Doctor.

"And this young gentleman?" asked Casimir, jerking a nod in the direction of Jean-Marie.

"He too"— the Doctor bowed.

"Well; and if it is a fair question, who is he?" pursued the brother-in-law.

"Jean-Marie," answered the Doctor, "combines the functions of a son and stable-boy. He began as the latter, but he rose rapidly to the more honourable rank in our affections. He is, I may say, the greatest comfort in our lives."

"Ha!" said Casimir. "And previous to becoming one of you?"

"Jean-Marie has lived a remarkable existence; his experience has been eminently formative," replied Desprez. "If I had to choose an education for my son, I should have chosen such another. Beginning life with mountebanks and thieves, passing onward to the society and friendship of philosophers, he may be said to have skimmed the volume of human life."

"Thieves?" repeated the brother-in-law, with a meditative air.

The Doctor could have bitten his tongue out. He foresaw what was coming, and prepared his mind for a vigorous defence.

"Did you ever steal yourself?" asked Casimir, turning suddenly on Jean-Marie, and for the first time employing a single eyeglass which hung round his neck.

"Yes, sir," replied the boy, with a deep blush.

Casimir turned to the others with pursed lips, and nodded to them meaningly. "Hey?" said he; "how is that?"

"Jean-Marie is a teller of the truth," returned the Doctor, throwing out his bust.

"He has never told a lie," added madame. "He is the best of boys."

"Never told a lie, has he not?" reflected Casimir. "Strange, very strange. Give me your attention, my young friend," he continued. "You knew about this treasure?"

"He helped to bring it home," interposed the Doctor.

"Desprez, I ask you nothing but to hold your tongue," returned Casimir. "I mean to question this stable-boy of yours; and if you are so certain of his innocence, you can afford to let him answer for himself. Now, sir," he resumed, pointing his eyeglass straight at Jean-Marie. "You knew it could be stolen with impunity? You knew you could not be prosecuted? Come! Did you, or did you not?"

"I did," answered Jean-Marie, in a miserable whisper. He sat there changing colour like a revolving pharos, twisting his fingers hysterically, swallowing air, the picture of guilt.

"You knew where it was put?" resumed the inquisitor.

"Yes," from Jean-Marie.

"You say you have been a thief before," continued Casimir. "Now how am I to know that you are not one still? I suppose you could climb the green gate?"

"Yes," still lower, from the culprit.

"Well, then, it was you who stole these things. You know it, and you dare not deny it. Look me in the face! Raise your sneak's eyes, and answer!"

But in place of anything of that sort Jean-Marie broke into a dismal howl and fled from the arbour. Anastasie, as she pursued to capture and reassure the victim, found time to send one Parthian arrow—"Casimir, you are a brute!"

"My brother," said Desprez, with the greatest dignity, "you take upon yourself a license——"

"Desprez," interrupted Casimir, "for Heaven's sake be a man of the world. You telegraph me to leave my business and come down here on yours. I come, I ask the business, you say 'Find me this thief!' Well, I find him; I say 'There he is!' You need not like it, but you have no manner of right to take offence."

"Well," returned the Doctor, "I grant that; I will even thank you for your mistaken zeal. But your hypothesis was so extravagantly monstrous——"

"Look here," interrupted Casimir; "was it you or Stasie?"

"Certainly not," answered the Doctor.

313

"Very well; then it was the boy. Say no more about it," said the brother-in-law, and he produced his cigar-case.

"I will say this much more," returned Desprez: "if that boy came and told me so himself, I should not believe him; and if I did believe him, so implicit is my trust, I should conclude that he had acted for the best."

"Well, well," said Casimir, indulgently. "Have you a light? I must be going. And by the way, I wish you would let me sell your Turks for you. I always told you, it meant smash. I tell you so again. Indeed, it was partly that which brought me down. You never acknowledged my letters—a most unpardonable habit."

"My good brother," replied the Doctor blandly, "I have never denied your ability in business; but I can perceive your limitations."

"Egad, my friend, I can return the compliment," observed the man of business. "Your limitation is to be downright irrational."

"Observe the relative position," returned the Doctor, with a smile. "It is your attitude to believe through thick and thin in one man's judgment—your own. I follow the same opinion, but critically and with open eyes. Which is the more irrational?—I leave it to yourself."

"Oh, my dear fellow!" cried Casimir, "stick to your Turks, stick to your stable-boy, go to the devil in general in your own way and be done with it. But don't ratiocinate with me—I can-

not bear it. And so, ta-ta. I might as well
have stayed away for any good I've done. Say
good-bye from me to Stasie, and to the sullen
hang-dog of a stable-boy, if you insist on it; I'm
off."

And Casimir departed. The Doctor, that
night, dissected his character before Anastasie.
"One thing, my beautiful," he said, "he has
learned one thing from his lifelong acquaintance
with your husband: the word *ratiocinate*. It
shines in his vocabulary, like a jewel in a muck-
heap. And, even so, he continually misapplies
it. For you must have observed he uses it as a
sort of taunt, in the case of *to ergotise*, implying,
as it were—the poor, dear fellow!—a vein of sophistry. As for his cruelty to Jean-Marie, it
must be forgiven him—it is not his nature, it is
the nature of his life. A man who deals with
money, my dear, is a man lost."

With Jean-Marie the process of reconciliation
had been somewhat slow. At first he was incon-
solable, insisted on leaving the family, went from
paroxysm to paroxysm of tears; and it was only
after Anastasie had been closeted for an hour
with him, alone, that she came forth, sought out
the Doctor, and, with tears in her eyes, acquainted that gentleman with what had passed.

"At first, my husband, he would hear of nothing," she said. "Imagine! if he had left us!
what would the treasure be to that? Horrible
treasure, it has brought all this about! At last,

after he has sobbed his very heart out, he agrees to stay on a condition—we are not to mention this matter, this infamous suspicion, not even to mention the robbery. On that agreement only, the poor, cruel boy will consent to remain among his friends."

"But this inhibition," said the Doctor, "this embargo—it cannot possibly apply to me?"

"To all of us," Anastasie assured him.

"My cherished one," Desprez protested, "you must have misunderstood. It cannot apply to me. He would naturally come to me."

"Henri," she said, "it does; I swear to you it does."

"This is a painful, a very painful circumstance," the Doctor said, looking a little black. "I cannot affect, Anastasie, to be anything but justly wounded. I feel this, I feel it, my wife, acutely."

"I knew you would," she said. "But if you had seen his distress! We must make allowances, we must sacrifice our feelings."

"I trust, my dear, you have never found me averse to sacrifices," returned the Doctor very stiffly.

"And you will let me go and tell him that you have agreed? It will be like your noble nature," she cried.

So it would, he perceived—it would be like his noble nature! Up jumped his spirits, triumphant at the thought. "Go, darling," he said nobly, "reassure him. The subject is buried; more—I make an effort, I have accustomed my will to these exertions—and it is forgotten."

A little after, but still with swollen eyes and looking mortally sheepish, Jean-Marie reappeared and went ostentatiously about his business. He was the only unhappy member of the party that sat down that night to supper. As for the Doctor, he was radiant. He thus sang the requiem of the treasure:—

"This has been, on the whole, a most amusing episode," he said. "We are not a penny the worse—nay, we are immensely gainers. Our philosophy has been exercised; some of the turtle is still left—the most wholesome of delicacies; I have my staff, Anastasie has her new dress, Jean-Marie is the proud possessor of a fashionable képi. Besides, we had a glass of Hermitage last night; the glow still suffuses my memory. I was growing positively niggardly with that Hermitage, positively niggardly. Let me take the hint: we had one bottle to celebrate the appearance of our visionary fortune; let us have a second to console us for its occultation. The third I hereby dedicate to Jean-Marie's wedding breakfast."

CHAPTER VII

THE FALL OF THE HOUSE OF DESPREZ

THE Doctor's house has not yet received the compliment of a description, and it is now high time that the omission were supplied, for the house is itself an actor in the stories, and one whose part is nearly at an end. Two stories in height, walls of a warm yellow, tiles of an ancient ruddy brown diversified with moss and lichen, it stood with one wall to the street in the angle of the Doctor's property. It was roomy, draughty, and inconvenient. The large rafters were here and there engraven with rude marks and patterns; the hand-rail of the stair was carved in countrified arabesque; a stout timber pillar, which did duty to support the dining-room roof, bore mysterious characters on its darker side, runes, according to the Doctor; nor did he fail, when he ran over the legendary history of the house and its possessors, to dwell upon the Scandinavian scholar who had left them. Floors, doors, and rafters made a great variety of angles; every room had a particular inclination; the gable had tilted towards the garden, after the manner of a leaning tower, and one of the former proprietors had buttressed the building from that side with a great strut of wood, like the derrick of a crane. Altogether, it had many marks of ruin; it was a house for the rats to desert; and nothing but its excellent brightness—the window-glass polished and shining, the paint well scoured, the brasses radiant, the very prop all wreathed about with climbing flowers—nothing but its air of a well-tended, smiling veteran, sitting, crutch and all, in the sunny corner of a garden, marked it as a house for comfortable people to inhabit. In poor or idle management it would soon have hurried into the blackguard stages of decay. As it was, the whole family loved it, and the Doctor was never better inspired than when he narrated its imaginary story and drew the character of its successive masters, from the Hebrew merchant who had re-edified its walls after the sack of the town, and past the mysterious engraver of the runes, down to the long-headed, dirty-handed boor from whom he had himself acquired it at a ruinous expense. As for any alarm about its security, the idea had never presented itself. What had stood four centuries might well endure a little longer.

Indeed, in this particular winter, after the finding and losing of the treasure, the Desprez had an anxiety of a very different order, and one which lay nearer their hearts. Jean-Marie was plainly not himself. He had fits of hectic activity, when he made unusual exertions to please, spoke more and faster, and redoubled in attention to his lessons. But these were interrupted by spells of melancholia and brooding silence, when the boy was little better than unbearable.

"Silence," the Doctor moralised—"you see, Anastasie, what comes of silence. Had the boy properly unbosomed himself, the little disappointment about the treasure, the little annoyance about Casimir's incivility, would long ago have been forgotten. As it is, they prey upon him like a disease. He loses flesh, his appetite is variable, and, on the whole, impaired. I keep him on the strictest regimen, I exhibit the most powerful tonics; both in vain."

"Don't you think you drug him too much?" asked madame, with an irrepressible shudder.

"Drug?" cried the Doctor; "I drug? Anastasie, you are mad!"

Time went on, and the boy's health still slowly declined. The Doctor blamed the weather, which was cold and boisterous. He called in his *confrère* from Bourron, took a fancy for him, magnified his capacity, and was pretty soon under treatment himself—it scarcely appeared for what complaint. He and Jean-Marie had each medicine to take at different periods of the day. The Doctor used to lie in wait for the exact moment, watch in hand. "There is nothing like regularity," he would say, fill out the doses, and dilate on the virtues of the draught; and if the boy seemed none the better, the Doctor was not at all the worse.

Gunpowder Day, the boy was particularly low. It was scowling, squally weather. Huge broken companies of cloud sailed swiftly overhead; raking gleams of sunlight swept the village, and were followed by intervals of darkness and white, flying rain. At times the wind lifted up its voice and bellowed. The trees were all scourging themselves along the meadows, the last leaves flying like-dust.

The Doctor, between the boy and the weather, was in his element; he had a theory to prove. He sat with his watch out and a barometer in front of him, waiting for the squalls and noting their effect upon the human pulse. "For the true philosopher," he remarked delightedly, "every fact in nature is a toy." A letter came to him; but, as its arrival coincided with the approach of another gust, he merely crammed it into his pocket, gave the time to Jean-Marie, and the next moment they were both counting their pulses as if for a wager.

At nightfall the wind rose into a tempest. It besieged the hamlet, apparently from every side, as if with batteries of cannon; the houses shook and groaned; live coals were blown upon the floor. The uproar and terror of the night kept people long awake, sitting with pallid faces giving ear.

It was twelve before the Desprez family retired. By half-past one, when the storm was already somewhat past its height, the Doctor was awakened from a troubled slumber, and sat up. A noise still rang in his ears, but whether of this world or the world of dreams he was not certain. Another clap of wind followed. It was accompanied by a sickening movement of the whole house, and in the subsequent lull Desprez could hear the tiles pouring like a cataract into the loft above his head. He plucked Anastasie bodily out of bed.

"Run!" he cried, thrusting some wearing apparel into her hands; "the house is falling! To the garden!"

She did not pause to be twice bidden; she was down the stair in an instant. She had never before suspected herself of such activity. The Doctor meanwhile, with the speed of a piece of pantomime business, and undeterred by broken shins, proceeded to rout out Jean-Marie, tore Aline from her virgin slumbers, seized her by the hand, and tumbled down-stairs and into the garden, with the girl tumbling behind him, still not half awake.

The fugitives rendezvoused in the arbour by some common instinct. Then came a bull's-eye flash of struggling moonshine, which disclosed their four figures standing huddled from the wind in a raffle of flying drapery, and not without a considerable need for more. At the humiliating spectacle Anastasie clutched her

322

night-dress desperately about her and burst loudly into tears. The Doctor flew to console her; but she elbowed him away. She suspected everybody of being the general public, and thought the darkness was alive with eyes.

Another gleam and another violent gust arrived together; the house was seen to rock on its foundation, and, just as the light was once more eclipsed, a crash which triumphed over the shouting of the wind announced its fall, and for a moment the whole garden was alive with skipping tiles and brickbats. One such missile grazed the Doctor's ear; another descended on the bare foot of Aline, who instantly made night hideous with her shrieks.

By this time the hamlet was alarmed, lights flashed from the windows, hails reached the party, and the Doctor answered, nobly contending against Aline and the tempest. But this prospect of help only awakened Anastasie to a more active stage of terror.

"Henri, people will be coming," she screamed in her husband's ear.

"I trust so," he replied.

"They cannot. I would rather die," she wailed.

"My dear," said the Doctor reprovingly, "you are excited. I gave you some clothes. What have you done with them?"

"Oh, I don't know—I must have thrown them away! Where are they?" she sobbed.

Desprez groped about in the darkness. "Admirable!" he remarked; "my grey velveteen trousers! This will exactly meet your necessities."

"Give them to me!" she cried fiercely; but as soon as she had them in her hands her mood appeared to alter—she stood silent for a moment, and then pressed the garment back upon the Doctor. "Give it to Aline," she said—"poor girl."

"Nonsense!" said the Doctor. "Aline does not know what she is about. Aline is beside herself with terror; and at any rate, she is a peasant. Now I am really concerned at this exposure for a person of your housekeeping habits; my solicitude and your fantastic modesty both point to the same remedy—the pantaloons." He held them ready.

"It is impossible. You do not understand," she said with dignity.

By this time rescue was at hand. It had been found impracticable to enter by the street, for the gate was blocked with masonry, and the nodding ruin still threatened further avalanches. But between the Doctor's garden and the one on the right hand there was that very picturesque contrivance—a common well; the door on the Desprez side had chanced to be unbolted, and now, through the arched aperture a man's bearded face and an arm supporting a lantern were introduced into the world of windy darkness, where Anastasie concealed her woes. The light struck here and there among the tossing apple boughs, it glinted on the grass; but the lantern and the glowing face became the centre of the world. Anastasie crouched back from the intrusion.

"This way!" shouted the man. "Are you all safe?"

Aline, still screaming, ran to the newcomer, and was presently hauled head-foremost through the wall.

"Now, Anastasie, come on; it is your turn," said the husband.

"I cannot," she replied.

"Are we all to die of exposure, madame?" thundered Doctor Desprez.

"You can go!" she cried. "Oh, go, go away! I can stay here; I am quite warm."

The Doctor took her by the shoulders with an oath.

"Stop!" she screamed. "I will put them on."

She took the detested lendings in her hand once more; but her repulsion was stronger than shame. "Never!" she cried, shuddering, and flung them far away into the night.

Next moment the Doctor had whirled her to the well. The man was there and the lantern; Anastasie closed her eyes and appeared to herself to be about to die. How she was transported through the arch she knew not; but once on the other side she was received by the neighbour's wife, and enveloped in a friendly blanket.

Beds were made ready for the two women, clothes of very various sizes for the Doctor and Jean-Marie; and for the remainder of the night, while madame dozed in and out on the borderland of hysterics, her husband sat beside the fire and held forth to the admiring neighbours. He showed them, at length, the causes of the accident; for years, he explained, the fall had been impending; one sign had followed another, the joints had opened, the plaster had cracked, the old walls bowed inward; last, not three weeks ago, the cellar-door had begun to work with difficulty in its grooves. "The cellar!" he said, gravely shaking his head over a glass of mulled wine. "That reminds me of my poor vintages. By a manifest providence the Hermitage was nearly at an end. One bottle—I lose but one bottle of that incomparable wine. It had been set apart against Jean-Marie's wedding. Well, I must lay down some more; it will be an interest in life. I am, however, a man somewhat advanced in years. My great work is now buried in the fall of my humble roof; it will never be completed—my name will have been writ in water. And yet you find me calm—I would say cheerful. Can your priest do more?"

By the first glimpse of day the party sallied forth from the fireside into the street. The wind had fallen, but still charioted a world of troubled clouds; the air bit like frost; and the party, as they stood about the ruins in the rainy twilight of the morning, beat upon their breasts and blew into their hands for warmth. The house had entirely fallen, the walls outward, the roof in; it was a mere heap of rubbish, with here and there a forlorn spear of broken rafter. A sentinel was placed over the ruins to protect the property, and the party adjourned to Tentaillon's to break their fast at the Doctor's expense. The bottle circulated somewhat freely; and before they left the table it had begun to snow.

For three days the snow continued to fall, and the ruins, covered with tarpaulin and watched by sentries, were left undisturbed. The Desprez meanwhile had taken up their abode at Tentaillon's. Madame spent her time in the kitchen, concocting little delicacies, with the admiring aid of Madame Tentaillon, or sitting by the fire in thoughtful abstraction. The fall of the house affected her wonderfully little; that blow had been parried by another; and in her mind she was continually fighting over again the battle of the trousers. Had she done right? Had she done wrong? And now she would applaud her determination; and anon, with a horrid flush of unavailing penitence, she would regret the trousers. No juncture in her life had so much exercised her judgment. In the meantime the Doctor had become vastly pleased with his situation. Two of the summer boarders still lingered behind the rest, prisoners for lack of a remittance; they were both English, but one of them spoke French pretty fluently, and was, besides, a humorous, agile-minded fellow, with whom the Doctor could reason by the hour, secure of comprehension. Many were the glasses they emptied, many the topics they discussed.

"Anastasie," the Doctor said on the third morning, "take an example from your husband, from Jean-Marie. The excitement has done more for the boy than all my tonics, he takes his turn as sentry with positive gusto. As for me, you behold me. I have made friends with the Egyptians; and my Pharaoh is, I swear it, a most agreeable companion. You alone are hipped. About a house—a few dresses? What are they in comparison to the *Pharmacopœia* —the labour of years lying buried below stones and sticks in this depressing hamlet? The snow falls; I shake it from my cloak! Imitate me. Our income will be impaired, I grant it, since we must rebuild; but moderation, patience, and philosophy will gather about the hearth. In the meanwhile, the Tentaillons are obliging; the table, with your additions, will pass; only the wine is execrable—well, I shall send for some to-day. My Pharaoh will be gratified to drink a decent glass; aha! and I shall see if he possesses that acme of organisation—a palate. If he has a palate, he is perfect."

"Henri," she said, shaking her head, "you are a man; you cannot understand my feelings; no woman could shake off the memory of so public a humiliation."

The Doctor could not restrain a titter. "Pardon me, darling," he said; "but really, to the philosophical intelligence, the incident appears so small a trifle. You looked extremely well——"

"Henri!" she cried.

"Well, well, I will say no more," he replied. "Though, to be sure, if you had consented to indue—— *À propos,*" he broke off, "and my trousers! They are lying in the snow—my favourite trousers!" And he dashed in quest of Jean-Marie.

Two hours afterwards the boy returned to the inn with a spade under one arm and a curious sop of clothing under the other.

The Doctor ruefully took it in his hands. "They have been!" he said. "Their tense is past. Excellent pantaloons, you are no more! Stay! something in the pocket," and he produced a piece of paper. "A letter! ay, now I mind me; it was received on the morning of the gale, when I was absorbed in delicate investigations. It is still legible. From poor, dear Casimir! It is as well," he chuckled, "that I have educated him to patience. Poor Casimir and his correspondence—his infinitesimal, timorous, idiotic correspondence!"

He had by this time cautiously unfolded the

wet letter; but, as he bent himself to decipher the writing, a cloud descended on his brow.

"*Bigre!*" he cried, with a galvanic start.

And then the letter was whipped into the fire, and the Doctor's cap was on his head in the turn of a hand.

"Ten minutes! I can catch it, if I run," he cried. "It is always late. I go to Paris. I shall telegraph."

"Henri! what is wrong?" cried his wife.

"Ottoman Bonds!" came from the disappearing Doctor; and Anastasie and Jean-Marie were left face to face with the wet trousers. Desprez had gone to Paris, for the second time in seven years; he had gone to Paris with a pair of wooden shoes, a knitted spencer, a black blouse, a country nightcap, and twenty francs in his pocket. The fall of the house was but a secondary marvel; the whole world might have fallen and scarce left his family more petrified.

CHAPTER VIII

THE WAGES OF PHILOSOPHY

ON the morning of the next day, the Doctor, a mere spectre of himself, was brought back in the custody of Casimir. They found Anastasie and the boy sitting together by the fire; and Desprez, who had exchanged his toilette for a ready-made rig-out of poor materials, waved his hand as he entered, and sank speechless on the nearest chair. Madame turned direct to Casimir.

"What is wrong?" she cried.

"Well," replied Casimir, "what have I told you all along? It has come. It is a clean shave, this time; so you may as well bear up and make the best of it. House down, too, eh? Bad luck, upon my soul."

"Are we—are we—ruined?" she gasped.

The Doctor stretched out his arms to her. "Ruined," he replied, "you are ruined by your sinister husband."

Casimir observed the consequent embrace through his eyeglass; then he turned to Jean-Marie. "You hear?" he said. "They are ruin-

331

ed; no more pickings, no more house, no more fat cutlets. It strikes me, my friend, that you had best be packing; the present speculation is about worked out." And he nodded to him meaningly.

"Never!" cried Desprez, springing up. "Jean-Marie, if you prefer to leave me, now that I am poor, you can go; you shall receive your hundred francs, if so much remains to me. But if you will consent to stay"—the Doctor wept a little—"Casimir offers me a place—as clerk," he resumed. "The emoluments are slender, but they will be enough for three. It is too much already to have lost my fortune; must I lose my son?"

Jean-Marie sobbed bitterly, but without a word.

"I don't like boys who cry," observed Casimir. "This one is always crying. Here! you clear out of this for a little; I have business with your master and mistress, and these domestic feelings may be settled after I am gone. March!" and he held the door open.

Jean-Marie slunk out, like a detected thief.

By twelve they were all at table but Jean-Marie.

"Hey?" said Casimir. "Gone, you see. Took the hint at once."

"I do not, I confess," said Desprez, "I do not seek to excuse his absence. It speaks a want of heart that disappoints me sorely."

"Want of manners," corrected Casimir. "Heart, he never had. Why, Desprez, for a clever fellow, you are the most gullible mortal in creation. Your ignorance of human nature and human business is beyond belief. You are swindled by heathen Turks, swindled by vagabond children, swindled right and left, up-stairs and down-stairs. I think it must be your imagination. I thank my stars I have none."

"Pardon me," replied Desprez, still humbly, but with a return of spirit at sight of a distinction to be drawn; "pardon me, Casimir. You possess, even to an eminent degree, the commercial imagination. It was the lack of that in me—it appears it is my weak point—that has led to these repeated shocks. By the commercial imagination the financier forecasts the destiny of his investments, marks the falling house——"

"Egad," interrupted Casimir: "our friend the stable-boy appears to have his share of it."

The Doctor was silenced; and the meal was continued and finished principally to the tune of the brother-in-law's not very consolatory conversation. He entirely ignored the two young English painters, turning a blind eyeglass to their salutations, and continuing his remarks as if he were alone in the bosom of his family; and with every second word he ripped another stitch out of the air-balloon of Desprez's vanity. By

the time coffee was over the poor Doctor was as
limp as a napkin.

"Let us go and see the ruins," said Casimir.

They strolled forth into the street. The fall
of the house, like the loss of a front tooth, had
quite transformed the village. Through the
gap the eye commanded a great stretch of open
snowy country, and the place shrank in comparison. It was like a room with an open door.
The sentinel stood by the green gate, looking
very red and cold, but he had a pleasant word
for the Doctor and his wealthy kinsman.

Casimir looked at the mound of ruins, he tried
the quality of the tarpaulin. "H'm," he said,
"I hope the cellar arch has stood. If it has, my
good brother, I will give you a good price for the
wines."

"We shall start digging to-morrow," said the
sentry. "There is no more fear of snow."

"My friend," returned Casimir sententiously,
"you had better wait till you get paid."

The Doctor winced, and began dragging his
offensive brother-in-law towards Tentaillon's.
In the house there would be fewer auditors, and
these already in the secret of his fall.

"Hullo," cried Casimir, "there goes the stable-
boy with his luggage; no, egad, he is taking it
into the inn."

And sure enough, Jean-Marie was seen to
cross the snowy street and enter Tentaillon's,
staggering under a large hamper.

The Doctor stopped with a sudden, wild hope.

"What can he have?" he said. "Let us go and see." And he hurried on.

"His luggage, to be sure," answered Casimir. "He is on the move—thanks to the commercial imagination."

"I have not seen that hamper for—for ever so long," remarked the Doctor.

"Nor will you see it much longer," chuckled Casimir; "unless, indeed, we interfere. And by the way, I insist on an examination."

"You will not require," said Desprez, positively with a sob; and, casting a moist, triumphant glance at Casimir, he began to run.

"What the devil is up with him, I wonder?" Casimir reflected; and then, curiosity taking the upper hand, he followed the Doctor's example and took to his heels.

The hamper was so heavy and large, and Jean-Marie himself so little and so weary, that it had taken him a great while to bundle it up-stairs to the Desprez private room; and he had just set it down on the floor in front of Anastasie, when the Doctor arrived, and was closely followed by the man of business. Boy and hamper were both in a most sorry plight; for the one had passed four months underground in a certain cave on the way to Achères, and the other had run about five miles, as hard as his legs would carry him, half that distance under a staggering weight.

"Jean-Marie," cried the Doctor, in a voice that was only too seraphic to be called hysterical, "is it——? It is!" he cried. "Oh, my son, my son!" And he sat down upon the hamper and sobbed like a little child.

"You will not go to Paris now," said Jean-Marie sheepishly.

"Casimir," said Desprez, raising his wet face, "do you see that boy, that angel boy? He is the thief; he took the treasure from a man unfit to be intrusted with its use; he brings it back to me when I am sobered and humbled. These, Casimir, are the Fruits of my Teaching, and this moment is the Reward of my Life."

"*Tiens!*" said Casimir.

MEMOIR OF
FLEEMING JENKIN

On the death of Fleeming Jenkin, his family and friends determined to publish a section of his various papers; by way of introduction, the following pages were drawn up; and the whole, forming two considerable volumes, has been issued in England. In the States, it has not been thought advisable to reproduce the whole; and the memoir appearing alone, shorn of that other matter which was at once its occasion and its justification, so large an account of a man so little known may seem to a stranger out of all proportion. But Jenkin was a man much more remarkable than the mere bulk or merit of his work approves him. It was in the world, in the commerce of friendship, by his brave attitude towards life, by his high moral value and unwearied intellectual effort, that he struck the minds of his contemporaries. His was an individual figure, such as authors delight to draw, and all men to read of, in the pages of a novel. His was a face worth painting for its own sake. If the sitter shall not seem to have justified the portrait, if Jenkin, after his death, shall not continue to make new friends, the fault will be altogether mine.

R. L. S.

Saranac, Oct. 1887.

CONTENTS

CHAPTER I

CHAPTER II   1833–1851

CHAPTER III   1851–1858

CONTENTS

MEMOIR OF
FLEEMING JENKIN

CHAPTER I

The Jenkins of Stowting—Fleeming's grandfather—Mrs.
Buckner's fortune—Fleeming's father; goes to sea; at St. Helena;
meets King Tom; service in the West Indies; end of his career
—The Campbell-Jacksons—Fleeming's mother—Fleeming's
Uncle John.

N the reign of Henry VIII, a
family of the name of Jenkin,
claiming to come from York,
and bearing the arms of Jenkin
ap Philip of St. Melans, are
found reputably settled in the
county of Kent. Persons of strong genealogical
pinion pass from William Jenkin, Mayor of
Folkestone in 1555, to his contemporary "John
Jenkin, of the Citie of York, Receiver General
of the County," and thence, by way of Jenkin
ap Philip, to the proper summit of any Cambrian
pedigree—a prince; "Guaith Voeth, Lord of
Cardigan," the name and style of him. It may
suffice, however, for the present, that these Kentish Jenkins must have undoubtedly derived from
Wales, and being a stock of some efficiency, they

341

struck root and grew to wealth and consequence
in their new home.

Of their consequence we have proof enough in
the fact that not only was William Jenkin (as
already mentioned) Mayor of Folkestone in
1555, but no less than twenty-three times in the
succeeding century and a half, a Jenkin (William,
Thomas, Henry, or Robert) sat in the same
place of humble honour. Of their wealth we
know that, in the reign of Charles I, Thomas
Jenkin of Eythorne was more than once in the
market buying land, and notably, in 1633, acquired the manor of Stowting Court. This was
an estate of some 320 acres, six miles from
Hythe, in the Bailiwick and Hundred of Stowting, and the Lathe of Shipway, held of the
Crown *in capite* by the service of six men and a
constable to defend the passage of the sea at
Sandgate. It had a chequered history before
it fell into the hands of Thomas of Eythorne,
having been sold and given from one to another
—to the Archbishop, to Heringods, to the Bur-
ghershes, to Pavelys, Trivets, Cliffords, Wen-
locks, Beauchamps, Nevilles, Kempes, and
Clarkes: a piece of Kentish ground condemned
to see new faces and to be no man's home. But
from 1633 onward it became the anchor of the
Jenkin family in Kent; and though passed on
from brother to brother, held in shares between
uncle and nephew, burthened by debts and join-
tures, and at least once sold and bought in

again, it remains to this day in the hands of the direct line. It is not my design, nor have I the necessary knowledge, to give a history of this obscure family. But this is an age when genealogy has taken a new lease of life, and become for the first time a human science; so that we no longer study it in quest of the Guaith Voeths, but to trace out some of the secrets of descent and destiny; and as we study, we think less of Sir Bernard Burke and more of Mr. Galton. Not only do our character and talents lie upon the anvil and receive their temper during generations; but the very plot of our life's story unfolds itself on a scale of centuries, and the biography of the man is only an episode in the epic of the family. From this point of view I ask the reader's leave to begin this notice of a remarkable man who was my friend, with the accession of his great-grandfather, John Jenkin.

This John Jenkin, a grandson of Damaris Kingsley, of the family of *Westward Ho!* was born in 1727, and married Elizabeth, daughter of Thomas Frewen, of Church House, Northiam. The Jenkins had now been long enough intermarrying with their Kentish neighbours to be Kentish folk themselves in all but name; and with the Frewens in particular their connection is singularly involved. John and his wife were each descended in the third degree from another Thomas Frewen, Vicar of Northiam, and brother to Accepted Frewen, Archbishop of York.

John's mother had married a Frewen for a second husband. And the last complication was to be added by the Bishop of Chichester's brother, Charles Buckner, Vice-Admiral of the White, who was twice married, first to a paternal cousin of Squire John, and second to Anne, only sister of the Squire's wife, and already the widow of another Frewen. The reader must bear Mrs. Buckner in mind; it was by means of that lady that Fleeming Jenkin began life as a poor man. Meanwhile, the relationship of any Frewen to any Jenkin at the end of these evolutions presents a problem almost insoluble; and we need not wonder if Mrs. John, thus exercised in her immediate circle, was in her old age "a great genealogist of all Sussex families, and much consulted." The names Frewen and Jenkin may almost seem to have been interchangeable at will; and yet Fate proceeds with such particularity that it was perhaps on the point of name that the family was ruined.

The John Jenkins had a family of one daughter and five extravagant and unpractical sons. The eldest, Stephen, entered the Church and held the living of Salehurst, where he offered, we may hope, an extreme example of the clergy of the age. He was a handsome figure of a man; jovial and jocular; fond of his garden, which produced under his care the finest fruits of the neighbourhood; and like all the family, very choice in horses. He drove tandem; like Jehu, furiously. His saddle-horse, Captain (for the names of horses are piously preserved in the family chronicle which I follow), was trained to break into a gallop as soon as the vicar's foot was thrown across its back; nor would the rein be drawn in the nine miles between Northiam and the Vicarage door. Debt was the man's proper element; he used to skulk from arrest in the chancel of his church; and the speed of Captain may have come sometimes handy. At an early age this unconventional parson married his cook, and by her he had two daughters and one son. One of the daughters died unmarried; the other imitated her father, and married "imprudently." The son, still more gallantly continuing the tradition, entered the army, loaded himself with debt, was forced to sell out, took refuge in the Marines, and was lost on the Dogger Bank in the war-ship *Minotaur*. If he did not marry below him, like his father, his sister, and a certain great-uncle William, it was perhaps because he never married at all.

The second brother, Thomas, who was employed in the General Post Office, followed in all material points the example of Stephen, married "not very creditably," and spent all the money he could lay his hands on. He died without issue; as did the fourth brother, John, who was of weak intellect and feeble health, and the fifth brother, William, whose brief career as one of Mrs. Buckner's satellites will fall to be considered later on. So soon, then, as the *Minotaur* had struck upon the Dogger Bank, Stowting and the line of the Jenkin family fell on the shoulders of the third brother, Charles.

Facility and self-indulgence are the family marks; facility (to judge by these imprudent marriages) being at once their quality and their defect; but in the case of Charles, a man of exceptional beauty and sweetness both of face and disposition, the family fault had quite grown to be a virtue, and we find him in consequence the drudge and milk-cow of his relatives. Born in 1766, Charles served at sea in his youth, and smelt both salt-water and powder. The Jenkins had inclined hitherto, as far as I can make out, to the land service. Stephen's son had been a soldier; William (fourth of Stowting) had been an officer of the unhappy Braddock's in America, where, by the way, he owned and afterwards sold an estate on the James River, called after the parental seat; of which I should like well to hear if it still bears the name. It was probably by the influence of Captain Buckner, already connected with the family by his first marriage, that Charles Jenkin turned his mind in the direction of the navy; and it was in Buckner's own ship, the *Prothée*, 64, that the lad made his only campaign. It was in the days of Rodney's war, when the *Prothée*, we read, captured two large privateers to windward of Barbadoes, and was "materially and distinguishedly engaged" in both the actions with De Grasse. While at sea Charles kept a journal, and made strange archaic pilot-book sketches, part plan, part elevation, some of which survive for the amusement of posterity. He did a good deal of surveying, so that here we may perhaps lay our finger on the beginning of Fleeming's education as an engineer. What is still more strange, among the relics of the handsome midshipman and his stay in the gun-room of the *Prothée*, I find a code of signals graphically represented, for all the world as it would have been done by his grandson.

On the declaration of peace, Charles, because he had suffered from scurvy, received his mother's orders to retire; and he was not the man to refuse a request, far less to disobey a command. Thereupon he turned farmer, a trade he was to practise on a large scale; and we find him married to a Miss Schirr, a woman of some fortune, the daughter of a London merchant. Stephen, the not very reverend, was still alive, galloping about the country or skulking in his chancel. It does not appear whether he let or sold the paternal manor to Charles; one or other, it must have been; and the sailor-farmer settled at Stowting, with his wife, his mother, his unmarried sister, and his sick brother John. Out of the six people of whom his nearest family consisted, three were in his own house,

and two others (the horse-leeches, Stephen and
Thomas) he appears to have continued to assist
with more amiability than wisdom. He hunted,
belonged to the Yeomanry, owned famous
horses, Maggie and Lucy, the latter coveted by
royalty itself. "Lord Rokeby, his neighbour,
called him kinsman," writes my artless chron-
icler, "and altogether life was very cheery."
At Stowting his three sons, John, Charles, and
Thomas Frewen, and his younger daughter,
Anna, were all born to him; and the reader should
here be told that it is through the report of this
second Charles (born 1801) that he has been
looking on at these confused passages of family
history.

In the year 1805 the ruin of the Jenkins was
begun. It was the work of a fallacious lady already mentioned, Aunt Anne Frewen, a sister of
Mrs. John. Twice married, first to her cousin
Charles Frewen, clerk to the Court of Chancery,
Brunswick Herald, and Usher of the Black Rod,
and secondly to Admiral Buckner, she was denied
issue in both beds, and being very rich—she
died worth about £60,000, mostly in land—
she was in perpetual quest of an heir. The mir-
age of this fortune hung before successive members of the Jenkin family until her death in 1825
when it dissolved and left the latest Alnaschar
face to face with bankruptcy. The grandniece,
Stephen's daughter, the one who had not "married imprudently," appears to have been the

first; for she was taken abroad by the golden
aunt, and died in her care at Ghent in 1792.
Next she adopted William, the youngest of the
five nephews; took him abroad with her—it
seems as if that were in the formula; was shut
up with him in Paris by the Revolution; brought
him back to Windsor, and got him a place in
the King's Body Guard, where he attracted the
notice of George III by his proficiency in German. In 1797, being on guard at St. James's
Palace, William took a cold which carried him
off; and Aunt Anne was once more left heirless.
Lastly, in 1805, perhaps moved by the Admiral,
who had a kindness for his old midshipman, perhaps pleased by the good looks and the good nature of the man himself, Mrs. Buckner turned
her eyes upon Charles Jenkin. He was not only
to be the heir, however, he was to be the chief
hand in a somewhat wild scheme of family farm-
ing. Mrs. Jenkin, the mother, contributed 164
acres of land; Mrs. Buckner, 570, some at Northiam, some farther off; Charles let one-half of
Stowting to a tenant, and threw the other and
various scattered parcels into the common enterprise; so that the whole farm amounted to
near upon a thousand acres, and was scattered
over thirty miles of country. The ex-seaman of
thirty-nine, on whose wisdom and ubiquity the
scheme depended, was to live in the meanwhile
without care or fear. He was to check himself in
nothing; his two extravagances, valuable horses

and worthless brothers, were to be indulged in comfort; and whether the year quite paid itself or not, whether successive years left accumulated savings or only a growing deficit, the fortune of the golden aunt should in the end repair all.

On this understanding Charles Jenkin transported his family to Church House, Northiam: Charles the second, then a child of three, among the number. Through the eyes of the boy we have glimpses of the life that followed: of Admiral and Mrs. Buckner driving up from Windsor in a coach and six, two post-horses and their own four, of the house full of visitors, the great roasts at the fire, the tables in the servants' hall laid for thirty or forty for a month together; of the daily press of neighbours, many of whom, Frewens, Lords, Bishops, Batchellors, and Dynes, were also kinsfolk; and the parties "under the great spreading chestnuts of the old fore court," where the young people danced and made merry to the music of the village band. Or perhaps, in the depth of winter, the father would bid young Charles saddle his pony; they would ride the thirty miles from Northiam to Stowting, with the snow to the pony's saddle-girths, and be received by the tenants like princes.

This life of delights, with the continual visible comings and goings of the golden aunt, was well qualified to relax the fibre of the lads. John, the heir, a yeoman and a fox-hunter, "loud and

notorious with his whip and spurs," settled down
into a kind of Tony Lumpkin, waiting for the
shoes of his father and his aunt. Thomas Frewen, the youngest, is briefly dismissed as "a
handsome beau"; but he had the merit or the
good fortune to become a doctor of medicine,
so that when the crash came he was not empty-
handed for the war of life. Charles, at the day-
school of Northiam, grew so well acquainted with
the rod, that his floggings became matter of
pleasantry and reached the ears of Admiral
Buckner. Hereupon that tall, rough-voiced formidable uncle entered with the lad into a cove-
nant: every time that Charles was thrashed he
was to pay the Admiral a penny; every day that
he escaped, the process was to be reversed. "I
recollect," writes Charles, "going crying to my
mother to be taken to the Admiral to pay my
debt." It would seem by these terms the speculation was a losing one; yet it is probable it
paid indirectly by bringing the boy under remark. The Admiral was no enemy to dunces;
he loved courage, and Charles, while yet little
more than a baby, would ride the great horse
into the pond. Presently it was decided that
here was the stuff of a fine sailor; and at an early
period the name of Charles Jenkin was entered
on a ship's books.

From Northiam he was sent to another school
at Boonshill, near Rye, where the master took
"infinite delight" in strapping him. "It keeps

me warm and makes you grow," he used to say. And the stripes were not altogether wasted, for the dunce, though still very "raw," made progress with his studies. It was known, moreover, that he was going to sea, always a ground of preeminence with schoolboys; and in his case the glory was not altogether future, it wore a present form when he came driving to Rye behind four horses in the same carriage with an Admiral. "I was not a little proud, you may believe," says he.

In 1814, when he was thirteen years of age, he was carried by his father to Chichester to the Bishop's Palace. The Bishop had heard from his brother the Admiral that Charles was likely to do well, and had an order from Lord Melville for the lad's admission to the Royal Naval College at Portsmouth. Both the Bishop and the Admiral patted him on the head and said, "Charles will restore the old family"; by which I gather with some surprise that, even in these days of open house at Northiam and golden hope of my aunt's fortune, the family was supposed to stand in need of restoration. But the past is apt to look brighter than nature, above all to those enamoured of their genealogy; and the ravages of Stephen and Thomas must have always given matter of alarm.

What with the flattery of bishops and admirals, the fine company in which he found himself at Portsmouth, his visits home, with their gaiety and greatness of life, his visits to Mrs. Buckner (soon a widow) at Windsor, where he had a pony kept for him, and visited at Lord Melville's and Lord Harcourt's and the Leveson-Gowers, he began to have "bumptious notions," and his head was "somewhat turned with fine people"; as to some extent it remained throughout his innocent and honourable life.

In this frame of mind the boy was appointed to the *Conqueror*, Captain Davie, humorously known as Gentle Johnnie. The captain had earned this name by his style of discipline, which would have figured well in the pages of Marryat: "Put the prisoner's head in a bag and give him another dozen!" survives as a specimen of his commands; and the men were often punished twice or thrice in a week. On board the ship of this disciplinarian, Charles and his father were carried in a billy-boat from Sheerness in December, 1816: Charles with an outfit suitable to his pretensions, a twenty-guinea sextant and 120 dollars in silver, which were ordered into the care of the gunner. "The old clerks and mates," he writes, "used to laugh and jeer me for joining the ship in a billy-boat, and when they found I was from Kent, vowed I was an old Kentish smuggler. This to my pride, you will believe, was not a little offensive."

The *Conqueror* carried the flag of Vice-Admiral Plampin, commanding at the Cape and St. Helena; and at that all-important islet, in

July, 1817, she relieved the flagship of Sir Pulteney Malcolm. Thus it befell that Charles Jenkin, coming too late for the epic of the French wars, played a small part in the dreary and disgraceful after-piece of St. Helena. Life on the guardship was onerous and irksome. The anchor was never lifted, sail never made, the great guns were silent; none was allowed on shore except on duty; all day the movements of the imperial captive were signalled to and fro; all night the boats rowed guard around the accessible portions of the coast. This prolonged stagnation and petty watchfulness in what Napoleon himself called that "unchristian" climate, told cruelly on the health of the ship's company. In eighteen months, according to O'Meara, the *Conqueror* had lost one hundred and ten men and invalided home one hundred and seven, "being more than a third of her complement." It does not seem that our young midshipman so much as once set eyes on Bonaparte; and yet in other ways Jenkin was more fortunate than some of his comrades. He drew in water-colour; not so badly as his father, yet ill enough; and this art was so rare aboard the *Conqueror* that even his humble proficiency marked him out and procured him some alleviations. Admiral Plampin had succeeded Napoleon at the Briars; and here he had young Jenkin staying with him to make sketches of the historic house. One of these is before me as I write, and gives a strange notion

354

of the arts in our old English Navy. Yet it was
again as an artist that the lad was taken for a
run to Rio, and apparently for a second outing
in a ten-gun brig. These, and a cruise of six
weeks to windward of the island undertaken by
the *Conqueror* herself in quest of health, were the
only breaks in three years of murderous inaction;
and at the end of that period Jenkin was invalided home, having "lost his health entirely."

As he left the deck of the guard-ship the historic part of his career came to an end. For
forty-two years he continued to serve his country obscurely on the seas, sometimes thanked
for inconspicuous and honourable services, but
denied any opportunity of serious distinction.
He was first two years in the *Larne*, Captain
Tait, hunting pirates and keeping a watch on
the Turkish and Greek squadrons in the Archipelago. Captain Tait was a favourite with Sir
Thomas Maitland, High Commissioner of the
Ionian Islands—King Tom as he was called—
who frequently took passage in the *Larne*. King
Tom knew every inch of the Mediterranean, and
was a terror to the officers of the watch. He
would come on deck at night; and with his broad
Scots accent, "Well, sir," he would say, "what
depth of water have ye? Well now, sound; and
ye'll just find so or so many fathoms," as the
case might be; and the obnoxious passenger was
generally right. On one occasion, as the ship
was going into Corfu, Sir Thomas came up the

hatchway and cast his eyes towards the gallows. "Bangham"—Charles Jenkin heard him say to his aide-de-camp, Lord Bangham—"where the devil is that other chap? I left four fellows hanging there; now I can only see three. Mind there is another there to-morrow." And sure enough there was another Greek dangling the next day. "Captain Hamilton, of the *Cambrian*, kept the Greeks in order afloat," writes my author, "and King Tom ashore."

From 1823 onward, the chief scene of Charles Jenkin's activities was in the West Indies, where he was engaged off and on till 1844, now as a subaltern, now in a vessel of his own, hunting out pirates, "then very notorious" in the Leeward Islands, cruising after slavers, or carrying dollars and provisions for the Government. While yet a midshipman, he accompanied Mr. Cockburn to Caraccas and had a sight of Bolivar. In the brigantine *Griffon*, which he commanded in his last years in the West Indies, he carried aid to Guadeloupe after the earthquake, and twice earned the thanks of Government: once for an expedition to Nicaragua to extort, under threat of a blockade, proper apologies and a sum of money due to certain British merchants; and once during an insurrection in San Domingo, for the rescue of certain others from a perilous imprisonment and the recovery of a "chest of money" of which they had been robbed. Once, on the other hand, he earned his share of public censure. This was in 1837, when he commanded the *Romney*, lying in the inner harbour of Havannah. The *Romney* was in no proper sense a man-of-war; she was a slave-hulk, the bonded warehouse of the Mixed Slave Commission; where negroes, captured out of slavers under Spanish colours, were detained provisionally till the Commission should decide upon their case and either set them free or bind them to apprenticeship. To this ship, already an eyesore to the authorities, a Cuban slave made his escape. The position was invidious; on one side were the tradition of the British flag and the state of public sentiment at home; on the other, the certainty that if the slave were kept, the *Romney* would be ordered at once out of the harbour, and the object of the Mixed Commission compromised. Without consultation with any other officer, Captain Jenkin (then lieutenant) returned the man to shore and took the Captain-General's receipt. Lord Palmerston approved his course; but the zealots of the anti-slave-trade movement (never to be named without respect) were much dissatisfied; and thirty-nine years later, the matter was again canvassed in Parliament, and Lord Palmerston and Captain Jenkin defended by Admiral Erskine in a letter to the *Times* (March 13, 1876).

In 1845, while still lieutenant, Charles Jenkin acted as Admiral Pigot's flag captain in the Cove of Cork, where there were some thirty pennants;

and about the same time, closed his career by an act of personal bravery. He had proceeded with his boats to the help of a merchant vessel, whose cargo of combustibles had taken fire and was smouldering under hatches; his sailors were in the hold, where the fumes were already heavy, and Jenkin was on deck directing operations, when he found his orders were no longer answered from below: he jumped down without hesitation and slung up several insensible men with his own hand. For this act, he received a letter from the Lords of the Admiralty expressing a sense of his gallantry; and pretty soon after was promoted Commander, superseded, and could never again obtain employment.

In 1828 or 1829, Charles Jenkin was in the same watch with another midshipman, Robert Colin Campbell-Jackson, who introduced him to his family in Jamaica. The father, the Honourable Robert Jackson, Custos Rotulorum of Kingston, came of a Yorkshire family, said to be originally Scotch; and on the mother's side, counted kinship with some of the Forbeses. The mother was Susan Campbell, one of the Campbells of Auchenbreck. Her father Colin, a merchant in Greenock, is said to have been the heir to both the estate and the baronetcy; he claimed neither, which casts a doubt upon the fact; but he had pride enough himself, and taught enough pride to his family, for any station or descent in Christendom. He had four daugh-

ters. One married an Edinburgh writer, as I
have it on a first account—a minister, according
to another—a man at least of reasonable station,
but not good enough for the Campbells of Auchenbreck; and the erring one was instantly dis-
carded. Another married an actor of the name
of Adcock, whom (as I receive the tale) she had
seen acting in a barn; but the phrase should perhaps be regarded rather as a measure of the
family annoyance, than a mirror of the facts.
The marriage was not in itself unhappy; Adcock
was a gentleman by birth and made a good husband; the family reasonably prospered, and one
of the daughters married no less a man than
Clarkson Stanfield. But by the father, and the
two remaining Miss Campbells, people of fierce
passions and a truly Highland pride, the deroga-
tion was bitterly resented. For long the sisters
lived estranged, then Mrs. Jackson and Mrs.
Adcock were reconciled for a moment, only to
quarrel the more fiercely; the name of Mrs.
Adcock was proscribed, nor did it again pass her
sister's lips, until the morning when she announced: "Mary Adcock is dead; I saw her in
her shroud last night." Second-sight was hereditary in the house; and sure enough, as I have
it reported, on that very night Mrs. Adcock had
passed away. Thus, of the four daughters, two
had, according to the idiotic notions of their
friends, disgraced themselves in marriage; the
others supported the honour of the family with

a better grace, and married West Indian mag-
nates of whom, I believe, the world has never
heard and would not care to hear: so strange a
thing is this hereditary pride. Of Mr. Jackson,
beyond the fact that he was Fleeming's grandfather, I know naught. His wife, as I have said,
was a woman of fierce passions; she would tie
her house slaves to the bed and lash them with
her own hand; and her conduct to her wild and
down-going sons, was a mixture of almost insane
self-sacrifice and wholly insane violence of temper. She had three sons and one daughter.
Two of the sons went utterly to ruin, and reduced their mother to poverty. The third went
to India, a slim, delicate lad, and passed so
wholly from the knowledge of his relatives that
he was thought to be long dead. Years later,
when his sister was living in Genoa, a red-beard-
ed man of great strength and stature, tanned by
years in India, and his hands covered with bar-
baric gems, entered the room unannounced, as
she was playing the piano, lifted her from her
seat, and kissed her. It was her brother, suddenly returned out of a past that was never very
clearly understood, with the rank of general,
many strange gems, many cloudy stories of adventure, and next his heart, the daguerreotype
of an Indian prince with whom he had mixed
blood.

The last of this wild family, the daughter,
Henrietta Camilla, became the wife of the mid-

shipman Charles, and the mother of the subject
of this notice, Fleeming Jenkin. She was a
woman of parts and courage. Not beautiful,
she had a far higher gift, the art of seeming so;
played the part of a belle in society, while far
lovelier women were left unattended; and up to
old age, had much of both the exigency and the
charm that mark that character. She drew naturally, for she had no training, with unusual
skill; and it was from her, and not from the two
naval artists, that Fleeming inherited his eye
and hand. She played on the harp and sang
with something beyond the talent of an amateur.
At the age of seventeen, she heard Pasta in
Paris; flew up in a fire of youthful enthusiasm;
and the next morning, all alone and without introduction, found her way into the presence of
the *prima donna* and begged for lessons. Pasta
made her sing, kissed her when she had done,
and though she refused to be her mistress, placed
her in the hands of a friend. Nor was this all;
for when Pasta returned to Paris, she sent for
the girl (once at least) to test her progress. But
Mrs. Jenkin's talents were not so remarkable as
her fortitude and strength of will; and it was in
an art for which she had no natural taste (the
art of literature) that she appeared before the
public. Her novels, though they attained and
merited a certain popularity both in France and
England, are a measure only of her courage.
They were a task, not a beloved task; they were

written for money in days of poverty, and they served their end. In the least thing as well as in the greatest, in every province of life as well as in her novels, she displayed the same capacity of taking infinite pains, which descended to her son. When she was about forty (as near as her age was known) she lost her voice; set herself at once to learn the piano, working eight hours a day; and attained to such proficiency that her collaboration in chamber music was courted by professionals. And more than twenty years later, the old lady might have been seen dauntlessly beginning the study of Hebrew. This is the more ethereal part of courage; nor was she wanting in the more material. Once when a neighbouring groom, a married man, had seduced her maid, Mrs. Jenkin mounted her horse, rode over to the stable entrance and horsewhipped the man with her own hand.

How a match came about between this talented and spirited girl and the young midshipman, is not very easy to conceive. Charles Jenkin was one of the finest creatures breathing; loyalty, devotion, simple natural piety, boyish cheerfulness, tender and manly sentiment in the old sailor fashion, were in him inherent and inextinguishable either by age, suffering, or injustice. He looked, as he was, every inch a gentleman; he must have been everywhere notable, even among handsome men, both for his face and his gallant bearing; not so much that of a sailor,

you would have said, as like one of those gentle
and graceful soldiers that, to this day, are the
most pleasant of Englishmen to see. But though
he was in these ways noble, the dunce scholar of
Northiam was to the end no genius. Upon all
points that a man must understand to be a gentleman, to be upright, gallant, affectionate and
dead to self, Captain Jenkin was more knowing
than one among a thousand; outside of that, his
mind was very largely blank. He had indeed a
simplicity that came near to vacancy; and in the
first forty years of his married life, this want
grew more accentuated. In both families imprudent marriages had been the rule; but neither
Jenkin nor Campbell had ever entered into a
more unequal union. It was the captain's good
looks, we may suppose, that gained for him this
elevation; and in some ways and for many years
of his life, he had to pay the penalty. His wife,
impatient of his incapacity and surrounded by
brilliant friends, used him with a certain con-
tempt. She was the managing partner; the life
was hers, not his; after his retirement they lived
much abroad, where the poor captain, who could
never learn any language but his own, sat in the
corner mumchance; and even his son, carried
away by his bright mother, did not recognise
for long the treasures of simple chivalry that lay
buried in the heart of his father. Yet it would
be an error to regard this marriage as unfortunate. It not only lasted long enough to justify

itself in a beautiful and touching epilogue, but it gave to the world the scientific work and what (while time was) were of far greater value, the delightful qualities of Fleeming Jenkin. The Kentish-Welsh family, facile, extravagant, generous to a fault and far from brilliant, had given the father, an extreme example of its humble virtues. On the other side, the wild, cruel, proud, and somewhat blackguard stock of the Scotch Campbell-Jacksons, had put forth, in the person of the mother, all its force and courage.

The marriage fell in evil days. In 1823, the bubble of the golden aunt's inheritance had burst. She died holding the hand of the nephew she had so wantonly deceived; at the last she drew him down and seemed to bless him, surely with some remorseful feeling; for when the will was opened, there was not found so much as the mention of his name. He was deeply in debt; in debt even to the estate of his deceiver, so that he had to sell a piece of land to clear himself. "My dear boy," he said to Charles, "there will be nothing left for you. I am a ruined man." And here follows for me the strangest part of this story. From the death of the treacherous aunt, Charles Jenkin, senior, had still some nine years to live; it was perhaps too late for him to turn to saving, and perhaps his affairs were past restoration. But his family at least had all this while to prepare; they were still young men, and knew what they had to look for at their father's death; and yet when that happened in September, 1831, the heir was still apathetically waiting. Poor John, the days of his whips and spurs, and Yeomanry dinners, were quite over; and with that incredible softness of the Jenkin nature, he settled down for the rest of a long life, into something not far removed above a peasant. The mill farm at Stowting had been saved out of the wreck; and here he built himself a house on the Mexican model and made the two ends meet with rustic thrift, gathering dung with his own hands upon the road and not at all abashed at his employment. In dress, voice, and manner, he fell into mere country plainness; lived without the least care for appearances, the least regret for the past or discontent with the present; and when he came to die, died with Stoic cheerfulness, announcing that he had had a comfortable time and was yet well pleased to go. One would think there was little active virtue to be inherited from such a race; and yet in this same voluntary peasant, the special gift of Fleeming Jenkin was already half developed. The old man to the end was perpetually inventing; his strange, ill-spelled, unpunctuated correspondence is full (when he does not drop into cookery receipts) of pumps, road-engines, steam-diggers, steam-ploughs, and steam-threshing machines; and I have it on Fleeming's word that what he did was full of ingenuity—only, as if by some cross destiny, useless. These disappointments he not only took with imperturbable good humour, but rejoiced with a particular relish over his nephew's success in the same field. "I glory in the professor," he wrote to his brother; and to Fleeming himself, with a touch of simple drollery, "I was much pleased with your lecture, but why did you hit me so hard with Conisure's" (connoisseur's, *quasi* amateur's) "engineering? Oh, what presumption!—either of you or *my*self!" A quaint, pathetic figure, this of uncle John, with his dung-cart and his inventions; and the romantic fancy of his Mexican house; and his craze about the Lost Tribes, which seemed to the worthy man the key of all perplexities; and his quiet conscience, looking back on a life not altogether vain, for he was a good son to his father while his father lived, and when evil days approached, he had proved himself a cheerful Stoic.

It followed from John's inertia, that the duty of winding up the estate fell into the hands of Charles. He managed it with no more skill than might be expected of a sailor ashore, saved a bare livelihood for John and nothing for the rest. Eight months later, he married Miss Jackson; and with her money, bought in some two-thirds of Stowting. In the beginning of the little family history which I have been following to so great an extent, the Captain mentions, with a delightful pride: "A Court Baron and Court Leet are regularly held by the Lady of the Man-

or, Mrs. Henrietta Camilla Jenkin"; and indeed
the pleasure of so describing his wife, was the
most solid benefit of the investment; for the purchase was heavily encumbered and paid them
nothing till some years before their death. In
the meanwhile, the Jackson family also, what
with wild sons, an indulgent mother and the impending emancipation of the slaves, was moving
nearer and nearer to beggary; and thus of two
doomed and declining houses, the subject of this
memoir was born, heir to an estate and to no
money, yet with inherited qualities that were to
make him known and loved.

CHAPTER II

1833–1851

Birth and Childhood—Edinburgh—Frankfort-on-the-Main—
Paris—The Revolution of 1848—The Insurrection—Flight to
Italy—Sympathy with Italy—The Insurrection in Genoa—A
Student in Genoa—The Lad and his Mother.

HENRY CHARLES FLEEMING JENKIN
(Fleeming, pronounced *Flemming*, to his
friends and family) was born in a Government
building on the coast of Kent, near Dungeness,
where his father was serving at the time in the
Coastguard, on March 25, 1833, and named
after Admiral Fleeming, one of his father's pro-
tectors in the navy.

His childhood was vagrant like his life. Once
he was left in the care of his grandmother Jackson, while Mrs. Jenkin sailed in her husband's
ship and stayed a year at the Havannah. The
tragic woman was besides from time to time a
member of the family; she was in distress of
mind and reduced in fortune by the misconduct
of her sons; her destitution and solitude made it
a recurring duty to receive her; her violence continually enforced fresh separations. In her pas-

sion of a disappointed mother, she was a fit
object of pity; but her grandson, who heard her
load his own mother with cruel insults and re-
proaches, conceived for her an indignant and
impatient hatred, for which he blamed himself
in later life.

It is strange from this point of view to see his
childish letters to Mrs. Jackson; and to think
that a man, distinguished above all by stubborn
truthfulness, should have been brought up to
such dissimulation. But this is of course un-
avoidable in life; it did no harm to Jenkin; and
whether he got harm or benefit from a so early
acquaintance with violent and hateful scenes,
is more than I can guess. The experience, at
least, was formative; and in judging his character it should not be forgotten. But Mrs. Jackson was not the only stranger in their gates; the
Captain's sister, Aunt Anna Jenkin, lived with
them until her death; she had all the Jenkin
beauty of countenance, though she was unhappily deformed in body and of frail health;
and she even excelled her gentle and ineffectual
family in all amiable qualities. So that each of
the two races from which Fleeming sprang, had
an outpost by his very cradle; the one he instinctively loved, the other hated; and the life-
long war in his members had begun thus early
by a victory for what was best.

We can trace the family from one country
place to another in the south of Scotland; where

the child learned his taste for sport by riding home the pony from the moors. Before he was nine he could write such a passage as this about a Hallowe'en observance: "I pulled a middling-sized cabbage-runt with a pretty sum of gold about it. No witches would run after me when I was sowing my hempseed this year; my nuts blazed away together very comfortably to the end of their lives, and when mamma put hers in which were meant for herself and papa they blazed away in the like manner." Before he was ten he could write, with a really irritating precocity, that he had been "making some pictures from a book called *Les Français peints par eux-mêmes*. . . . It is full of pictures of all classes, with a description of each in French. The pictures are a little caricatured, but not much." Doubtless this was only an echo from his mother, but it shows the atmosphere in which he breathed. It must have been a good change for this art critic to be the playmate of Mary Macdonald, their gardener's daughter at Barjarg, and to sup with her family on potatoes and milk; and Fleeming himself attached some value to this early and friendly experience of another class.

His education, in the formal sense, began at Jedburgh. Thence he went to the Edinburgh Academy, where Clerk Maxwell was his senior and Tait his classmate; bore away many prizes; and was once unjustly flogged by Rector Williams.

He used to insist that all his bad schoolfellows
had died early, a belief amusingly characteristic of the man's consistent optimism. In 1846
the mother and son proceeded to Frankfort-on-
the-Main, where they were soon joined by the
father, now reduced to inaction and to play
something like third fiddle in his narrow household. The emancipation of the slaves had de-
prived them of their last resource beyond the
half-pay of a captain; and life abroad was not
only desirable for the sake of Fleeming's education, it was almost enforced by reasons of economy. But it was, no doubt, somewhat hard
upon the captain. Certainly that perennial boy
found a companion in his son; they were both
active and eager, both willing to be amused,
both young, if not in years, then in character.
They went out together on excursions and
sketched old castles, sitting side by side; they
had an angry rivalry in walking, doubtless equally sincere upon both sides; and indeed we may
say that Fleeming was exceptionally favoured,
and that no boy had ever a companion more innocent, engaging, gay, and airy. But although
in this case it would be easy to exaggerate its import, yet, in the Jenkin family also, the tragedy
of the generations was proceeding, and the child
was growing out of his father's knowledge. His
artistic aptitude was of a different order. Already he had his quick sight of many sides of
life; he already overflowed with distinctions and

generalisations, contrasting the dramatic art and
national character of England, Germany, Italy,
and France. If he were dull, he would write
stories and poems. "I have written," he says
at thirteen, "a very long story in heroic measure,
300 lines, and another Scotch story and innumerable bits of poetry"; and at the same age he had
not only a keen feeling for scenery, but could do
something with his pen to call it up. I feel I do
always less than justice to the delightful memory of Captain Jenkin; but with a lad of this
character, cutting the teeth of his intelligence,
he was sure to fall into the background.

The family removed in 1847 to Paris, where
Fleeming was put to school under one Deluc.
There he learned French, and (if the captain is
right) first began to show a taste for mathematics. But a far more important teacher than
Deluc was at hand; the year 1848, so momentous
for Europe, was momentous also for Fleeming's
character. The family politics were Liberal;
Mrs. Jenkin, generous before all things, was sure
to be upon the side of exiles; and in the house
of a Paris friend of hers, Mrs. Turner—already
known to fame as Shelley's Cornelia de Boin-
ville—Fleeming saw and heard such men as
Manin, Gioberti, and the Ruffinis. He was thus
prepared to sympathise with revolution; and
when the hour came, and he found himself in
the midst of stirring and influential events, the
lad's whole character was moved. He corre-

sponded at that time with a young Edinburgh
friend, one Frank Scott; and I am here going
to draw somewhat largely on this boyish correspondence. It gives us at once a picture of the
Revolution and a portrait of Jenkin at fifteen;
not so different (his friends will think) from the
Jenkin of the end—boyish, simple, opinionated,
delighting in action, delighting before all things
in any generous sentiment.

"February 23, 1848.

"When at 7 o'clock to-day I went out, I met
a large band going round the streets, calling on
the inhabitants to illuminate their houses and
bearing torches. This was all very good fun,
and everybody was delighted; but as they
stopped rather long and were rather turbulent
in the Place de la Madeleine, near where we live"
[in the Rue Caumartin] "a squadron of dragoons came up, formed, and charged at a hand-
gallop. This was a very pretty sight; the crowd
was not too thick, so they easily got away; and
the dragoons only gave blows with the back of
the sword, which hurt but did not wound. I
was as close to them as I am now to the other
side of the table; it was rather impressive, however. At the second charge they rode on the
pavement and knocked the torches out of the
fellows' hands; rather a shame, too—wouldn't
be stood in England. . . .

"[At] ten minutes to ten . . . I went a

373

long way along the Boulevards, passing by the
office of Foreign Affairs, where Guizot lives, and
where to-night there were about a thousand
troops protecting him from the fury of the populace.   After this was passed, the number of the
people thickened, till about half a mile further
on, I met a troop of vagabonds, the wildest vagabonds in the world—Paris vagabonds, well
armed, having probably broken into gunsmiths'
shops and taken the guns and swords.   They
were about a hundred.   These were followed by
about a thousand (I am rather diminishing than
exaggerating numbers all through), indifferently
armed with rusty sabres, sticks, etc.   An un-
countable troop of gentlemen, workmen, shop-
keepers' wives (Paris women dare anything),
ladies' maids, common women—in fact, a crowd
of all classes, though by far the greater number
were of the better-dressed class—followed.   Indeed, it was a splendid sight: the mob in front
chanting the '*Marseillaise*,' the national war-
hymn, grave and powerful, sweetened by the
night air—though night in these splendid streets
was turned into day, every window was filled
with lamps, dim torches were tossing in the
crowd . . . for Guizot has late this night
given in his resignation, and this was an im-
provised illumination.

"I and my father had turned with the crowd,
and were close behind the second troop of vagabonds.   Joy was on every face.   I remarked to

papa that 'I would not have missed the scene
for anything, I might never see such a splendid
one,' when *plong* went one shot—every face
went pale—*r-r-r-r-r* went the whole detachment,
[and] the whole crowd of gentlemen and ladies
turned and cut. Such a scene!—ladies, gentlemen, and vagabonds went sprawling in the mud,
not shot but tripped up; and those that went
down could not rise, they were trampled over.
. . . I ran a short time straight on and did
not fall, then turned down a side street, ran
fifty yards and felt tolerably safe; looked for
papa, did not see him; so walked on quickly, giving the news as I went." [It appears, from another letter, the boy was the first to carry word
of the firing to the Rue St. Honoré; and that his
news wherever he brought it was received with
hurrahs. It was an odd entrance upon life for
a little English lad, thus to play the part of rumour in such a crisis of the history of France.]

"But now a new fear came over me. I had
little doubt but my papa was safe, but my fear
was that he should arrive at home before me and
tell the story; in that case I knew my mamma
would go half mad with fright, so on I went as
quick as possible. I heard no more discharges.
When I got half way home, I found my way
blocked up by troops. That way or the Boulevards I must pass. In the Boulevards they were
fighting, and I was afraid all other passages
might be blocked up . . . and I should

have to sleep in a hotel in that case, and then my mamma——however, after a long *détour*, I found a passage and ran home, and in our street joined papa.

" . . . I'll tell you to-morrow the other facts gathered from newspapers and papa. . . . To-night I have given you what I have seen with my own eyes an hour ago, and began trembling with excitement and fear. If I have been too long on this one subject, it is because it is yet before my eyes."

"Monday, 24th.

"It was that fire raised the people. There was fighting all through the night in the Rue Notre Dame de Lorette, on the Boulevards where they had been shot at, and at the Porte St. Denis. At ten o'clock, they resigned the house of the Minister of Foreign Affairs (where the disastrous volley was fired) to the people, who immediately took possession of it. I went to school, but [was] hardly there when the row in that quarter commenced. Barricades began to be fixed. Everyone was very grave now; the *externes* went away, but no one came to fetch me, so I had to stay. No lessons could go on. A troop of armed men took possession of the barricades, so it was supposed I should have to sleep there. The revolters came and asked for arms, but Deluc (head-master) is a National Guard, and he said he had only his own and he

wanted them; but he said he would not fire on
them. Then they asked for wine, which he gave
them. They took good care not to get drunk,
knowing they would not be able to fight. They
were very polite and behaved extremely well.

"About 12 o'clock a servant came for a boy
who lived near me, [and] Deluc thought it best
to send me with him. We heard a good deal of
firing near, but did not come across any of the
parties. As we approached the railway, the
barricades were no longer formed of palings,
planks, or stones; but they had got all the omni-
buses as they passed, sent the horses and passen-
gers about their business, and turned them over.
A double row of overturned coaches made a
capital barricade, with a few paving-stones.

"When I got home I found to my astonishment that in our fighting quarter it was much
quieter. Mamma had just been out seeing the
troops in the Place de la Concorde, when suddenly the Municipal Guard, now fairly exasper-
ated, prevented the National Guard from proceeding, and fired at them; the National Guard
had come with their muskets not loaded, but
at length returned the fire. Mamma saw the
National Guard fire. The Municipal Guard
were round the corner. She was delighted, for
she saw no person killed, though many of the
Municipals were. . . .

"I immediately went out with my papa
(mamma had just come back with him) and

went to the Place de la Concorde. There was
an enormous quantity of troops in the Place.
Suddenly the gates of the gardens of the Tuileries
opened; we rushed forward, out galloped an
enormous number of cuirassiers, in the middle
of which were a couple of low carriages, said
first to contain the Count de Paris and the
Duchess of Orleans, but afterwards they said
it was the King and Queen; and then I heard
he had abdicated. I returned and gave the
news.

"Went out again up the Boulevards. The
house of the Minister of Foreign Affairs was
filled with people and '*Hôtel du Peuple*' written
on it; the Boulevards were barricaded with fine
old trees that were cut down and stretched all
across the road. We went through a great
many little streets, all strongly barricaded, and
sentinels of the people at the principal of them.
The streets were very unquiet, filled with armed
men and women, for the troops had followed the
ex-King to Neuilly and left Paris in the power
of the people. We met the captain of the Third
Legion of the National Guard (who had principally protected the people), badly wounded by
a Municipal Guard, stretched on a litter. He
was in possession of his senses. He was surrounded by a troop of men crying 'Our brave
captain—we have him yet—he's not dead! *Vive
la Réforme!*' This cry was responded to by all,
and every one saluted him as he passed. I do

not know if he was mortally wounded. That Third Legion has behaved splendidly.

"I then returned, and shortly afterwards went out again to the garden of the Tuileries. They were given up to the people and the palace was being sacked. The people were firing blank cartridges to testify their joy, and they had a cannon on the top of the palace. It was a sight to see a palace sacked and armed vagabonds firing out of the windows, and throwing shirts, papers, and dresses of all kinds out of the windows. They are not rogues, these French; they are not stealing, burning, or doing much harm. In the Tuileries they have dressed up some of the statues, broken some, and stolen nothing but queer dresses. I say, Frank, you must not hate the French; hate the Germans if you like. The French laugh at us a little, and call out *Goddam* in the streets; but to-day, in civil war, when they might have put a bullet through our heads, I never was insulted once.

"At present we have a provisional Government, consisting of Odion [*sic*] Barrot, Lamartine, Marast, and some others; among them a common workman, but very intelligent. This is a triumph of liberty—rather!

"Now then, Frank, what do you think of it? I in a revolution and out all day. Just think, what fun! So it was at first, till I was fired at yesterday; but to-day I was not frightened, but it turned me sick at heart, I don't know why.

There has been no great bloodshed, [though] I certainly have seen men's blood several times. But there's something shocking to see a whole armed populace, though not furious, for not one single shop has been broken open, except the gunsmiths' shops, and most of the arms will probably be taken back again. For the French have no cupidity in their nature; they don't like to steal—it is not in their nature. I shall send this letter in a day or two, when I am sure the post will go again. I know I have been a long time writing, but I hope you will find the matter of this letter interesting, as coming from a person resident on the spot; though probably you don't take much interest in the French, but I can think, write, and speak on no other subject.

"*Feb. 25.*

"There is no more fighting, the people have conquered; but the barricades are still kept up, and the people are in arms, more than ever fearing some new act of treachery on the part of the ex-King. The fight where I was was the principal cause of the Revolution. I was in little danger from the shot, for there was an immense crowd in front of me, though quite within gun-shot. [By another letter, a hundred yards from the troops.] I wished I had stopped there.

"The Paris streets are filled with the most extraordinary crowds of men, women, and children, ladies and gentlemen. Every person joyful. The bands of armed men are perfectly polite. Mamma and aunt to-day walked through armed crowds alone, that were firing blank cartridges in all directions. Every person made way with the greatest politeness, and one common man with a blouse, coming by accident against her, immediately stopped to beg her pardon in the politest manner. There are few drunken men. The Tuileries is still being run over by the people; they only broke two things, a bust of Louis Philippe and one of Marshal Bugeaud, who fired on the people. . . .

"I have been out all day again to-day, and precious tired I am. The Republican party seem the strongest, and are going about with red ribbons in their button-holes. . . .

"The title of 'Mister' is abandoned; they say nothing but 'Citizen,' and the people are shaking hands amazingly. They have got to the top of the public monuments, and, mingling with bronze or stone statues, five or six make a sort of *tableau vivant*, the top man holding up the red flag of the Republic; and right well they do it, and very picturesque they look. I think I shall put this letter in the post to-morrow, as we got a letter to-night.

(On Envelope.)

"M. Lamartine has now by his eloquence conquered the whole armed crowd of citizens threatening to kill him if he did not immediately proclaim the Republic and red flag. He said he could not yield to the citizens of Paris alone, that the whole country must be consulted, that he chose the tricolour, for it had followed and accompanied the triumphs of France all over the world, and that the red flag had only been dipped in the blood of the citizens. For sixty hours he has been quieting the people: he is at the head of everything. Don't be prejudiced, Frank, by what you see in the papers. The French have acted nobly, splendidly; there has been no brutality, plundering, or stealing. . . . I did not like the French before; but in this respect they are the finest people in the world. I am so glad to have been here."

And there one could wish to stop with this apotheosis of liberty and order read with the generous enthusiasm of a boy; but as the reader knows, it was but the first act of the piece. The letters, vivid as they are, written as they were by a hand trembling with fear and excitement, yet do injustice, in their boyishness of tone, to the profound effect produced. At the sound of these songs and shot of cannon, the boy's mind awoke. He dated his own appreciation of the art of acting from the day when he saw and heard Rachel recite the "*Marseillaise*" at the Français, the tricolour in her arms. What is still more strange, he had been up to then invincibly indifferent to music, insomuch that he could not distinguish "God save the Queen" from "Bonnie Dundee"; and now, to the chanting of the mob, he amazed his family by learning and singing "*Mourir pour la Patrie.*" But the letters, though they prepare the mind for no such revolution in the boy's tastes and feelings, are yet full of entertaining traits. Let the reader note Fleeming's eagerness to influence his friend Frank, an incipient Tory (no less) as further history displayed; his unconscious indifference to his father and devotion to his mother, betrayed in so many significant expressions and omissions; the sense of dignity of this diminutive "person resident on the spot," who was so happy as to escape insult; and the strange picture of the household—father, mother, son, and even poor Aunt Anna—all day in the streets in the thick of this rough business, and the boy packed off alone to school in a distant quarter on the very morrow of the massacre.

They had all the gift of enjoying life's texture as it comes; they were all born optimists. The name of liberty was honoured in that family, its spirit also, but within stringent limits; and some of the foreign friends of Mrs. Jenkin were, as I have said, men distinguished on the Liberal side. Like Wordsworth, they beheld

> "France standing on the top of golden hours
> And human nature seeming born again."

At once, by temper and belief, they were formed to find their element in such a decent and whiggish convulsion, spectacular in its course, moderate in its purpose. For them,

> "Bliss was it in that dawn to be alive,
> But to be young was very heaven."

And I cannot but smile when I think that (again like Wordsworth) they should have so specially disliked the consequence.

It came upon them by surprise. Liberal friends of the precise right shade of colour had assured them, in Mrs. Turner's drawing-room, that all was for the best; and they rose on February 28 without fear. About the middle of the day they heard the sound of musketry, and the next morning they were awakened by the cannonade. The French, who had behaved so "splendidly," pausing, at the voice of Lamartine, just where judicious Liberals could have desired—the French, who had "no cupidity in their nature," were now about to play a variation on the theme rebellion. The Jenkins took refuge in the house of Mrs. Turner, the house of the false prophets, "Anna going with Mrs. Turner, that she might be prevented speaking English, Fleeming, Miss H. and I" (it is the mother who writes) "walking together. As we reached the Rue de Clichy, the report of the cannon sounded close to our ears and made our hearts sick, I assure you. The fighting was at the barrier Rochechouart, a few streets off. All Saturday and Sunday we were a prey to great alarm, there came so many reports that the insurgents were getting the upper hand. One could tell the state of affairs from the extreme quiet or the sudden hum in the street. When the news was bad, all the houses closed and the people disappeared; when better, the doors half opened and you heard the sound of men again. From the upper windows we could see each discharge from the Bastille—I mean the smoke rising—and also the flames and smoke from the Boulevard la Chapelle. We were four ladies, and only Fleeming by way of a man, and difficulty enough we had to keep him from joining the National Guards—his pride and spirit were both fired. You cannot picture to yourself the multitudes of soldiers, guards, and armed men of all sorts we watched—not close to the window, however, for such havoc had been made among them by the firing from the windows, that as the battalions marched by, they cried, '*Fermez vos fenêtres*' and it was very painful to watch their looks of anxiety and suspicion as they marched by."

"The Revolution," writes Fleeming to Frank Scott, "was quite delightful: getting popped at and run at by horses, and giving sous for the wounded into little boxes guarded by the raggedest, picturesquest delightfullest sentinels; but the insurrection! ugh, I shudder to think at [*sic*] it." He found it "not a bit of fun sitting boxed up in the house four days almost. . . .

I was the only *gentleman* to four ladies, and didn't they keep me in order! I did not dare to show my face at a window, for fear of catching a stray ball or being forced to enter the National Guard; [for] they would have it I was a man full-grown, French, and every way fit to fight. And my mamma was as bad as any of them; she that told me I was a coward last time if I stayed in the house a quarter of an hour! But I drew, examined the pistols, of which I found lots with caps, powder, and ball, while sometimes murderous intentions of killing a dozen insurgents and dying violently overpowered by numbers. . . ." We may drop this sentence here: under the conduct of its boyish writer, it was to reach no legitimate end.

Four days of such a discipline had cured the family of Paris; the same year Fleeming was to write, in answer apparently to a question of Frank Scott's, "I could find no national game in France but revolutions"; and the witticism was justified in their experience. On the first possible day, they applied for passports, and were advised to take the road to Geneva. It appears it was scarce safe to leave Paris for England. Charles Reade, with keen dramatic gusto, had just smuggled himself out of that city in the bottom of a cab. English gold had been found on the insurgents, the name of England was in evil odour; and it was thus—for strategic reasons, so to speak—that Fleeming found himself on the way to that Italy where he was to complete his education, and for which he cherished to the end a special kindness.

It was in Genoa they settled; partly for the sake of the captain, who might there find naval comrades; partly because of the Ruffinis, who had been friends of Mrs. Jenkin in their time of exile and were now considerable men at home; partly, in fine, with hopes that Fleeming might attend the University; in preparation for which he was put at once to school. It was the year of Novara; Mazzini was in Rome; the dry bones of Italy were moving; and for people of alert and liberal sympathies the time was inspiriting. What with exiles turned Ministers of State, Universities thrown open to Protestants, Fleeming himself the first Protestant student in Genoa, and thus, as his mother writes, "a living instance of the progress of liberal ideas"—it was little wonder if the enthusiastic young woman and the clever boy were heart and soul upon the side of Italy. It should not be forgotten that they were both on their first visit to that country; the mother still "child enough" to be delighted when she saw "real monks"; and both mother and son thrilling with the first sight of snowy Alps, the blue Mediterranean, and the crowded port and the palaces of Genoa. Nor was their zeal without knowledge. Ruffini, deputy for Genoa and soon to be head of the University, was at their side; and by means of him the family appear to have had access to much Italian society. To the end, Fleeming professed his admiration of the Piedmontese and his unalterable confidence in the future of Italy under their conduct; for Victor Emanuel, Cavour, the first La Marmora and Garibaldi, he had varying degrees of sympathy and praise: perhaps highest for the King, whose good sense and temper filled him with respect—perhaps least for Garibaldi, whom he loved but yet mistrusted.

But this is to look forward: these were the days not of Victor Emanuel but of Charles Albert; and it was on Charles Albert that mother and son had now fixed their eyes as on the sword-bearer of Italy. On Fleeming's sixteenth birthday, they were, the mother writes, "in great anxiety for news from the army. You can have no idea what it is to live in a country where such a struggle is going on. The interest is one that absorbs all others. We eat, drink, and sleep to the noise of drums and musketry. You would enjoy and almost admire Fleeming's enthusiasm and earnestness—and courage, I may say—for we are among the small minority of English who side with the Italians. The other day, at dinner at the Consul's, boy as he is, and in spite of my admonitions, Fleeming defended the Italian cause, and so well that he 'tripped up the heels of his adversary' simply from being well-informed on the subject and honest. He is as true as steel, and for no one will he bend right or left. . . . Do not fancy him a Bobadil," she adds, "he is only a very true candid boy. I am so glad he remains in all respects but information a great child."

If this letter is correctly dated, the cause was already lost and the King had already abdicated when these lines were written. No sooner did the news reach Genoa, than there began "tumultuous movements"; and the Jenkins received hints it would be wise to leave the city. But they had friends and interests; even the captain had English officers to keep him company, for Lord Hardwicke's ship, the *Vengeance*, lay in port; and supposing the danger to be real, I cannot but suspect the whole family of a divided purpose, prudence being possibly weaker than curiosity. Stay, at least, they did, and thus rounded their experience of the revolutionary year. On Sunday, April 1, Fleeming and the captain went for a ramble beyond the walls, leaving Aunt Anna and Mrs. Jenkin to walk on the bastions with some friends. On the way back, this party turned aside to rest in the Church of the Madonna delle Grazie. "We had remarked," writes Mrs. Jenkin, "the entire absence of sentinels on the ramparts, and how the cannons were left in solitary state; and I had just remarked 'How quiet everything is!' when suddenly we heard the drums begin to beat and distant shouts. *Accustomed as we are* to revolutions, we never thought of being frightened."

For all that, they resumed their return home. On the way they saw men running and vociferating, but nothing to indicate a general disturbance, until, near the Duke's palace, they came upon and passed a shouting mob dragging along with it three cannons. It had scarcely passed before they heard "a rushing sound"; one of the gentlemen thrust back the party of ladies under a shed, and the mob passed again. A fine-looking young man was in their hands; and Mrs. Jenkin saw him with his mouth open as if he sought to speak, saw him tossed from one to another like a ball, and then saw him no more. "He was dead a few instants after, but the crowd hid that terror from us. My knees shook under me and my sight left me." With this street tragedy, the curtain rose upon their second revolution.

The attack on Spirito Santo, and the capitulation and departure of the troops speedily followed. Genoa was in the hands of the Republicans, and now came a time when the English residents were in a position to pay some return for hospitality received. Nor were they backward. Our Consul (the same who had the benefit of correction from Fleeming) carried the Intendente on board the *Vengeance*, escorting him through the streets, getting along with him on board a shore boat, and when the insurgents levelled their muskets, standing up and naming himself, "*Console Inglese*." A friend of the Jenkins,

Captain Glynne, had a more painful, if a less dramatic part. One Colonel Nosozzo had been killed (I read) while trying to prevent his own artillery from firing on the mob; but in that hell's cauldron of a distracted city, there were no distinctions made, and the colonel's widow was hunted for her life. In her grief and peril, the Glynnes received and hid her; Captain Glynne sought and found her husband's body among the slain, saved it for two days, brought the widow a lock of the dead man's hair; but at last, the mob still strictly searching, seems to have abandoned the body, and conveyed his guest on board the *Vengeance*. The Jenkins also had their refugees, the family of an *employé* threatened by a decree. "You should have seen me making a Union Jack to nail over our door," writes Mrs. Jenkin. "I never worked so fast in my life. Monday and Tuesday," she continues, "were tolerably quiet, our hearts beating fast in the hope of La Marmora's approach, the streets barricaded, and none but foreigners and women allowed to leave the city." On Wednesday, La Marmora came indeed, but in the ugly form of a bombardment; and that evening the Jenkins sat without lights about their drawing-room window, "watching the huge red flashes of the cannon" from the Brigato and La Specula forts, and hearkening, not without some awful pleasure, to the thunder of the cannonade.

Lord Hardwicke intervened between the reb-

els and La Marmora; and there followed a
troubled armistice, filled with the voice of panic.
Now the *Vengeance* was known to be cleared for
action; now it was rumoured that the galley
slaves were to be let loose upon the town, and
now that the troops would enter it by storm.
Crowds, trusting in the Union Jack over the
Jenkins' door, came to beg them to receive their
linen and other valuables; nor could their instances be refused; and in the midst of all this
bustle and alarm, piles of goods must be examined and long inventories made. At last the
captain decided things had gone too far. He
himself apparently remained to watch over the
linen; but at five o'clock on the Sunday morning,
Aunt Anna, Fleeming, and his mother were
rowed in a pour of rain on board an English
merchantman, to suffer "nine mortal hours of
agonising suspense." With the end of that
time, peace was restored. On Tuesday morning
officers with white flags appeared on the bastions; then, regiment by regiment, the troops
marched in, two hundred men sleeping on the
ground floor of the Jenkins' house, thirty thousand in all entering the city, but without disturbance, old La Marmora being a commander
of a Roman sternness.

With the return of quiet, and the reopening of
the Universities, we behold a new character, Signor Flaminio: the professors, it appears, made
no attempt upon the Jenkin; and thus readily

italianised the Fleeming. He came well recommended; for their friend Ruffini was then, or
soon after, raised to be the head of the University; and the professors were very kind and
attentive, possibly to Ruffini's *protégé*, perhaps
also to the first Protestant student. It was no
joke for Signor Flaminio at first; certificates had
to be got from Paris and from Rector Williams;
the classics must be furbished up at home that
he might follow Latin lectures; examinations
bristled in the path, the entrance examination
with Latin and English essay, and oral trials
(much softened for the foreigner) in Horace,
Tacitus, and Cicero, and the first University examination only three months later, in Italian
eloquence, no less, and other wider subjects.
On one point the first Protestant student was
moved to thank his stars: that there was no
Greek required for the degree. Little did he
think, as he set down his gratitude, how much,
in later life and among cribs and dictionaries, he
was to lament this circumstance; nor how much
of that later life he was to spend acquiring, with
infinite toil, a shadow of what he might then
have got with ease and fully. But if his Genoese education was in this particular imperfect,
he was fortunate in the branches that more immediately touched on his career. The physical
laboratory was the best mounted in Italy. Ban-
calari, the professor of natural philosophy, was
famous in his day; by what seems even an odd

coincidence, he went deeply into electro-magnetism; and it was principally in that subject that Signor Flaminio, questioned in Latin and answering in Italian, passed his Master of Arts degree with first-class honours. That he had secured the notice of his teachers, one circumstance sufficiently proves. A philosophical society was started under the presidency of Mamiani, "one of the examiners and one of the leaders of the Moderate party"; and out of five promising students brought forward by the professors to attend the sittings and present essays, Signor Flaminio was one. I cannot find that he ever read an essay; and indeed I think his hands were otherwise too full. He found his fellow-students "not such a bad set of chaps," and preferred the Piedmontese before the Genoese; but I suspect he mixed not very freely with either. Not only were his days filled with university work, but his spare hours were fully dedicated to the arts under the eye of a beloved task-mistress. He worked hard and well in the art school, where he obtained a silver medal "for a couple of legs the size of life drawn from one of Raphael's cartoons." His holidays were spent in sketching; his evenings, when they were free, at the theatre. Here at the opera he discovered besides a taste for a new art, the art of music; and it was, he wrote, "as if he had found out a heaven on earth." "I am so anxious that whatever he professes to know, he should really perfectly possess," his mother wrote, "that I spare no pains"; neither to him nor to myself, she might have added. And so when he begged to be allowed to learn the piano, she started him with characteristic barbarity on the scales; and heard in consequence "heart-rending groans" and saw "anguished claspings of hands" as he lost his way among their arid intricacies.

In this picture of the lad at the piano, there is something, for the period, girlish. He was indeed his mother's boy; and it was fortunate his mother was not altogether feminine. She gave her son a womanly delicacy in morals, to a man's taste—to his own taste in later life—too finely spun, and perhaps more elegant than healthful. She encouraged him besides in drawing-room interests. But in other points her influence was man-like. Filled with the spirit of thoroughness, she taught him to make of the least of these accomplishments a virile task; and the teaching lasted him through life. Immersed as she was in the day's movements and buzzed about by leading Liberals, she handed on to him her creed in politics: an enduring kindness for Italy, and a loyalty, like that of many clever women, to the Liberal party with but small regard to men or measures. This attitude of mind used often to disappoint me in a man so fond of logic; but I see now how it was learned from the bright eyes of his mother, and to the sound of the cannonades of 1848. To some of her defects, be-

sides, she made him heir.   Kind as was the bond
that united her to her son, kind, and even pretty,
she was scarce a woman to adorn a home; loving as she did to shine; careless as she was of
domestic, studious of public graces.   She probably rejoiced to see the boy grow up in somewhat of the image of herself, generous, excessive,
enthusiastic, external; catching at ideas, bran-
dishing them when caught; fiery for the right,
but always fiery; ready at fifteen to correct a
consul, ready at fifty to explain to any artist his
own art.

The defects and advantages of such a training
were obvious in Fleeming throughout life.   His
thoroughness was not that of the patient scholar,
but of an untrained woman with fits of passionate study; he had learned too much from dogma,
given indeed by cherished lips; and precocious
as he was in the use of the tools of the mind, he
was truly backward in knowledge of life and of
himself.   Such as it was at least, his home and
school training was now complete; and you are
to conceive the lad as being formed in a household of meagre revenue, among foreign surroundings, and under the influence of an imperious
drawing-room queen; from whom he learned a
great refinement of morals, a strong sense of
duty, much forwardness of bearing, all manner
of studious and artistic interests, and many
ready-made opinions which he embraced with a
son's and a disciple's loyalty.

CHAPTER III

1851–1858

Return to England—Fleeming at Fairbairn's—Experience in
a Strike—Dr. Bell and Greek Architecture—The Gaskells—
Fleeming at Greenwich—The Austins—Fleeming and the
Austins—His Engagement—Fleeming and Sir W. Thomson.

IN 1851, the year of Aunt Anna's death, the
family left Genoa and came to Manchester,
where Fleeming was entered in Fairbairn's works
as an apprentice. From the palaces and Alps,
the Mole, the blue Mediterranean, the humming
lanes and the bright theatres of Genoa, he fell—
and he was sharply conscious of the fall—to the
dim skies and the foul ways of Manchester. England he found on his return "a horrid place," and
there is no doubt the family found it a dear one.

The story of the Jenkin finances is not easy
to follow. The family, I am told, did not practise frugality, only lamented that it should be
needful; and Mrs. Jenkin, who was always com-
plaining of "those dreadful bills," was "always
a good deal dressed." But at this time of
the return to England, things must have gone

397

further. A holiday tour of a fortnight, Fleeming feared would be beyond what he could afford, and he only projected it "to have a castle in the air." And there were actual pinches. Fresh from a warmer sun, he was obliged to go without a great-coat, and learned on railway journeys to supply the place of one with wrappings of old newspaper.

From half-past eight till six, he must "file and chip vigorously in a moleskin suit and infernally dirty." The work was not new to him, for he had already passed some time in a Genoese shop; and to Fleeming no work was without interest. Whatever a man can do or know, he longed to know and do also. "I never learned anything," he wrote, "not even standing on my head, but I found a use for it." In the spare hours of his first telegraph voyage, to give an instance of his greed of knowledge, he meant "to learn the whole art of navigation, every rope in the ship and how to handle her on any occasion"; and once when he was shown a young lady's holiday collection of seaweeds, he must cry out, "It showed me my eyes had been idle." Nor was his the case of the mere literary smatterer, content if he but learn the names of things. In him, to do and to do well, was even a dearer ambition than to know. Anything done well, any craft, despatch, or finish, delighted and inspired him. I remember him with a twopenny Japanese box of three drawers, so exactly fitted that, when one was driven home, the others started from their places; the whole spirit of Japan, he told me, was pictured in that box; that plain piece of carpentry was as much inspired by the spirit of perfection as the happiest drawing or the finest bronze; and he who could not enjoy it in the one was not fully able to enjoy it in the others. Thus, too, he found in Leonardo's engineering and anatomical drawings a perpetual feast; and of the former he spoke even with emotion. Nothing indeed annoyed Fleeming more than the attempt to separate the fine arts from the arts of handicraft; any definition or theory that failed to bring these two together, according to him, had missed the point; and the essence of the pleasure received lay in seeing things well done. Other qualities must be added; he was the last to deny that; but this of perfect craft, was at the bottom of all. And on the other hand, a nail ill-driven, a joint ill-fitted, a tracing clumsily done, anything to which a man had set his hand and not set it aptly, moved him to shame and anger. With such a character, he would feel but little drudgery at Fairbairn's. There would be something daily to be done, slovenliness to be avoided, and a higher mark of skill to be attained; he would chip and file, as he had practised scales, impatient of his own imperfection, but resolute to learn.

And there was another spring of delight. For

he was now moving daily among those strange creations of man's brain, to some so abhorrent, to him of an interest so inexhaustible: in which iron, water, and fire are made to serve as slaves, now with a tread more powerful than an elephant's, and now with a touch more precise and dainty than a pianist's. The taste for machinery was one that I could never share with him, and he had a certain bitter pity for my weakness. Once when I had proved, for the hundredth time, the depth of this defect, he looked at me askance: "And the best of the joke," said he, "is that he thinks himself quite a poet." For to him the struggle of the engineer against brute forces and with inert allies, was nobly poetic. Habit never dulled in him the sense of the greatness of the aims and obstacles of his profession. Habit only sharpened his inventor's gusto in contrivance, in triumphant artifice, in the Odyssean subtleties, by which wires are taught to speak, and iron hands to weave, and the slender ship to brave and to outstrip the tempest. To the ignorant the great results alone are admirable; to the knowing, and to Fleeming in particular, rather the infinite device and sleight of hand that made them possible.

A notion was current at the time that, in such a shop as Fairbairn's, a pupil would never be popular unless he drank with the workmen and imitated them in speech and manner. Fleeming, who would do none of these things, they accepted as a friend and companion; and this was the subject of remark in Manchester, where some memory of it lingers till to-day. He thought it one of the advantages of his profession to be brought into a close relation with the working classes; and for the skilled artisan he had a great esteem, liking his company, his virtues, and his taste in some of the arts. But he knew the classes too well to regard them, like a platform speaker, in a lump. He drew, on the other hand, broad distinctions; and it was his profound sense of the difference between one working man and another that led him to devote so much time, in later days, to the furtherance of technical education. In 1852 he had occasion to see both men and masters at their worst, in the excitement of a strike; and very foolishly (after their custom) both would seem to have behaved. Beginning with a fair show of justice on either side, the masters stultified their cause by obstinate impolicy, and the men disgraced their order by acts of outrage. "On Wednesday last," writes Fleeming, "about three thousand banded round Fairbairn's door at 6 o'clock: men, women, and children, factory boys and girls, the lowest of the low in a very low place. Orders came that no one was to leave the works; but the men inside (Knobsticks as they are called) were precious hungry and thought they would venture. Two of my com-

panions and myself went out with the very first,
and had the full benefit of every possible groan
and bad language." But the police cleared a
lane through the crowd, the pupils were suffered
to escape unhurt, and only the Knobsticks followed home and kicked with clogs; so that
Fleeming enjoyed, as we may say, for nothing,
that fine thrill of expectant valour with which
he had sallied forth into the mob. "I never before felt myself so decidedly somebody, instead
of nobody," he wrote.

Outside as inside the works, he was "pretty
merry and well-to-do," zealous in study, welcome
to many friends, unwearied in loving-kindness
to his mother. For some time he spent three
nights a week with Dr. Bell, "working away at
certain geometrical methods of getting the Greek
architectural proportions": a business after
Fleeming's heart, for he was never so pleased as
when he could marry his two devotions, art and
science. This was besides, in all likelihood, the
beginning of that love and intimate appreciation
of things Greek, from the least to the greatest,
from the *Agamemnon* (perhaps his favourite
tragedy) down to the details of Grecian tailoring,
which he used to express in his familiar phrase:
"The Greeks were the boys." Dr. Bell—the
son of George Joseph, the nephew of Sir Charles,
and though he made less use of it than some, a
sharer in the distinguished talents of his race—
had hit upon the singular fact that certain

geometrical intersections gave the proportions of the Doric order. Fleeming, under Dr. Bell's direction, applied the same method to the other orders, and again found the proportions accurately given. Numbers of diagrams were prepared; but the discovery was never given to the world, perhaps because of the dissensions that arose between the authors. For Dr. Bell believed that "these intersections were in some way connected with, or symbolical of, the antagonistic forces at work"; but his pupil and helper, with characteristic trenchancy, brushed aside this mysticism, and interpreted the discovery as "a geometrical method of dividing the spaces or (as might be said) of setting out the work, purely empirical and in no way connected with any laws of either force or beauty." "Many a hard and pleasant fight we had over it," wrote Jenkin, in later years; "and impertinent as it may seem, the pupil is still unconvinced by the arguments of the master." I do not know about the antagonistic forces in the Doric order; in Fleeming they were plain enough; and the Bobadil of these affairs with Dr. Bell was still, like the corrector of Italian consuls, "a great child in everything but information." At the house of Colonel Cleather, he might be seen with a family of children; and with these, there was no word of the Greek orders; with these Fleeming was only an uproarious boy and an entertaining draughtsman; so that his coming was the

signal for the young people to troop into the
playroom, where sometimes the roof rang with
romping, and sometimes they gathered quietly
about him as he amused them with his pencil.

In another Manchester family, whose name
will be familiar to my readers—that of the Gaskells—Fleeming was a frequent visitor. To Mrs.
Gaskell, he would often bring his new ideas, a
process that many of his later friends will understand and, in their own cases, remember. With
the girls, he had "constant fierce wrangles,"
forcing them to reason out their thoughts and
to explain their prepossessions; and I hear from
Miss Gaskell that they used to wonder how he
could throw all the ardour of his character into
the smallest matters, and to admire his unselfish
devotion to his parents. Of one of these wrangles, I have found a record most characteristic
of the man. Fleeming had been laying down his
doctrine that the end justifies the means, and
that it is quite right "to boast of your six men-
servants to a burglar or to steal a knife to prevent a murder"; and the Miss Gaskells, with
girlish loyalty to what is current, had rejected
the heresy with indignation. From such pas-·
sages-at-arms, many retire mortified and ruffled;
but Fleeming had no sooner left the house than
he fell into delighted admiration of the spirit of
his adversaries. From that it was but a step
to ask himself "what truth was sticking in their
heads"; for even the falsest form of words (in

Fleeming's life-long opinion) reposed upon some truth, just as he could "not even allow that people admire ugly things, they admire what is pretty in the ugly thing." And before he sat down to write his letter, he thought he had hit upon the explanation. "I fancy the true idea," he wrote, "is that you must never do yourself or any one else a moral injury—make any man a thief or a liar—for any end"; quite a different thing, as he would have loved to point out, from never stealing or lying. But this perfervid disputant was not always out of key with his audience. One whom he met in the same house announced that she would never again be happy. "What does that signify?" cried Fleeming. "We are not here to be happy, but to be good." And the words (as his hearer writes to me) became to her a sort of motto during life.

From Fairbairn's and Manchester, Fleeming passed to a railway survey in Switzerland, and thence again to Mr. Penn's at Greenwich, where he was engaged as draughtsman. There in 1856, we find him in "a terribly busy state, finishing up engines for innumerable gun-boats and steam frigates for the ensuing campaign." From half-past eight in the morning till nine or ten at night, he worked in a crowded office among uncongenial comrades, "saluted by chaff, generally low, personal, and not witty," pelted with oranges and apples, regaled with dirty stories, and seeking to suit himself with his surroundings or (as he writes) trying to be as little like himself as possible. His lodgings were hard by, "across a dirty green and through some half-built streets of two-storied houses"; he had Carlyle and the poets, engineering and mathematics, to study by himself in such spare time as remained to him; and there were several ladies, young and not so young, with whom he liked to correspond. But not all of these could compensate for the absence of that mother, who had made herself so large a figure in his life, for sorry surroundings, unsuitable society, and work that leaned to the mechanical. "Sunday," says he, "I generally visit some friends in town and seem to swim in clearer water, but the dirty green seems all the dirtier when I get back. Luckily I am fond of my profession, or I could not stand this life." It is a question in my mind, if he could have long continued to stand it without loss. "We are not here to be happy, but to be good," quoth the young philosopher; but no man had a keener appetite for happiness than Fleeming Jenkin. There is a time of life besides when, apart from circumstances, few men are agreeable to their neighbours and still fewer to themselves; and it was at this stage that Fleeming had arrived, later than common and even worse provided. The letter from which I have quoted is the last of his correspondence with Frank Scott, and his last confidential letter to one of his own sex. "If you consider

it rightly," he wrote long after, "you will find
the want of correspondence no such strange
want in men's friendships. There is, believe me,
something noble in the metal which does not
rust though not burnished by daily use." It is
well said; but the last letter to Frank Scott is
scarcely of a noble metal. It is plain the writer
has outgrown his old self, yet not made acquaintance with the new. This letter from a busy
youth of three-and-twenty, breathes of seventeen: the sickening alternations of conceit and
shame, the expense of hope *in vacuo*, the lack of
friends, the longing after love; the whole world
of egoism under which youth stands groaning,
a voluntary Atlas.

With Fleeming this disease was never seemingly severe. The very day before this (to me)
distasteful letter, he had written to Miss Bell
of Manchester in a sweeter strain; I do not
quote the one, I quote the other; fair things are
the best. "I keep my own little lodgings," he
writes, "but come up every night to see mamma"
(who was then on a visit to London) "if not
kept too late at the works; and have singing lessons once more, and sing '*Donne l'amore è scaltro
pargoletto';* and think and talk about you; and
listen to mamma's projects *de* Stowting. Everything turns to gold at her touch, she's a fairy
and no mistake. We go on talking till I have a
picture in my head, and can hardly believe at
the end that the original is Stowting. Even

you don't know half how good mamma is; in
other things too, which I must not mention.
She teaches me how it is not necessary to be
very rich to do much good. I begin to understand that mamma would find useful occupation and create beauty at the bottom of a vol-
cano. She has little weaknesses, but is a real
generous-hearted woman, which I suppose is the
finest thing in the world." Though neither
mother nor son could be called beautiful, they
make a pretty picture; the ugly, generous, ardent woman weaving rainbow illusions; the ugly,
clear-sighted, loving son sitting at her side in
one of his rare hours of pleasure, half-beguiled,
half-amused, wholly admiring, as he listens.
But as he goes home, and the fancy pictures
fade, and Stowting is once more burthened with
debt, and the noisy companions and the long
hours of drudgery once more approach, no wonder if the dirty green seems all the dirtier or if
Atlas must resume his load.

But in healthy natures this time of moral
teething passes quickly of itself, and is easily
alleviated by fresh interests; and already, in
the letter to Frank Scott, there are two words
of hope: his friends in London, his love for his
profession. The last might have saved him; for
he was ere long to pass into a new sphere, where
all his faculties were to be tried and exercised,
and his life to be filled with interest and effort.
But it was not left to engineering: another and

more influential aim was to be set before him. He must, in any case, have fallen in love; in any case, his love would have ruled his life; and the question of choice was, for the descendant of two such families, a thing of paramount importance. Innocent of the world, fiery, generous, devoted as he was, the son of the wild Jacksons and the facile Jenkins might have been led far astray. By one of those partialities that fill men at once with gratitude and wonder, his choosing was directed well. Or are we to say that by a man's choice in marriage, as by a crucial merit, he deserves his fortune? One thing at least reason may discern: that a man but partly chooses, he also partly forms, his helpmate; and he must in part deserve her, or the treasure is but won for a moment to be lost. Fleeming chanced, if you will (and indeed all these opportunitities are as "random as blindman's-buff") upon a wife who was worthy of him; but he had the wit to know it, the courage to wait and labour for his prize, and the tenderness and chivalry that are required to keep such prizes precious. Upon this point he has himself written well, as usual with fervent optimism, but as usual (in his own phrase) with a truth sticking in his head.

"Love," he wrote, "is not an intuition of the person most suitable to us, most required by us; of the person with whom life flowers and bears fruit. If this were so, the chances of our meeting that person would be small indeed: our intuition would often fail; the blindness of love would then be fatal as it is proverbial. No, love works differently, and in its blindness lies its strength. Man and woman, each strongly desires to be loved, each opens to the other that heart of ideal aspirations which they have often hid till then; each, thus knowing the ideal of the other, tries to fulfil that ideal, each partially succeeds. The greater the love, the greater the success; the nobler the ideal of each, the more durable, the more beautiful the effect. Meanwhile the blindness of each to the other's defects enables the transformation to proceed [unobserved], so that when the veil is withdrawn (if it ever is, and this I do not know) neither knows that any change has occurred in the person whom they loved. Do not fear, therefore. I do not tell you that your friend will not change, but as I am sure that her choice cannot be that of a man with a base ideal, so I am sure the change will be a safe and a good one. Do not fear that anything you love will vanish—he must love it too."

Among other introductions in London, Fleeming had presented a letter from Mrs. Gaskell to the Alfred Austins. This was a family certain to interest a thoughtful young man. Alfred, the youngest and least known of the Austins, had been a beautiful golden-haired child, petted and kept out of the way of both sport and study by

a partial mother. Bred an attorney, he had
(like both his brothers) changed his way of life,
and was called to the bar when past thirty. A
Commission of Inquiry into the state of the
poor in Dorsetshire gave him an opportunity of
proving his true talents; and he was appointed
a Poor Law Inspector, first at Worcester, next
at Manchester, where he had to deal with the po-
tato famine and the Irish immigration of the
'forties, and finally in London, where he again
distinguished himself during an epidemic of
cholera. He was then advanced to the Permanent Secretaryship of Her Majesty's Office of
Works and Public Buildings; a position which he
filled with perfect competence, but with an extreme of modesty; and on his retirement, in
1868, he was made a Companion of the Bath.
While apprentice to a Norwich attorney, Alfred
Austin was a frequent visitor in the house of Mr.
Barron, a rallying-place in those days of intellectual society. Edward Barron, the son of a rich
saddler or leather merchant in the Borough, was
a man typical of the time. When he was a
child, he had once been patted on the head in
his father's shop by no less a man than Samuel
Johnson, as the Doctor went round the Borough canvassing for Mr. Thrale; and the child
was true to this early consecration. "A life of
lettered ease spent in provincial retirement," it
is thus that the biographer of that remarkable
man, William Taylor, announces his subject;

and the phrase is equally descriptive of the life
of Edward Barron. The pair were close friends:
"W. T. and a pipe render everything agreeable,"
writes Barron in his diary in 1828; and in 1833,
after Barron had moved to London and Taylor
had tasted the first public failure of his powers,
the latter wrote: "To my ever dearest Mr. Barron say, if you please, that I miss him more than
I regret him—that I acquiesce in his retirement
from Norwich, because I could ill brook his observation of my increasing debility of mind."
This chosen companion of William Taylor must
himself have been no ordinary man; and he was
the friend besides of Borrow, whom I find him
helping in his Latin. But he had no desire for
popular distinction, lived privately, married a
daughter of Dr. Enfield of Enfield's *Speaker*, and
devoted his time to the education of his family,
in a deliberate and scholarly fashion, and with
certain traits of stoicism, that would surprise a
modern. From these children we must single
out his youngest daughter, Eliza, who learned
under his care to be a sound Latin, an elegant
Grecian, and to suppress emotion without outward sign after the manner of the Godwin school.
This was the more notable, as the girl really
derived from the Enfields; whose high-flown
romantic temper I wish I could find space to il-
lustrate. She was but seven years old, when
Alfred Austin remarked and fell in love with her;
and the union thus early prepared was singularly

full. Where the husband and wife differed, and
they did so on momentous subjects, they differed with perfect temper and content; and in
the conduct of life, and in depth and durability of
love, they were at one. Each full of high spirits,
each practised something of the same repression:
no sharp word was uttered in their house. The
same point of honour ruled them; a guest was
sacred and stood within the pale from criticism.
It was a house, besides, of unusual intellectual
tension. Mrs. Austin remembered, in the early
days of the marriage, the three brothers, John,
Charles, and Alfred, marching to and fro, each
with his hands behind his back, and "reasoning
high" till morning; and how, like Dr. Johnson,
they would cheer their speculations with as
many as fifteen cups of tea. And though, before the date of Fleeming's visit, the brothers
were separated, Charles long ago retired from
the world at Brandeston, and John already near
his end in the "rambling old house" at Wey-
bridge, Alfred Austin and his wife were still a
centre of much intellectual society, and still, as
indeed they remained until the last, youthfully
alert in mind. There was but one child of the
marriage, Anne, and she was herself something
new for the eyes of the young visitor; brought
up, as she had been, like her mother before her,
to the standard of a man's acquirements. Only
one art had she been denied, she must not learn
the violin—the thought was too monstrous even

for the Austins; and indeed it would seem as if
that tide of reform which we may date from the
days of Mary Wollstonecraft had in some degree even receded; for though Miss Austin was
suffered to learn Greek, the accomplishment was
kept secret like a piece of guilt. But whether
this stealth was caused by a backward movement in public thought since the time of Edward
Barron, or by the change from enlightened Norwich to barbarian London, I have no means of
judging.

When Fleeming presented his letter, he fell in
love at first sight with Mrs. Austin and the life
and atmosphere of the house. There was in the
society of the Austins, outward, stoical conform-
ers to the world, something gravely suggestive
of essential eccentricity, something unpreten-
tiously breathing of intellectual effort, that could
not fail to hit the fancy of this hot-brained
boy. The unbroken enamel of courtesy, the self-
restraint, the dignified kindness of these married
folk, had besides a particular attraction for their
visitor. He could not but compare what he
saw, with what he knew of his mother and himself. Whatever virtues Fleeming possessed, he
could never count on being civil; whatever brave,
true-hearted qualities he was able to admire in
Mrs. Jenkin, mildness of demeanour was not one
of them. And here he found persons who were
the equals of his mother and himself in intellect
and width of interest, and the equals of his

father in mild urbanity of disposition. Show
Fleeming an active virtue, and he always loved
it. He went away from that house struck
through with admiration, and vowing to himself
that his own married life should be upon that
pattern, his wife (whoever she might be) like
Eliza Barron, himself such another husband as
Alfred Austin. What is more strange, he not
only brought away, but left behind him, golden
opinions. He must have been—he was, I am
told—a trying lad; but there shone out of him
such a light of innocent candour, enthusiasm,
intelligence, and appreciation, that to persons
already some way forward in years, and thus
able to enjoy indulgently the perennial comedy
of youth, the sight of him was delightful. By a
pleasant coincidence, there was one person in the
house whom he did not appreciate and who did
not appreciate him: Anne Austin, his future
wife. His boyish vanity ruffled her; his appearance, never impressive, was then, by reason of
obtrusive boyishness, still less so; she found occasion to put him in the wrong by correcting a
false quantity; and when Mr. Austin, after doing
his visitor the almost unheard-of honour of accompanying him to the door, announced "That
was what young men were like in my time"—
she could only reply, looking on her handsome
father, "I thought they had been better looking."

This first visit to the Austins took place in

1855; and it seems it was some time before
Fleeming began to know his mind; and yet longer
ere he ventured to show it. The corrected
quantity, to those who knew him well, will seem
to have played its part; he was the man always to
reflect over a correction and to admire the cas-
tigator. And fall in love he did; not hurriedly
but step by step, not blindly but with critical
discrimination; not in the fashion of Romeo, but,
before he was done, with all Romeo's ardour
and more than Romeo's faith. The high favour
to which he presently rose in the esteem of Alfred Austin and his wife, might well give him
ambitious notions; but the poverty of the present and the obscurity of the future were there
to give him pause; and when his aspirations began to settle round Miss Austin, he tasted, perhaps for the only time in his life, the pangs of
diffidence. There was indeed opening before
him a wide door of hope. He had changed into
the service of Messrs. Liddell & Gordon; these
gentlemen had begun to dabble in the new field
of marine telegraphy; and Fleeming was already
face to face with his life's work. That impotent
sense of his own value, as of a ship aground,
which makes one of the agonies of youth, began
to fall from him. New problems which he was
endowed to solve, vistas of new inquiry which
he was fitted to explore, opened before him continually. His gifts had found their avenue and
goal. And with this pleasure of effective exer-

cise, there must have sprung up at once the hope
of what is called by the world success. But
from these low beginnings, it was a far look up-
ward to Miss Austin: the favour of the loved one
seems always more than problematical to any
lover; the consent of parents must be always
more than doubtful to a young man with a small
salary and no capital except capacity and hope.
But Fleeming was not the lad to lose any good
thing for the lack of trial; and at length, in
the autumn of 1857, this boyish-sized, boyish-
mannered, and superlatively ill-dressed young
engineer entered the house of the Austins, with
such sinkings as we may fancy, and asked leave
to pay his addresses to the daughter. Mrs.
Austin already loved him like a son, she was
but too glad to give him her consent; Mr. Austin
reserved the right to inquire into his character;
from neither was there a word about his pros-
pects, by neither was his income mentioned.
"Are these people," he wrote, struck with wonder at this dignified disinterestedness, "are these
people the same as other people?" It was not
till he was armed with this permission, that Miss
Austin even suspected the nature of his hopes:
so strong, in this unmannerly boy, was the principle of true courtesy; so powerful, in this impetuous nature, the springs of self-repression.
And yet a boy he was; a boy in heart and mind;
and it was with a boy's chivalry and frankness
that he won his wife. His conduct was a model

of honour, hardly of tact; to conceal love from the loved one, to court her parents, to be silent and discreet till these are won, and then without preparation to approach the lady—these are not arts that I would recommend for imitation. They lead to final refusal. Nothing saved Fleeming from that fate, but one circumstance that cannot be counted upon—the hearty favour of the mother, and one gift that is inimitable and that never failed him throughout life, the gift of a nature essentially noble and outspoken. A happy and high-minded anger flashed through his despair: it won for him his wife.

Nearly two years passed before it was possible to marry: two years of activity, now in London; now at Birkenhead, fitting out ships, inventing new machinery for new purposes, and dipping into electrical experiment; now in the *Elba* on his first telegraph cruise between Sardinia and Algiers: a busy and delightful period of bounding ardour, incessant toil, growing hope and fresh interests, with behind and through all, the image of his beloved. A few extracts from his correspondence with his betrothed will give the note of these truly joyous years. "My profession gives me all the excitement and interest I ever hope for, but the sorry jade is obviously jealous of you."—"'Poor Fleeming,' in spite of wet, cold, and wind, clambering over moist, tarry slips, wandering among pools of slush in waste places inhabited by wandering locomotives, grows visibly stronger, has dismissed his office cough and cured his toothache."—"The whole of the paying out and lifting machinery must be designed and ordered in two or three days, and I am half crazy with work. I like it though: it's like a good ball, the excitement carries you through."—"I was running to and from the ships and warehouse through fierce gusts of rain and wind till near eleven, and you cannot think what a pleasure it was to be blown about and think of you in your pretty dress."—"I am at the works till ten and sometimes till eleven. But I have a nice office to sit in, with a fire to myself, and bright brass scientific instruments all around me, and books to read, and experiments to make, and enjoy myself amazingly. I find the study of electricity so entertaining that I am apt to neglect my other work." And for a last taste,—"Yesterday I had some charming electrical experiments. What shall I compare them to—a new song? a Greek play?"

It was at this time besides that he made the acquaintance of Professor, now Sir William, Thomson. To describe the part played by these two in each other's lives would lie out of my way. They worked together on the Committee on Electrical Standards; they served together at the laying down or the repair of many deep-sea cables; and Sir William was regarded by Fleeming, not only with the "worship" (the word is his own) due to great scientific gifts, but with

FLEEMING JENKIN

an ardour of personal friendship not frequently excelled. To their association, Fleeming brought the valuable element of a practical understanding; but he never thought or spoke of himself where Sir William was in question; and I recall, quite in his last days, a singular instance of this modest loyalty to one whom he admired and loved. He drew up a paper, in a quite personal interest, of his own services; yet even here he must step out of his way, he must add, where it had no claim to be added, his opinion that, in their joint work, the contributions of Sir William had been always greatly the most valuable. Again, I shall not readily forget with what emotion he once told me an incident of their associated travels. On one of the mountain ledges of Madeira, Fleeming's pony bolted between Sir William and the precipice above; by strange good fortune and thanks to the steadiness of Sir William's horse, no harm was done; but for the moment, Fleeming saw his friend hurled into the sea, and almost by his own act: it was a memory that haunted him.

CHAPTER IV

1859–1868

ON Saturday, Feb. 26, 1859, profiting by a holiday of four days, Fleeming was married to Miss Austin at Northiam: a place connected not only with his own family but with that of his bride as well. By Tuesday morning, he was at work again, fitting out cableships at Birkenhead. Of the walk from his lodgings to the works, I find a graphic sketch in one of his letters: "Out over the railway bridge, along a wide road raised to the level of a ground floor above the land, which, not being built upon, harbours puddles, ponds, pigs and Irish hovels; —so to the dock warehouses, four huge piles of building with no windows, surrounded by a wall about twelve feet high;—in through the large gates, round which hang twenty or thirty rusty Irish, playing pitch and toss and waiting for employment;—on along the railway, which came in at the same gates and which branches down between each vast block—past a pilot-engine butting refractory trucks into their places—on to the last block, [and] down the branch, sniffing the guano-scented air and detecting the old bones. The hartshorn flavour of the guano becomes very strong, as I near the docks where, across the *Elba's* decks, a huge vessel is discharging her cargo of the brown dust, and where huge vessels have been discharging that same cargo for the last five months." This was the walk he took his young wife on the morrow of his return. She had been used to the society of lawyers and civil servants, moving in that circle which seems to itself the pivot of the nation and is in truth only a clique like another; and Fleeming was to her the nameless assistant of a nameless firm of engineers, doing his inglorious business, as she now saw for herself, among unsavoury surroundings. But when their walk brought them within view of the river, she beheld a sight to her of the most novel beauty: four great, sea-going ships dressed out with flags. "How lovely!" she cried. "What is it for?"—"For you," said Fleeming. Her surprise was only equalled by her pleasure. But perhaps, for what we may call private fame, there is no life like that of the engineer; who is a great man in out-of-the-way places, by the dockside or on the desert island or in populous ships, and remains quite unheard of in the coteries of London. And Fleeming had already made his

mark among the few who had an opportunity
of knowing him.

His marriage was the one decisive incident of
his career; from that moment until the day of
his death, he had one thought to which all the
rest were tributary, the thought of his wife.　No
one could know him even slightly, and not
remark the absorbing greatness of that sentiment; nor can any picture of the man be drawn
that does not in proportion dwell upon it.　This
is a delicate task; but if we are to leave behind
us (as we wish) some presentment of the friend
we have lost, it is a task that must be undertaken.

For all his play of mind and fancy, for all his
indulgence—and, as time went on, he grew indulgent—Fleeming had views of duty that were
even stern.　He was too shrewd a student of his
fellow-men to remain long content with rigid
formulæ of conduct.　Iron-bound, impersonal
ethics, the procrustean bed of rules, he soon saw
at their true value as the deification of averages.
"As to Miss (I declare I forget her name) being
bad," I find him writing, "people only mean
that she has broken the Decalogue—which is not
at all the same thing.　People who have kept in
the high-road of Life really have less opportunity for taking a comprehensive view of it than
those who have leaped over the hedges and
strayed up the hills; not but what the hedges are
very necessary, and our stray travellers often

have a weary time of it. So, you may say, have those in the dusty roads." Yet he was himself a very stern respecter of the hedgerows; sought safety and found dignity in the obvious path of conduct; and would palter with no simple and recognised duty of his epoch. Of marriage in particular, of the bond so formed, of the obligations incurred, of the debt men owe to their children, he conceived in a truly antique spirit: not to blame others, but to constrain himself. It was not to blame, I repeat, that he held these views; for others, he could make a large allowance; and yet he tacitly expected of his friends and his wife a high standard of behaviour. Nor was it always easy to wear the armour of that ideal.

Acting upon these beliefs; conceiving that he had indeed "given himself" (in the full meaning of these words) for better, for worse; painfully alive to his defects of temper and deficiency in charm; resolute to make up for these; thinking last of himself: Fleeming was in some ways the very man to have made a noble, uphill fight of an unfortunate marriage. In other ways, it is true, he was one of the most unfit for such a trial. And it was his beautiful destiny to remain to the last hour the same absolute and romantic lover, who had shown to his new bride the flag-draped vessels in the Mersey. No fate is altogether easy; but trials are our touchstone, trials overcome our reward; and it was given to

Fleeming to conquer. It was given to him to live for another, not as a task, but till the end as an enchanting pleasure. "People may write novels," he wrote in 1869, "and other people may write poems, but not a man or woman among them can write to say how happy a man may be, who is desperately in love with his wife after ten years of marriage." And again in 1885, after more than twenty-six years of marriage, and within but five weeks of his death: "Your first letter from Bournemouth," he wrote, "gives me heavenly pleasure—for which I thank Heaven and you too—who are my heaven on earth." The mind hesitates whether to say that such a man has been more good or more fortunate.

Any woman (it is the defect of her sex) comes sooner to the stable mind of maturity than any man; Jenkin was to the end of a most deliberate growth. In the next chapter, when I come to deal with his telegraphic voyages and give some taste of his correspondence, the reader will still find him at twenty-five an arrant schoolboy. His wife besides was more thoroughly educated than he. In many ways she was able to teach him, and he proud to be taught; in many ways she outshone him, and he delighted to be outshone. All these superiorities, and others that, after the manner of lovers, he no doubt forged for himself, added as time went on to the humility of his original love. Only once, in all I know of his career, did he show a touch of smallness. He could not learn to sing correctly; his wife told him so and desisted from her lessons; and the mortification was so sharply felt that for years he could not be induced to go to a concert, instanced himself as a typical man without an ear, and never sang again. I tell it; for the fact that this stood singular in his behaviour, and really amazed all who knew him, is the happiest way I can imagine to commend the tenor of his simplicity; and because it illustrates his feeling for his wife. Others were always welcome to laugh at him; if it amused them, or if it amused him, he would proceed undisturbed with his occupation, his vanity invulnerable. With his wife it was different: his wife had laughed at his singing; and for twenty years the fibre ached. Nothing, again, was more notable than the formal chivalry of this unmannered man to the person on earth with whom he was the most familiar. He was conscious of his own innate and often rasping vivacity and roughness; and he was never forgetful of his first visit to the Austins and the vow he had registered on his return. There was thus an artificial element in his punctilio that at times might almost raise a smile. But it stood on noble grounds; for this was how he sought to shelter from his own petulance the woman who was to him the symbol of the household and to the end the beloved of his youth.

I wish in this chapter to chronicle small beer;

taking a hasty glance at some ten years of married life and of professional struggle; and reserving till the next all the more interesting matter of his cruises. Of his achievements and their worth, it is not for me to speak: his friend and partner, Sir William Thomson, has contributed a note on the subject, which will be found in the Appendix, and to which I must refer the reader. He is to conceive in the meanwhile for himself Fleeming's manifold engagements: his service on the Committee on Electrical Standards, his lectures on electricity at Chatham, his chair at the London University, his partnership with Sir William Thomson and Mr. Varley in many ingenious patents, his growing credit with engineers and men of science; and he is to bear in mind that of all this activity and acquist of reputation, the immediate profit was scanty. Soon after his marriage, Fleeming had left the service of Messrs. Liddell & Gordon, and entered into a general engineering partnership with Mr. Forde, a gentleman in a good way of business. It was a fortunate partnership in this, that the parties retained their mutual respect unlessened and separated with regret; but men's affairs, like men, have their times of sickness, and by one of these unaccountable variations, for hard upon ten years the business was disappointing and the profits meagre. "Inditing drafts of German railways which will never get made": it is thus I find Fleeming, not without a touch of bitterness, describe his occupation. Even the patents hung fire at first. There was no salary to rely on; children were coming and growing up; the prospect was often anxious. In the days of his courtship, Fleeming had written to Miss Austin a dissuasive picture of the trials of poverty, assuring her these were no figments but truly bitter to support: he told her this, he wrote, beforehand, so that when the pinch came and she suffered, she should not be disappointed in herself nor tempted to doubt her own magnanimity: a letter of admirable wisdom and solicitude. But now that the trouble came, he bore it very lightly. It was his principle, as he once prettily expressed it, "to enjoy each day's happiness, as it arises, like birds or children." His optimism, if driven out at the door, would come in again by the window; if it found nothing but blackness in the present, would hit upon some ground of consolation in the future or the past. And his courage and energy were indefatigable. In the year 1863, soon after the birth of their first son, they moved into a cottage at Claygate near Esher; and about this time, under manifold troubles both of money and health, I find him writing from abroad: "The country will give us, please God, health and strength. I will love and cherish you more than ever, you shall go where you wish, you shall receive whom you wish—and as for money you shall have that too. I cannot be mistaken. I have now measured myself with many men. I do not feel weak, I do not feel that I shall fail. In many things I have succeeded, and I will in this. And meanwhile the time of waiting, which, please Heaven, shall not be long, shall also not be so bitter. Well, well, I promise much, and do not know at this moment how you and the dear child are. If he is but better, courage, my girl, for I see light."

This cottage at Claygate stood just without the village, well surrounded with trees and commanding a pleasant view. A piece of the garden was turfed over to form a croquet-green, and Fleeming became (I need scarce say) a very ardent player. He grew ardent, too, in gardening. This he took up at first to please his wife, having no natural inclination; but he had no sooner set his hand to it, than, like everything else he touched, it became with him a passion. He budded roses, he potted cuttings in the coach-house; if there came a change of weather at night, he would rise out of bed to protect his favourites; when he was thrown with a dull companion, it was enough for him to discover in the man a fellow gardener; on his travels, he would go out of his way to visit nurseries and gather hints; and to the end of his life, after other occupations prevented him putting his own hand to the spade, he drew up a yearly programme for his gardener, in which all details were regulated. He had begun by this time to write.

His paper on Darwin, which had the merit of convincing on one point the philosopher himself, had indeed been written before this in London lodgings; but his pen was not idle at Claygate; and it was here he wrote (among other things) that review of *Fecundity, Fertility, Sterility, and Allied Topics*, which Dr. Matthews Duncan prefixed by way of introduction to the second edition of the work. The mere act of writing seems to cheer the vanity of the most incompetent; but a correction accepted by Darwin, and a whole review borrowed and reprinted by Matthews Duncan, are compliments of a rare strain, and to a man still unsuccessful must have been precious indeed. There was yet a third of the same kind in store for him; and when Munro himself owned that he had found instruction in the paper on Lucretius, we may say that Fleeming had been crowned in the capitol of reviewing.

Croquet, charades, Christmas magic lanterns for the village children, an amateur concert or a review article in the evening; plenty of hard work by day; regular visits to meetings of the British Association, from one of which I find him characteristically writing: "I cannot say that I have had any amusement yet, but I am enjoying the dulness and dry bustle of the whole thing"; occasional visits abroad on business, when he would find the time to glean (as I have said) gardening hints for himself, and old folksongs or new fashions of dress for his wife; and

the continual study and care of his children:
these were the chief elements of his life. Nor
were friends wanting. Captain and Mrs. Jenkin, Mr. and Mrs. Austin, Clerk Maxwell, Miss
Bell of Manchester, and others came to them
on visits. Mr. Hertslet of the Foreign Office,
his wife and his daughter, were neighbours and
proved kind friends; in 1867 the Howitts came
to Claygate and sought the society of "the two
bright, clever young people";[1] and in a house
close by, Mr. Frederick Ricketts came to live
with his family. Mr. Ricketts was a valued
friend during his short life; and when he was
lost with every circumstance of heroism in the
La Plata, Fleeming mourned him sincerely.

I think I shall give the best idea of Fleeming
in this time of his early married life, by a few
sustained extracts from his letters to his wife,
while she was absent on a visit in 1864.

"*Nov. 11.*—Sunday was too wet to walk to
Isleworth, for which I was sorry, so I stayed and
went to Church and thought of you at Ardwick
all through the Commandments, and heard
Dr. —— expound in a remarkable way a proph-
ecy of St. Paul's about Roman Catholics, which,
mutatis mutandis, would do very well for Protestants in some parts. Then I made a little
nursery of Borecole and Enfield market cab-
bage, grubbing in wet earth with leggings and

---

[1] "Reminiscences of My Later Life," by Mary Howitt. *Good
Words*, May, 1886.

grey coat on. Then I tidied up the coach-house to my own and Christine's admiration. Then encouraged by *bouts-rimés* I wrote you a copy of verses; high time I think; I shall just save my tenth year of knowing my lady-love without inditing poetry or rhymes to her.

"Then I rummaged over the box with my father's letters and found interesting notes from myself. One I should say my first letter, which little Austin I should say would rejoice to see and shall see—with a drawing of a cottage and a spirited 'cob.' What was more to the purpose, I found with it a paste-cutter which Mary begged humbly for Christine and I generously gave this morning.

"Then I read some of Congreve. There are admirable scenes in the manner of Sheridan; all wit and no character, or rather one character in a great variety of situations and scenes. I could show you some scenes, but others are too coarse even for my stomach hardened by a course of French novels.

"All things look so happy for the rain.

"*Nov. 16.*—Verbenas looking well. . . . I am but a poor creature without you; I have naturally no spirit or fun or enterprise in me. Only a kind of mechanical capacity for ascertaining whether two really is half four, etc.; but when you are near me I can fancy that I too shine and vainly suppose it to be my proper light; whereas by my extreme darkness when you are

not by, it clearly can only be by a reflected bril-
liance that I seem aught but dull. Then for
the moral part of me: if it were not for you and
little Odden, I should feel by no means sure that
I had any affection power in me. . . . Even
the muscular me suffers a sad deterioration in
your absence. I don't get up when I ought to,
I have snoozed in my chair after dinner; I do
not go in at the garden with my wonted vigour,
and feel ten times as tired as usual with a walk
in your absence; so you see, when you are not
by, I am a person without ability, affections
or vigour, but droop dull, selfish, and spiritless;
can you wonder that I love you?

"*Nov. 17.*— . . . I am very glad we married young. I would not have missed these five
years, no, not for any hopes; they are my own.

"*Nov. 30.*—I got through my Chatham lecture very fairly though almost all my apparatus
went astray. I dined at the mess, and got home
to Isleworth the same evening; your father very
kindly sitting up for me.

"*Dec. 1.*—Back at dear Claygate. Many
cuttings flourish, especially those which do honour to your hand. Your Californian annuals
are up and about. Badger is fat, the grass
green. . . .

"*Dec. 3.*—Odden will not talk of you, while
you are away, having inherited, as I suspect,
his father's way of declining to consider a subject which is painful, as your absence is. . . .

I certainly should like to learn Greek and I think
it would be a capital pastime for the long winter
evenings. . . . How things are misrated!
I declare croquet is a noble occupation compared to the pursuits of business men. As for
so-called idleness—that is, one form of it—I
vow it is the noblest aim of man. When idle,
one can love, one can be good, feel kindly to all,
devote oneself to others, be thankful for existence, educate one's mind, one's heart, one's
body. When busy, as I am busy now or have
been busy to-day, one feels just as you sometimes felt when you were too busy, owing to
want of servants.

"*Dec.* 5.—On Sunday I was at Isleworth,
chiefly engaged in playing with Odden. We
had the most enchanting walk together through
the brickfields. It was very muddy, and, as
he remarked, not fit for Nanna, but fit for us
men. The dreary waste of bared earth, thatched
sheds and standing water, was a paradise to
him; and when we walked up planks to deserted
mixing and crushing mills, and actually saw
where the clay was stirred with long iron prongs,
and chalk or lime ground with 'a tind of a mill,'
his expression of contentment and triumphant
heroism knew no limit to its beauty. Of course
on returning I found Mrs. Austin looking out
at the door in an anxious manner, and thinking
we had been out quite long enough. . . . I
am reading Don Quixote chiefly and am his fer-

vent admirer, but I am so sorry he did not place
his affections on a Dulcinea of somewhat worth-
ier stamp.   In fact I think there must be a mistake about it.   Don Quixote might and would
serve his lady in most preposterous fashion, but
I am sure he would have chosen a lady of merit.
He imagined her to be such no doubt, and drew
a charming picture of her occupations by the
banks of the river; but in his other imaginations
there was some kind of peg on which to hang
the false costumes he created; windmills are big,
and wave their arms like giants; sheep in the
distance are somewhat like an army; a little
boat on the river-side must look much the same
whether enchanted or belonging to millers; but
except that Dulcinea is a woman, she bears no
resemblance at all to the damsel of his imagination."

At the time of these letters, the oldest son
only was born to them.   In September of the
next year, with the birth of the second, Charles
Frewen, there befell Fleeming a terrible alarm
and what proved to be a lifelong misfortune.
Mrs. Jenkin was taken suddenly and alarm-
ingly ill; Fleeming ran a matter of two miles
to fetch the doctor, and drenched with sweat
as he was, returned with him at once in an
open gig.   On their arrival at the house, Mrs.
Jenkin half unconsciously took and kept hold
of her husband's hand.   By the doctor's orders,
windows and doors were set open to create a

thorough draught, and the patient was on no account to be disturbed. Thus, then, did Fleeming pass the whole of that night, crouching on the floor in the draught, and not daring to move lest he should wake the sleeper. He had never been strong; energy had stood him instead of vigour; and the result of that night's exposure was flying rheumatism varied by settled sciatica. Sometimes it quite disabled him, sometimes it was less acute; but he was rarely free from it until his death. I knew him for many years; for more than ten we were closely intimate; I have lived with him for weeks; and during all this time, he only once referred to his infirmity and then perforce as an excuse for some trouble he put me to, and so slightly worded that I paid no heed. This is a good measure of his courage under sufferings of which none but the untried will think lightly. And I think it worth noting how this optimist was acquainted with pain. It will seem strange only to the superficial. The disease of pessimism springs never from real troubles, which it braces men to bear, which it delights men to bear well. Nor does it readily spring at all, in minds that have conceived of life as a field of ordered duties, not as a chase in which to hunt gratifications. "We are not here to be happy, but to be good"; I wish he had mended the phrase: "We are not here to be happy, but to try to be good," comes nearer the modesty of truth. With such old-

FLEEMING JENKIN

fashioned morality, it is possible to get through
life and see the worst of it, and feel some of
the worst of it, and still acquiesce piously and
even gladly in man's fate. Feel some of the
worst of it, I say; for some of the rest of the
worst is, by this simple faith, excluded.

It was in the year 1868, that the clouds finally
rose. The business in partnership with Mr.
Forde began suddenly to pay well; about the
same time the patents showed themselves a
valuable property; and but a little after, Fleeming was appointed to the new chair of engineering in the University of Edinburgh. Thus, almost at once, pecuniary embarrassments passed
for ever out of his life. Here is his own epilogue
to the time at Claygate, and his anticipations
of the future in Edinburgh.

" . . . The dear old house at Claygate is not let and the pretty garden a mass of
weeds. I feel rather as if we had behaved unkindly to them. We were very happy there,
but now that it is over I am conscious of the
weight of anxiety as to money which I bore all
the time. With you in the garden, with Austin
in the coach-house, with pretty songs in the
little, low white room, with the moonlight in
the dear room up-stairs, ah, it was perfect; but
the long walk, wondering, pondering, fearing,
scheming, and the dusty jolting railway, and
the horrid fusty office with its endless disappointments, they are well gone. It is well

enough to fight and scheme and bustle about in the eager crowd here [in London] for a while now and then, but not for a lifetime. What I have now is just perfect. Study for winter, action for summer, lovely country for recreation, a pleasant town for talk. . . ."

CHAPTER V

1858–1873

Notes of Telegraph Voyages.

BUT it is now time to see Jenkin at his life's work. I have before me certain imperfect series of letters written, as he says, "at hazard, for one does not know at the time what is important and what is not": the earlier addressed to Miss Austin, after the betrothal; the later to Mrs. Jenkin, the young wife. I should premise that I have allowed myself certain editorial freedoms, leaving out and splicing together much as he himself did with the Bona cable: thus edited the letters speak for themselves, and will fail to interest none who love adventure or activity. Addressed as they were to her whom he called his "dear engineering pupil," they give a picture of his work so clear that a child may understand, and so attractive that I am half afraid their publication may prove harmful, and still further crowd the ranks of a profession already overcrowded. But their most engaging quality is the picture of the writer;

439

with his indomitable self-confidence and courage, his readiness in every pinch of circumstance or change of plan, and his ever fresh enjoyment of the whole web of human experience, nature, adventure, science, toil and rest, society and solitude. It should be borne in mind that the writer of these buoyant pages was, even while he wrote, harassed by responsibility, stinted in sleep, and often struggling with the prostration of sea-sickness. To this last enemy, which he never overcame, I have omitted, in my search after condensation, a good many references; if they were all left, such was the man's temper, they would not represent one hundredth part of what he suffered, for he was never given to complaint. But indeed he had met this ugly trifle, as he met every thwart circumstance of life, with a certain pleasure of pugnacity; and suffered it not to check him, whether in the exercise of his profession or the pursuit of amusement.

I

"Birkenhead: April 18, 1858.

"Well, you should know, Mr. ——, having a contract to lay down a submarine telegraph from Sardinia to Africa, failed three times in the attempt. The distance from land to land is about 140 miles. On the first occasion, after proceeding some 70 miles, he had to cut the cable —the cause I forget: he tried again, same result; then picked up about 20 miles of the lost cable, spliced on a new piece, and very nearly got across that time, but ran short of cable, and when but a few miles off Galita in very deep water, had to telegraph to London for more cable to be manufactured and sent out whilst he tried to stick to the end: for five days, I think, he lay there sending and receiving messages, but heavy weather coming on the cable parted and Mr. —— went home in despair—at least I should think so.

"He then applied to those eminent engineers, R. S. Newall & Co., who made and laid down a cable for him last autumn—Fleeming Jenkin (at the time in considerable mental agitation) having the honour of fitting out the *Elba* for that purpose." [On this occasion, the *Elba* has no cable to lay; but] "is going out in the beginning of May to endeavour to fish up the cables Mr. —— lost. There are two ends at or near the shore: the third will probably not be found within 20 miles from land. One of these ends will be passed over a very big pulley or sheave at the bows, passed six times round a big barrel or drum; which will be turned round by a steam engine on deck, and thus wind up the cable, while the *Elba* slowly steams ahead. The cable is not wound round and round the drum as your silk is wound on its reel, but on the contrary never goes round more than six times, going off at one side as it comes on at the other, and going down into the hold of the *Elba* to be coiled along in a big coil or skein.

"I went down to Gateshead to discuss with Mr. Newall the form which this tolerably simple idea should take, and have been busy since I came here drawing, ordering, and putting up the machinery—uninterfered with, thank goodness, by any one. I own I like responsibility; it flatters one, and then, your father might say, I have more to gain than to lose. Moreover I do like this bloodless, painless combat with wood and iron, forcing the stubborn rascals to do my will, licking the clumsy cubs into an active shape, seeing the child of to-day's thought working to-morrow in full vigour at his appointed task.

"*May 12.*

"By dint of bribing, bullying, cajoling, and going day by day to see the state of things ordered, all my work is very nearly ready now but those who have neglected these precautions are of course disappointed. Five hundred fathoms of chain [were] ordered by —— some three weeks since, to be ready by the 10th without fail; he sends for it to-day—150 fathoms all they can let us have by the 15th—and how the rest is to be got, who knows? He ordered a boat a month since and yesterday we could see nothing of her but the keel and about two planks. I could multiply instances without end. At first one goes nearly mad with vexation at these things; but one finds so soon that they are the rule, that then it becomes necessary to feign a rage one does not feel. I look upon it as the natural order of things, that if I order a thing, it will not be done—if by accident it gets done, it will certainly be done wrong: the only remedy being to watch the performance at every stage.

"To-day was a grand field-day. I had steam up and tried the engine against pressure or resistance. One part of the machinery is driven by a belt or strap of leather. I always had my doubts this might slip; and so it did, wildly. I had made provision for doubling it, putting on two belts instead of one. No use—off they went, slipping round and off the pulleys instead of driving the machinery. Tighten them—no use. More strength there—down with the lever —smash something, tear the belts, but get them tight—now then, stand clear, on with the steam —and the belts slip away as if nothing held them. Men begin to look queer; the circle of quidnuncs make sage remarks. Once more— no use. I begin to know I ought to feel sheepish and beat, but somehow I feel cocky instead. I laugh and say, 'Well, I am bound to break something down'—and suddenly see. 'Oho, there's the place; get weight on there, and the belt won't slip.' With much labour, on go the belts again. 'Now then, a spar thro' there and six men's weight on; mind you 're not carried away.' —'Ay, ay, sir.' But evidently no one believes in the plan. 'Hurrah, round she goes—stick to your spar. All right, shut off steam.' And the difficulty is vanquished.

"This or such as this (not always quite so bad) occurs hour after hour, while five hundred tons of coal are rattling down into the holds and bunkers, riveters are making their infernal row all round, and riggers bend the sails and fit the rigging:—a sort of Pandemonium, it appeared to young Mrs. Newall, who was here on Monday and half-choked with guano; but it suits the likes o' me.

"S. S. Elba, River Mersey: May 17.

"We are delayed in the river by some of the ship's papers not being ready. Such a scene at the dock gates. Not a sailor will join till the last moment; and then, just as the ship forges ahead through the narrow pass, beds and baggage fly on board, the men half tipsy clutch at the rigging, the captain swears, the women scream and sob, the crowd cheer and laugh, while one or two pretty little girls stand still and cry outright, regardless of all eyes.

"These two days of comparative peace have quite set me on my legs again. I was getting worn and weary with anxiety and work. As usual I have been delighted with my shipwrights. I gave them some beer on Saturday, making a s..ort oration. To-day when they went ashore and I came on board, they gave three cheers, whether for me or the ship I hardly know, but I had just bid them good-bye, and the ship was out of hail; but I was startled and hardly liked to claim the compliment by acknowledging it.

"*S. S. Elba: May 25.*

"My first intentions of a long journal have been fairly frustrated by sea-sickness. On Tuesday last about noon we started from the Mersey in very dirty weather, and were hardly out of the river when we met a gale from the southwest and a heavy sea, both right in our teeth; and the poor *Elba* had a sad shaking. Had I not been very sea-sick, the sight would have been exciting enough, as I sat wrapped in my oilskins on the bridge; [but] in spite of all my efforts to talk, to eat, and to grin, I soon collapsed into imbecility; and I was heartily thankful towards evening to find myself in bed.

"Next morning, I fancied it grew quieter and, as I listened, heard, 'Let go the anchor,' whereon I concluded we had run into Holyhead Harbour, as was indeed the case. All that day we lay in Holyhead, but I could neither read nor write nor draw. The captain of another steamer which had put in came on board, and we all went for a walk on the hill; and in the evening there was an exchange of presents. We gave some tobacco I think, and received a cat, two pounds of fresh butter, a Cumberland ham, *Westward Ho!* and Thackeray's *English Humor-*

ists. I was astonished at receiving two such fair books from the captain of a little coasting screw. Our captain said he [the captain of the screw] had plenty of money, five or six hundred a year at least.—'What in the world makes him go rolling about in such a craft, then?'—'Why, I fancy he's reckless; he's desperate in love with that girl I mentioned, and she won't look at him.' Our honest, fat, old captain says this very grimly in his thick, broad voice.

"My head won't stand much writing yet, so I will run and take a look at the blue night sky off the coast of Portugal.

"*May 26.*

"A nice lad of some two-and-twenty, A—— by name, goes out in a nondescript capacity as part purser, part telegraph clerk, part generally useful person. A—— was a great comfort during the miseries [of the gale]; for when with a dead head wind and a heavy sea, plates, books, papers, stomachs were being rolled about in sad confusion, we generally managed to lie on our backs, and grin, and try discordant staves of the *Flowers of the Forest* and the *Low-Backed Car*. We could sing and laugh, when we could do nothing else; though A—— was ready to swear after each fit was past, that that was the first time he had felt anything, and at this moment would declare in broad Scotch that he'd never been sick at all, qualifying the oath with 'except for a minute now and then.' He brought a cornet-à-piston to practise on, having had three weeks' instruction on that melodious instrument; and if you could hear the horrid sounds that come! especially at heavy rolls. When I hint he is not improving, there comes a confession: 'I don't feel quite right yet, you see!' But he blows away manfully, and in self-defence I try to roar the tune louder.

11:30 P. M.

"Long past Cape St. Vincent now. We went within about 400 yards of the cliffs and lighthouse in a calm moonlight, with porpoises springing from the sea, the men crooning long ballads as they lay idle on the forecastle, and the sails flapping uncertain on the yards. As we passed, there came a sudden breeze from land, hot and heavy scented; and now as I write its warm rich flavour contrasts strongly with the salt air. we have been breathing.

"I paced the deck with H——, the second mate, and in the quiet night drew a confession that he was engaged to be married, and gave him a world of good advice. He is a very nice, active, little fellow, with a broad Scotch tongue and 'dirty, little rascal' appearance. He had a sad disappointment at starting. Having been second mate on the last voyage, when the first mate was discharged, he took charge of the *Elba* all the time she was in port, and of course looked forward to being chief mate this trip. Liddell promised him the post. He had not authority to do this; and when Newall heard of it, he appointed another man. Fancy poor H——having told all the men and most of all, his sweetheart! But more remains behind; for when it came to signing articles, it turned out that O——, the new first mate, had not a certificate which allowed him to have a second mate. Then came rather an affecting scene. For H—— proposed to sign as chief (he having the necessary higher certificate) but to act as second for the lower wages. At first O—— would not give in, but offered to go as second. But our brave little H—— said, no: 'The owners wished Mr. O—— to be chief mate, and chief mate he should be.' So he carried the day, signed as chief and acts as second. Shakespeare and Byron are his favourite books. I walked into Byron a little, but can well understand his stirring up a rough, young sailor's romance. I lent him *Westward Ho!* from the cabin; but to my astonishment he did not care much for it; he said it smelt of the shilling railway library; perhaps I had praised it too highly. Scott is his standard for novels. I am very happy to find good taste by no means confined to gentlemen, H—— having no pretensions to that title. He is a man after my own heart.

"Then I came down to the cabin and heard young A——'s schemes for the future. His

highest picture is a commission in the Prince
of Vizianagram's irregular horse. His eldest
brother is tutor to his Highness's children, and
grand vizier, and magistrate, and on his Highness's household staff, and seems to be one of
those Scotch adventurers one meets with and
hears of in queer berths—raising cavalry, building palaces, and using some petty Eastern king's
long purse with their long Scotch heads.

"Off Bona: June 4.

"I read your letter carefully, leaning back in
a Maltese boat to present the smallest surface
of my body to a grilling sun, and sailing from the
Elba to Cape Hamrah, about three miles distant.
How we fried and sighed! At last, we reached
land under Fort Genova, and I was carried
ashore pick-a-back, and plucked the first flower
I saw for Annie. It was a strange scene, far
more novel than I had imagined: the high, steep
banks covered with rich, spicy vegetation of
which I hardly knew one plant. The dwarf
palm with fan-like leaves, growing about two
feet high, formed the staple of the verdure. As
we brushed through them, the gummy leaves of
a cistus stuck to the clothes; and with its small
white flower and yellow heart, stood for our
English dog-rose. In place of heather, we had
myrtle and lentisque with leaves somewhat similar. That large bulb with long flat leaves? Do
not touch it if your hands are cut; the Arabs

use it as blisters for their horses. Is that the same sort? No, take that one up; it is the bulb of a dwarf palm, each layer of the onion peels off, brown and netted, like the outside of a cocoanut. It is a clever plant that; from the leaves we get a vegetable horsehair:—and eat the bottom of the centre spike. All the leaves you pull have the same aromatic scent. But here a little patch of cleared ground shows old friends, who seem to cling by abused civilisation:—fine, hardy thistles, one of them bright yellow, though;—honest, Scotch-looking, large daisies or gowans;—potatoes here and there, looking but sickly; and dark sturdy fig-trees looking cool and at their ease in the burning sun.

"Here we are at Fort Genova, crowning the little point, a small old building, due to my old Genoese acquaintance who fought and traded bravely once upon a time. A broken cannon of theirs forms the threshold: and through a dark, low arch, we enter upon broad terraces sloping to the centre, from which rain water may collect and run into that well. Large-breeched French troopers lounge about and are most civil; and the whole party sit down to breakfast in a little white-washed room, from the door of which the long mountain coastline and the sparkling sea show of an impossible blue through the openings of a white-washed rampart. I try a sea-egg, one of those prickly fellows—sea-urchins they are called sometimes; the shell is of a lovely purple, and when opened, there are rays of yellow adhering to the inside; these I eat, but they are very fishy.

"We are silent and shy of one another, and soon go out to watch while turbaned, blue-breeched, bare-legged Arabs dig holes for the land telegraph posts on the following principle: one man takes a pick and bangs lazily at the hard earth; when a little is loosened, his mate with a small spade lifts it on one side; and *da capo*. They have regular features and look quite in place among the palms. Our English workmen screw the earthenware insulators on the posts, strain the wire, and order Arabs about by the generic term of Johnny. I find W—— has nothing for me to do, and that in fact no one has anything to do. Some instruments for testing have stuck at Lyons, some at Cagliari; and nothing can be done—or at any rate, is done. I wander about, thinking of you and staring at big, green grasshoppers—locusts, some people call them—and smelling the rich brushwood. There was nothing for a pencil to sketch, and I soon got tired of this work, though I have paid willingly much money for far less strange and lovely sights.

"Off Cape Spartivento: June 8.

"At two this morning, we left Cagliari; at five cast anchor here. I got up and began preparing for the final trial; and shortly afterwards every one else of note on board went ashore to make experiments on the state of the cable, leaving me with the prospect of beginning to lift at 12 o'clock. I was not ready by that time; but the experiments were not concluded and moreover the cable was found to be imbedded some four or five feet in sand, so that the boat could not bring off the end. At three, Messrs. Liddell, etc., came on board in good spirits, having found two wires good or in such a state as permitted messages to be transmitted freely. The boat now went to grapple for the cable some way from shore while the *Elba* towed a small lateen craft which was to take back the consul to Cagliari some distance on its way. On our return we found the boat had been unsuccessful; she was allowed to drop astern, while we grappled for the cable in the *Elba* [without more success]. The coast is a low mountain range covered with brushwood or heather—pools of water and a sandy beach at their feet. I have not yet been ashore, my hands having been very full all day.

"June 9.

"Grappling for the cable outside the bank had been voted too uncertain; [and the day was spent in] efforts to pull the cable off through the sand which has accumulated over it. By getting the cable tight on to the boat, and letting the swell pitch her about till it got slack, and then tightening again with blocks and pulleys, we managed to get out from the beach towards the ship at the rate of about twenty yards an hour. When they had got about 100 yards from shore, we ran round in the *Elba* to try and help them, letting go the anchor in the shallowest possible water; this was about sunset. Suddenly some one calls out he sees the cable at the bottom; there it was sure enough, apparently wriggling about as the waves rippled. Great excitement; still greater when we find our own anchor is foul of it and has been the means of bringing it to light. We let go a grapnel, get the cable clear of the anchor on to the grapnel— the captain in an agony lest we should drift ashore meanwhile—hand the grappling line into the big boat, steam out far enough, and anchor again. A little more work and one end of the cable is up over the bows round my drum. I go to my engine and we start hauling in. All goes pretty well, but it is quite dark. Lamps are got at last, and men arranged. We go on for a quarter of a mile or so from shore and then stop at about half-past nine with orders to be up at three. Grand work at last! A number of the *Saturday Review* here; it reads so hot and feverish, so tomb-like and unhealthy, in the midst of dear Nature's hills and sea, with good wholesome work to do. Pray that all go well to-morrow.

"June 10.

"Thank heaven for a most fortunate day. At three o'clock this morning in a damp, chill mist

453

all hands were roused to work. With a small
delay, for one or two improvements I had seen
to be necessary last night, the engine started
and since that time I do not think there has been
half an hour's stoppage. A rope to splice, a
block to change, a wheel to oil, an old rusted
anchor to disengage from the cable which
brought it up, these have been our only obstruc-
tions. Sixty, seventy, eighty, a hundred, a hundred and twenty revolutions at last, my little
engine tears away. The even black rope comes
straight out of the blue heaving water; passes
slowly round an open-hearted, good-tempered
looking pulley, five feet diameter; aft past a vicious nipper, to bring all up should anything go
wrong; through a gentle guide; on to a huge
bluff drum, who wraps him round his body and
says 'Come you must,' as plain as drum can
speak: the chattering pawls say 'I've got him,
I've got him, he can't get back'; whilst black
cable, much slacker and easier in mind and body,
is taken by a slim V-pulley and passed down into the huge hold, where half a dozen men put
him comfortably to bed after his exertion in
rising from his long bath. In good sooth, it is
one of the strangest sights I know to see that
black fellow rising up so steadily in the midst
of the blue sea. We are more than half way
to the place where we expect the fault; and already the one wire, supposed previously to be
quite bad near the African coast, can be spoken

through. I am very glad I am here, for my machines are my own children and I look on their little failings with a parent's eye and lead them into the path of duty with gentleness and firmness. I am naturally in good spirits, but keep very quiet, for misfortunes may arise at any instant; moreover to-morrow my paying-out apparatus will be wanted should all go well, and that will be another nervous operation. Fifteen miles are safely in; but no one knows better than I do that nothing is done till all is done.

"June 11.

"9 A. M.—We have reached the splice supposed to be faulty, and no fault has been found. The two men learned in electricity, L—— and W——, squabble where the fault is.

"*Evening.*—A weary day in a hot broiling sun; no air. After the experiments, L—— said the fault might be ten miles ahead; by that time, we should be according to a chart in about a thousand fathoms of water—rather more than a mile. It was most difficult to decide whether to go on or not. I made preparations for a heavy pull, set small things to rights and went to sleep. About four in the afternoon, Mr. Liddell decided to proceed, and we are now (at seven) grinding it in at the rate of a mile and three-quarters per hour, which appears a grand speed to us. If the paying-out only works well!

I have just thought of a great improvement in
it; I can't apply it this time, however.—The
sea is of an oily calm, and a perfect fleet of brigs
and ships surrounds us, their sails hardly filling
in the lazy breeze.   The sun sets behind the dim
coast of the Isola San Pietro, the coast of Sardinia, high and rugged, becomes softer and softer
in the distance, while to the westward still the
isolated rock of Toro springs from the horizon.—
It would amuse you to see how cool (in head)
and jolly everybody is.   A testy word now and
then shows the wires are strained a little, but
every one laughs and makes his little jokes as
if it were all in fun: yet we are all as much in
earnest as the most earnest of the earnest bas-
tard German school or demonstrative of Frenchmen.   I enjoy it very much.

"June 12.

"5:30 A. M.—Out of sight of land: about thirty
nautical miles in the hold; the wind rising a
little; experiments being made for a fault, while
the engine slowly revolves to keep us hanging
at the same spot: depth supposed about a mile.
The machinery has behaved admirably.   Oh!
that the paying-out were over!   The new machinery there is but rough, meant for an experiment in shallow water, and here we are in a mile
of water.

"6:30.—I have made my calculations and find
the new paying-out gear cannot possibly answer

456

at this depth, some portion would give way. Luckily, I have brought the old things with me and am getting them rigged up as fast as may be. Bad news from the cable. Number four has given in some portion of the last ten miles: the fault in number three is still at the bottom of the sea: number two is now the only good wire; and the hold is getting in such a mess, through keeping bad bits out and cutting for splicing and testing, that there will be great risk in paying out. The cable is somewhat strained in its ascent from one mile below us; what it will be when we get to two miles is a problem we may have to determine.

"9 P.M.—A most provoking unsatisfactory day. We have done nothing. The wind and sea have both risen. Too little notice has been given to the telegraphists who accompany this expedition; they had to leave all their instruments at Lyons in order to arrive at Bona in time; our tests are therefore of the roughest, and no one really knows where the faults are. Mr. L—— in the morning lost much time; then he told us, after we had been inactive for about eight hours, that the fault in number three was within six miles; and at six o'clock in the evening, when all was ready for a start to pick up these six miles, he comes and says there must be a fault about thirty miles from Bona! By this time it was too late to begin paying out to-day, and we must lie here moored in a thousand fathoms till light to-morrow morning. The ship pitches a good deal, but the wind is going down.

"*June 13, Sunday.*

The wind has not gone down, however. It now (at 10:30) blows a pretty stiff gale. The sea has also risen; and the *Elba's* bows rise and fall about 9 feet. We make twelve pitches to the minute, and the poor cable must feel very seasick by this time. We are quite unable to do anything, and continue riding at anchor in one thousand fathoms, the engines going constantly so as to keep the ship's bows up to the cable, which by this means hangs nearly vertical and sustains no strain but that caused by its own weight and the pitching of the vessel. We were all up at four, but the weather entirely forbade work for to-day, so some went to bed and most lay down, making up our leeway, as we nautically term our loss of sleep. I must say Liddell is a fine fellow and keeps his patience and temper wonderfully; and yet how he does fret and fume about trifles at home! This wind has blown now for 36 hours, and yet we have telegrams from Bona to say the sea there is as calm as a mirror. It makes one laugh to remember one is still tied to the shore. Click, click, click, the pecker is at work: I wonder what Herr P—— says to Herr L——, —tests, tests, tests, nothing more. This will be a very anxious day.

FLEEMING JENKIN

"Another day of fatal inaction.

"9.30.—The wind has gone down a deal; but even now there are doubts whether we shall start to-day.   When shall I get back to you?

"9 P. M.—Four miles from land.   Our run has been successful and eventless.   Now the work is nearly over I feel a little out of spirits— why, I should be puzzled to say—mere wantonness, or reaction perhaps after suspense.

"Up this morning at three, coupled my self-acting gear to the brake and had the satisfaction of seeing it pay out the last four miles in very good style.   With one or two little improvements, I hope to make it a capital thing.   The end has just gone ashore in two boats, three out of four wires good.   Thus ends our first expedition.   By some odd chance a *Times* of June the 7th has found its way on board through the agency of a wretched old peasant who watches the end of the line here.   A long account of breakages in the Atlantic trial trip.   To-night we grapple for the heavy cable, eight tons to the mile.   I long to have a tug at him; he may puzzle me, and though misfortunes or rather difficulties are a bore at the time, life when working with cables is tame without them.

"2. P.M.—Hurrah, he is hooked, the big fellow, almost at the first cast. He hangs under our bows looking so huge and imposing that I could find it in my heart to be afraid of him.

"*June 17.*

"We went to a little bay called Chia, where a freshwater stream falls into the sea, and took in water. This is rather a long operation, so I went a walk up the valley with Mr. Liddell. The coast here consists of rocky mountains 800 to 1,000 feet high covered with shrubs of a brilliant green. On landing, our first amusement was watching the hundreds of large fish who lazily swam in shoals about the river; the big canes on the further side hold numberless tortoises, we are told, but see none, for just now they prefer taking a siesta. A little further on, and what is this with large pink flowers in such abundance? —the oleander in full flower. At first I fear to pluck them, thinking they must be cultivated and valuable; but soon the banks show a long line of thick, tall shrubs, one mass of glorious pink and green. Set these in a little valley, framed by mountains whose rocks gleam out blue and purple colours such as pre-Raphaelites only dare attempt, shining out hard and weird-like amongst the clumps of castor-oil plants, cistus, arbor vitæ and many other evergreens, whose names, alas! I know not; the cistus is brown now, the rest all deep or brilliant green.

Large herds of cattle browse on the baked deposit at the foot of these large crags. One or two half-savage herdsmen in sheepskin kilts, etc., ask for cigars; partridges whirr up on either side of us; pigeons coo and nightingales sing amongst the blooming oleander. We get six sheep and many fowls, too, from the priest of the small village; and then run back to Spartivento and make preparations for the morning.

"June 18.

"The big cable is stubborn and will not behave like his smaller brother. The gear employed to take him off the drum is not strong enough; he gets slack on the drum and plays the mischief. Luckily for my own conscience, the gear I had wanted was negatived by Mr. Newall. Mr. Liddell does not exactly blame me, but he says we might have had a silver pulley cheaper than the cost of this delay. He has telegraphed for more men to Cagliari, to try to pull the cable off the drum into the hold, by hand. I look as comfortable as I can, but feel as if people were blaming me. I am trying my best to get something rigged which may help us; I wanted a little difficulty, and feel much better.—The short length we have picked up was covered at places with beautiful sprays of coral, twisted and twined with shells of those small, fairy animals we saw in the aquarium at home; poor little things, they died at once, with their little bells and delicate bright tints.

461

"*12 o'clock.*—Hurrah, victory! for the present anyhow. Whilst in our first dejection, I thought I saw a place where a flat roller would remedy the whole misfortune; but a flat roller at Cape Spartivento, hard, easily unshipped, running freely! There was a grooved pulley used for the paying-out machinery with a spindle wheel which might suit me. I filled him up with tarry spunyarn, nailed sheet copper round him, bent some parts in the fire; and we are paying-in without more trouble now. You would think some one would praise me; no, no more praise than blame before; perhaps now they think better of me, though.

"10 P. M.—We have gone on very comfortably for nearly six miles. An hour and a half was spent washing down; for along with many coloured polypi, from corals, shells and insects, the big cable brings up much mud and rust, and makes a fishy smell by no means pleasant: the bottom seems to teem with life.

—But now we are startled by a most unpleasant, grinding noise; which appeared at first to come from the large low pulley, but when the engines stopped, the noise continued; and we now imagine it is something slipping down the cable, and the pulley but acts as sounding-board to the big fiddle. Whether it is only an anchor or one of the two other cables, we know not. We hope it is not the cable just laid down.

FLEEMING JENKIN

"10 A. M.—All our alarm groundless, it would appear: the odd noise ceased after a time, and there was no mark sufficiently strong on the large cable to warrant the suspicion that we had cut another line through. I stopped up on the look-out till three in the morning, which made 23 hours between sleep and sleep. One goes dozing about, though, most of the day, for it is only when something goes wrong that one has to look alive. Hour after hour, I stand on the forecastle-head, picking off little specimens of polypi and coral, or lie on the saloon deck reading back numbers of the *Times*—till something hitches, and then all is hurly-burly once more. There are awnings all along the ship, and a most ancient, fish-like smell beneath.

"*1 o'clock.*—Suddenly a great strain in only 95 fathoms of water—belts surging and general dismay; grapnels being thrown out in the hope of finding what holds the cable.—Should it prove the young cable! We are apparently crossing its path—not the working one, but the lost child; Mr. Liddell *would* start the big one first though it was laid first; he wanted to see the job done, and meant to leave us to the small one unaided by his presence.

"3.30.—Grapnel caught something, lost it again; it left its marks on the prongs. Started lifting gear again; and after hauling in some 50 fathoms—grunt, grunt, grunt—we hear the

463

other cable slipping down our big one, playing the selfsame tune we heard last night—louder, however.

"10 P.M.—The pull on the deck engines became harder and harder. I got steam up in a boiler on deck, and another little engine starts hauling at the grapnel. I wonder if there ever was such a scene of confusion: Mr. Liddell and W—— and the captain all giving orders contradictory, etc., on the forecastle; D——, the foreman of our men, the mates, etc., following the example of our superiors; the ship's engine and boilers below, a 50-horse engine on deck, a boiler 14 feet long on deck beside it, a little steam-winch tearing round; a dozen Italians (20 have come to relieve our hands, the men we telegraphed for to Cagliari) hauling at the rope; wiremen, sailors, in the crevices left by ropes and machinery; everything that could swear swearing—I found myself swearing like a trooper at last. We got the unknown difficulty within ten fathoms of the surface; but then the forecastle got frightened that, if it was the small cable which we had got hold of, we should certainly break it by continuing the tremendous and increasing strain. So at last Mr. Liddell decided to stop; cut the big cable, buoying its end; go back to our pleasant watering-place at Chia, take more water and start lifting the small cable. The end of the large one has even now regained its sandy bed; and three buoys—one to grapnel foul of

464

the supposed small cable, two to the big cable—
are dipping about on the surface. One more—a
flag-buoy—will soon follow, and then straight
for shore.

"*June 20.*

"It is an ill-wind, etc. I have an unexpected
opportunity of forwarding this engineering letter; for the craft which brought out our Italian
sailors must return to Cagliari to-night, as the
little cable will take us nearly to Galita, and the
Italian skipper could hardly find his way from
thence. To-day—Sunday—not much rest. Mr.
Liddell is at Spartivento telegraphing. We
are at Chia, and shall shortly go to help our
boat's crew in getting the small cable on board,
We dropped them some time since in order that
they might dig it out of the sand as far as possible.

"*June 21.*

"Yesterday—Sunday as it was—all hands
were kept at work all day, coaling, watering,
and making a futile attempt to pull the cable
from the shore on board through the sand. This
attempt was rather silly after the experience we
had gained at Cape Spartivento. This morning
we grappled, hooked the cable at once, and have
made an excellent start. Though I have called
this the small cable, it is much larger than the
Bona one.—Here comes a break down and a bad
one.

"June 22.

"We got over it, however; but it is a warning to me that my future difficulties will arise from parts wearing out. Yesterday the cable was often a lovely sight, coming out of the water one large incrustation of delicate, net-like corals and long, white curling shells. No portion of the dirty black wires was visible; instead we had a garland of soft pink with little scarlet sprays and white enamel intermixed. All was fragile, however, and could hardly be secured in safety; and inexorable iron crushed the tender leaves to atoms.—This morning at the end of my watch, about 4 o'clock, we came to the buoys, proving our anticipations right concerning the crossing of the cables. I went to bed for four hours, and on getting up, found a sad mess. A tangle of the six-wire cable hung to the grapnel which had been left buoyed, and the small cable had parted and is lost for the present. Our hauling of the other day must have done the mischief.

"June 23.

"We contrived to get the two ends of the large cable and to pick the short end up. The long end, leading us seaward, was next put round the drum and a mile of it picked up; but then, fearing another tangle, the end was cut and buoyed, and we returned to grapple for the three-wire cable. All this is very tiresome for me. The buoying and dredging are managed entirely by W——, who has had much experience in this sort of thing; so I have not enough to do and get very homesick. At noon the wind freshened and the sea rose so high that we had to run for land and are once more this evening anchored at Chia.

"June 24.

"The whole day spent in dredging without success. This operation consists in allowing the ship to drift slowly across the line where you expect the cable to be, while at the end of a long rope, fast either to the bow or stern, a grapnel drags along the ground. This grapnel is a small anchor, made like four pot-hooks tied back to back. When the rope gets taut, the ship is stopped and the grapnel hauled up to the surface in the hopes of finding the cable on its prongs.—I am much discontented with myself for idly lounging about and reading *Westward Ho!* for the second time, instead of taking to electricity or picking up nautical information. I am uncommonly idle. The sea is not quite so rough, but the weather is squally and the rain comes in frequent gusts.

"June 25.

"To-day about 1 o'clock we hooked the three-wire cable, buoyed the long sea-end, and picked up the short [or shore] end. Now it is dark and we must wait for morning before lifting the buoy

we lowered to-day and proceeding seawards.—
The depth of water here is about 600 feet, the
height of a respectable English hill; our fishing
line was about a quarter of a mile long. It
blows pretty fresh, and there is a great deal of
sea.

"*26th.*

"This morning it came on to blow so heavily
that it was impossible to take up our buoy. The
Elba recommenced rolling in true Baltic style
and towards noon we ran for land.

"*27th, Sunday.*

"This morning was a beautiful calm. We
reached the buoys at about 4.30 and commenced
picking up at 6.30. Shortly a new cause of
anxiety arose. Kinks came up in great quan-
tities, about thirty in the hour. To have a true
conception of a kink, you must see one: it is a
loop drawn tight, all the wires get twisted and
the gutta-percha inside pushed out. These
much diminish the value of the cable, as they
must all be cut out, the gutta-percha made good,
and the cable spliced. They arise from the
cable having been badly laid down so that it
forms folds and tails at the bottom of the sea.
These kinks have another disadvantage: they
weaken the cable very much.—At about six
o'clock [P. M.] we had some twelve miles lifted,
when I went to the bows; the kinks were exceedingly tight and were giving way in a most alarm-

468

ing manner. I got a cage rigged up to prevent the end (if it broke) from hurting any one, and sat down on the bowsprit, thinking I should describe kinks to Annie:—suddenly I saw a great many coils and kinks altogether at the surface. I jumped to the gutta-percha pipe, by blowing through which the signal is given to stop the engine. I blow, but the engine does not stop; again—no answer: the coils and kinks jam in the bows and I rush aft shouting, 'Stop!' Too late: the cable had parted and must lie in peace at the bottom. Some one had pulled the gutta-percha tube across a bare part of the steam pipe and melted it. It had been used hundreds of times in the last few days and gave no symptoms of failing. I believe the cable must have gone at any rate; however, since it went in my watch and since I might have secured the tubing more strongly, I feel rather sad. . . .

"June 28.

"Since I could not go to Annie I took down Shakespeare, and by the time I had finished *Antony and Cleopatra*, read the second half of *Troilus* and got some way in *Coriolanus*, I felt it was childish to regret the accident had happened in my watch, and moreover I felt myself not much to blame in the tubing matter—it had been torn down, it had not fallen down; so I went to bed, and slept without fretting, and woke this morning in the same good mood—for which thank you and our friend Shakespeare. I am happy to say Mr. Liddell said the loss of the cable did not much matter; though this would have been no consolation had I felt myself to blame. This morning we have grappled for and found another length of small cable which Mr. —— dropped in 100 fathoms of water. If this also gets full of kinks, we shall probably have to cut it after ten miles or so, or more probably still it will part of its own free will or weight.

"10 P.M.—This second length of three-wire cable soon got into the same condition as its fellow—i.e. came up twenty kinks an hour—and after seven miles were in, parted on the pulley over the bows at one of the said kinks; during my watch again, but this time no earthly power could have saved it. I had taken all manner of precautions to prevent the end doing any damage when the smash came, for come I knew it must. We now return to the six-wire cable. As I sat watching the cable to-night, large phosphorescent globes kept rolling from it and fading in the black water.

"*June 29.*

"To-day we returned to the buoy we had left at the end of the six-wire cable, and after much trouble from a series of tangles, got a fair start at noon. You will easily believe a tangle of iron rope inch and a half diameter is not easy to unravel, especially with a ton or so hanging to the ends. It is now eight o'clock and we have about six and a half miles safe: it becomes very exciting, however, for the kinks are coming fast and furious.

"July 2.

"Twenty-eight miles safe in the hold. The ship is now so deep, that the men are to be turned out of their aft hold, and the remainder coiled there; so the good *Elba's* nose need not burrow too far into the waves. There can only be about 10 or 12 miles more, but these weigh 80 or 100 tons.

"July 5.

"Our first mate was much hurt in securing a buoy on the evening of the 2nd. As interpreter [with the Italians] I am useful in all these cases; but for no fortune would I be a doctor to witness these scenes continually. Pain is a terrible thing.—Our work is done: the whole of the six-wire cable has been recovered; only a small part of the three-wire, but that wire was bad and, owing to its twisted state, the value small. We may therefore be said to have been very successful."

II

I have given this cruise nearly in full. From the notes, unhappily imperfect, of two others, I will take only specimens; for in all there are fea-

471

tures of similarity and it is possible to have too much even of submarine telegraphy and the romance of engineering. And first from the cruise of 1859 in the Greek Islands and to Alexandria, take a few traits, incidents, and pictures.

"*May 10, 1859.*

"We had a fair wind and we did very well, seeing a little bit of Cerig or Cythera, and lots of turtle-doves wandering about over the sea and perching, tired and timid, in the rigging of our little craft. Then Falconera, Antimilo, and Milo, topped with huge white clouds, barren, deserted, rising bold and mysterious from the blue, chafing sea;—Argentiera, Siphano, Scapho, Paros, Antiparos, and late at night Syra itself. *Adam Bede* in one hand, a sketch-book in the other, lying on rugs under an awning, I enjoyed a very pleasant day.

"*May 14.*

"Syra is semi-Eastern. The pavement, huge shapeless blocks sloping to a central gutter; from this bare two-storied houses, sometimes plaster many coloured, sometimes rough-hewn marble, rise, dirty and ill-finished, to straight, plain, flat roofs; shops guiltless of windows, with signs in Greek letters; dogs, Greeks in blue, baggy Zouave breeches and a fez, a few narghilehs and a sprinkling of the ordinary continental shopboys. —In the evening I tried one more walk in Syra with A——, but in vain endeavoured to amuse myself or to spend money; the first effort resulting in singing *Doodah* to a passing Greek or two, the second in spending, no, in making A—— spend, threepence on coffee for three.

"*May 16.*

"On coming on deck, I found we were at anchor in Canea bay, and saw one of the most lovely sights man could witness. Far on either hand stretch bold mountain capes, Spada and Maleka, tender in colour, bold in outline; rich sunny levels lie beneath them, framed by the azure sea. Right in front, a dark brown fortress girdles white mosques and minarets. Rich and green, our mountain capes here join to form a setting for the town, in whose dark walls—still darker—open a dozen high-arched caves in which the huge Venetian galleys used to lie in wait. High above all, higher and higher yet, up into the firmament, range after range of blue and snow-capped mountains. I was bewildered and amazed, having heard nothing of this great beauty. The town when entered is quite Eastern. The streets are formed of open stalls under the first story, in which squat tailors, cooks, sherbet-vendors and the like, busy at their work or smoking narghilehs. Cloths stretched from house to house keep out the sun. Mules rattle through the crowd; curs yelp between your legs; negroes are as hideous and bright clothed as usual; grave Turks with long chibouques continue to march solemnly without breaking them; a little Arab in one dirty rag pokes fun at two splendid little Turks with brilliant fezzes; wiry mountaineers in dirty, full, white kilts, shouldering long guns and one hand on their pistols, stalk untamed past a dozen Turkish soldiers, who look sheepish and brutal in worn cloth jacket and cotton trousers. A headless, wingless lion of St. Mark still stands upon a gate, and has left the mark of his strong clutch. Of ancient times when Crete was Crete, not a trace remains; save perhaps in the full, well-cut nostril and firm tread of that mountaineer, and I suspect that even his sires were Albanians, mere outer barbarians.

"*May 17*.

"I spent the day at the little station where the cable was landed, which has apparently been first a Venetian monastery and then a Turkish mosque. At any rate the big dome is very cool, and the little ones hold [our electric] batteries capitally. A handsome young Bashi-bazouk guards it, and a still handsomer mountaineer is the servant; so I draw them and the monastery and the hill till I'm black in the face with heat and come on board to hear the Canea cable is still bad.

"*May 23*.

"We arrived in the morning at the east end of Candia, and had a glorious scramble over the

474

mountains, which seem built of adamant. Time
has worn away the softer portions of the rock,
only leaving sharp jagged edges of steel. Sea-
eagles soaring above our heads; old tanks, ruins,
and desolation at our feet. The ancient Arsinoë
stood here; a few blocks of marble with the cross
attest the presence of Venetian Christians; but
now—the desolation of desolations. Mr. Liddell and I separated from the rest, and when we
had found a sure bay for the cable, had a tremendous lively scramble back to the boat. These
are the bits of our life which I enjoy, which have
some poetry, some grandeur in them.

"*May 29* (?).

"Yesterday we ran round to the new harbour
[of Alexandria], landed the shore end of the cable
close to Cleopatra's bath, and made a very satis-
factory start about one in the afternoon. We
had scarcely gone 200 yards when I noticed that
the cable ceased to run out, and I wondered why
the ship had stopped. People ran aft to tell me
not to put such a strain on the cable; I answered
indignantly that there was no strain; and suddenly it broke on every one in the ship at once
that we were aground. Here was a nice mess.
A violent scirocco blew from the land; making
one's skin feel as if it belonged to some one else
and didn't fit, making the horizon dim and yellow with fine sand, oppressing every sense and
raising the thermometer 20 degrees in an hour,

but making calm water round us which enabled the ship to lie for the time in safety. The wind might change at any moment, since the scirocco was only accidental; and at the first wave from seaward bump would go the poor ship, and there would [might] be an end of our voyage. The captain, without waiting to sound, began to make an effort to put the ship over what was supposed to be a sandbank; but by the time soundings were made, this was found to be impossible, and he had only been jamming the poor *Elba* faster on a rock. Now every effort was made to get her astern, an anchor taken out, a rope brought to a winch I had for the cable, and the engines backed; but all in vain. A small Turkish Government steamer, which is to be our consort, came to our assistance, but of course very slowly, and much time was occupied before we could get a hawser to her. I could do no good after having made a chart of the soundings round the ship, and went at last on to the bridge to sketch the scene. But at that moment the strain from the winch and a jerk from the Turkish steamer got off the boat, after we had been some hours aground. The carpenter reported that she had made only two inches of water in one compartment; the cable was still uninjured astern, and our spirits rose; when, will you believe it? after going a short distance astern, the pilot ran us once more fast aground on what seemed to me nearly the same spot. The very same scene was gone through as on the first occasion, and dark came on whilst the wind shifted, and we were still aground. Dinner was served up, but poor Mr. Liddell could eat very little; and bump, bump, grind, grind, went the ship fifteen or sixteen times as we sat at dinner. The slight sea, however, did enable us to bump off. This morning we appear not to have suffered in any way; but a sea is rolling in, which a few hours ago would have settled the poor old *Elba*.

"June —.

"The Alexandria cable has again failed; after paying out two-thirds of the distance successfully, an unlucky touch in deep water snapped the line. Luckily the accident occurred in Mr. Liddell's watch. Though personally it may not really concern me, the accident weighs like a personal misfortune. Still, I am glad I was present—a failure is probably more instructive than a success; and this experience may enable us to avoid misfortune in still greater undertakings.

"June —.

"We left Syra the morning after our arrival on Saturday the 4th. This we did (first) because we were in a hurry to do something and (second) because, coming from Alexandria, we had four days' quarantine to perform. We were all mustered along the side while the doctor counted us; the letters were popped into a little tin box and taken away to be smoked; the guardians put on board to see that we held no communication with the shore—without them we should still have had four more days' quarantine; and with twelve Greek sailors besides, we started merrily enough picking up the Canea cable. . . . To our utter dismay, the yarn covering began to come up quite decayed, and the cable, which when laid should have borne half a ton, was now in danger of snapping with a tenth part of that strain. We went as slow as possible in fear of a break at every instant. My watch was from eight to twelve in the morning, and during that time we had barely secured three miles of cable. Once it broke inside the ship, but I seized hold of it in time—the weight being hardly anything—and the line for the nonce was saved. Regular nooses were then planted inboard with men to draw them taut, should the cable break inboard. A——, who should have relieved me, was unwell, so I had to continue my look-out; and about one o'clock the line again parted, but was again caught in the last noose, with about four inches to spare. Five minutes afterwards it again parted and was yet once more caught. Mr. Liddell (whom I had called) could stand this no longer; so we buoyed the line and ran into a bay in Siphano, waiting for calm weather, though I was by no means of opinion that the slight sea and wind had been the cause of our failures.—All next day (Monday) we lay off Siphano, amusing ourselves on shore with fowling-pieces and navy revolvers. I need not say we killed nothing; and luckily we did not wound any of ourselves. A guardiano accompanied us, his functions being limited to preventing actual contact with the natives, for they might come as near and talk as much as they pleased. These isles of Greece are sad, interesting places. They are not really barren all over, but they are quite destitute of verdure; and tufts of thyme, wild mastic or mint, though they sound well, are not nearly so pretty as grass. Many little churches, glittering white, dot the islands; most of them, I believe, abandoned during the whole year with the exception of one day sacred to their patron saint. The villages are mean, but the inhabitants do not look wretched and the men are good sailors. There is something in this Greek race yet; they will become a powerful Levantine nation in the course of time.—What a lovely moonlight evening that was! the barren island cutting the clear sky with fantastic outline, marble cliffs on either hand fairly gleaming over the calm sea. Next day, the wind still continuing, I proposed a boating excursion and decoyed A——, L——, and S—— into accompanying me. We took the little gig, and sailed away merrily enough round a point to a beautiful white bay, flanked with two glistening little churches, fronted by beautiful distant islands; when suddenly, to my horror, I discovered the *Elba* steaming full speed out from the island. Of course we steered after her; but the wind that instant ceased, and we were left in a dead calm. There was nothing for it but to unship the mast, get out the oars and pull. The ship was nearly certain to stop at the buoy; and I wanted to learn how to take an oar, so here was a chance with a vengeance. L—— steered, and we three pulled—a broiling pull it was about half way across to Palikandro —still we did come in, pulling an uncommon good stroke, and I had learned to hang on my oar. L—— had pressed me to let him take my place; but though I was very tired at the end of the first quarter of an hour, and then every successive half hour, I would not give in. I nearly paid dear for my obstinacy, however; for in the evening I had alternate fits of shivering and burning."

III

The next extracts, and I am sorry to say the last, are from Fleeming's letters of 1860, when he was back at Bona and Spartivento and for the first time at the head of an expedition. Unhappily these letters are not only the last, but the series is quite imperfect; and this is the more to be lamented as he had now begun to use a pen more skilfully, and in the following notes

there is at times a touch of real distinction in
the manner.

"Cagliari: October 5, 1860.

"All Tuesday I spent examining what was on
board the *Elba*, and trying to start the repairs
of the Spartivento land line, which has been entirely neglected, and no wonder, for no one has
been paid for three months, no, not even the
poor guards who have to keep themselves, their
horses and their families, on their pay. Wednesday morning, I started for Spartivento and got
there in time to try a good many experiments.
Spartivento looks more wild and savage than
ever, but is not without a strange deadly beauty:
the hills covered with bushes of a metallic green
with coppery patches of soil in between; the val-
leys filled with dry salt mud and a little stagnant
water; where that very morning the deer had
drunk, where herons, curlews, and other fowl
abound, and where, alas! malaria is breeding
with this rain. (No fear for those who do not
sleep on shore.) A little iron hut had been
placed there since 1858; but the windows had
been carried off, the door broken down, the roof
pierced all over. In it, we sat to make experiments; and how it recalled Birkenhead! There
was Thomson, there was my testing board, the
strings of gutta-percha; Harry P—— even, bat-
tering with the batteries; but where was my darling Annie? Whilst I sat feet in sand, with

Harry alone inside the hut—mats, coats, and wood to darken the window—the others visited the murderous old friar, who is of the order of Scaloppi, and for whom I brought a letter from his superior, ordering him to pay us attention; but he was away from home, gone to Cagliari in a boat with the produce of the farm belonging to his convent. Then they visited the tower of Chia, but could not get in because the door is thirty feet off the ground; so they came back and pitched a magnificent tent which I brought from the *Bahiana* a long time ago—and where they will live (if I mistake not) in preference to the friar's, or the owl- and bat-haunted tower. MM. T—— and S—— will be left there: T——, an intelligent, hard-working Frenchman, with whom I am well pleased; he can speak English and Italian well, and has been two years at Genoa. S—— is a French-German with a face like an ancient Gaul, who has been sergeant-major in the French line and who is, I see, a great, big, muscular *fainéant*. We left the tent pitched and some stores in charge of a guide, and ran back to Cagliari.

"Certainly, being at the head of things is pleasanter than being subordinate. We all agree very well; and I have made the testing-office into a kind of private room where I can come and write to you undisturbed, surrounded by my dear, bright brass things which all of them remind me of our nights at Birkenhead. Then I

can work here, too, and try lots of experiments;
you know how I like that! and now and then I
read—Shakespeare principally. Thank you so
much for making me bring him: I think I must
get a pocket edition of *Hamlet* and *Henry the
Fifth*, so as never to be without them.

"*Cagliari: October 7.*

"[The town was full?] . . . of red-shirted
English Garibaldini. A very fine-looking set
of fellows they are, too: the officers rather raffish,
but with medals Crimean and Indian; the men
a very sturdy set, with many lads of good birth
I should say. They still wait their consort the
Emperor and will, I fear, be too late to do anything. I meant to have called on them, but
they are all gone into barracks some way from
the town, and I have been much too busy to go
far.

"The view from the ramparts was very strange
and beautiful. Cagliari rises on a very steep
rock, at the mouth of a wide plain circled by
large hills and three-quarters filled with lagoons;
it looks, therefore, like an old island citadel.
Large heaps of salt mark the border between
the sea and the lagoons; thousands of flamingoes
whiten the centre of the huge shallow marsh;
hawks hover and scream among the trees under
the high mouldering battlements.—A little lower
down, the band played. Men and ladies bowed
and pranced, the costumes posed, church bells

tinkled, processions processed, the sun set behind thick clouds capping the hills; I pondered on you and enjoyed it all.

"Decidedly I prefer being master to being man: boats at all hours, stewards flying for marmalade, captain inquiring when ship is to sail, clerks to copy my writing, the boat to steer when we go out—I have run her nose on several times; decidedly, I begin to feel quite a little king. Confound the cable, though! I shall never be able to repair it.

"Bona: October 14.

"We left Cagliari at 4.30 on the 9th and soon got to Spartivento. I repeated some of my experiments, but found Thomson, who was to have been my grand stand-by, would not work on that day in the wretched little hut. Even if the windows and door had been put in, the wind, which was very high, made the lamp flicker about and blew it out; so I sent on board and got old sails, and fairly wrapped the hut up in them; and then we were as snug as could be, and I left the hut in glorious condition with a nice little stove in it. The tent which should have been forthcoming from the curé's for the guards, had gone to Cagliari; but I found another, [a] green, Turkish tent, in the *Elba* and soon had him up. The square tent left on the last occasion was standing all right and tight in spite of wind and rain. We landed provisions, two beds, plates, knives, forks, candles, cooking utensils, and were ready for a start at 6 P.M.; but the wind meanwhile had come on to blow at such a rate that I thought better of it, and we stopped. T—— and S—— slept ashore, however, to see how they liked it; at least they tried to sleep, for S——, the ancient sergeant-major, had a toothache, and T—— thought the tent was coming down every minute. Next morning they could only complain of sand and a leaky coffee-pot, so I leave them with a good conscience. The little encampment looked quite picturesque: the green round tent, the square white tent and the hut all wrapped up in sails, on a sand hill, looking on the sea and masking those confounded marshes at the back. One would have thought the Cagliaritans were in a conspiracy to frighten the two poor fellows, who (I believe) will be safe enough if they do not go into the marshes after nightfall. S—— brought a little dog to amuse them, such a jolly, ugly little cur without a tail, but full of fun; he will be better than quinine.

"The wind drove a barque, which had anchored near us for shelter, out to sea. We started, however, at 2 P.M., and had a quick passage but a very rough one, getting to Bona by daylight [on the 11th]. Such a place as this is for getting anything done! The health boat went away from us at 7.30 with W—— on board; and we heard nothing of them till 9.30, when W—— came back with two fat Frenchmen who are to look on on the part of the Government.

They are exactly alike: only one has four bands
and the other three round his cap, and so I know
them. Then I sent a boat round to Fort Gênois
[Fort Genova of 1858], where the cable is landed,
with all sorts of things and directions, whilst I
went ashore to see about coals and a room at the
fort. We hunted people in the little square in
their shops and offices, but only found them in
cafés. One amiable gentleman wasn't up at
9.30, was out at 10, and as soon as he came back
the servant said he would go to bed and not get
up till 3: he came, however, to find us at a café,
and said that, on the contrary, two days in the
week he did not do so! Then my two fat friends
must have their breakfast after their 'something'
at a café; and all the shops shut from 10 to 2;
and the post does not open till 12; and there was
a road to Fort Gênois, only a bridge had been
carried away, etc. At last I got off, and we
rowed round to Fort Gênois, where my men had
put up a capital gipsy tent with sails, and there
was my big board and Thomson's number 5 in
great glory. I soon came to the conclusion there
was a break. Two of my faithful Cagliaritans
slept all night in the little tent, to guard it and
my precious instruments; and the sea, which
was rather rough, silenced my Frenchmen.

"Next day I went on with my experiments,
whilst a boat grappled for the cable a little way
from shore and buoyed it where the *Elba* could
get hold. I brought all back to the *Elba*, tried

my machinery and was all ready for a start next morning. But the wretched coal had not come yet; Government permission from Algiers to be got; lighters, men, baskets, and I know not what forms to be got or got through—and everybody asleep! Coals or no coals, I was determined to start next morning; and start we did at four in the morning, picked up the buoy with our deck engine, popped the cable across a boat, tested the wires to make sure the fault was not behind us, and started picking up at 11. Everything worked admirably, and about 2 P. M., in came the fault. There is no doubt the cable was broken by coral-fishers; twice they have had it up to their own knowledge.

"Many men have been ashore to-day and have come back tipsy, and the whole ship is in a state of quarrel from top to bottom, and they will gossip just within my hearing. And we have had, moreover, three French gentlemen and a French lady to dinner, and I had to act host and try to manage the mixtures to their taste. The good-natured little Frenchwoman was most amusing; when I asked her if she would have some apple tart—'*Mon Dieu*,' with heroic resignation, '*je veux bien*'; or a little *plombodding*—'*Mais ce que vous voudrez, Monsieur!*'

"*S. S. Elba, somewhere not far from Bona: Oct. 19.*

"Yesterday [after three previous days of useless grappling] was destined to be very eventful.

We began dredging at daybreak and hooked at once every time in rocks; but by capital luck, just as we were deciding it was no use to continue in that place, we hooked the cable: up it came, was tested, and lo! another complete break, a quarter of a mile off. I was amazed at my own tranquillity under these disappointments, but I was not really half so fussy as about getting a cab. Well, there was nothing for it but grappling again, and, as you may imagine, we were getting about six miles from shore. But the water did not deepen rapidly; we seemed to be on the crest of a kind of submarine mountain in prolongation of Cape de Gonde, and pretty havoc we must have made with the crags. What rocks we did hook! No sooner was the grapnel down than the ship was anchored; and then came such a business: ship's engines going, deck engine thundering, belt slipping, fear of breaking ropes: actually breaking grapnels. It was always an hour or more before we could get the grapnel down again. At last we had to give up the place, though we knew we were close to the cable, and go further to sea in much deeper water; to my great fear, as I knew the cable was much eaten away and would stand but little strain. Well, we hooked the cable first dredge this time, and pulled it slowly and gently to the top, with much trepidation. Was it the cable? was there any weight on? it was evidently too small. Imagine my dismay when the cable did come up, but hanging loosely, thus:

instead of taut, thus:

showing certain signs of a break close by. For a moment I felt provoked, as I thought, 'Here we are in deep water, and the cable will not stand lifting!' I tested at once, and by the very first wire found it had broken towards shore and was good towards sea. This was of course very pleasant; but from that time to this, though the wires test very well, not a signal has come from Spartivento. I got the cable into a boat, and a gutta-percha line from the ship to the boat, and we signalled away at a great rate—but no signs of life. The tests, however, make me pretty sure one wire at least is good; so I determined to lay down cable from where we were to the shore, and go to Spartivento to see what had happened there. I fear my men are ill. The night was lovely, perfectly calm; so we lay close to the boat and signals were continually sent, but with no result. This morning I laid the cable down to Fort Gênois in style; and now we are picking up odds and ends of cable between the different breaks, and getting our buoys on board, etc. To-morrow I expect to leave for Spartivento."

IV

And now I am quite at an end of journal-keeping; diaries and diary letters being things of youth which Fleeming had at length outgrown. But one or two more fragments from his correspondence may be taken, and first this brief sketch of the laying of the Norderney cable; mainly interesting as showing under what defects of strength and in what extremities of pain this cheerful man must at times continue to go about his work.

"I slept on board 29th September, having arranged everything to start by daybreak from where we lay in the roads: but at daybreak a heavy mist hung over us so that nothing of land or water could be seen. At midday it lifted suddenly and away we went with perfect weather, but could not find the buoys Forde left, that evening. I saw the captain was not strong in navigation, and took matters next day much more into my own hands and before nine o'clock found the buoys (the weather had been so fine, we had anchored in the open sea near Texel). It took us till the evening to reach the buoys, get the cable on board, test the first half, speak to Lowestoft, make the splice, and start. H—— had not finished his work at Norderney, so I was alone on board for Reuter. Moreover the buoys to guide us in our course were not placed, and the captain had very vague ideas about keeping his course; so I had to do a good deal, and only lay down as I was for two hours in the night. I managed to run the course perfectly. Everything went well, and we found Norderney just where we wanted it next afternoon, and if the shore end had been laid, could have finished there and then, October 1st. But when we got to Norderney, we found the *Caroline* with shore-end lying apparently aground, and could not understand her signals; so we had to anchor suddenly and I went off in a small boat with the captain to the *Caroline*. It was cold by this time, and my arm was rather stiff and I was tired; I hauled myself up on board the *Caroline* by a rope and found H—— and two men on board. All the rest were trying to get the shore-end on shore, but had failed and apparently had stuck on shore, and the waves were getting up. We had anchored in the right place and next morning we hoped the shore-end would be laid, so we had only to go back. It was of course still colder and quite night. I went to bed and hoped to sleep, but, alas, the rheumatism got into the joints and caused me terrible pain so that I could not sleep. I bore it as long as I could in order to disturb no one, for all were tired; but at last I could bear it no longer and managed to wake the steward and got a mustard poultice, which took the pain from the shoulder;

but then the elbow got very bad, and I had to
call the second steward and get a second poultice, and then it was daylight, and I felt very ill
and feverish. The sea was now rather rough—
too rough rather for small boats, but luckily a
sort of thing called a scoot came out, and we got
on board her with some trouble, and got on
shore after a good tossing about which made us
all sea-sick. The cable sent from the *Caroline*
was just 60 yards too short and did not reach
the shore, so although the *Caroline* did make the
splice late that night, we could neither test nor
speak. Reuter was at Norderney, and I had to
do the best I could, which was not much, and
went to bed early; I thought I should never sleep
again, but in sheer desperation got up in the middle of the night and gulped a lot of raw whis-
key and slept at last. But not long. A Mr.
F—— washed my face and hands and dressed
me; and we hauled the cable out of the sea,
and got it joined to the telegraph station, and
on October 3rd telegraphed to Lowestoft first
and then to London. Miss Clara Volkman, a
niece of Mr. Reuter's, sent the first message to
Mrs. Reuter, who was waiting (Varley used
Miss Clara's hand as a kind of key), and I sent
one of the first messages to Odden. I thought a
message addressed to him would not frighten
you, and that he would enjoy a message through
papa's cable. I hope he did. They were all
very merry, but I had been so lowered by pain

that I could not enjoy myself in spite of the success."

V

Of the 1869 cruise in the *Great Eastern,* I give what I am able; only sorry it is no more, for the sake of the ship itself, already almost a legend even to the generation that saw it launched.

"*June 17, 1869.*—Here are the names of our staff in whom I expect you to be interested, as future *Great Eastern* stories may be full of them: Theophilus Smith, a man of Latimer Clark's; Leslie C. Hill, my prizeman at University College; Lord Sackville Cecil; King, one of the Thomsonian Kings; Laws, goes for Willoughby Smith, who will also be on board; Varley, Clark, and Sir James Anderson, make up the sum of all you know anything of. A Captain Halpin commands the big ship. There are four smaller vessels. The *Wm. Cory,* which laid the Norderney cable, has already gone to St. Pierre to lay the shore-ends. The *Hawk* and *Chiltern* have gone to Brest to lay shore-ends. The *Hawk* and *Scanderia* go with us across the Atlantic and we shall at St. Pierre be transshipped into one or the other.

"*June 18, somewhere in London.*—The shore-end is laid, as you may have seen, and we are all under pressing orders to march, so we start from London to-night at 5.10.

"*June 20, off Ushant.*—I am getting quite

fond of the big ship. Yesterday morning in the quiet sunlight, she turned so slowly and lazily in the great harbour at Portland, and by and by slipped out past the long pier with so little stir, that I could hardly believe we were really off. No men drunk, no women crying, no singing or swearing, no confusion or bustle on deck—nobody apparently aware that they had anything to do. The look of the thing was that the ship had been spoken to civilly and had kindly undertaken to do everything that was necessary without any further interference. I have a nice cabin with plenty of room for my legs in my berth and have slept two nights like a top. Then we have the ladies' cabin set apart as an engineer's office, and I think this decidedly the nicest place in the ship: 35 ft. x 20 ft. broad— four tables, three great mirrors, plenty of air and no heat from the funnels which spoil the great dining-room. I saw a whole library of books on the walls when here last, and this made me less anxious to provide light literature; but alas, to-day I find that they are every one Bibles or Prayer-books. Now one cannot read many hundred Bibles. . . . As for the motion of the ship it is not very much, but 'twill suffice. Thomson shook hands and wished me well. I *do* like Thomson. . . . Tell Austin that the *Great Eastern* has six masts and four funnels. When I get back I will make a little model of her for all the chicks and pay out cotton reels.

. . . Here we are at 4.20 at Brest. We leave probably to-morrow morning.

"*July 12. Great Eastern.*—Here as I write we run our last course for the buoy at the St. Pierre shore-end. It blows and lightens, and our good ship rolls, and buoys are hard to find; but we must soon now finish our work, and then this letter will start for home. . . . Yesterday we were mournfully groping our way through the wet grey fog, not at all sure where we were, with one consort lost and the other faintly answering the roar of our great whistle through the mist. As to the ship which was to meet us, and pioneer us up the deep channel, we did not know if we should come within twenty miles of her; when suddenly up went the fog, out came the sun, and there, straight ahead, was the *Wm. Cory*, our pioneer, and a little dancing boat, the *Gulnare*, sending signals of welcome with many-coloured flags. Since then we have been steaming in a grand procession; but now at 2 A. M. the fog has fallen, and the great roaring whistle calls up the distant answering notes all around us. Shall we, or shall we not find the buoy?

"*July 13.*—All yesterday we lay in the damp dripping fog, with whistles all round and guns firing so that we might not bump up against one another. This little delay has let us get our reports into tolerable order. We are now at 7 o'clock getting the cable end again, with the main cable buoy close to us."

A telegram of July 20: "I have received your four welcome letters. The Americans are charming people."

VI

And here, to make an end, are a few random bits about the cruise to Pernambuco:—

"*Plymouth, June 21, 1873.*—I have been down to the sea-shore and smelt the salt sea and like it; and I have seen the *Hooper* pointing her great bow sea-ward, while light smoke rises from her funnels telling that the fires are being lighted; and sorry as I am to be without you, something inside me answers to the call to be off and doing.

"*Lalla Rookh, Plymouth, June 22.*—We have been a little cruise in the yacht over to the Eddystone lighthouse, and my sea-legs seem very well on. Strange how alike all these starts are— first on shore, steaming hot days with a smell of bone-dust and tar and salt water; then the little puffing, panting steam-launch that bustles out across a port with green woody sides, little yachts sliding about, men-of-war training-ships, and then a great big black hulk of a thing with a mass of smaller vessels sticking to it like parasites; and that is one's home being coaled. Then comes the champagne lunch where every one says all that is polite to every one else, and then the uncertainty when to start. So far as we know *now*, we are to start to-morrow morning at daybreak; letters that come later are to be sent to Pernambuco by first mail. . . . My father has sent me the heartiest sort of Jack Tar's cheer.

"*S. S. Hooper, off Funchal, June 29.*—Here we are off Madeira at seven o'clock in the morning. Thomson has been sounding with his special toy ever since half-past three (1087 fathoms of water). I have been watching the bay and long jagged islands start into being out of the dull night. We are still some miles from land; but the sea is calmer than Loch Eil often was, and the big *Hooper* rests very contentedly after a pleasant voyage and favourable breezes. I have not been able to do any real work except the testing [of the cable], for though not seasick, I get a little giddy when I try to think on board. . . . The ducks have just had their daily souse and are quacking and gabbling in a mighty way outside the door of the captain's deck cabin where I write. The cocks are crowing, and new-laid eggs are said to be found in the coops. Four mild oxen have been untethered and allowed to walk along the broad iron decks—a whole drove of sheep seem quite content while licking big lumps of bay salt. Two exceedingly impertinent goats lead the cook a perfect life of misery. They steal round the galley and *will* nibble the carrots or turnips if his back is turned for one minute; and then he throws something at them and misses them; and they scuttle off laughing impudently, and flick one ear at him from a safe distance. This is the most impudent gesture I ever saw. Winking is nothing to it. The ear normally hangs down behind; the goat turns sideways to her enemy—by a little knowing cock of the head flicks one ear over one eye, and squints from behind it for half a minute—tosses her head back, skips a pace or two further off, and repeats the manœuvre. The cook is very fat and cannot run after that goat much.

"*Pernambuco, Aug. 1.*—We landed here yesterday, all well and cable sound, after a good passage. . . . I am on familiar terms with cocoa-nuts, mangoes, and bread-fruit trees, but I think I like the negresses best of anything I have seen. In turbans and loose sea-green robes, with beautiful black-brown complexions and a stately carriage, they really are a satisfaction to my eye. The weather has been windy and rainy; the *Hooper* has to lie about a mile from the town, in an open roadstead, with the whole swell of the Atlantic driving straight on shore. The little steam-launch gives all who go in her a good ducking, as she bobs about on the big rollers; and my old gymnastic practice stands me in good stead on boarding and leaving her. We clamber down a rope-ladder hanging from the high stern, and then, taking a rope in one hand, swing into the launch at the moment when she can contrive to steam up under us—bobbing about like an apple thrown into a tub all the while. The President of the province and his suite tried to come off to a State luncheon on board on Sunday; but the launch being rather heavily laden, behaved worse than usual, and some green seas stove in the President's hat and made him wetter than he had probably ever been in his life; so after one or two rollers, he turned back; and indeed he was wise to do so, for I don't see how he could have got on board. . . . Being fully convinced that the world will not continue to go round unless I pay it personal attention, I must run away to my work."

CHAPTER VI

1869–1885

THE remaining external incidents of Fleeming's life, pleasures, honours, fresh interests, new friends, are not such as will bear to be told at any length or in the temporal order. And it is now time to lay narration by, and to look at the man he was and the life he lived, more largely.

Edinburgh, which was henceforth to be his home, is a metropolitan small town; where college professors and the lawyers of the Parliament House give the tone, and persons of leisure, attracted by educational advantages, make up much of the bulk of society. Not, therefore, an unlettered place, yet not pedantic, Edinburgh will compare favourably with much larger cities. A hard and disputatious element has been commented on by strangers: it would not touch Fleeming, who was himself regarded, even in this metropolis of disputation, as a thorny tablemate. To golf unhappily he did not take, and golf is a cardinal virtue in the city of the winds. Nor did he become an archer of the Queen's Body Guard, which is the Chiltern Hundreds of the distasted golfer. He did not even frequent the Evening Club, where his colleague Tait (in my day) was so punctual and so genial. So that in some ways he stood outside of the lighter and kindlier life of his new home. I should not like to say that he was generally popular; but there as elsewhere, those who knew him well enough to love him, loved him well. And he, upon his side, liked a place where a dinner-party was not of necessity unintellectual, and where men stood up to him in argument.

The presence of his old classmate, Tait, was one of his early attractions to the chair; and now that Fleeming is gone again, Tait still remains, ruling and really teaching his great classes. Sir Robert Christison was an old friend of his mother's; Sir Alexander Grant, Kelland, and Sellar, were new acquaintances and highly valued; and these too, all but the last, have been taken from their friends and labours. Death has been busy in the Senatus. I will speak elsewhere of Fleeming's demeanour to his students; and it will be enough to add here that his relations with his colleagues in general were pleasant to himself.

Edinburgh, then, with its society, its university work, its delightful scenery, and its skating in the winter, was thenceforth his base of operations. But he shot meanwhile erratic in many directions: twice to America, as we have seen, on telegraph voyages; continually to London on business; often to Paris; year after year to the Highlands to shoot, to fish, to learn reels and Gaelic, to make the acquaintance and fall in love with the character of Highlanders; and once to Styria, to hunt chamois and dance with peasant maidens. All the while, he was pursuing the course of his electrical studies, making fresh inventions, taking up the phonograph, filled with theories of graphic representation; reading, writing, publishing, founding sanitary associations, interested in technical education, investigating the laws of metre, drawing, acting, directing private theatricals, going a long way to see an actor—a long way to see a picture; in the very bubble of the tideway of contemporary interests. And all the while he was busied about his father and mother, his wife, and in particular his sons; anxiously watching, anxiously guiding these, and plunging with his whole fund of youthfulness into their sports and interests. And all the while he was himself maturing —not in character or body, for these remained young—but in the stocked mind, in the tolerant knowledge of life and man, in pious acceptance of the universe.   Here is a farrago for a chapter: here is a world of interests and activities, human, artistic, social, scientific, at each of which he sprang with impetuous pleasure, on each of which he squandered energy, the arrow drawn to the head, the whole intensity of his spirit bent, for the moment, on the momentary purpose. It was this that lent such unusual interest to his society, so that no friend of his can forget that figure of Fleeming coming charged with some new discovery: it is this that makes his character so difficult to represent.   Our fathers, upon some difficult theme, would invoke the Muse; I can but appeal to the imagination of the reader. When I dwell upon some one thing, he must bear in mind it was only one of a score; that the unweariable brain was teeming at the very time with other thoughts; that the good heart had left no kind duty forgotten.

I

In Edinburgh, for a considerable time, Fleeming's family, to three generations, was united: Mr. and Mrs. Austin at Hailes, Captain and Mrs. Jenkin in the suburb of Merchiston, Fleeming himself in the city.   It is not every family that could risk with safety such close inter-domestic dealings; but in this also Fleeming was particularly favoured.   Even the two extremes, Mr.

Austin and the Captain, drew together. It is
pleasant to find that each of the old gentlemen
set a high value on the good looks of the other,
doubtless also on his own; and a fine picture
they made as they walked the green terrace at
Hailes, conversing by the hour. What they
talked of is still a mystery to those who knew
them; but Mr. Austin always declared that on
these occasions he learned much. To both of
these families of elders, due service was paid of
attention; to both, Fleeming's easy circumstances had brought joy; and the eyes of all were
on the grandchildren. In Fleeming's scheme
of duties, those of the family stood first; a man
was first of all a child, nor did he cease to be so,
but only took on added obligations, when he became in turn a father. The care of his parents
was always a first thought with him, and their
gratification his delight. And the care of his
sons, as it was always a grave subject of study
with him, and an affair never neglected, so it
brought him a thousand satisfactions. "Hard
work they are," as he once wrote, "but what fit
work!" And again: "O, it's a cold house
where a dog is the only representative of a
child!" Not that dogs were despised; we shall
drop across the name of Jack, the harum-scarum
Irish terrier, ere we have done; his own dog
Plato went up with him daily to his lectures,
and still (like other friends) feels the loss and
looks visibly for the reappearance of his master;

and Martin, the cat, Fleeming has himself immortalised, to the delight of Mr. Swinburne, in the columns of the *Spectator*. Indeed, there was nothing in which men take interest, in which he took not some; and yet always most in the strong human bonds, ancient as the race and woven of delights and duties.

He was even an anxious father; perhaps that is the part where optimism is hardest tested. He was eager for his sons; eager for their health, whether of mind or body; eager for their education; in that, I should have thought, too eager. But he kept a pleasant face upon all things, believed in play, loved it himself, shared boyishly in theirs, and knew how to put a face of entertainment upon business, and a spirit of education into entertainment. If he was to test the progress of the three boys, this advertisement would appear in their little manuscript paper:—"Notice: The Professor of Engineering in the University of Edinburgh intends at the close of the scholastic year to hold examinations in the following subjects: (1) For boys in the fourth class of the Academy—Geometry and Algebra; (2) For boys at Mr. Henderson's school—Dictation and Recitation; (3) For boys taught exclusively by their mothers—Arithmetic and Reading." Prizes were given; but what prize would be so conciliatory as this boyish little joke? It may read thin here; it would smack racily in the playroom. Whenever his sons "started a new fad" (as one of them writes to me) they "had only to tell him about it, and he was at once interested and keen to help." He would discourage them in nothing unless it was hopelessly too hard for them; only, if there was any principle of science involved, they must understand the principle; and whatever was attempted, that was to be done thoroughly. If it was but play, if it was but a puppet-show they were to build, he set them the example of being no sluggard in play. When Frewen, the second son, embarked on the ambitious design to make an engine for a toy steamboat, Fleeming made him begin with a proper drawing—doubt-less to the disgust of the young engineer; but once that foundation laid, helped in the work with unflagging gusto, "tinkering away," for hours, and assisted at the final trial "in the big bath" with no less excitement than the boy. "He would take any amount of trouble to help us," writes my correspondent. "We never felt an affair was complete till we had called him to see, and he would come at any time, in the middle of any work." There was indeed one recognised play-hour, immediately after the des-patch of the day's letters; and the boys were to be seen waiting on the stairs until the mail should be ready and the fun could begin. But at no other time did this busy man suffer his work to interfere with that first duty to his children; and there is a pleasant tale of the inventive Master

Frewen, engaged at the time upon a toy crane, bringing to the study where his father sat at work a half-wound reel that formed some part of his design, and observing, "Papa, you might finiss windin' this for me; I am so very busy to-day."

I put together here a few brief extracts from Fleeming's letters, none very important in itself, but all together building up a pleasant picture of the father with his sons.

"*Jan. 15th, 1875.*—Frewen contemplates suspending soap bubbles by silk threads for experimental purposes. I don't think he will manage that. Bernard" [the youngest] "volunteered to blow the bubbles with enthusiasm."

"*Jan. 17th.*—I am learning a great deal of electrostatics in consequence of the perpetual cross-examination to which I am subjected. I long for you on many grounds, but one is that I may not be obliged to deliver a running lecture on abstract points of science, subject to cross-examination by two acute students. Bernie does not cross-examine much; but if any one gets discomfited, he laughs a sort of little silver-whistle giggle, which is trying to the unhappy blunderer."

"*May 9th.*—Frewen is deep in parachutes. I beg him not to drop from the top landing in one of his own making."

"*June 6th, 1876.*—Frewen's crank axle is a failure just at present—but he bears up."

"*June 14th.*—The boys enjoy their riding. It gets them whole funds of adventures. One of their caps falling off is matter for delightful reminiscences; and when a horse breaks his step, the occurrence becomes a rear, a shy, or a plunge as they talk it over. Austin, with quiet confidence, speaks of the greater pleasure in riding a spirited horse, even if he does give a little trouble. It is the stolid brute that he dislikes. (N. B. You can still see six inches between him and the saddle when his pony trots.) I listen and sympathise and throw out no hint that their achievements are not really great."

"*June 18th.*—Bernard is much impressed by the fact that I can be useful to Frewen about the steamboat" [which the latter irrepressible inventor was making]. "He says, quite with awe, 'He would not have got on nearly so well if you had not helped him.'"

"*June 27th.*—I do not see what I could do without Austin. He talks so pleasantly and is so truly good all through."

"*July 7th.*—My chief difficulty with Austin is to get him measured for a pair of trousers. Hitherto I have failed, but I keep a stout heart and mean to succeed. Frewen the observer, in describing the paces of two horses, says, 'Polly takes twenty-seven steps to get round the school. I couldn't count Sophy, but she takes more than a hundred.'"

"*Feb. 18th, 1877.*—We all feel very lonely

without you. Frewen had to come up and sit in my room for company last night and I actually kissed him, a thing that has not occurred for years. Jack, poor fellow, bears it as well as he can, and has taken the opportunity of having a fester on his foot, so he is lame and has it bathed, and this occupies his thoughts a good deal."

"*Feb. 19th.*—As to Mill, Austin has not got the list yet. I think it will prejudice him very much against Mill—but that is not my affair. Education of that kind! . . . I would as soon cram my boys with food and boast of the pounds they had eaten, as cram them with literature."

But if Fleeming was an anxious father, he did not suffer his anxiety to prevent the boys from any manly or even dangerous pursuit. Whatever it might occur to them to try, he would carefully show them how to do it, explain the risks, and then either share the danger himself or, if that were not possible, stand aside and wait the event with that unhappy courage of the looker-on. He was a good swimmer, and taught them to swim. He thoroughly loved all manly exercises; and during their holidays, and principally in the Highlands, helped and encouraged them to excel in as many as possible—to shoot, to fish, to walk, to pull an oar, to hand, reef and steer, and to run a steam-launch. In all of these, and in all parts of Highland life, he shared delightedly. He was well on to forty when he took once more to shooting, he was forty-three when he killed his first salmon, but no boy could have more single-mindedly rejoiced in these pursuits. His growing love for the Highland character, perhaps also a sense of the difficulty of the task, led him to take up at forty-one the study of Gaelic; in which he made some shadow of progress, but not much: the fastnesses of that elusive speech retaining to the last their independence. At the house of his friend Mrs. Blackburn, who plays the part of a Highland lady as to the manner born, he learned the delightful custom of kitchen dances, which became the rule at his own house and brought him into yet nearer contact with his neighbours. And thus, at forty-two, he began to learn the reel; a study to which he brought his usual smiling earnestness; and the steps, diagrammatically represented by his own hand, are before me as I write.

It was in 1879 that a new feature was added to the Highland life: a steam-launch, called the *Purgle*, the Styrian corruption of Walpurga, after a friend to be hereafter mentioned. "The steam-launch goes," Fleeming wrote. "I wish you had been present to describe two scenes of which she has been the occasion already: one during which the population of Ullapool, to a baby, was harnessed to her hurrahing—and the other in which the same population sat with its legs over a little pier, watching Frewen and Bernie getting up steam for the first time." The *Purgle* was got with educational intent; and it served its purpose so well, and the boys knew their business so practically, that when the summer was at an end, Fleeming, Mrs. Jenkin, Frewen the engineer, Bernard the stoker, and Kenneth Robertson, a Highland seaman, set forth in her to make the passage south. The first morning they got from Loch Broom into Gruinard bay, where they lunched upon an island; but the wind blowing up in the afternoon, with sheets of rain, it was found impossible to beat to sea; and very much in the situation of castaways upon an unknown coast, the party landed at the mouth of Gruinard river. A shooting-lodge was spied among the trees; there Fleeming went; and though the master, Mr. Murray, was from home, though the two Jenkin boys were of course as black as colliers, and all the castaways so wetted through that, as they stood in the passage, pools formed about their feet and ran before them into the house, yet Mrs. Murray kindly entertained them for the night. On the morrow, however, visitors were to arrive; there would be no room and, in so out-of-the-way a spot, most probably no food for the crew of the *Purgle;* and on the morrow about noon, with the bay white with spindrift and the wind so strong that one could scarcely stand against it, they got up

steam and skulked under the land as far as
Sanda Bay. Here they crept into a seaside cave,
and cooked some food; but the weather now
freshening to a gale, it was plain they must moor
the launch where she was, and find their way
overland to some place of shelter. Even to get
their baggage from on board was no light business; for the dingy was blown so far to leeward
every trip, that they must carry her back by
hand along the beach. But this once managed
and a cart procured in the neighbourhood, they
were able to spend the night in a pot-house at
Ault Bea. Next day the sea was unapproachable; but the next they had a pleasant passage
to Poolewe, hugging the cliffs, the falling swell
bursting close by them in the gullies, and the
black scarts that sat like ornaments on the top
of every stack and pinnacle looking down into
the *Purgle* as she passed. The climate of Scotland had not done with them yet: for three days
they lay storm-stayed in Poolewe, and when they
put to sea on the morning of the fourth, the sailors prayed them for God's sake not to attempt
the passage. Their setting out was indeed
merely tentative; but presently they had gone
too far to return, and found themselves committed to double Rhu Reay with a foul wind and
a cross sea. From half-past eleven in the morning until half-past five at night, they were in
immediate and unceasing danger. Upon the
least mishap, the *Purgle* must either have been

swamped by the seas or bulged upon the cliffs of that rude headland. Fleeming and Robertson took turns baling and steering; Mrs. Jenkin, so violent was the commotion of the boat, held on with both hands; Frewen, by Robertson's direction, ran the engine, slacking and pressing her to meet the seas; and Bernard, only twelve years old, deadly sea-sick, and continually thrown against the boiler, so that he was found next day to be covered with burns, yet kept an even fire. It was a very thankful party that sat down that evening to meat in the hotel at Gairloch. And perhaps, although the thing was new in the family, no one was much surprised when Fleeming said grace over that meal. Thenceforward he continued to observe the form, so that there was kept alive in his house a grateful memory of peril and deliverance. But there was nothing of the muff in Fleeming; he thought it a good thing to escape death, but a becoming and a healthful thing to run the risk of it; and what is rarer, that which he thought for himself, he thought for his family also. In spite of the terrors of Rhu Reay, the cruise was persevered in and brought to an end under happier conditions.

One year, instead of the Highlands, Alt-Aussee, in the Steiermark, was chosen for the holidays; and the place, the people, and the life delighted Fleeming. He worked hard at German, which he had much forgotten since he was a boy; and what is highly characteristic, equally hard at the *patois*, in which he learned to excel. He won a prize at a Schützen-fest; and though he hunted chamois without much success, brought down more interesting game in the shape of the Styrian peasants, and in particular of his gillie, Joseph. This Joseph was much of a character; and his appreciations of Fleeming have a fine note of their own. The bringing up of the boys he deigned to approve of: "*fast so gut wie ein Bauer,*" was his trenchant criticism. The attention and courtly respect with which Fleeming surrounded his wife, was something of a puzzle to the philosophic gillie; he announced in the village that Mrs. Jenkin—*die silberne Frau,* as the folk had prettily named her from some silver ornaments—was a "*geborene Gräfin*" who had married beneath her; and when Fleeming explained what he called the English theory (though indeed it was quite his own) of married relations, Joseph, admiring but unconvinced, avowed it was "*gar schön.*" Joseph's cousin, Walpurga Moser, to an orchestra of clarionet and zither, taught the family the country dances, the Steierisch and the Ländler, and gained their hearts during the lessons. Her sister Loys, too, who was up at the Alp with the cattle, came down to church on Sundays, made acquaintance with the Jenkins, and must have them up to see the sunrise from her house upon the Loser, where they had supper and all slept in the loft among the hay. The Mosers were not

lost sight of; Walpurga still corresponds with
Mrs. Jenkin, and it was a late pleasure of Fleeming's to choose and despatch a wedding present
for his little mountain friend. This visit was
brought to an end by a ball in the big inn par-
lour; the refreshments chosen, the list of guests
drawn up, by Joseph; the best music of the
place in attendance; and hosts and guests in
their best clothes. The ball was opened by Mrs.
Jenkin dancing Steierisch with a lordly Bauer, in
grey and silver and with a plumed hat; and
Fleeming followed with Walpurga Moser.

There ran a principle through all these holiday pleasures. In Styria, as in the Highlands,
the same course was followed: Fleeming threw
himself as fully as he could into the life and
occupations of the native people, studying everywhere their dances and their language, and con-
forming, always with pleasure, to their rustic
etiquette. Just as the ball at Alt-Aussee was
designed for the taste of Joseph, the parting
feast at Attadale was ordered in every particular
to the taste of Murdoch the Keeper. Fleeming
was not one of the common, so-called gentlemen,
who take the tricks of their own coterie to be
eternal principles of taste. He was aware, on
the other hand, that rustic people dwelling in
their own places follow ancient rules with fastid-
ious precision, and are easily shocked and embarrassed by what (if they used the word) they
would have to call the vulgarity of visitors from

town. And he, who was so cavalier with men of his own class, was sedulous to shield the more tender feelings of the peasant; he, who could be so trying in a drawing-room, was even punctilious in the cottage. It was in all respects a happy virtue. It renewed his life, during these holidays, in all particulars. It often entertained him with the discovery of strange survivals; as when, by the orders of Murdoch, Mrs. Jenkin must publicly taste of every dish before it was set before her guests. And thus to throw himself into a fresh life and a new school of manners was a grateful exercise of Fleeming's mimetic instinct; and to the pleasures of the open air, of hardships supported, of dexterities improved and displayed, and of plain and elegant society, added a spice of drama.

II

Fleeming was all his life a lover of the play and all that belonged to it. Dramatic literature he knew fully. He was one of the not very numerous people who can read a play; a knack, the fruit of much knowledge and some imagination, comparable to that of reading score. Few men better understood the artificial principles on which a play is good or bad; few more unaffectedly enjoyed a piece of any merit of construction. His own play was conceived with a double design; for he had long been filled with his theory of the true story of Griselda; used to gird at

Father Chaucer for his misconception; and was, perhaps first of all, moved by the desire to do justice to the Marquis of Saluces, and perhaps only in the second place, by the wish to treat a story (as he phrased it) like a sum in arithmetic. I do not think he quite succeeded; but I must own myself no fit judge. Fleeming and I were teacher and taught as to the principles, disputatious rivals in the practice, of dramatic writing.

Acting had always, ever since Rachel and the *Marseillaise*, a particular power on him. "If I do not cry at the play," he used to say, "I want to have my money back." Even from a poor play with poor actors, he could draw pleasure. "Giacometti's *Elisabetta*," I find him writing, "fetched the house vastly. Poor Queen Elizabeth! And yet it was a little good." And again, after a night of Salvini: "I do not suppose any one with feelings could sit out *Othello*, if Iago and Desdemona were acted." Salvini was, in his view, the greatest actor he had seen. We were all indeed moved and bettered by the visit of that wonderful man.—"I declare I feel as if I could pray!" cried one of us, on the return from *Hamlet*.—"That is prayer," said Fleeming. W. B. Hole and I, in a fine enthusiasm of gratitude, determined to draw up an address to Salvini, did so, and carried it to Fleeming; and I shall never forget with what coldness he heard and deleted the eloquence of our draft, nor with what spirit (our vanities once properly mortified) he threw himself into the business of collecting signatures. It was his part, on the ground of his Italian, to see and arrange with the actor; it was mine to write in the *Academy* a notice of the first performance of *Macbeth*. Fleeming opened the paper, read so far, and flung it on the floor. "No," he cried, "that won't do. You were thinking of yourself, not of Salvini!" The criticism was shrewd as usual, but it was unfair through ignorance; it was not of myself that I was thinking, but of the difficulties of my trade which I had not well mastered. Another unalloyed dramatic pleasure which Fleeming and I shared the year of the Paris Exposition, was the *Marquis de Villemer*, that blameless play, performed by Madeleine Brohan, Delaunay, Worms, and Broisat—an actress, in such parts at least, to whom I have never seen full justice rendered. He had his fill of weeping on that occasion; and when the piece was at an end, in front of a café, in the mild midnight air, we had our fill of talk about the art of acting.

But what gave the stage so strong a hold on Fleeming was an inheritance from Norwich, from Edward Barron, and from Enfield of the *Speaker*. The theatre was one of Edward Barron's elegant hobbies; he read plays, as became Enfield's son-in-law, with a good discretion; he wrote plays for his family, in which Eliza Barron used to shine in the chief parts; and later in life, after the Norwich home was broken up,

his little granddaughter would sit behind him
in a great armchair, and be introduced, with his
stately elocution, to the world of dramatic literature. From this, in a direct line, we can deduce
the charades at Claygate; and after money
came, in the Edinburgh days, that private
theatre which took up so much of Fleeming's
energy and thought. The company—Mr. and
Mrs. R. O. Carter of Colwall, W. B. Hole, Captain Charles Douglas, Mr. Kunz, Mr. Burnett,
Professor Lewis Campbell, Mr. Charles Baxter,
and many more—made a charming society for
themselves and gave pleasure to their audience.
Mr. Carter in Sir Toby Belch it would be hard
to beat. Mr. Hole in broad farce, or as the herald in the *Trachiniæ*, showed true stage talent.
As for Mrs. Jenkin, it was for her the rest of us
existed and were forgiven; her powers were an
endless spring of pride and pleasure to her husband; he spent hours hearing and schooling her
in private; and when it came to the performance, though there was perhaps no one in the
audience more critical, none was more moved
than Fleeming. The rest of us did not aspire so
high. There were always five performances and
weeks of busy rehearsal; and whether we came
to sit and stifle as the prompter, to be the dumb
(or rather the inarticulate) recipients of Carter's
dog whip in the *Taming of the Shrew*, or, having
earned our spurs, to lose one more illusion in a
leading part, we were always sure at least of a

long and an exciting holiday in mirthful company.

In this laborious annual diversion, Fleming's part was large. I never thought him an actor, but he was something of a mimic, which stood him in stead. Thus he had seen Got in Poirier; and his own Poirier, when he came to play it, breathed meritoriously of the model. The last part I saw him play was Triplet, and at first I thought it promised well. But alas! the boys went for a holiday, missed a train, and were not heard of at home till late at night. Poor Fleeming, the man who never hesitated to give his sons a chisel or a gun, or to send them abroad in a canoe or on a horse, toiled all day at his rehearsal, growing hourly paler, Triplet growing hourly less meritorious. And though the return of the children, none the worse for their little adventure, brought the colour back into his face, it could not restore him to his part. I remember finding him seated on the stairs in some rare moment of quiet during the subsequent performances. "Hullo, Jenkin," said I, "you look down in the mouth."—"My dear boy," said he, "haven't you heard me? I have not had one decent intonation from beginning to end."

But indeed he never supposed himself an actor; took a part, when he took any, merely for convenience, as one takes a hand at whist; and found his true service and pleasure in the more congenial business of the manager. Augier, Racine, Shakespeare, Aristophanes in Hookham Frere's translation, Sophocles and Æschylus in Lewis Campbell's, such were some of the authors whom he introduced to his public. In putting these upon the stage, he found a thousand exercises for his ingenuity and taste, a thousand problems arising which he delighted to study, a thousand opportunities to make these infinitesimal improvements which are so much in art and for the artist. Our first Greek play had been costumed by the professional costumer, with unforgettable results of comicality and indecorum: the second, the *Trachiniæ* of Sophocles, he took in hand himself, and a delightful task he made of it. His study was then in antiquarian books, where he found confusion, and on statues and bas-reliefs, where he at last found clearness; after an hour or so at the British Museum, he was able to master "the chitôn, sleeves and all"; and before the time was ripe, he had a theory of Greek tailoring at his fingers' ends, and had all the costumes made under his eye as a Greek tailor would have made them. "The Greeks made the best plays and the best statues, and were the best architects: of course, they were the best tailors, too," said he; and was never weary, when he could find a tolerant listener, of dwelling on the simplicity, the economy, the elegance both of means and effect, which made their system so delightful.

But there is another side to the stage-manager's employment. The discipline of acting is detestable; the failures and triumphs of that business appeal too directly to the vanity; and even in the course of a careful amateur performance such as ours, much of the smaller side of man will be displayed. Fleeming, among conflicting vanities and levities, played his part to my admiration. He had his own view; he might be wrong; but the performances (he would remind us) were after all his, and he must decide. He was, in this as in all other things, an iron taskmaster, sparing not himself nor others. If you were going to do it at all, he would see that it was done as well as you were able. I have known him to keep two culprits (and one of these his wife) repeating the same action and the same two or three words for a whole weary afternoon. And yet he gained and retained warm feelings from far the most of those who fell under his domination, and particularly (it is pleasant to remember) from the girls. After the slipshod training and the incomplete accomplishments of a girls' school, there was something at first annoying, at last exciting and bracing, in this high standard of accomplishment and perseverance.

III

It did not matter why he entered upon any study or employment, whether for amusement,

like the Greek tailoring or the Highland reels,
whether from a desire to serve the public as with
his sanitary work, or in the view of benefiting
poorer men as with his labours for technical
education, he "pitched into it" (as he would
have said himself) with the same headlong zest.
I give in the Appendix[1] a letter from Colonel
Fergusson, which tells fully the nature of the
sanitary work and of Fleeming's part and success in it. It will be enough to say here that it
was a scheme of protection against the blunder-
ing of builders and the dishonesty of plumbers.
Started with an eye rather to the houses of the
rich, Fleeming hoped his Sanitary Associations
would soon extend their sphere of usefulness
and improve the dwellings of the poor. In this
hope he was disappointed; but in all other ways
the scheme exceedingly prospered, associations
sprang up and continue to spring up in many
quarters, and wherever tried they have been
found of use.

Here, then, was a serious employment; it has
proved highly useful to mankind; and it was begun besides, in a mood of bitterness, under the
shock of what Fleeming would so sensitively
feel—the death of a whole family of children.
Yet it was gone upon like a holiday jaunt. I
read in Colonel Fergusson's letter that his school-
mates bantered him when he began to broach
his scheme; so did I at first, and he took the

[1]Not reprinted in this edition—Ed.

banter as he always did with enjoyment, until he suddenly posed me with the question: "And now do you see any other jokes to make? Well, then," said he, "that's all right. I wanted you to have your fun out first; now we can be serious." And then with a glowing heat of pleasure, he laid his plans before me, revelling in the details, revelling in hope. It was as he wrote about the joy of electrical experiment: "What shall I compare them to? A new song?—a Greek play?" Delight attended the exercise of all his powers; delight painted the future. Of these ideal visions, some (as I have said) failed of their fruition. And the illusion was characteristic. Fleeming believed we had only to make a virtue cheap and easy, and then all would practise it; that for an end unquestionably good, men would not grudge a little trouble and a little money, though they might stumble at laborious pains and generous sacrifices. He could not believe in any resolute badness. "I cannot quite say," he wrote in his young manhood, "that I think there is no sin or misery. This I can say: I do not remember one single malicious act done to myself. In fact it is rather awkward when I have to say the Lord's Prayer. I have nobody's trespasses to forgive." And to the point, I remember one of our discussions. I said it was a dangerous error not to admit there were bad people; he, that it was only a confession of blindness on our part, and that we

probably called others bad only so far as we were
wrapped in ourselves and lacking in the trans-
migratory forces of imagination. I undertook
to describe to him three persons irredeemably
bad and whom he should admit to be so. In
the first case, he denied my evidence: "You cannot judge a man upon such testimony," said he.
For the second, he owned it made him sick to
hear the tale; but then there was no spark of
malice, it was mere weakness I had described,
and he had never denied nor thought to set a
limit to man's weakness. At my third gentleman, he struck his colours. "Yes," said he,
"I'm afraid that *is* a bad man." And then
looking at me shrewdly: "I wonder if it isn't a
very unfortunate thing for you to have met him."
I showed him radiantly how it was the world we
must know, the world as it was, not a world ex-
purgated and prettified with optimistic rainbows.
"Yes, yes," said he; "but this badness is such an
easy, lazy explanation. Won't you be tempted
to use it, instead of trying to understand people?"

In the year 1878, he took a passionate fancy
for the phonograph: it was a toy after his heart,
a toy that touched the skirts of life, art, and
science, a toy prolific of problems and theories.
Something fell to be done for a University
Cricket-Ground Bazaar. "And the thought
struck him," Mr. Ewing writes to me, "to exhibit Edison's phonograph, then the very newest scientific marvel. The instrument itself was

not to be purchased—I think no specimen had then crossed the Atlantic—but a copy of the *Times* with an account of it was at hand, and by the help of this we made a phonograph which to our great joy talked, and talked, too; with the purest American accent. It was so good that a second instrument was got ready forth-with. Both were shown at the Bazaar: one by Mrs. Jenkin to people willing to pay half a crown for a private view and the privilege of hearing their own voices, while Jenkin, perfervid as usual, gave half-hourly lectures on the other in an adjoining room—I, as his lieutenant, taking turns. The thing was in its way a little triumph. A few of the visitors were deaf, and hugged the belief that they were the victims of a new kind of fancy-fair swindle. Of the others, many who came to scoff remained to take raffle tickets; and one of the phonographs was finally disposed of in this way."

The other remained in Fleeming's hands, and was a source of infinite occupation. Once it was sent to London, "to bring back on the tinfoil the tones of a lady distinguished for clear vocalisations; at another time Sir Robert Christison was brought in to contribute his powerful bass"; and there scarcely came a visitor about the house, but he was made the subject of experiment. The visitors, I am afraid, took their parts lightly: Mr. Hole and I, with unscientific laughter, commemorating various shades of

Scottish accent, or proposing to "teach the poor dumb animal to swear." But Fleeming and Mr. Ewing, when we butterflies were gone, were laboriously ardent. Many thoughts that occupied the later years of my friend were caught from the small utterance of that toy. Thence came his inquiries into the roots of articulate language and the foundations of literary art; his papers on vowel sounds, his papers in the *Saturday Review* upon the laws of verse, and many a strange approximation, many a just note, thrown out in talk and now forgotten. I pass over dozens of his interests, and dwell on this trifling matter of the phonograph, because it seems to me that it depicts the man. So, for Fleeming, one thing joined into another, the greater with the less. He cared not where it was he scratched the surface of the ultimate mystery—in the child's toy, in the great tragedy, in the laws of the tempest, or in the properties of energy or mass—certain that whatever he touched, it was a part of life —and however he touched it, there would flow for his happy constitution interest and delight. "All fables have their morals," says Thoreau, "but the innocent enjoy the story." There is a truth represented for the imagination in these lines of a noble poem, where we were told that, in our highest hours of visionary clearness, we can but

"see the children sport upon the shore
And hear the mighty waters rolling evermore."

To this clearness Fleeming had attained; and although he heard the voice of the eternal seas and weighed its message, he was yet able, until the end of his life, to sport upon these shores of death and mystery with the gaiety and innocence of children.

IV

It was as a student that I first knew Fleeming, as one of that modest number of young men who sat under his ministrations in a soul-chilling class-room at the top of the University buildings. His presence was against him as a professor: no one, least of all students, would have been moved to respect him at first sight: rather short in stature, markedly plain, boyishly young in manner, cocking his head like a terrier with every mark of the most engaging vivacity and readiness to be pleased, full of words, full of paradox, a stranger could scarcely fail to look at him twice, a man thrown with him in a train could scarcely fail to be engaged by him in talk, but a student would never regard him as academical. Yet he had that fibre in him that order always existed in his class-room. I do not remember that he ever addressed me in language; at the least sign of unrest, his eye would fall on me and I was quelled. Such a feat is comparatively easy in a small class; but I have misbehaved in smaller classes and under eyes more Olympian than Fleeming Jenkin's. He was simply a man

from whose reproof one shrank; in manner the
least buckrammed of mankind, he had, in serious moments, an extreme dignity of goodness.
So it was that he obtained a power over the
most insubordinate of students, but a power of
which I was myself unconscious. I was inclined
to regard any professor as a joke, and Fleeming
as a particularly good joke, perhaps the broad-
est in the vast pleasantry of my curriculum. I
was not able to follow his lectures; I somehow
dared not misconduct myself, as was my customary solace; and I refrained from attending.
This brought me at the end of the session into a
relation with my contemned professor that com-
pletely opened my eyes. During the year, bad
student as I was, he had shown a certain leaning
to my society; I had been to his house, he had
asked me to take a humble part in his theatricals; I was a master in the art of extracting a certificate even at the cannon's mouth; and I was under no apprehension. But when I approached
Fleeming, I found myself in another world; he
would have naught of me. "It is quite useless for *you* to come to me, Mr. Stevenson.
There may be doubtful cases, there is no doubt
about yours. You have simply *not* attended
my class." The document was necessary to
me for family considerations; and presently I
stooped to such pleadings and rose to such ad-
jurations, as made my ears burn to remember.
He was quite unmoved; he had no pity for me.

"You are no fool," said he, "and you chose your course." I showed him that he had misconceived his duty, that certificates were things of form, attendance a matter of taste. Two things, he replied, had been required for graduation, a certain competency proved in the final trials and a certain period of genuine training proved by certificate; if he did as I desired, not less than if he gave me hints for an examination, he was aiding me to steal a degree. "You see, Mr. Stevenson, these are the laws and I am here to apply them," said he. I could not say but that this view was tenable, though it was new to me; I changed my attack: it was only for my father's eye that I required his signature, it need never go to the Senatus, I had already certificates enough to justify my year's attendance. "Bring them to me; I cannot take your word for that," said he. "Then I will consider." The next day I came charged with my certificates, a humble assortment. And when he had satisfied himself, "Remember," said he, "that I can promise nothing, but I will try to find a form of words." He did find one, and I am still ashamed when I think of his shame in giving me that paper. He made no reproach in speech, but his manner was the more eloquent; it told me plainly what a dirty business we were on; and I went from his presence, with my certificate indeed in my possession, but with no answerable sense of triumph.

That was the bitter beginning of my love for Fleeming; I never thought lightly of him afterwards.

Once, and once only, after our friendship was truly founded, did we come to a considerable difference. It was, by the rules of poor humanity, my fault and his. I had been led to dabble in society journalism; and this coming to his ears, he felt it like a disgrace upon himself. So far he was exactly in the right; but he was scarce happily inspired when he broached the subject at his own table and before guests who were strangers to me. It was the sort of error he was always ready to repent, but always certain to repeat; and on this occasion he spoke so freely that I soon made an excuse and left the house with the firm purpose of returning no more. About a month later, I met him at dinner at a common friend's. "Now," said he, on the stairs, "I engage you—like a lady to dance—for the end of the evening. You have no right to quarrel with me and not give me a chance." I have often said and thought that Fleeming had no tact; he belied the opinion then. I remember perfectly how, so soon as we could get together, he began his attack: "You may have grounds of quarrel with me; you have none against Mrs. Jenkin; and before I say another word, I want you to promise you will come to *her* house as usual." An interview thus begun could have but one ending: if the quarrel were the fault of both, the merit of the reconciliation was entirely Fleeming's.

When our intimacy first began, coldly enough, accidentally enough on his part, he had still something of the Puritan, something of the inhuman narrowness of the good youth. It fell from him slowly, year by year, as he continued to ripen, and grow milder, and understand more generously the mingled characters of men. In the early days he once read me a bitter lecture; and I remember leaving his house in a fine spring afternoon, with the physical darkness of despair upon my eyesight. Long after he made me a formal retraction of the sermon and a formal apology for the pain he had inflicted; adding drolly, but truly, "You see, at that time I was so much younger than you!" And yet even in those days there was much to learn from him; and above all his fine spirit of piety, bravely and trustfully accepting life, and his singular delight in the heroic.

His piety was, indeed, a thing of chief importance. His views (as they are called) upon religious matters varied much: and he could never be induced to think them more or less than views. "All dogma is to me mere form," he wrote; "dogmas are mere blind struggles to express the inexpressible. I cannot conceive that any single proposition whatever in religion is true in the scientific sense: and yet all the while I think the religious view of the world is the most

true view. Try to separate from the mass of
their statements that which is common to Socrates, Isaiah, David, St. Bernard, the Jan-
senists, Luther, Mahomet, Bunyan—yes, and
George Eliot: of course you do not believe that
this something could be written down in a set
of propositions like Euclid, neither will you deny
that there is something common and this something very valuable. . . . I shall be sorry if
the boys ever give a moment's thought to the
question of what community they belong to—I
hope they will belong to the great community."
I should observe that as time went on his conformity to the Church in which he was born
grew more complete, and his views drew nearer
the conventional. "The longer I live, my dear
Louis," he wrote but a few months before his
death, "the more convinced I become of a direct
care by God—which is reasonably impossible—
but there it is." And in his last year he took
the Communion.

But at the time when I fell under his influence,
he stood more aloof; and this made him the
more impressive to a youthful atheist. He had
a keen sense of language and its imperial influence on men; language contained all the great
and sound metaphysics, he was wont to say; and
a word once made and generally understood, he
thought a real victory of man and reason. But
he never dreamed it could be accurate, knowing
that words stand symbol for the indefinable. I

came to him once with a problem which had
puzzled me out of measure: What is a cause?
why out of so many innumerable millions of
conditions, all necessary, should one be singled
out and ticketed "the cause"? "You do not
understand," said he. "A cause is the answer
to a question: it designates that condition which
I happen to know and you happen not to know."
It was thus, with partial exception of the mathe-
matical, that he thought of all means of reasoning: they were in his eyes but means of communication, so to be understood, so to be judged,
and only so far to be credited. The mathe-
matical he made, I say, exception of: number
and measure he believed in to the extent of their
significance, but that significance, he was never
weary of reminding you, was slender to the verge
of nonentity. Science was true, because it told
us almost nothing. With a few abstractions it
could deal, and deal correctly; conveying honestly faint truths. Apply its means to any con-
crete fact of life, and this high dialect of the
wise became a childish jargon.

Thus the atheistic youth was met at every
turn by a scepticism more complete than his
own, so that the very weapons of the fight were
changed in his grasp to swords of paper. Certainly the Church is not right, he would argue,
but certainly not the anti-Church either. Men
are not such fools as to be wholly in the wrong,
nor yet are they so placed as to be ever wholly

in the right. Somewhere, in mid-air between the disputants, like hovering Victory in some design of a Greek battle, the truth hangs undiscerned. And in the meanwhile what matter these uncertainties? Right is very obvious; a great consent of the best of mankind, a loud voice within us (whether of God, or whether by inheritance, and in that case still from God), guide and command us in the path of duty. He saw life very simple; he did not love refinements; he was a friend to much conformity in unessentials. For (he would argue) it is in this life as it stands about us, that we are given our problem; the manners of the day are the colours of our palette, they condition, they constrain us; and a man must be very sure he is in the right, must (in a favourite phrase of his) be "either very wise or very vain," to break with any general consent in ethics. I remember taking his advice upon some point of conduct. "Now," he said, "how do you suppose Christ would have advised you?" and when I had answered that he would not have counselled me anything unkind or cowardly, "No," he said, with one of his shrewd strokes at the weakness of his hearer, "nor anything amusing." Later in life, he made less certain in the field of ethics. "The old story of the knowledge of good and evil is a very true one," I find him writing; only (he goes on) "the effect of the original dose is much worn out, leaving Adam's descendants

with the knowledge that there is such a thing—
but uncertain where." His growing sense of
this ambiguity made him less swift to condemn,
but no less stimulating in counsel. "You grant
yourself certain freedoms. Very well," he would
say, "I want to see you pay for them some other
way. You positively cannot do this: then there
positively must be something else that you can
do, and I want to see you find that out and do
it." Fleeming would never suffer you to think
that you were living, if there were not, somewhere in your life, some touch of heroism, to do
or to endure.

This was his rarest quality. Far on in middle
age, when men begin to lie down with the bestial
goddesses, Comfort and Respectability, the
strings of his nature still sounded as high a note
as a young man's. He loved the harsh voice of
duty like a call to battle. He loved courage, enterprise, brave natures, a brave word, an ugly
virtue; everything that lifts us above the table
where we eat or the bed we sleep upon. This
with no touch of the motive-monger or the ascetic. He loved his virtues to be practical, his
heroes to be great eaters of beef; he loved the
jovial Heracles, loved the astute Odysseus;
not the Robespierres and Wesleys. A fine buoyant sense of life and of man's unequal character ran through all his thoughts. He could
not tolerate the spirit of the pickthank; being
what we are, he wished us to see others with a

generous eye of admiration, not with the smallness of the seeker after faults. If there shone
anywhere a virtue, no matter how incongruous-
ly set, it was upon the virtue we must fix our
eyes. I remember having found much entertainment in Voltaire's *Saül*, and telling him what
seemed to me the drollest touches. He heard
me out, as usual when displeased, and then
opened fire on me with red-hot shot. To be-
little a noble story was easy: it was not literature, it was not art, it was not morality; there
was no sustenance in such a form of jesting,
there was (in his favourite phrase) "no nitrogenous food" in such literature. And then he
proceeded to show what a fine fellow David was;
and what a hard knot he was in about Bathshe-
ba, so that (the initial wrong committed) honour might well hesitate in the choice of conduct;
and what owls those people were who marvelled
because an Eastern tyrant had killed Uriah, instead of marvelling that he had not killed the
prophet also. "Now if Voltaire had helped me
to feel that," said he, "I could have seen some
fun in it." He loved the comedy which shows
a hero human, and yet leaves him a hero, and
the laughter which does not lessen love.

It was this taste for what is fine in human-
kind, that ruled his choice in books. These
should all strike a high note, whether brave or
tender, and smack of the open air. The noble
and simple presentation of things noble and sim-

ple, that was the "nitrogenous food" of which
he spoke so much, which he sought so eagerly,
enjoyed so royally. He wrote to an author, the
first part of whose story he had seen with sympathy, hoping that it might continue in the same
vein. "That this may be so," he wrote, "I long
with the longing of David for the water of Beth-
lehem. But no man need die for the water a
poet can give, and all can drink it to the end of
time, and their thirst be quenched and the pool
never dry—and the thirst and the water are
both blessed." It was in the Greeks particularly that he found this blessed water; he loved "a
fresh air" which he found "about the Greek
things even in translations"; he loved their freedom from the mawkish and the rancid. The
tale of David in the Bible, the *Odyssey*, Sophocles, Æschylus, Shakespeare, Scott; old Dumas
in his chivalrous note; Dickens rather than
Thackeray, and *A Tale of Two Cities* out of
Dickens: such were some of his preferences. To
Ariosto and Boccaccio he was always faithful;
Burnt Njal was a late favourite; and he found
at least a passing entertainment in the *Arcadia*
and the *Grand Cyrus*. George Eliot he outgrew,
finding her latterly only sawdust in the mouth;
but her influence, while it lasted, was great, and
must have gone some way to form his mind.
He was easily set on edge, however, by didactic
writing; and held that books should teach no
other lesson but what "real life would teach,

were it as vividly presented." Again, it was the thing made that took him, the drama in the book; to the book itself, to any merit of the making, he was long strangely blind. He would prefer the *Agamemnon* in the prose of Mr. Buckley, ay, to Keats. But he was his mother's son, learning to the last. He told me one day that literature was not a trade; that it was no craft; that the professed author was merely an amateur with a door-plate. "Very well," said I, "the first time you get a proof, I will demonstrate that it is as much a trade as bricklaying, and that you do not know it." By the very next post, a proof came. I opened it with fear; for he was indeed, as the reader will see by these volumes, a formidable amateur; always wrote brightly, because he always thought trenchantly; and sometimes wrote brilliantly, as the worst of whistlers may sometimes stumble on a perfect intonation. But it was all for the best in the interests of his education; and I was able, over that proof, to give him a quarter of an hour such as Fleeming loved both to give and to receive. His subsequent training passed out of my hands into those of our common friend, W. E. Henley. "Henley and I," he wrote, "have fairly good times wigging one another for not doing better. I wig him because he won't try to write a real play, and he wigs me because I can't try to write English." When I next saw him, he was full of his new acquisitions.

"And yet I have lost something too," he said regretfully. "Up to now Scott seemed to me quite perfect, he was all I wanted. Since I have been learning this confounded thing, I took up one of the novels, and a great deal of it is both careless and clumsy."

V

He spoke four languages with freedom, not even English with any marked propriety. What he uttered was not so much well said, as excellently acted: so we may hear every day the inexpressive language of a poorly-written drama assume character and colour in the hands of a good player. No man had more of the *vis comica* in private life; he played no character on the stage, as he could play himself among his friends. It was one of his special charms; now when the voice is silent and the face still, it makes it impossible to do justice to his power in conversation. He was a delightful companion to such as can bear bracing weather; not to the very vain; not to the owlishly wise, who cannot have their dogmas canvassed; not to the painfully refined, whose sentiments become articles of faith. The spirit in which he could write that he was "much revived by having an opportunity of abusing Whistler to a knot of his special admirers," is a spirit apt to be misconstrued. He was not a dogmatist, even about Whistler. "The house is full of pretty things,"

he wrote, when on a visit; "but Mrs. ———'s taste
in pretty things has one very bad fault: it is not
my taste." And that was the true attitude of
his mind; but these eternal differences it was his
joy to thresh out and wrangle over by the hour.
It was no wonder if he loved the Greeks; he was
in many ways a Greek himself; he should have
been a sophist and met Socrates; he would have
loved Socrates, and done battle with him
staunchly and manfully owned his defeat; and
the dialogue, arranged by Plato, would have
shown even in Plato's gallery. He seemed in
talk aggressive, petulant, full of a singular energy; as vain you would have said as a peacock,
until you trod on his toes, and then you saw that
he was at least clear of all the sicklier elements
of vanity. Soundly rang his laugh at any jest
against himself. He wished to be taken, as
he took others, for what was good in him without dissimulation of the evil, for what was wise
in him without concealment of the childish. He
hated a draped virtue, and despised a wit on its
own defence. And he drew (if I may so express
myself) a human and humorous portrait of himself with all his defects and qualities, as he thus
enjoyed in talk the robust sports of the intelligence; giving and taking manfully, always without pretence, always with paradox, always with
exuberant pleasure; speaking wisely of what he
knew, foolishly of what he knew not; a teacher,
a learner, but still combative; picking holes in

what was said even to the length of captious-
ness, yet aware of all that was said rightly; ju-
bilant in victory, delighted by defeat: a Greek
sophist, a British schoolboy.

Among the legends of what was once a very
pleasant spot, the old Savile Club, not then di-
vorced from Savile Row, there are many memories of Fleeming.   He was not popular at first,
being known simply as "the man who dines here
and goes up to Scotland"; but he grew at last,
I think, the most generally liked of all the members.   To those who truly knew and loved him,
who had tasted the real sweetness of his nature,
Fleeming's porcupine ways had always been a
matter of keen regret.   They introduced him
to their own friends with fear; sometimes recalled the step with mortification.   It was not
possible to look on with patience while a man so
lovable thwarted love at every step.   But the
course of time and the ripening of his nature
brought a cure.   It was at the Savile that he
first remarked a change; it soon spread beyond
the walls of the club.   Presently I find him writing: "Will you kindly explain what has happened
to me?   All my life I have talked a good deal,
with the almost unfailing result of making people
sick of the sound of my tongue.   It appeared to
me that I had various things to say, and I had
no malevolent feelings, but nevertheless the result was that expressed above.   Well, lately
some change has happened.   If I talk to a per-

son one day, they must have me the next. Faces
light up when they see me.—'Ah, I say, come
here,'—'come and dine with me.' It's the most
preposterous thing I ever experienced. It is
curiously pleasant. You have enjoyed it all your
life, and therefore cannot conceive how bewil-
dering a burst of it is for the first time at forty-
nine." And this late sunshine of popularity still
further softened him. He was a bit of a porcupine to the last, still shedding darts; or rather he
was to the end a bit of a schoolboy, and must still
throw stones; but the essential toleration that un-
derlay his disputatiousness, and the kindness that
made of him a tender sick-nurse and a generous
helper, shone more conspicuously through. A
new pleasure had come to him; and as with all
sound natures, he was bettered by the pleasure.

I can best show Fleeming in this later stage
by quoting from a vivid and interesting letter of
M. Émile Trélat's. Here, admirably expressed,
is how he appeared to a friend of another nation,
whom he encountered only late in life. M. Trélat
will pardon me if I correct, even before I quote
him; but what the Frenchman supposed to flow
from some particular bitterness against France,
was only Fleeming's usual address. Had M. Trélat been Italian, Italy would have fared as ill; and
yet Italy was Fleeming's favourite country.

Vous savez comment j'ai connu Fleeming Jenkin! C'était en
Mai 1878. Nous étions tous deux membres du jury de l'Exposition Universelle. On n'avait rien fait qui vaille à la première

séance de notre classe, qui avait eu lieu le matin. Tout le monde avait parlé et reparlé pour ne rien dire. Cela durait depuis huit heures; il était midi. Je demandai la parole pour une motion d'ordre, et je proposai que la séance fût levée à la condition que chaque membre français *emportât* à déjeuner un juré étranger. Jenkin applaudit. "Je vous emmène déjeuner," lui criai-je. "Je veux bien." . . . Nous partîmes; en chemin nous vous rencontrions; il vous présente et nous allons déjeuner tous trois auprès du Trocadéro.

Et, depuis ce temps, nous avons été de vieux amis. Non seulement nous passions nos journées au jury, où nous étions toujours ensemble, côte-à-côte, mais nos habitudes s'étaient faites telles que, non contents de déjeuner en face l'un de l'autre, je le ramenais dîner presque tous les jours chez moi. Cela dura une quinzaine: puis il fut rappelé en Angleterre. Mais il revint, et nous fîmes encore une bonne étape de vie intellectuelle, morale et philosophique. Je crois qu'il me rendait déjà tout ce que j'éprouvais de sympathie et d'estime, et que je ne fus pas pour rien dans son retour à Paris.

Chose singulière! nous nous étions attachés l'un à l'autre par les sous-entendus bien plus que par la matière de nos conversations. À vrai dire, nous étions presque toujours en discussion; et il nous arrivait de nous rire au nez l'un et l'autre pendant des heures, tant nous nous étonnions réciproquement de la diversité de nos points de vue. Je le trouvais si Anglais, et il me trouvait si Français! Il était si franchement révolté de certaines choses qu'il voyait chez nous, et je comprenais si mal certaines choses qui se passaient chez vous! Rien de plus intéressant que ces contacts qui étaient des contrastes, et que ces rencontres d'idées qui étaient des choses; rien de si attachant que les échappées de cœur ou d'esprit auxquelles ces petits conflits donnaient à tout moment cours. C'est dans ces conditions que, pendant son séjour à Paris en 1878, je conduisis un peu partout mon nouvel ami. Nous allâmes chez Madame Edmond Adam, où il vit passer beaucoup d'hommes politiques avec lesquels il causa. Mais c'est chez les ministres qu'il fût intéressé. Le moment était, d'ailleurs, curieux en France. Je me rappelle que, lorsque je le présentai au Ministre du Commerce, il fit cette spirituelle repartie: "C'est la seconde fois que je viens en France sous la République. La première fois, c'était en 1848, elle s'était coiffée de travers: je suis bien heureux de saluer aujourd'hui votre excellence, quand elle a mis son chapeau droit." Une fois je le menai voir couronner la Rosière de Nanterre. Il y suivit les cérémonies civiles et religieuses; il y assista au banquet donné par le Maire; il y vit notre De Lesseps, auquel il porta un toast. Le soir, nous revînmes tard à Paris; il faisait chaud; nous étions un peu fatigués; nous entrâmes dans un des rares cafés encore ouverts. Il devint silencieux.—"N'êtes-vous pas content de votre journée?" lui dis-je.—"O, si! mais je réfléchis, et je me dis que vous êtes un peuple gai—tous ces braves gens étaient gais aujourd'hui. C'est une vertu, la gaieté, et vous l'avez en France, cette vertu!" Il me disait cela mélancoliquement; et c'était la première fois que je lui entendais faire une louange adressée à la France. . . . Mais il ne faut pas que vous voyiez là une plainte de ma part. Je serais un ingrat si je me plaignais; car il me disait souvent: "Quel bon Français vous faites!" Et il m'aimait à cause de cela, quoiqu'il semblât n'aimer pas la France. C'était là un trait de son originalité. Il est vrai qu'il s'en tirait en disant que je ne ressemblai pas à mes compatriotes, ce à quoi il ne connaissait rien!—Tout cela était fort curieux; car, moi-même, je l'aimais quoiqu'il en eût à mon pays!

En 1879 il amena son fils Austin à Paris. J'attirai celui-ci. Il déjeunait avec moi deux fois par semaine. Je lui montrai ce qu'était l'intimité française en le tutoyant paternellement. Cela resserra beaucoup nos liens d'intimité avec Jenkin. . . . Je fis inviter mon ami au congrès de l'*Association française pour l'avancement des sciences*, qui se tenait à Rheims en 1880. Il y vint. J'eus le plaisir de lui donner la parole dans la section du génie civil et militaire, que je présidais. Il y fit une très intéressante communication, qui me montrait une fois de plus l'originalité de ses vues et la sûreté de sa science. C'est à l'issue de ce congrès que je passai lui faire visite à Rochefort, où je le trouvai installé en famille et où je présentai pour la première fois mes hommages à son éminente compagne. Je le vis là sous un jour nouveau et touchant pour moi. Madame Jenkin, qu'il entourait si galamment, et ses deux jeunes fils donnaient encore plus de relief à sa personne. J'emportai des quelques heures que je passai à côté de lui dans ce charmant paysage un souvenir ému.

FLEEMING JENKIN

J'étais allé en Angleterre en 1882 sans pouvoir gagner Edimbourg. J'y retournai en 1883 avec la commission d'assainissement de la ville de Paris, dont je faisais partie. Jenkin me rejoignit. Je le fis entendre par mes collègues; car il était fondateur d'une société de salubrité. Il eut un grand succès parmi nous. Mais ce voyage me restera toujours en mémoire parce que c'est là que se fixa définitivement notre forte amitié. Il m'invita un jour à dîner à son club et au moment de me faire asseoir à côté de lui, il me retint et me dit: "Je voudrais vous demander de m'accorder quelque chose. C'est mon sentiment que nos relations ne peuvent pas se bien continuer si vous ne me donnez pas la permission de vous tutoyer. Voulez-vous que nous nous tutoyions?" Je lui pris les mains et je lui dis qu'une pareille proposition venant d'un Anglais, et d'un Anglais de sa haute distinction, c'était une victoire, dont je serais fier toute ma vie. Et nous commencions à user de cette nouvelle forme dans nos rapports. Vous savez avec quelle finesse il parlait le français: comme il en connaissait tous les tours, comme il jouait avec ses difficultés, et même avec ses petites gamineries. Je crois qu'il a été heureux de pratiquer avec moi ce tutoiement, qui ne s'adapte pas à l'anglais, et qui est si français. Je ne puis vous peindre l'étendue et la variété de nos conversations de la soirée. Mais ce que je puis vous dire, c'est que, sous la caresse du *tu*, nos idées se sont élevées. Nous avions toujours beaucoup ri ensemble; mais nous n'avions jamais laissé des banalités s'introduire dans nos échanges de pensées. Ce soir-là, notre horizon intellectuel s'est élargi, et nous y avons poussé des reconnaissances profondes et lointaines. Après avoir vivement causé à table, nous avons longuement causé au salon; et nous nous séparions le soir à Trafalgar Square, après avoir longé les trottoirs, stationné aux coins des rues et deux fois rebroussé chemin en nous reconduisant l'un l'autre. Il était près d'une heure du matin! Mais quelle belle passe d'argumentation, quels beaux échanges de sentiments, quelles fortes confidences patriotiques nous avions fournies! J'ai compris ce soir-là que Jenkin ne détestait pas la France, et je lui serrai fort les mains en l'embrassant. Nous nous quittions aussi amis qu'on puisse l'être; et notre affection s'était par lui étendue et comprise dans un *tu* français.

CHAPTER VII

1875–1885

AND now I must resume my narrative for that melancholy business that concludes all human histories. In January of the year 1875, while Fleeming's sky was still unclouded, he was reading Smiles. "I read my engineers' lives steadily," he writes, "but find biographies depressing. I suspect one reason to be that misfortunes and trials can be graphically described, but happiness and the causes of happiness either cannot be or are not. A grand new branch of literature opens to my view: a drama in which people begin in a poor way and end, after getting gradually happier, in an ecstasy of enjoyment. The common novel is not the thing at all. It gives struggle followed by relief. I want each act to close on a new and triumphant happiness, which has been steadily growing all the while. This is the real antithesis of

547

tragedy, where things get blacker and blacker and end in hopeless woe. Smiles has not grasped my grand idea, and only shows a bitter struggle followed by a little respite before death. Some feeble critic might say my new idea was not true to nature. I'm sick of this old-fashioned notion of art. Hold a mirror up, indeed! Let's paint a picture of how things ought to be and hold that up to nature, and perhaps the poor old woman may repent and mend her ways." The "grand idea" might be possible in art; not even the ingenuity of nature could so round in the actual life of any man. And yet it might almost seem to fancy that she had read the letter and taken the hint; for to Fleeming the cruelties of fate were strangely blended with tenderness, and when death came, it came harshly to others, to him not unkindly.

In the autumn of that same year 1875, Fleeming's father and mother were walking in the garden of their house at Merchiston, when the latter fell to the ground. It was thought at the time to be a stumble; it was in all likelihood a premonitory stroke of palsy. From that day, there fell upon her an abiding panic fear; that glib, superficial part of us that speaks and reasons could allege no cause, science itself could find no mark of danger, a son's solicitude was laid at rest; but the eyes of the body saw the approach of a blow, and the consciousness of the body trembled at its coming. It came in a moment; the brilliant, spirited old lady leapt from her bed, raving. For about six months, this stage of her disease continued with many painful and many pathetic circumstances; her husband who tended her, her son who was unwearied in his visits, looked for no change in her condition but the change that comes to all. "Poor mother," I find Fleeming writing, "I cannot get the tones of her voice out of my head. . . . I may have to bear this pain for a long time; and so I am bearing it and sparing myself whatever pain seems useless. Mercifully I do sleep, I am so weary that I must sleep." And again later: "I could do very well, if my mind did not revert to my poor mother's state whenever I stop attending to matters immediately before me." And the next day: "I can never feel a moment's pleasure without having my mother's suffering recalled by the very feeling of happiness. A pretty, young face recalls hers by contrast—a careworn face recalls it by association. I tell you, for I can speak to no one else; but do not suppose that I wilfully let my mind dwell on sorrow."

In the summer of the next year, the frenzy left her; it left her stone deaf and almost entirely aphasic, but with some remains of her old sense and courage. Stoutly she set to work with dictionaries, to recover her lost tongues; and had already made notable progress, when a third stroke scattered her acquisitions. Thenceforth, for nearly ten years, stroke followed upon stroke, each still further jumbling the threads of her intelligence, but by degrees so gradual and with such partiality of loss and survival, that her precise state was always and to the end a matter of dispute. She still remembered her friends: she still loved to learn news of them upon the slate; she still read and marked the list of the subscription library; she still took an interest in the choice of a play for the theatricals, and could remember and find parallel passages; but alongside of these surviving powers, were lapses as remarkable, she misbehaved like a child, and a servant had to sit with her at table. To see her so sitting, speaking with the tones of a deaf-mute not always to the purpose, and to remember what she had been, was a moving appeal to all who knew her. Such was the pathos of these two old people in their affliction, that even the reserve of cities was melted and the neighbours vied in sympathy and kindness. Where so many were more than usually helpful, it is hard to draw distinctions; but I am directed and I delight to mention in particular the good Dr. Joseph Bell, Mr. Thomas, and Mr. Archibald Constable, with both their wives, the Rev. Mr. Belcombe (of whose good heart and taste I do not hear for the first time—the news had come to me by way of the Infirmary), and their next-door neighbour, unwearied in service, Miss Hannah Mayne. Nor should I omit to mention that John Ruffini continued to write to Mrs. Jenkin till his own death, and the clever lady known to the world as Vernon Lee until the end: a touching, a becoming attention to what was only the wreck and survival of their brilliant friend.

But he to whom this affliction brought the greatest change was the Captain himself. What was bitter in his lot, he bore with unshaken courage; only once, in these ten years of trial, has Mrs. Fleeming Jenkin seen him weep; for the rest of the time his wife—his commanding officer, now become his trying child—was served not with patience alone, but with a lovely happiness of temper. He had belonged all his life to the ancient, formal, speech-making, compliment-presenting school of courtesy; the dictates of this code partook in his eyes of the nature of a duty; and he must now be courteous for two. Partly from a happy illusion, partly in a tender fraud, he kept his wife before the world as a still active partner. When he paid a call, he would have her write "with love" upon a card; or if that (at the moment) was too much he would go armed with a bouquet and present it in her name. He even wrote letters for her to copy and sign: an innocent substitution, which may have caused surprise to Ruffini or to Vernon Lee, if they ever received, in the hand of Mrs. Jenkin, the very obvious reflections of her husband. He had always adored this wife whom he now tended and sought to represent in correspondence: it was now, if not before, her turn to repay the compliment; mind enough was left her to perceive his unwearied kindness; and as her moral qualities seemed to survive quite unimpaired, a childish love and gratitude were his reward.   She would interrupt a conversation to cross the room and kiss him.   If she grew excited (as she did too often) it was his habit to come behind her chair and pat her shoulder; and then she would turn round, and clasp his hand in hers, and look from him to her visitor with a face of pride and love; and it was at such moments only that the light of humanity revived in her eyes.   It was hard for any stranger, it was impossible for any that loved them, to behold these mute scenes, to recall the past, and not to weep.   But to the Captain, I think it was all happiness.   After these so long years, he had found his wife again; perhaps kinder than ever before; perhaps now on a more equal footing; certainly, to his eyes, still beautiful.   And the call made on his intelligence had not been made in vain.   The merchants of Aux Cayes, who had seen him tried in some "counter-revolution" in 1845, wrote to the consul of his "able and decided measures," "his cool, steady judgment and discernment" with admiration; and of himself, as "a credit and an ornament to H. M. Naval Service."   It is plain he must have sunk in all his powers, during the years when he was only a figure, and often a dumb figure, in his wife's drawing-room; but with this new term of service, he brightened visibly. He showed tact and even invention in managing his wife, guiding or restraining her by the touch, holding family worship so arranged that she could follow and take part in it. He took (to the world's surprise) to reading—voyages, biographies, Blair's *Sermons*, even (for her letters' sake) a work of Vernon Lee's, which proved, however, more than he was quite prepared for. He shone more, in his remarkable way, in society; and twice he had a little holiday to Glenmorven, where, as may be fancied, he was the delight of the Highlanders. One of his last pleasures was to arrange his dining-room. Many and many a room (in their wandering and thriftless existence) had he seen his wife furnish "with exquisite taste" and perhaps with "considerable luxury": now it was his turn to be the decorator. On the wall he had an engraving of Lord Rodney's action, showing the *Prothée*, his father's ship, if the reader recollects; on either side of this, on brackets, his father's sword, and his father's telescope, a gift from Admiral Buckner, who had used it himself during the engagement; higher yet, the head of his grandson's first stag, portraits of his son and his son's wife, and a couple of old Windsor jugs from Mrs. Buckner's. But his simple trophy was not yet complete; a device had to be worked and framed and hung below the engraving; and for this he applied to his daughter-in-law: "I want you to work me something, Annie. An anchor at each side—an anchor—stands for an old sailor, you know— stands for hope, you know—an anchor at each side, and in the middle THANKFUL." It is not easy, on any system of punctuation, to represent the Captain's speech. Yet I hope there may shine out of these facts, even as there shone through his own troubled utterance, some of the charm of that delightful spirit.

In 1881, the time of the golden wedding came round for that sad and pretty household. It fell on a Good Friday, and its celebration can scarcely be recalled without both smiles and tears. The drawing-room was filled with presents and beautiful bouquets; these, to Fleeming and his family, the golden bride and bridegroom displayed with unspeakable pride, she so painfully excited that the guests feared every moment to see her stricken afresh, he guiding and moderating her with his customary tact and understanding, and doing the honours of the day with more than his usual delight. Thence they were brought to the dining-room, where the Captain's idea of a feast awaited them: tea and champagne, fruit and toast and childish little luxuries, set forth pell-mell and pressed at random on the guests. And here he must make a speech for himself and his wife, praising their destiny, their marriage, their son, their daughter-in-law, their grandchildren, their manifold causes of gratitude: surely the most innocent speech, the old, sharp contemner of his innocence now watching him with eyes of admiration. Then it was time for the guests to depart; and they went away, bathed, even to the youngest child, in tears of inseparable sorrow and gladness, and leaving the golden bride and bridegroom to their own society and that of the hired nurse.

It was a great thing for Fleeming to make, even thus late, the acquaintance of his father; but the harrowing pathos of such scenes consumed him. In a life of tense intellectual effort, a certain smoothness of emotional tenor were to be desired; or we burn the candle at both ends. Dr. Bell perceived the evil that was being done; he pressed Mrs. Jenkin to restrain her husband from too frequent visits; but here was one of those clear-cut, indubitable duties for which Fleeming lived, and he could not pardon even the suggestion of neglect.

And now, after death had so long visibly but still innocuously hovered above the family, it began at last to strike and its blows fell thick and heavy. The first to go was uncle John Jenkin, taken at last from his Mexican dwelling and the lost tribes of Israel; and nothing in this remarkable old gentleman's life became him like the leaving it. His sterling, jovial acquiescence in man's destiny was a delight to Fleeming. "My visit to Stowting has been a very strange but not at all a painful one," he wrote. "In case you ever wish to make a person die as he ought to die in a novel," he said to me, "I must tell you all about my old uncle." He was to see a nearer instance before long; for this family of Jenkin, if they were not very aptly fitted to live, had the art of manly dying. Uncle John was but an outsider after all; he had dropped out of hail of his nephew's way of life and station in society, and was more like some shrewd, old, humble friend who should have kept a lodge; yet he led the procession of becoming deaths, and began in the mind of Fleeming that train of tender and grateful thought, which was like a preparation for his own. Already I find him writing in the plural of "these impending deaths"; already I find him in quest of consolation. "There is little pain in store for these wayfarers," he wrote, "and we have hope—more than hope, trust."

On May 19, 1884, Mr. Austin was taken. He was seventy-eight years of age, suffered sharply with all his old firmness, and died happy in the knowledge that he had left his wife well cared for. This had always been a bosom concern, for the Barrons were long-lived and he believed that she would long survive him. But their union had been so full and quiet that Mrs. Austin languished under the separation. In their last years, they would sit all evening in their own drawing-room hand in hand: two old people who, for all their fundamental differences, had yet grown together and become all the world in each other's eyes and hearts; and it was felt to be a kind release, when eight months after, on January 14, 1885, Eliza Barron followed Alfred Austin. "I wish I could save you from all pain," wrote Fleeming six days later to his sorrowing wife, "I would if I could—but my way is not God's way; and of this be assured,—God's way is best."

In the end of the same month, Captain Jenkin caught cold and was confined to bed. He was so unchanged in spirit that at first there seemed no ground of fear; but his great age began to tell, and presently it was plain he had a summons. The charm of his sailor's cheerfulness and ancient courtesy, as he lay dying, is not to be described. There he lay, singing his old sea songs; watching the poultry from the window with a child's delight; scribbling on the slate little messages to his wife, who lay bed-ridden in another room; glad to have Psalms read aloud to him, if they were of a pious strain—checking, with an "I don't think we need read that, my dear," any that were gloomy or bloody. Fleeming's wife coming to the house and asking one of the nurses for news of Mrs. Jenkin, "Madam, I do not know," said the nurse; "for I am really so carried away by the Captain that I can think of nothing else." One of the last messages scribbled to his wife and sent her with a glass of the champagne that had been ordered for himself, ran, in his most finished vein of childish madrigal: "The Captain bows to you, my love, across the table." When the end was near and it was thought best that Fleeming should no longer go home but sleep at Merchiston, he broke his news to the Captain with some trepidation, knowing that it carried sentence of death. "Charming, charming—charming arrangement," was the Captain's only commentary. It was the proper thing for a dying man, of Captain Jenkin's school of manners, to make some expression of his spiritual state; nor did he neglect the observance. With his usual abruptness, "Fleeming," said he, "I suppose you and I feel about all this as two Christian gentlemen should." A last pleasure was secured for him. He had been waiting with painful interest for news of Gordon and Khartoum; and by great good fortune, a false report reached him that the city was relieved, and the men of Sussex (his old neighbours) had been the first to enter. He sat up in bed and gave three cheers for the Sussex regiment. The subsequent correction, if it came in time, was prudently withheld from the dying man. An hour before midnight on the fifth of February, he passed away: aged eighty-four.

Word of his death was kept from Mrs. Jenkin; and she survived him no more than nine and forty hours. On the day before her death, she

FLEEMING JENKIN

received a letter from her old friend Miss Bell of
Manchester, knew the hand, kissed the envelope,
and laid it on her heart; so that she too died upon a pleasure. Half an hour after midnight, on
the eighth of February, she fell asleep: it is supposed in her seventy-eighth year.

Thus, in the space of less than ten months, the
four seniors of this family were taken away; but
taken with such features of opportunity in time
or pleasant courage in the sufferer, that grief was
tempered with a kind of admiration. The effect
on Fleeming was profound. His pious optimism
increased and became touched with something
mystic and filial. "The grave is not good, the
approaches to it are terrible," he had written at
the beginning of his mother's illness: he thought
so no more, when he had laid father and mother
side by side at Stowting. He had always loved
life; in the brief time that now remained to him,
he seemed to be half in love with death. "Grief
is no duty," he wrote to Miss Bell; "it was all
too beautiful for grief," he said to me; but the
emotion, call it by what name we please, shook
him to his depths; his wife thought he would
have broken his heart when he must demolish
the Captain's trophy in the dining-room, and he
seemed thenceforth scarcely the same man.

These last years were indeed years of an excessive demand upon his vitality; he was not
only worn out with sorrow, he was worn out by
hope. The singular invention to which he gave

559

the name of telpherage, had of late consumed
his time, overtaxed his strength and overheated
his imagination. The words in which he first
mentioned his discovery to me—"I am simply
Alnaschar"—were not only descriptive of his
state of mind, they were in a sense prophetic;
since whatever fortune may await his idea in the
future, it was not his to see it bring forth fruit.
Alnaschar he was indeed; beholding about him a
world all changed, a world filled with telpherage
wires; and seeing not only himself and family
but all his friends enriched. It was his pleasure,
when the company was floated, to endow those
whom he liked with stock; one, at least, never
knew that he was a possible rich man until the
grave had closed over his stealthy benefactor.
And however Fleeming chafed among material
and business difficulties, this rainbow vision
never faded; and he, like his father and his
mother, may be said to have died upon a pleasure. But the strain told, and he knew that it
was telling. "I am becoming a fossil," he had
written five years before, as a kind of plea for a
holiday visit to his beloved Italy. "Take care!
If I am Mr. Fossil, you will be Mrs. Fossil, and
Jack will be Jack Fossil, and all the boys will be
little fossils, and then we shall be a collection."
There was no fear more chimerical for Fleeming; years brought him no repose; he was as
packed with energy, as fiery in hope, as at the
first; weariness, to which he began to be no

stranger, distressed, it did not quiet him. He feared for himself, not without ground, the fate which had overtaken his mother; others shared the fear. In the changed life now made for his family, the elders dead, the sons going from home upon their education, even their tried domestic (Mrs. Alice Dunns) leaving the house after twenty-two years of service, it was not unnatural that he should return to dreams of Italy. He and his wife were to go (as he told me) on "a real honeymoon tour." He had not been alone with his wife "to speak of," he added, since the birth of his children. But now he was to enjoy the society of her to whom he wrote, in these last days, that she was his "Heaven on earth." Now he was to revisit Italy, and see all the pictures and the buildings and the scenes that he admired so warmly, and lay aside for a time the irritations of his strenuous activity. Nor was this all. A trifling operation was to restore his former lightness of foot; and it was a renovated youth that was to set forth upon this re-enacted honeymoon.

The operation was performed; it was of a trifling character, it seemed to go well, no fear was entertained; and his wife was reading aloud to him as he lay in bed, when she perceived him to wander in his mind. It is doubtful if he ever recovered a sure grasp upon the things of life; and he was still unconscious when he passed away, June the twelfth, 1885, in the fifty-third year of his age. He passed; but something in his gallant vitality had impressed itself upon his friends, and still impresses. Not from one or two only, but from many, I hear the same tale of how the imagination refuses to accept our loss and instinctively looks for his re-appearing, and how memory retains his voice and image like things of yesterday. Others, the well-beloved too, die and are progressively forgotten; two years have passed since Fleeming was laid to rest beside his father, his mother, and his Uncle John; and the thought and the look of our friend still haunt us.